WHAT
I'VE
DONE

ALSO BY MELINDA LEIGH

WHAT I'VE DONE

MELINDA LEIGH

Montlake
Romance

Published by Montlake Romance, Seattle

www.apub.com

Amazon, the Amazon logo, and Montlake Romance are trademarks of Amazon.com, Inc., or its affiliates.

ISBN-13: 9781503903050
ISBN-10: 1503903052

Cover design by Eileen Carey

Printed in the United States of America

To Charlie
After twenty-four years together,
our life keeps getting better.

Chapter One

Haley gasped, sucking air into her lungs like a person who had just surfaced after being underwater too long. Oxygen flooded her, and consciousness returned with a rush of sensation that swept over her skin and left it tingling. Pain throbbed through her head as she opened her eyes. Her vision blurred. The blur spun, and she quickly shut her eyes again.

What happened?

Shimmering lights and loud music flashed in her mind. It had been Piper's birthday, and she'd talked Haley into going dancing to celebrate, even though Haley would have preferred to hang out in her pajamas, eat pizza, and play video games. Haley had run into Noah and his friends. She and Noah had ordered drinks and nachos. They'd danced.

Then what?

She blinked. A dim and unfamiliar ceiling fan took shape. She was not in her own bed. Heart racing, she glanced at the pillow next to hers. Vacant. Whose bed was she in? Regret followed close on the heels of the agony splitting her head.

She slammed her eyelids down, rolled to her side, and curled into a fetal position.

This was why she wasn't a drinker.

This was why she preferred gaming to clubbing.

Had she gone home with Noah? The last thing she remembered was him chatting her up, bringing her a second cosmo. Though she didn't have much tolerance for alcohol, two drinks certainly weren't enough to make her black out. She hadn't had a hangover since college. She'd learned her lesson about overindulging in alcohol during The Great Tequila Incident of freshman year.

But that was before she'd gotten sick. Now she rarely drank, and she never overindulged.

Dizziness swam through her head. *Duh*. She wasn't hungover. She needed her medication, and for that, she needed to find her purse. Her stupid Addison's disease was a pain in the butt. She'd take her meds, then call an Uber and go home. She'd figure the rest out later. Though she hadn't planned to hook up with anyone, she always carried extra medication with her in case of an emergency.

But last night hadn't been an emergency. She'd gone home with someone. Shame washed over her, leaving her cold and hollow.

Please let it have been Noah.

It had to have been him. Piper wouldn't have let her leave with a stranger, even if Haley hadn't been a best friend last night. She winced as she remembered how much time she'd spent with Noah during a girls' night out. She and her girlfriend always watched each other's backs. Always. Piper wouldn't let something as stupid as a little jealousy bypass their safety pact.

Right?

In the back of her mind, something didn't feel normal, but she shushed the nagging voice. She'd take her meds, her brain would clear, and things would start making sense.

She opened her eyes and blinked a few times. Her vision was still blurry. The light filtering in through the blinds told her it was daytime. Dehydration was a frequent issue with her disease. Her purse sat on the nightstand next to a half-empty bottle of water. She pulled the purse to her and searched for her phone. She didn't find it, but she did spot her prescription bottle. She swallowed a tablet and drained the water bottle.

An envelope on the nightstand caught her attention. She reached for it. Through the clear window, the label read *Noah Carter* above a Grey's Hollow address.

Relief swept over her. Though they'd met only a few times, the chemistry between her and Noah had been palpable. He was a very cute web designer who had consulted for the bank where she was a social media coordinator.

Haley had a weakness for nerds.

Her focus shifted to a crusty substance on her hand. Haley spread her hand in front of her face. Something dark and dry and rust-colored was smeared on her fingers. It took a moment before confusion shifted to clarity.

Blood?

Disbelief sliced through her haze. She sat upright, the quick motion turning her stomach over. Her gaze cut across the bed. The same rusty marks streaked the bedding, though the dark red was barely visible on the charcoal-gray comforter. Definitely blood. Fear rushed through her. Her heartbeat doubled its rhythm. She turned her hand over but saw no cuts on her skin, nor could she feel any sharp pain anywhere on her body.

She swallowed, her stomach sour. This couldn't be happening. It must be a nightmare.

With panic gearing up inside her, Haley scooted back against the headboard, getting as far away from the stains as possible. But there was no escaping them. In horror, she stared at her body. She was naked, and her hands, arms, and legs were streaked with dried blood. Panic surged as she searched her skin for injuries. She found a scratch on her arm, but there was no way that scratch had produced the volume of blood on the bedding.

If it wasn't her blood, whose was it?

Noah's?

Coldness spread through her limbs, and she trembled as she scrambled to the edge of the bed.

The double bed faced a dresser and chair. On the wall to her left, two doors stood open. One led into a hall. Through the other she could see into the closet, where men's shirts hung in a row, some still in clear plastic dry-cleaning bags.

Shivering, she climbed out of the bed, her legs shaky and weak, her mouth dry from nerves and dehydration. Frigid air wafted from the doorway. Goose bumps rose on her arms. Where was her phone? Dropping to her knees on the carpet, she looked under the bed. Dust. A sock.

And more blood.

Rusty drops of it led across the pale-gray carpet toward the open door. Even without any clear memory, she knew that the blood had dripped from her hands.

Standing, she took two steps to the window and peered through the blinds. A long lawn and driveway sloped toward the street a hundred feet away. A small red house sat on the other side of the road.

Turning, she crept barefoot to the doorway and eased from the room into the even colder hall. Her heart hammered hard enough to rattle her breastbone and vibrate in her throat. The bathroom was just outside the bedroom door. It was white-tiled, empty, and clean. She glanced through another doorway into a second bedroom furnished as a home office. There was no one inside.

Her gaze snapped back to the trail of blood that meandered down the hallway.

She hesitated, listening. *Was anyone else here?* Seconds ticked by, punctuated by the echo of her pulse in her ears. All she could hear was the distant whine of a leaf blower coming from outside. No sounds emanated from the living areas of the house.

Whatever she was going to find at the end of the trail wasn't going to be good. But she couldn't stop herself. Her feet tracked a line parallel to the blood. The air grew colder, and the dots became more numerous. Clumping together.

As if the blood had dripped less as she'd walked toward the bedroom.

The hallway opened into a living room. Her gaze panned over the furniture and carpet. Her black dress lay crumpled on the floor. Her high heels were under the coffee table. She crossed the room, snatched her dress from the floor, and tugged it over her head. The snug fit, lauded as hot by Piper the night before, felt binding and uncomfortable. It was better than being naked, but the skimpy garment did little to ward off the cold, damp air of early March in upstate New York.

Or the sense that she was acutely vulnerable.

The blood trail beckoned her to follow it through a doorway that led to the back of the house, toward the source of the wind. She walked to the threshold of the kitchen, the sight stopping her forward motion as if she'd stepped in deep, wet cement.

The blood.

The rusty trail led to a sickeningly large smear on the gray floor tiles. In the center of the blood lay a knife.

An image flashed in her mind, and she knew the knife had once been in her hand.

A second line of blood led from the smear out the open door. This trail was not composed of dots but one long streak. Through the doorway, Haley could see the large backyard and the woods in the distance.

The blood crossed the threshold and continued onto the porch.

Her legs threatened to give out as she stumbled out the back door. At the bottom of the porch steps, she saw him.

No.

Her breath froze in her throat. Her knees buckled. The sky spun. She put a hand on the nearby railing to steady herself.

Clearly crawling or dragging himself, Noah had turned right, toward the nearest neighbor's house, but he hadn't gotten far. He was sprawled on his side, his arms flung forward. His eyes, once a warm brown, were empty and opaque. He was wearing the same dorky Doctor Who T-shirt she'd thought was so adorable the night before. Saturated, the spinning TARDIS was barely recognizable.

Numb, she sank to her knees beside the body. The cold didn't register on the bare skin of her legs. One hand reached for Noah. She brushed a lock of hair off his forehead. A bug crawled across his face. She snatched her hand away as if burned.

She sank back onto her heels. Gasping, she stared down at her open palms and the blood on her hands. A scream ripped from her throat.

What have I done?

Chapter Two

"Lincoln Sharp, private investigator." Closing the door on the March wind, Sharp assessed the woman in the foyer of Sharp Investigations. "How can I help you?"

"My name is Olivia Cruz. You can call me Olivia." She unbuttoned her khaki trench coat. Black slacks and a pale-blue blouse draped a fit-looking body. She was short, even in her pointy high heels. Her dark eyes, deep-brown hair, and olive skin suggested some Hispanic ancestry. "I'm looking for Morgan Dane."

Morgan, a former prosecutor turned criminal defense attorney, rented an office in Sharp's converted duplex.

"Ms. Dane isn't in this morning. You should call and make an appointment."

"I tried that." Olivia slid her hand into a sleek black bag and withdrew a business card. "She hasn't returned my message."

Sharp read the card she handed him.

"You're a reporter," he said with disdain.

If she had told him that when she'd introduced herself, he wouldn't have let her through the front door. Her small smile said she knew it.

Damn. He was too old to get fooled by a pretty face.

"Yes." She nodded, completely ignoring the obvious contempt in his voice. "But at the moment, I'm working on a true crime book about the Chelsea Clark kidnapping."

Several months before, Morgan had been hired by Chelsea Clark's husband. In turn, Morgan had engaged Sharp Investigations to find the missing woman. The man who had kidnapped Chelsea had committed suicide in prison, so there was no upcoming trial that would prevent Morgan from discussing the case. But Sharp still doubted that Morgan would speak to a reporter. She respected the Clark family's privacy, and frankly, the case had been horrific. Who would want to dredge it all up again?

A reporter looking to cash in on the suffering of others, that's who.

Sharp reached for the door, anxious to get rid of her. "Look, Ms. Cruz—"

"Olivia," she said.

Sharp ignored the correction. Reporters were best dealt with on a strictly professional level.

"I don't interfere with Ms. Dane's decisions," he said. "I'll give her your card and pass along the message."

But she didn't budge. "She's currently representing Roger McFarland."

Morgan had only taken the case a few days before, and it wasn't very high profile. The fact that Cruz knew about it gave him pause. He remained silent, however. Once again, Morgan had hired Sharp Investigations to do the legwork. As her agent, he was bound by her client confidentiality.

"You don't have to respond." Ms. Cruz waved a hand. "I have some information on Mr. McFarland that Ms. Dane will want."

Sharp gritted his teeth. "How did you come by this information?"

"I have my sources."

Irritated, Sharp gave her his interrogation stare, a permanent byproduct of his long police career. But she was clearly not intimidated by his bad attitude.

Unfazed, she continued, her tone cool. "I am offering this information to Ms. Dane as a show of good faith."

8

Suspicion rattled in Sharp's gut. He had no love for reporters. They stuck their nose in cases where they weren't wanted, publicized sensitive information, and generally mucked up investigations. As a defense attorney, Morgan had had her own share of difficulty with the media. It was no wonder she wasn't taking any calls from members of the press.

"No strings attached." Olivia caught and held his gaze.

He had a well-developed bullshit meter, and he didn't sense any duplicity in her. But then she'd played him well enough to get in the door, hadn't she? That didn't happen very often.

And she was a *reporter.*

"McFarland lied during his arraignment." Olivia grew serious.

Sharp kept his cop face firmly in place.

But *shit.*

Ms. Cruz's head tilted, as if she were trying to see through his stony expression. "I know you frequently work with Ms. Dane. I also know you and your partner have been talking to Roger McFarland's associates, so I am assuming you were therefore hired to work the case."

"You seem to know a lot about us."

Arrogance quirked the corner of her mouth. Then she grew serious again. "A client's perjury creates a serious ethical dilemma for a defense attorney."

Morgan took ethics very seriously.

Sharp sighed. "If you give me the information, I'll relay it to her."

Olivia pursed her lips, seemingly considering his offer. Then she nodded. "McFarland was convicted of felony battery six years ago in Florida."

McFarland had neglected to list a Florida residence under previous addresses. Private investigators did not have access to the FBI's national criminal databases and had to rely on regional sources. Sharp had run a search for criminal records on McFarland in New York State. He'd also checked for arrest records with the sheriff's office and conviction records with Randolph County. Sharp would have eventually uncovered the residence gap and the felony conviction, but searches took time.

"He attacked his girlfriend in a jealous rage when she broke up with him," Olivia said. "He beat her up pretty badly. Yet during his arraignment here in New York, he denied having any prior felony convictions."

Because McFarland knew the prior conviction for a similar violent crime would diminish his chances of being granted bail. A battery charge in Florida was the equivalent of assault in New York. Bail would be revisited after this morning's preliminary hearing. Prior convictions were one of the court's main considerations when granting bail. Sharp knew that Morgan would not lie in court, but her job was to do everything in her power to defend McFarland. Telling the court about the previous felony would harm her client. Ethical dilemma indeed.

"Did he do time?" Sharp asked.

She shook her head. "He made a deal, got probation, and paid a fine. The girlfriend refused to testify."

She'd probably been too scared.

Since both prosecutor and defense had only been working McFarland's case for a few days, neither side had completed their investigation. Morgan didn't even have all the discovery documents yet. Ninety percent of cases were plea-bargained. No one would bother with the substantial effort involved in preparing the case unless it appeared they would go to trial. The sheriff's department or prosecutor's office should have discovered the Florida conviction, but occasionally, details got lost in the county's massive caseload.

"Do you have anything else to add?" Sharp asked.

"Only this." Her mouth tightened with resolve. "I cannot in good conscience sit on this information. My source at the courthouse says McFarland's preliminary hearing is on the docket for midmorning and will probably be heard between ten thirty and eleven."

Sharp glanced at his watch. Nine o'clock.

She continued. "I will give you until ten o'clock, and then I will call the prosecutor's office. ADA Esposito will know about McFarland's perjury before today's hearing."

Which meant that Sharp couldn't table Morgan's ethical dilemma by simply not telling her about her client's lie. She'd be ambushed in court.

"So considerate of you," he said dryly.

A flash of anger lit her eyes. "Think what you want of me. McFarland lied to the judge knowing the truth would likely come out before his trial. Do you really think he intends to show up for it?"

Sharp brooded. She was right, not that he was going to admit it to her. McFarland's case wouldn't be tried for months. He had the money and motive to run.

"He's committed two violent felonies." She tied her belt around her waist with an irritated snap. "Repeat offenders don't change. He'll do it again. I don't want any future victims on my conscience." Her chin came up, and their gazes met. She searched his eyes, her face smoothing out again. "And neither do you."

Damn. She was right about that too. Working for the defense had its drawbacks.

"I will pass the information along to Ms. Dane." Sharp opened the door, signaling that their discussion was over. He didn't have time to waste. Morgan needed to know the truth, *after* he had verified that it was accurate. "Thank you, Ms. Cruz."

"Olivia," she corrected. The corner of her mouth curved. She pivoted on a skinny heel, stepped over the threshold, and turned toward a white Prius parked at the curb.

"Goodbye, *Ms. Cruz*." Sharp closed the door on her low laugh.

He hurried into his office. Two phone calls and ten minutes later, he had verified that Roger McFarland did indeed have a felony battery conviction in Florida.

Morgan's new client was a perjuring scumbag with a capital *S*.

Maybe she would fire him. The last thing Sharp wanted to do was play an active part in keeping McFarland out of jail. The dude deserved to be behind bars. But Sharp understood why Morgan had taken him on as a client. He'd produced a fat retainer. Her fledgling practice had already represented several charity cases. She had three kids to send to college. She both deserved and needed to be paid for her work. Why did it seem like only guilty people had enough money to pay for a good lawyer?

But then, in his five years as a private investigator, Sharp had worked more than a few distasteful cases. But somehow it seemed worse for Morgan to defend scumbags. She was too classy to deal with slime like McFarland. But now Sharp needed to pack away his judgy attitude and let her know that her case was in the crapper.

He dialed Morgan's number. After she didn't answer, he called Lance.

"Where are you?" he asked as soon as Lance answered.

"Outside the courthouse making some calls."

"Where is Morgan?"

"Inside, talking to McFarland before the case is called. I passed the ADA in the hallway. He was headed toward Morgan. If they wheel and deal, we might be able to get out of here early. The sooner she finishes with McFarland, the better."

"Agreed." Sharp gave Lance a rundown on what the reporter had to say.

"I'll go find her. Talk to you later, Sharp." Lance ended the call.

Restless, Sharp paced his office. He had reports to type, invoices to send, and bills to pay. The sound of a car door closing caught his attention. He looked out the window.

A Mercedes sedan was parked in the driveway. A woman got out and walked toward the building. Her head was down as she looked at her phone, but something about her seemed vaguely familiar. He went to the foyer and opened the front door.

She slid her phone into her purse and looked up. Under short, spiky red hair, her face was pale and her mouth tight. Their eyes met, and recognition nearly tripped him.

It couldn't be.

But he knew it was. After all these years . . .

"Hello, Lincoln," she said.

Chapter Three

"I hired you to make this go away."

In the corridor outside the courtroom, Morgan Dane stared at her client. Roger McFarland was the owner of McFarland Landscaping. Square from the flat buzz of his red hair to his fireplug body, he wasn't a particularly big man, but he was solid in a way that suggested he'd moved plenty of earth in his thirty-five years.

She lowered her voice as three lawyers rushed past them. "I've told you that these charges are not going away."

McFarland dismissed her comment with a wave of his meaty, calloused hand. "I'll pay whatever fines are necessary. Just keep me out of jail."

With a bank account that was nearly as inflated as his ego, McFarland was accustomed to buying his way out of trouble. When he'd first come to her office and she'd agreed to take his case, he'd seemed remorseful, almost ashamed of his behavior. In hindsight, she strongly suspected that had been an act.

"You are charged with attempted murder," Morgan said. "We're still in the discovery process, but the evidence I've seen so far is strong."

How could she convince him that money wasn't enough? He'd crossed a line.

"That's why I wrote you such a big check." McFarland folded his arms and narrowed his eyes. One thing was certain—McFarland would not be going on the stand. He didn't have the sparkling personality to sway a jury. He looked like he broke knees for the mob.

And enjoyed it.

A former prosecutor turned defense attorney, Morgan had worked a couple of high-profile cases over the last six months, but she was still adjusting to working the other side of the courtroom.

"And it's my job to tell you the truth," she said.

"You got that kid off back in September." McFarland shrugged. "Do the same for me."

The kid had been innocent, while McFarland had been arrested standing over the unconscious body of his ex's new boyfriend, whom he'd assaulted in full view of dozens of witnesses. With McFarland's case, Morgan would be arguing admissibility of evidence and shades of guilt. She'd be examining every procedural element with a microscope to chisel away at the prosecutor's case. Most of her clients swore they were innocent. McFarland hadn't bothered. At least he'd known enough to clamp his mouth firmly shut when the police had attempted to question him.

"Your case is different." Morgan shifted the wool coat folded over her arm to check the time. Nine thirty. McFarland's case should be called within the next hour. She expected to be approached by the assistant district attorney before they went in front of the judge.

"Just do your fucking job," McFarland snapped.

Morgan ignored his nastiness. She didn't have to like McFarland to defend him. It was her job to make the ADA prove each charge. But it was a case like this that made her nostalgic for her time in the prosecutor's office and the perception of moral high ground she'd once stood on.

However, she now recognized that concept had been an illusion. Working the defense side of the courtroom had taught her that the system was more flawed than she'd realized, and reinforced the basic tenant of American law: every person was innocent until proven guilty.

Movement at the end of the hall caught her attention. Private investigator Lance Kruger weaved his way toward her, his short blond hair a head above the crowd. He wore the dark-blue suit he usually reserved for court, and he wore it very well.

Despite her determination to keep their relationship strictly professional when they were working, she couldn't help but marvel at what she felt for him after just six months. She'd never thought she'd find love again after her husband's death. But her heart warmed as Lance walked closer.

"Excuse me for a minute." She stepped away from McFarland to join Lance on the other side of the wide corridor. At nearly six feet tall in her heels, she was just a couple of inches shorter than him.

She leaned close to his ear. "Any luck with the witnesses?"

Several people had stated that McFarland had threatened to kill the victim. Morgan was hoping a few of them would backtrack on their statements.

"Not yet." Lance's blue eyes were grim. "They're all sure he said he was going to kill the SOB."

At the moment, her only line of defense was a clerical error on the search warrant affidavit. Police had found evidence that McFarland had fashioned his weapon, a homemade blackjack, in his garage, along with a cash receipt for the raw materials indicating he'd planned the attack several days before carrying it out. Premeditation was the key to the attempted murder charge. Without the evidence uncovered during the search, the case was less cut-and-dried.

A tiny worm of doubt wiggled in Morgan's belly. Before he'd been killed in the line of duty, her father had been a cop. Her grandfather was a retired cop. Her brother was NYPD SWAT. One of her sisters was a Scarlet Falls police detective. The other was a forensic psychiatrist, and before her life had imploded with her husband's death, Morgan had been a prosecutor in Albany. Generations of Danes had devoted—even sacrificed—their lives to put criminals behind bars. Her feelings on being a defense attorney were definitely mixed.

She shook it off. She'd incinerated her bridges with the prosecutor's office last fall by defending her neighbor. This was the only career open to her now. She'd represent McFarland to the best of her ability and put her trust in the legal system. The courts would decide his guilt or innocence.

"Sharp just called." In a low voice, Lance told her about her client's lie.

Before she could wrap her head around Lance's announcement, Assistant District Attorney Anthony Esposito came around the corner and crooked a finger at her.

She strode ten yards down the corridor to confer with the ADA.

Esposito's dark eyes were smiling and smug. "Your client is going to jail."

"We'll see about that," Morgan bluffed.

He looked slick, from his gelled black hair to his shiny wingtips. Usually, she was struck with a twinge of sliminess when they were close, but this morning, the look he shot Morgan was filled with disappointment, and she felt as if their situations had been reversed.

Did he know her client had committed perjury?

"McFarland is as guilty as guilty gets," Esposito said, opening negotiations. "He isn't your usual underdog. He's a dirtball. Why would you even take on a client like him?"

"Because it's my job." She and her three little girls lived with her grandfather, so they'd always have a roof over their heads. But she would like to have some savings. She couldn't limit her practice to pro bono work. "And everyone is presumed innocent."

"Your client put a man in the hospital with a skull fracture. I have more witnesses to the attack than I can fit in a courtroom. I have a weapon with your client's fingerprints on it that matches the dent in the victim's skull and proof that he planned the attack days in advance."

Esposito gave his head a slow shake. "I've been wanting to beat you in court for months, but honestly, this case is so black and white, I can't even take much pleasure in the win."

The glee in Esposito's eyes disagreed. Morgan had bested him multiple times. Each loss had battered his ego. He licked his lips as if he could taste victory.

But he clearly didn't know about McFarland's prior conviction. Yet. But he soon would.

"He never intended to kill anyone," Morgan said.

Esposito lifted a you-must-be-kidding eyebrow. "Your client saw his ex-wife and her new man on Monday. He stopped at a hardware store on the way home for materials to make a weapon. He made said weapon in his garage, waited two days, until Wednesday, when he knew his ex and the new man would be at her favorite bar for happy hour. Then he knocked him out cold from behind and stomped on his unconscious body until three bouncers pulled him off. As he was dragged away, your client stated that he wanted to kill the man. The attack was premeditated, cold-blooded, and violent."

Morgan didn't argue with the facts. Instead, she pointed out the error on the search warrant.

Esposito shrugged, but he couldn't completely conceal a grimace of irritation. "It doesn't matter. Judge Marlow won't throw out the warrant, and even in the *very* unlikely event that he does, I have plenty of other ways to demonstrate premeditation without the evidence uncovered in the search."

"You'll have to."

"I appreciate your game face, but we both know your client will do time," Esposito said. "Let's save the taxpayers some money. Here's the best I can do. He pleads guilty to first-degree assault, and we'll give him seven years. He'll be out in three if he behaves himself. If he insists on going to trial, I'll get him on attempted murder. He'll serve at least ten to fifteen years. Judge Marlow is a hard-ass."

He was, and once the judge found out about the perjury, not only would he be more inclined to give McFarland the maximum sentence for the attempted murder, but her client would be facing additional charges—and more prison time.

"That's not much of a deal," Morgan deadpanned. On the inside, she wanted to throw confetti and do a cartwheel. It was a far better deal than she could have hoped for. If she could convince McFarland to take it, they would avoid a trial. The perjury issue would go away because, while she couldn't lie in court if the judge asked about prior convictions, she was also ethically prohibited from volunteering information to the ADA that might hurt her client. In this case, a quick plea would be a win.

"Take it or leave it." Esposito's lips pressed into a flat line. "You know the drill. If I have to present the case in front of the grand jury, I'll rescind the offer, and it's the only one you're going to get."

Esposito's deals were always now or never. Always so much drama with this man.

"I'll talk to my client." Morgan turned away. Above the crowd, she could see Lance walking away, his phone pressed to his ear.

McFarland leaned on the wall, but the tension in his expression as she approached him belied his casual pose. "Well?"

Morgan outlined the deal.

McFarland's neck and face flushed deep red. "What the fuck? What part of *I'm not going to jail* did you not understand?"

Frustrated, Morgan gritted her teeth. "Mr. McFarland, this is your decision, but I am advising you to take this deal or risk spending much more time in prison." She lowered her voice. "I know about the Florida conviction. You lied at your arraignment hearing."

He rolled his eyes. "So? You're my lawyer. I have attorney-client privilege. You can't tell anyone."

"At the end of this hearing, bail will be revisited. If the judge asks about prior convictions, I cannot lie. Your bail will likely be revoked, and you will also likely be charged with perjury. But even if it doesn't come out today, the prosecutor will discover the prior conviction before trial. If you take the deal he is offering today, I doubt anyone will find out about the perjury. You will avoid potential additional charges and prison time."

"You let me worry about that. I am not going to prison." He leaned closer, his gaze sharpening to a knifepoint. "We are going into that courtroom. If the judge asks about prior convictions, you're going to lie your pretty head off."

"I'm sorry. I can't do that." Morgan would not violate her professional ethics.

Rage sparked like a solar flare in his eyes. "You're no different from every other female. No loyalty." His nostrils flared, and a vein that snaked down his temple throbbed as his blood pressure spiked. "You're a nasty, backstabbing bitch."

His weight shifted, his arm arced, and his fist connected with her temple with a blinding impact. Morgan never saw the hook punch coming. Pain exploded through her head and eye. Her legs folded, and she dropped her tote bag and coat. Before she could register that he'd hit her, her tailbone was ringing on the tile, and a big brown shoe was heading toward her face. With no time to scramble away, she threw her hands in front of her face to block the kick and braced herself for impact.

Chapter Four

Lance ended his call. Someone shouted. He turned toward the commotion and the sound of running feet. The hairs on the back of his neck signaled trouble.

With apprehension building like a soundtrack crescendo, he threaded his way through the crowded hall and sped around the corner. At least six deputies gathered where Morgan had last been standing with her client. More deputies rushed down the hall toward the melee. Lance pressed forward, pushing his way past a group of onlookers. Worry for Morgan wrapped around his heart like barbed wire.

McFarland lay facedown on the tile, his hands cuffed behind his back. He yelled obscenities and thrashed under the weight of the two deputies pinning him to the floor.

Lance's pulse surged. What had McFarland done, and where was Morgan?

He didn't take a full breath until he spotted her sitting on the floor, her tote and wool coat on the floor beside her. Esposito crouched over her, supporting her shoulders with one hand behind her back, the other hand cupping her chin. Lance abandoned politeness and shoved people out of his way to get to her.

He dropped to one knee beside Morgan and took her hand, scanning her for possible injuries. A red blotch stained her temple and the outer rim of her eye socket. "What happened?"

"McFarland popped her." Esposito tilted Morgan's chin.

"What?" Anger burned a short fuse in Lance's chest. He looked back toward McFarland, still struggling with the deputies. "That son of a . . ."

"She's going to have a black eye tomorrow." Esposito looked around and pointed at a young clerk carrying a box of files. "Go find an ice pack."

The clerk nodded and scurried away. With an uncomfortable cough, Esposito dropped the hand holding Morgan's chin.

Lance turned his attention back to Morgan. How badly was she hurt? "How hard did he hit you?"

"I'm OK," Morgan said. But her pretty blue eyes were wide-open with shock. The blotch blooming beside her eye seemed to be darkening.

The mark made Lance wish McFarland would break free of the deputies. He wanted to teach him a lesson about the collision of fists and faces. His love for Morgan was absolute. The desire to protect her blotted out the refinements of civilization and left Lance stripped down to his primal instincts.

The deputies hauled McFarland to his feet and dragged him off, still cursing and resisting.

"Can you sit up by yourself?" Esposito asked.

When Morgan nodded, he removed his hand from her back and stood. "Don't rush to get up."

Lance scanned her face, reassessing. Beyond the red mark, he didn't like the vacant, *doe in the headlights* look in her eyes. "You should get checked out by a doctor."

"It was only one punch." Morgan blinked hard and stared up at the ADA. "Thank you. If you hadn't stepped in . . ."

Esposito flushed, tugged on his lapels, and smoothed his hair with one swipe of a thick hand.

His chin dipped in a curt nod. "As I said before, your client is a dirtball."

"Former client. He'll have to find another attorney." Morgan folded her long legs under her body. Lance held her hand and elbow and helped her stand. She wobbled, and he wrapped a steadying arm around her. And because he couldn't help himself, he pulled her closer and pressed a kiss to her hair.

Lance's relationship with Morgan wasn't a secret, but they kept their interactions professional in professional settings, mostly because Morgan insisted. Lance didn't give a rat's ass about other people's opinions. But then, as a PI, his reputation wasn't as critical as hers was as an attorney. But today, the only thing that mattered was that she was all right.

The clerk returned with a cold pack and handed it to Morgan. She thanked him and pressed it to the side of her face. Her flinch sent a fresh wave of hot anger through Lance's veins.

Esposito bent to pick up Morgan's tote bag and coat. He handed both to Lance. "Feel better, Ms. Dane." With a quick nod to Lance, Esposito walked away.

Morgan gave a statement to a deputy and agreed to make herself available for further questioning at a later date. Lance took her arm and led her toward the exit.

She repositioned the cold pack. Her hand trembled. "I'm not sure which was more shocking—the fact that my client punched me, or that Esposito came to my rescue. McFarland was getting ready to kick me in the head. Esposito body-slammed him."

Lance glanced over his shoulder at the retreating back of the ADA. "I wouldn't have expected it."

"Me either. He considers all defense attorneys bottom-feeders. Usually he treats me with complete disdain."

They stepped outside. The cold air wrapped around them, and Morgan shivered. Lance tucked her huge bag under his arm and held her coat open for her. Lowering the ice pack, she slid her arms into her coat and wrapped it tightly around her body. Lance tucked her against him, and they walked to his Jeep. He opened and closed her door before rounding the vehicle and sliding behind the wheel.

She fastened her seat belt, then dug through her bag. "Can you stop at the Minimart? I'm out of Tylenol."

"Sure." He drove to the convenience store, and they went inside.

Morgan took a box of pain relievers from the shelf, then ducked down the next aisle for a bag of Peanut M&M's. She paid at the register, and they left the store. Walking toward the Jeep, she shoved the medicine into her tote. She wobbled, one hand reaching out as if to balance herself. Lance reached for her as her knees buckled. She pitched forward, her face rushing toward the blacktop.

Lance lunged, catching her shoulders and easing her to the ground. Supporting her upper body with one arm, he turned her chin toward him. "Morgan?"

Her eyes fluttered open. She blinked hard. "What happened?"

"You fainted." Worried, Lance tilted her face to get a better look at her eyes. They looked normal, but he wasn't a doctor. She needed to see one of those ASAP. He wouldn't take no for an answer this time. She had three little girls who depended on her.

She frowned. "I don't faint." Her voice was indignant.

Lance shifted his body to pick her up.

"Wait." Morgan grabbed her tote. Then she snagged her candy from the asphalt where it had fallen.

"Seriously?" He scooped her into his arms.

"My blood sugar must be low. I don't need to be carried," she protested. "You can put me down."

"So you can hit your head again?" Lance hefted her higher in his arms and headed toward his Jeep. "I don't think so. We're going to the ER."

She didn't protest, which told him she felt much worse than she wanted to admit.

Chapter Five

Sharp froze. Her use of his first name brought the memories rushing back. No one had called him Lincoln in ages. His parents were both dead, he was an only child, and he hadn't spoken to his ex-wife in many years. But Eliza had also known him before he'd become a cop, before he'd acquired his nickname.

"Eliza?" Even with the evidence right in front of him, he couldn't believe she was here.

"I was afraid you might not remember me." She blew a piece of hair away from her eyes. "It's been a long time."

"I remember you," he said.

Don't just stand there, idiot.

He hurried down the steps and stood awkwardly in front of her, unsure how to greet her. He settled on a quick hug. They were old friends after all, no matter what else had transpired between them. "How are you?"

Twenty-five years before, her husband, Officer Ted Powell, had died, leaving Eliza to raise their baby, Haley, alone. The memory of Ted's death was etched permanently into Sharp's brain. Nor would he ever forget the way she'd accepted the folded flag, the fog crawling over the cemetery, or her three involuntary flinches as the honor guard sent off the twenty-one-gun salute. To this day, Sharp hated the sound of bagpipes.

The community and the Scarlet Falls PD had come together to support Eliza. But less than a year after her husband's death, she had moved to New York City, wanting a fresh start.

Maybe she'd also wanted to put some distance between her and Sharp.

"I need your help." Her voice broke. "I don't know who else to call."

The desperate edge in her voice put Sharp on alert and wiped away his nostalgia. "What's wrong?"

"It's Haley." Eliza's breath hitched. "She needs a lawyer."

In his mind, Sharp saw an infant in a pink blanket, but Haley would be an adult now.

A garbage truck rumbled down the street, and two cars pulled into the small parking lot of the real estate agency next door. Sensing Eliza's story would require privacy, he steered her up the front steps.

"Let's go inside." He held the door open for her.

In the foyer, he gestured toward his office. The largest room in the unit, it had once been a living room and accommodated a couch in addition to the usual office furniture.

Clearly agitated, Eliza paced.

"Haley called me this morning. She was nearly hysterical, almost incoherent." Eliza's eyes misted. She paused to collect herself. "She told me she was at the sheriff's station, and they wouldn't let her leave. They think she killed someone named Noah."

"She's at the Randolph County Sheriff's Station?" Sharp asked, confused.

"Yes."

"Why was Haley in town?"

"We live in Grey's Hollow." Eliza's eyes flickered away from his for a moment, then she got back to business. "Right after she called, two deputies showed up on my doorstep with a search warrant. They went through Haley's room and took her computer."

Sharp swallowed the fact that she'd never let him know she was back. Then he focused on her needs. "What did the warrant say?"

Eliza took a folded piece of paper from her purse. "They gave me a copy and a receipt for Haley's computer."

Sharp read the warrant. The police were looking for evidence in the murder of Noah Carter. The probable cause affidavit wasn't attached, so he didn't know how much evidence the police had on Haley. "They only took her computer, so that means they didn't find any other evidence."

"I don't even know who Noah Carter is." Eliza's voice broke.

"Me either. A missing woman case has dominated the news," Sharp said. The sheriff's department had been looking for twenty-five-year-old Shannon Yates since she'd been reported missing the previous Tuesday. Her car had been found Saturday afternoon, and the sheriff's department suspected that foul play had occurred. "But there was another story about a young man being stabbed. Is that the case?"

"I don't know." Eliza whirled and paced back toward him. "By the time I got that little bit of information out of Haley, someone in the background was yelling that her time was up. I told her not to say anything else. That I would get her a lawyer. And she hung up."

"Did you go to the station?" Sharp went behind his desk. He opened his computer and pulled up the local news station website.

She nodded. "Yes. As soon as the deputies left my house. I couldn't get past the front desk."

"What time was this?" Sharp asked, scrolling.

Eliza looked at her watch. "About an hour ago. I called a couple of local lawyers, but they don't handle criminal defense. Then I remembered seeing you on the news last fall after that big murder case. You were working with a lawyer. A woman. She seemed very smart."

"She is," Sharp said. "If anyone can help Haley, it's Morgan Dane."

"Haley's health is fragile. About seven years ago, in her freshman year of college, she was very sick. She lost weight. She was weak and had bouts of dizziness. The doctors originally thought it might have been a tumor." Eliza gulped and closed her eyes for a few seconds. "I was terrified."

"I can only imagine," Sharp said.

"We were relieved when she was diagnosed with Addison's disease. Her adrenal glands don't function properly. She needs to take medication every day or she can suffer dehydration, hypoglycemia, and dangerous drops in blood pressure, which is why her near incoherency this morning is particularly alarming. Haley always carries extra medication, but the police would have taken her purse."

"Did you explain this at the sheriff's office?"

"Yes. The deputy at the desk said he would tell the sheriff."

"How long can she go without her medication before she's in serious trouble?" Sharp asked, looking up from his computer.

"Normally, a few days without medication would make her tired and possibly dizzy, and she would feel better once she resumed taking the replacement hormones. But stress compounds the problem. Your adrenal glands respond to stress by producing extra cortisol. But Haley's body can't do that, and she must take extra medication when she's stressed. The short answer is, I don't know."

Sharp found the story he'd been looking for and skimmed it. "Noah Carter was stabbed to death in his home Friday night. A woman is being questioned as a person of interest in the case."

Eliza paled. "Haley couldn't possibly have done that."

"The best thing we can do is get Morgan over there." Sharp pulled out his cell and speed-dialed Morgan. After three rings, the call flipped to voice mail. He left a brief message, then tried Lance's number. He didn't answer either. Sharp sent Lance a text.

"We should get a call back quickly. Unless she's in court, Morgan usually answers her phone. She'll check her messages as soon as the hearing is over."

"It was a zoo in the sheriff's station. Several news vans were outside."

"The search for Shannon Yates is ongoing," Sharp said.

"I know," Eliza said. "I'm afraid Haley has been forgotten."

"They're not going to forget a murder suspect. It will still be a major case."

"But if she's in custody, then she's no longer a threat. The sheriff's office will put her on the back burner and focus on the search for the missing woman." Eliza's voice tightened.

She was right. The sheriff had a limited number of deputies. They would concentrate their efforts where they could affect the outcome of the case.

"OK. Let's go to the station. Maybe I can get someone's attention." Sharp knew many of the deputies, including the one who had stepped in to act as sheriff after the previous one had died back in November.

"Thank you." Eliza turned toward the door. The hand on her purse strap was clenched tightly enough to raise the tendons on the back of her hand. "I can't lose her."

"You won't." Sharp couldn't let that happen. It didn't matter how many years had passed since Ted's death. Some promises never expired.

July 1993

Sharp climbed out of his patrol car in the lot alongside the deli. Sweat dripped down his back before he'd closed the car door. The sun had gone down an hour before, but the sweltering heat had barely broken. The night air was thick and charged with the possibility of a thunderstorm. July humidity, his stiff uniform, and his duty belt were an uncomfortable combination.

Also on night shift, Ted Powell drove up in his black-and-white, parked next to him, and got out of the vehicle. Sweat beaded on his upper lip. Nasty smells emanated from the open dumpster as they walked past it.

"What do you want to drink?" Sharp led the way around the corner of the brick building. He opened the glass front door, and they stepped inside.

The scent of hot dogs filled his nose. In front of them, a small group of customers stood in line at the register.

Ted pivoted left, toward the ORDER HERE *sign suspended from the ceiling over the sandwich counter. "You want food?"*

"No, thanks." Sharp had packed his dinner. "The chemicals in deli meat will kill you."

"The baby has been awake for days." Ted rubbed an eye. "I need sustenance."

Sharp swallowed a small bite of envy. His own marital problems weren't his best friend's fault. He and Kristy had only been married for six months. Things would smooth out. "Good thing that little girl of yours is adorable."

One thing Sharp liked about working second shift was that by the time he got home, Kristy was asleep. And by the time he woke in the morning, she had left for work. He was avoiding her, which was a bad sign. They were still newlyweds. He should want *to go home to his wife.*

But she was pressuring him to quit the force. She couldn't sleep knowing that he might not come home. She had nightmares.

Being married to a cop wasn't easy. Not everyone could handle it.

"She is adorable, isn't she?" Smiling, Ted adjusted his belt under the small paunch he'd developed since they'd graduated from the academy together two years before. "Eliza put me on a diet. I'm starving. I'm getting an all-meat sub with a side of meat."

"If you went running with me, you wouldn't have that gut," Sharp said as he veered right toward the cold cases in the back of the store.

"Yeah. Yeah. Yeah." Ted had many great qualities. Athleticism wasn't one of them. "Grab me a Coke," he called over his shoulder.

"That'll kill you too," Sharp said.

"Stop nagging." Ted laughed. "I already have a wife."

Sharp walked down the junk food aisle and stopped in front of a refrigerator case. He selected a Coke, then moved two doors down and grabbed a bottle of unsweetened iced tea for himself.

A woman screamed from the front of the store, the sound high-pitched and terrified.

Sharp froze, his hand automatically going to his sidearm.

"Hands up!" a man shouted. Someone started sobbing.

A robbery.

Sharp's heart kicked into gear. He glanced at the curved mirror mounted in the corner of the ceiling. In the distorted reflection, the customers in line at the register held their hands over their heads. At the head of the line, a man in an army-green jacket pointed a revolver at the clerk. Under dirty black hair, his face shone with sweat, his eyes were wild, and his chest heaved.

The robber had angled his body sideways to have a view of the clerk, the five customers in line, and the front door. Agitated, he shifted his weight as his gaze darted back and forth.

Sharp registered the nightmare scenario: innocent people and an armed meth head.

The robber did not know two cops were in the store. If he'd approached from the front, he wouldn't have seen their patrol cars hidden behind the dumpsters.

Sharp looked for Ted but didn't have a view of the sandwich counter on the other side of the store. He set the drinks on the floor without making any noise and silenced his radio. Then he drew his weapon. Quieting his breath, he eased to the end of the aisle, put his back to a display of Hostess Cakes, and peered around it.

"Empty the register." The robber jerked the barrel of his gun toward the clerk.

With shaking hands, the clerk pressed a button on the register. The drawer opened with a clang. He scooped the cash into a bag and handed it to the armed man.

The robber glanced in the bag. His angry gaze cut to the clerk. "It's not enough."

"That's all I have." The clerk's voice trembled.

The robber raised the gun until it was aimed directly at the clerk's face. The barrel shook as if it had a vibrate setting. "Open the other register."

The clerk turned toward the second register on the other end of the counter. He opened it and removed a wad of bills.

"That's all that's here," the clerk cried, tears streaming down his face as he handed the cash across the counter.

Where is Ted?

Sharp couldn't use his radio. The robber would hear it, and the meth head was already unstable. If he saw two cops, he'd surely lose his shit.

The robber shook the gun harder. His face reddened, and his chest heaved with rapid breaths. "It's still not enough! I am not leaving here with a lousy hundred bucks."

Sharp didn't have a clear shot. There were too many customers in the way. He eased back and crept along the aisle. A man huddled on the floor, shaking. He raised a frightened gaze. Sharp motioned toward the floor, telling the man to stay down.

At the opposite end of the aisle, Sharp looked through a display of candy bars. Two customers were still in Sharp's line of fire. The small store was too crowded for a clean shot. The robber's body language and tone felt desperate. Sharp used another ceiling-mounted mirror to scan the distorted, bird's-eye view of the store. If he could work his way over one more aisle, he should have an unobstructed shot.

The robber shifted his aim from the clerk to the line of customers. He arced the gun back and forth. "I need more money or somebody dies."

Sharp crept around a revolving magazine rack. A shadow caught his attention. Twenty feet away, Ted crouched behind the ice machine, gun in hand. He pointed at Sharp and made a circular motion with his hand, indicating he wanted Sharp to circle around to the front of the store. Then he tapped his own chest and pointed down the aisle between them.

Sharp shook his head. There was no way he was letting Ted confront the robber while Sharp batted cleanup. Ted had a family.

Sharp pointed to his own chest and motioned down the next aisle. Without waiting for Ted to agree, he crouched lower and started down the aisle. In his peripheral vision, he saw Ted turn around and head toward the end of the aisle.

Sharp checked the overhead mirror and waited until Ted was in position. Their rough plan should work. Sharp would shout out, and the robber would turn toward him—and turn the gun away from the civilians. The robber would be flanked by Sharp and Ted, with the civilians out of the line of fire.

His heartbeat slammed through his chest. His pulse echoed in his ears. His vision tunneled down to the robber and the few feet around him.

With a quick breath, Sharp stood and pointed his weapon over an ice cream chest at the robber. As he shouted, "Police," a crack sounded from Ted's direction. A can of dog food rolled across the floor.

The robber spun away from Sharp and toward Ted, whose navy-blue uniform was just visible through the potato chip display. The revolver fired. Sharp pulled his trigger. Ted's gun went off. Someone screamed. The robber's legs folded. He slumped to the floor on his side. His fingers opened. Sharp shuffled forward, his gun still aimed at the robber's center mass. He kicked the gun away, holstered his own weapon, then handcuffed the robber. Blood seeped onto the floor from multiple gunshots in his torso, arm, and shoulder. He and Ted must have both hit their target.

With the threat neutralized, Sharp stood, chest heaving. Ten feet away, Ted collapsed onto his ass. He threw a hand out to brace himself. Blood poured down his shoulder from a wound in the side of his neck.

No.

Horrified, Sharp rushed forward and caught his friend around the shoulders, easing him to the floor.

"Officer down!" Sharp shouted into his radio mic to call for backup and an ambulance. He pressed both hands to the wound, trying to slow the bleeding. Panic roiled in his belly as blood welled between his fingers.

"Here." A woman handed a towel over Sharp's shoulder.

He used it to staunch the flow of blood, but the puddle on the linoleum was spreading no matter what he did. It soaked through the knees of his uniform trousers. The bullet must have severed Ted's carotid artery.

Red lights flashed outside the glass door as two more patrol cars turned into the parking lot.

Another patrol officer rushed in and sized up the situation. "Ambulance ETA is nine minutes."

Grief and anguish welled into Sharp's chest and throat. The pressure built until it felt as if it would crack him open. His vision blurred as a river of red continued to flow from Ted's neck.

Ted needed help now. He wouldn't make it another nine minutes. He might not make it ninety seconds.

There was nothing Sharp could do. Nothing. Helplessness flooded him.

Ted's hand moved to touch Sharp's wrist. His mouth moved, but no words came out, just a hiss of pink froth. A thin line of blood trickled from the corner of his mouth. His lips moved. Sharp leaned close to hear the words over the gurgle of blood in Ted's throat.

"Take care of Eliza and Haley," Ted rasped.

Sharp wanted to protest, to tell his friend that he'd be caring for his own wife and baby. But that wasn't what Ted needed. He wanted to know his family would be cared for.

They both knew Ted wasn't going to make it. It just wasn't possible. He might have a chance if there were an operating room and bags of blood right here, right now. But there weren't.

So, instead of making empty promises, Sharp said the words that would ease his friend's anxiety. "I will."

Tears filled Ted's eyes. His lips moved again. "Tell her I love her," he mouthed.

Unable to speak, his throat clogged with shock and sorrow, Sharp nodded.

Ted's grip on his wrist weakened and fell away. His breath rattled in his throat. Air bubbles welled in the blood coming from the bullet hole. His chest expanded in one more ragged, wet gasp, then settled, still and silent. His gaze left Sharp's and stared blankly at the ceiling.

Footsteps sounded behind Sharp. Someone pulled him away. Medics rushed in. One compressed the wound. The other started CPR. But the silence in the small store told the truth.

Ted was gone. He hadn't had a chance. The wound had been too grievous. The bullet had hit too many vital structures.

Hands gripped Sharp's shoulders. "Are you hit?"

He shook his head, his gaze still on his friend.

Reality overwhelmed him. Ted was dead. His wife and baby were alone. Who would tell Eliza?

Chapter Six

The ER was quiet when they arrived. Two hours later, Morgan was diagnosed with a mild concussion and released. Her head throbbed with its own pulse as she and Lance exited the building. He had pulled the Jeep up to the door. Holding an ice pack given to her in the ER, she climbed into the passenger seat, and he drove out of the parking lot.

Morgan rooted through her tote bag for the small bottle of pain relievers she'd purchased earlier. Her hands trembled hard enough to make the pills rattle inside the bottle.

Her own client had hit her.

Inside the courthouse in full view of the prosecutor, a half dozen deputies, and who knew how many surveillance cameras? She'd been threatened numerous times as a prosecutor but always by the opposing side. She hadn't expected an attack from the very person she'd been trying to defend. Being a private defense attorney should be less dangerous than working for the DA's office. As the mother of three children who had already lost one parent, Morgan had considered this aspect of her career change a benefit. Had she been wrong?

The event seemed surreal, except for the very real pain rocketing through her face and head. McFarland's fist had connected with her temple, but she felt its impact in her jaw and the back of her skull. Even her teeth ached.

Lance reached behind her seat and produced a bottle of water. He set it in the console cupholder.

"Thank you." She twisted the cap off the medicine bottle and tipped it into her hand. The pills spilled out over her lap.

"Damn." She picked two tablets off the seat of the Jeep, put them in her mouth, and washed them down. Setting the water in the cupholder, she gathered up the spilled medication and returned it to the bottle.

"Let's get you home."

Morgan was going to spend the rest of the day snuggling with her girls on her couch in her pajamas. She returned the pill bottle to her tote. Inside the bag, her phone vibrated. She reached for it. She hadn't checked her messages since they'd left the courthouse.

"You don't have to answer that." Lance frowned.

"It's Sharp." Morgan took the call. "We're in the Jeep. You're on speaker."

"Are you finished with McFarland for the day?" Sharp asked. "I have an urgent case for you."

"I'm definitely finished with McFarland," Morgan said. "What's going on?"

"A young woman named Haley Powell is being held at the sheriff's station. They've had her since Saturday afternoon, so they've been holding her for almost two days." Sharp detailed Haley's medical condition and her case in a few sentences, then his voice thickened. "I'd consider this a personal favor. Her mother and I go way back."

"I'm on my way to the sheriff's station now," Morgan said, even though all she really wanted to do was go home.

"We'll be waiting for you." Sharp disconnected.

Lance glanced over the console. "You didn't tell him you just left the ER."

"He didn't ask."

A long exhale from Lance conveyed his frustration. "Are you sure you're up to this?"

"The X-ray and CAT scan were clear. The doctor said I would make a full recovery."

"He also said you should rest." Lance's frown deepened.

She knew he wanted to protect her, but he also tried hard to respect her ability to handle her job. However, the emotion in Sharp's voice concerned her. Something was wrong.

"Sharp never asks for anything," she said. "And he's helped with two of my cases without being paid. He sounded upset."

"He did sound rough." Lance's brows dipped. "But you look like you're going to throw up."

"I look that bad?" Morgan lowered the sun visor and opened the mirror. "Ugh."

A fist-size goose egg decorated her temple, her hair had been pulled from its neat twist, and by tomorrow, she was definitely going to have a black eye. She removed the remaining hairpins and stuffed them in her tote. She considered the tube of concealer in her makeup bag, but the thought of touching the tender area to apply makeup stopped her from attempting to cover up the damage. She finger-combed her hair and let it fall alongside her face like a curtain. That was the best she could do.

"Unbelievably, you still look gorgeous." Lance stopped the car at a red light. He reached over and took her hand. "I love that you want to help Sharp, but you have to be honest about how you feel. You won't be any good to his friend if you make yourself sick." He picked up her hand and kissed her knuckles. "Plus, I love you, and I don't like to see you hurting."

"I love you too." She squeezed his fingers. "I know you're worried about me, but if Sharp needs me, I have to try to help him."

"I know."

The sheriff's station parking lot was full of news vans, and reporters were broadcasting updates from the sidewalk in front of the station. Lance parked on the street. Skirting the media circus, Morgan and Lance went inside, where the scene was equally chaotic.

"Looks like every deputy in the department has been called in," Lance said.

Morgan turned toward the corner of the crowded lobby and found Sharp waiting with a woman in her late forties.

At fifty-three, Sharp was fitter than most people half his age thanks to a strict exercise regimen and an organic, crunchy lifestyle. Clad in his usual jeans and T-shirt, he looked more tense than normal.

The woman's eyes widened with a quick flash of surprise as she blinked at Morgan's face, but she was too polite to say anything.

But Sharp had no such reservations. He strode across the tile. "What the hell happened to you?" He reached for Morgan's hair, lifting a piece out of the way and leaning in to get a closer look at her goose egg.

Morgan leaned back and pushed Sharp's hand away. "My client wasn't happy with my advice."

"McFarland hit you?" Sharp nearly snarled.

"I'm OK," Morgan said.

Sharp didn't look convinced. "I don't want to jeopardize your health."

"Sharp, I'm fully capable of doing my job."

He nodded. "Then I appreciate that you came right over here." He glanced behind him at the woman who stood ten feet away and lowered his voice. "Eliza's husband was my best friend." He paused, his face tightening as if he were struggling to contain his grief and articulate his feelings.

Morgan put a hand on his arm and nodded toward the woman. "Why don't you introduce me, and let me get to it?"

"Thank you." Sharp introduced them in a low voice. "Eliza, this is Morgan Dane. She's the best lawyer I've ever worked with. Morgan, Eliza Powell is a very old friend."

"Thank you for coming." Eliza sniffed. "I didn't know what to do when Haley called me, so I went to see Lincoln."

Lincoln?

Morgan had never heard him addressed by his first name. *Everyone* called him Sharp.

"Please." Eliza's voice broke. "I'm so worried about my daughter."

"Let me see what I can find out." Morgan turned toward the reception counter. Behind it, deputies and administrative staff worked phones and computers.

The sheriff's watchdog, Marge, approached the counter, lowered her reading glasses from her nose, and hooked them in the neck of her gray cardigan. In her sixties, Marge had worked for the sheriff's office longer than anyone else in the department.

"You're here to represent Haley Powell?" Marge asked with a pitying look at Morgan's face.

When her eye went full black, people were going to be able to see Morgan's injury from fifty yards away.

"Yes," Morgan said. "I need to see my client, and I'll need to speak with the sheriff as soon as he has a moment."

Marge nodded with what appeared to be approval.

Interesting.

"The sheriff is in right now," Marge said. "Considering all that's going on this morning with the search for the missing woman, there's no guarantee how long he'll be here. I'll take you back to see him first, if that's agreeable to you." Marge gestured to the corridor that led to the sheriff's office.

"Yes. Thank you." Morgan followed her. While she was anxious to see Haley, she didn't want to miss what might be her only opportunity to see the sheriff. She needed to know what specific charges were pending against Haley and why.

The sheriff stood when Morgan entered. Sixty-year-old Henry Colgate was just months away from retirement. He shoved a harried hand through the few wispy gray hairs left on his head.

"Ms. Dane." Colgate gestured to the chair that faced his desk. Papers, file folders, and pink message slips littered the surface. "Please close the door."

Morgan pushed it shut, then took a seat.

Narrowing his eyes at her face, he said, "I heard about what happened at the courthouse."

Of course he had. In addition to regular law enforcement for all of Randolph County, the sheriff was in charge of the county jail and courthouse. It was an immense responsibility for a man who had publicly declared he no intention of running for the office.

"It looks worse than it is," Morgan lied. Her face pulsed with pain. "I'm representing Haley Powell."

Nodding, Colgate settled behind the desk. Technically, Colgate was the acting sheriff. He'd been the chief deputy when the prior sheriff had died back in November. Colgate had stepped into the position. The job was obviously wearing him down. The bags under his eyes were deep and dark.

Morgan reaching into her bag for her legal pad and a pen. As she leaned over, the room did a quick spin around her. She clutched the armrest and closed her eyes for a few seconds.

"Ms. Dane? Are you all right?"

"Yes. Thank you." Morgan straightened. "Are you aware that my client has a serious medical condition?"

"No." His mouth twisted in a skeptical frown. "She didn't look sick when I talked to her, and she wasn't wearing a medical alert bracelet."

"Her mother was here this morning. She left a message for you." Morgan gave the clutter on Colgate's desk a pointed stare.

He sifted through the stack of messages. "I don't see it."

"Haley requires medication daily. She's been without it for two days." Morgan had no time to waste arguing. She made a note and moved on. "Has she been formally charged?"

41

Colgate shook his head. "Not yet, but I've been communicating with the prosecutor's office. I have no doubt murder charges will be filed later today."

"How long has she been here?"

"Since one p.m. Saturday."

"And *you* questioned her personally?"

Colgate leaned back in his chair. The springs squeaked. "I did."

"Without a lawyer present?"

"She didn't ask for a lawyer." He folded his hands on his small paunch. "And she didn't say anything about being sick or needing medicine either," he added in a defensive tone.

"How many times did you interview her?"

"Three," he said. "At the scene, here immediately after we brought her in, and again this morning."

Morgan checked her watch. "You brought her here at one p.m. on Saturday, and she sat in your holding cell for nearly two days. Did anyone else question her during that time?"

"No." Colgate flushed. "We're looking for a missing woman. We have limited resources."

A number of deputies had quit in the four months following the former sheriff's death. Colgate was shorthanded, and he was juggling two major cases. Any sheriff would likely have done the same under the circumstances. The rules for holding a suspect no longer than forty-eight hours were customarily extended when the time spanned a weekend. Technically, he could hold her another day.

Colgate hadn't done anything illegal. But Morgan still wasn't happy about the situation. Her young client had been sitting in a filthy cell without her medication for far too long.

The sheriff squirmed. "Haley Powell murdered Noah Carter. The arrest warrant will be here any minute."

"Based on what evidence?" Morgan looked up. The sheriff's department had to demonstrate probable cause before the prosecutor would issue an arrest warrant. Esposito might be overly aggressive, but his boss, District Attorney Bryce Walters, would tread carefully with a case as serious as murder. Bryce would make sure every technicality was addressed.

"Her fingerprints were on the weapon." Colgate shifted his weight forward and began ticking facts off on his fingers. "She was covered in blood. The blood type matched that of the victim. She was seen leaving the club with the victim at approximately one a.m. Saturday morning. The club gave us surveillance footage of them exiting the building together. Multiple witnesses stated they were cozy all evening, and we found a used condom in the bathroom trash can." Colgate folded his hands on his desk. "I'm pretty certain both your client's DNA and that of the victim will be confirmed on the condom."

"If she went home willingly with him, what was her motive?"

Colgate turned up a palm. "Who knows? She seems flaky. Maybe she changed her mind."

Morgan pounced on the crumb he'd tossed her. "Are you suggesting he raped her, and she defended herself?"

"No." Colgate pressed his lips together hard, clearly realizing his mistake. "I'm saying we don't know what her motive was yet."

Morgan leveled her gaze at him. "But it's a possibility."

Colgate exhaled hard through his nose. "Your client has not claimed self-defense. Nor did she say anything about being raped." He opened a file and put on a pair of reading glasses. "In fact, what she said to the deputies who responded to the original call was, 'What have *I* done?' At no point has she accused the victim of doing anything or claimed to be injured in any way." He looked at Morgan over the top of his glasses. "Once she got a hold of herself, she got quieter."

No doubt Colgate thought sitting in the holding cell might inspire her to talk.

Morgan set down her pen. "Now I'd like to see my client." She had more questions, but they would wait until she'd talked to Haley.

"One more thing." Colgate opened a file on his desk.

Morgan braced herself for what she suspected was coming: crime scene and/or autopsy photos. This wasn't her first rodeo. Stabbings could be particularly nasty. A knife could do more damage than a bullet.

The sheriff slid three photographs across the desk. In the first, a young man lay on his stomach, his arms stretched out ahead of him, as if he had been trying to pull himself though the grass. Photo number two was a long trail of blood, and the third picture was clearly where he had been killed.

Morgan had seen many photos of dead bodies, but the sight never failed to twist her heart into knots.

Colgate stabbed the photo of the body with a forefinger. "With three knife wounds, Noah tried to crawl for help, but he bled out before he was feet from the house."

"Where did the knife come from?" she asked.

"The block on the kitchen counter."

"Were there any other prints on the weapon?"

"No," Colgate said in a satisfied tone.

"Not even Noah Carter's?"

Colgate frowned. "No."

Interesting.

"This morning, I had to go to Noah's parents' house and tell them their son was dead," Colgate said.

"I'm sorry. That must have been awful for you, and I can't even imagine their grief." While she needed objectivity to do her job, Morgan never wanted to lose sight of the fact that cases were about people.

The sheriff's brows lifted a millimeter, as if he were surprised by her comment. "Haley Powell killed Noah Carter."

Morgan slid her notepad into her tote and stood. "I need to see my client."

Colgate pushed off his desk and got to his feet. They left his office, and he led her to an empty interview room. "I'll have Ms. Powell brought in."

"Thank you." Morgan set her tote on the floor next to a chair. She settled at the table with her legal pad and pen. A few minutes later, footsteps shuffled in the hall. Her first look at her client brought Morgan to her feet.

The petite girl wore a skimpy black dress. A blanket was draped over her shoulders, and her eyes were frighteningly blank. Flecks of dried blood dotted the skin of her upper arms and neck. Mascara ringed her eyes, and makeup smeared her face. Two nights in a holding cell would make anyone look ragged, but Haley didn't look like a suspect. She looked like a victim.

The deputy led her inside the room and steered her toward a chair.

Anger surged through Morgan's veins. "Remove those handcuffs."

The deputy spun Haley around like a doll and unlocked the cuffs. The girl didn't rub her wrists or flex her fingers the way that most suspects did when freed from handcuffs. She just stood there, barefoot and shivering, her arms hanging limply at her sides.

Morgan went to her, wrapping the rough blanket more tightly around her shoulders. "Where are her shoes?"

The deputy shrugged. "Locked up with her personal possessions. The heels were pointy."

Holding cells were rarely, if ever, cleaned. They were commonly covered in feces, vomit, and urine, and Haley had been left in one in her bare feet. More scare tactics from the sheriff?

The deputy left the room, locking the door behind him.

Taking the girl by the shoulders, Morgan guided her to a chair and eased her down into it. The girl wouldn't meet her gaze but stared at her hands instead.

"Haley, I'm Morgan Dane. Your mother hired me to be your lawyer. Do you know why you're here?"

Shrugging, Haley picked at her thumbnail. Blood oozed from the skin. Morgan took the girl's hands in her own. Haley's were ice-cold. Her nails had been painted dark blue, but the polish was peeling, and her nails were bitten below the quick.

"How do you feel? When was the last time you took your medication?" Morgan lifted the blanket. She didn't see any serious injuries, but a few bruises dotted Haley's pale, bare leg. Her feet were as filthy as Morgan would expect.

Haley's breath hitched, but she remained silent, shifting her focus from her hands to a spot over Morgan's shoulder.

Morgan crouched in front of the girl and rubbed her shoulders. "Are you hurt?"

For the first time, Haley's gaze rose to meet Morgan's, but the expression in her eyes looked distant. Several seconds passed before Haley seemed to fully focus.

She shook her head. "I don't think so."

Think?

"Haley, do you know where you are?"

The girl sniffed and nodded. "The police think I killed Noah." She might be an adult, but her voice was as soft as a child's.

Morgan's nerves chilled. "Can you tell me what happened?"

"I woke up. I was naked. There was blood on me. On everything. A trail went out the bedroom door. I followed it. My dress was in the family room on the floor. I couldn't find Noah. Then I did, and he was . . ." She groaned, bent double, and retched.

Morgan moved a plastic garbage pail from the corner to Haley's side. But the girl straightened and shook her head.

"You stayed at Noah's house Friday night?" Morgan asked.

Haley lifted a thin shoulder. "I guess so."

"You guess? You don't remember?"

She shook her head. "I was at that new club, Beats, with Piper. I remember talking to Noah. I liked him." Her chest heaved with a breath. "I think I went home with him. Then I woke up in his bed."

"How many drinks did you have?" Morgan asked.

"I don't remember." She winced. "But I never have more than two."

Not enough to cause even a petite person to black out. Did her condition affect her ability to metabolize alcohol? Or had she been drugged?

Haley had been seen leaving the club with Noah at one a.m. Saturday morning. If Haley had been slipped a drug, two and a half days had passed since she'd consumed it. That was far too long for many date-rape drugs to remain in her system. But there was still a chance.

Morgan stood, turned, and banged on the door, her own pain numbed by adrenaline and fury. The deputy opened the door.

"I want to see the sheriff," Morgan demanded. "Now."

The deputy withdrew. Morgan heard the scrape and click of the door lock.

A few minutes later, the door opened, and Colgate stepped inside.

"Is my client under arrest?" Morgan asked.

"I expect the arrest warrant shortly." Colgate's eyes narrowed warily. "The preliminary autopsy just came in. The DA is reviewing it."

"Haley has no memory of Friday night. She needs to be seen by a doctor immediately."

"*Now* she's claiming amnesia? How convenient." Colgate all but rolled his eyes. "She didn't claim to have amnesia when I interviewed her."

"Someone could have slipped a date-rape drug into her drink at the club. We both know it happens all the time. Or her Addison's disease could have flared up."

Colgate looked past Morgan at Haley. His face hardened. "I know you're a pretty slick lawyer, but even you can't spin these facts to favor your client. She isn't the victim here. She buried a knife in Noah Carter's belly."

Haley flinched as if he'd struck her.

"She doesn't remember what happened." Frustration clipped Morgan's words. "She needs to be examined at the hospital. Though if she were drugged and/or raped, it might be too late for the lab to confirm because you held her all weekend without doing anything."

Colgate's jaw sawed.

Morgan had had it. "If she isn't under arrest, I'm taking her to the hospital. I also want her to have a SAFE exam." Sexual assault forensics examiners were specifically trained to collect and preserve evidence of sexual assault. "Regardless of what did or did not happen to Haley, a SAFE nurse is the best chance at recovering trace evidence or DNA."

Colgate couldn't argue with that. He propped his hands on his hips. "I'm not letting her out of my custody. I'll have a deputy take her to the ER, though I think it's a bullshit claim. She doesn't have a scratch on her."

Muttering under his breath, Colgate turned away.

"Time is of the essence, Sheriff," Morgan called after him. But she already feared it was too late.

Chapter Seven

Plastic chairs and vending machines formed a small waiting area at the end of the hall in the emergency department.

Lance leaned on a snack machine, assessing the pallor in Morgan's face and the slight trembling of her fingers, which she was working hard to hide. "You should be resting."

"I know." She sniffed, and her voice dropped to a whisper. "There's nothing I'd like more than to go home and focus all my attention on an entire pint of Ben & Jerry's. But if I let go now, I'm not sure I could pull myself together again."

Her gaze broke away and traveled the hallway to where a deputy stood guard outside the room where Haley was being examined. The deputy had balked at being told to wait outside. But once he realized the ER staff was going to collect a rape kit in addition to treating Haley, he'd backed off after making sure the exam room had no other exits. The previous sheriff had been very old-school. There were no female deputies.

The situation was unusual. Normally, the person being examined was the victim, not the accused. But seriously, where was Haley going to go? She was sick, and she barely weighed a hundred pounds. She wasn't going to overpower the nurses and escape.

Lance didn't even want to think about what was going on inside the room. Collecting a rape kit involved an invasive exam that lasted several hours. The victim was swabbed and photographed in exactly the

---

places she had been violated. Even with a specially trained nurse, the procedure was traumatic.

Morgan drew a shaky breath. "It's bad enough that I got knocked on my butt in the courthouse and Esposito had to save me from my own client. Haley needs a tough lawyer today. If the sheriff or prosecutor's office smells weakness, my bargaining power on her behalf is diminished. We both know that part of my job is an act, and I'll be honest with you, I'm having a really hard time staying in character."

"I understand. I don't like it, but I understand." As much as he wanted to take her in his arms and comfort her, he respected her need to maintain her professional reputation.

He respected *her*. She was the strongest person he'd ever met. And underneath all that determination and intelligence was a heart of gold. Morgan was a rescuer. She took care of three small children, her elderly grandfather, and two stray dogs; and last summer, she'd opened her home to a sick young woman waiting for a kidney transplant. That girl had grown well enough that she now insisted on serving as Morgan's live-in nanny, but no matter how much Gianna tried to earn her keep, there was no denying that Morgan was the one taking care of her.

And Lance couldn't even begin to describe what Morgan had done for him. Nor could he consider how he would have gotten through his mother's mental health crisis back in November without her support.

"Just remember, you're only one person. You can't save everyone." He dropped his hand from her shoulder and gave her forearm a quick squeeze.

Nodding, Morgan closed her eyes for a few seconds. When she opened them, her resolve was back in full force. "But I want to help Haley, and she needs me to be on my game."

No one would work harder. Morgan would identify with Eliza too. They'd both lost their husbands and been left to raise their kids alone.

Morgan walked to the coffee machine in the corner. She brewed a cup and lifted it to her nose, inhaling the scent as if it were oxygen.

Sipping the coffee, she glanced down the hall. Twenty feet away from the deputy on guard duty, Eliza sat in a plastic chair against the wall, hugging a bag of fresh clothes she'd brought for her daughter. Sharp stood next to her chair, his hands shoved in the front pockets of his pants, as if he were having difficulty keeping himself from reaching out to touch Eliza.

After a testing sip, Morgan downed the coffee like a shot of tequila. Then she tossed the empty cup in the garbage can. She pulled out the pack of M&M's she'd bought earlier and tore off the top.

Lance opened his mouth to point out that healthy food would help her heal faster than would giving in to her sugar addiction. Then he thought better of it. Today was probably not the day.

Morgan turned to him, her expression thoughtful. "Does it bother you to work for the defendant?"

"Sometimes," he admitted. "But we all have a job to do. The legal system isn't perfect. The PI business isn't exactly all unicorns and rainbows."

"McFarland has made me second-guess my career change." She ate another piece of candy.

"It shouldn't. You've kept several innocent people out of jail," Lance reminded her. "Don't let one bad client undermine your efforts. Look what you've already done for Haley. She wouldn't be here getting a medical evaluation if it wasn't for you."

"I know." But she was still frowning. Or maybe that was just her headache. He hated the pain lines creased around her mouth and eyes.

Morgan ate more M&M's. "Don't look at me like that. As soon as it gets warm, I'm going to start working out."

"OK." Lance had heard that more than a few times. "I hate to echo Sharp, but regular exercise would give you more energy than candy."

A breaking news report banner on the TV in the corner caught Lance's attention. He pointed toward the television. "The state police found a body."

Morgan walked closer to the television. Reaching up, she increased the volume. A reporter stood on the side of a road, a forest at his back. Behind him, police vehicles lined the gravel shoulder. Grim-faced officers gathered in clusters.

The newscaster looked equally serious as he held his microphone out for a deputy.

The deputy said, "The body of a female in her midtwenties was found this morning by hikers in a section of woods near the state park. We suspect foul play is involved in her death. Identification of the victim is pending notification of her next of kin. The sheriff's office is investigating. That's all for now. No questions." With a nod and a lift of a hand, the detective stepped away from the mic.

"Could be Shannon Yates," Lance suggested.

"Yes," Morgan agreed. "She's the right age."

"The same age as Haley."

Morgan sighed. "Young women are prime targets." She nodded toward the other end of the hallway. "Do you know Eliza or Haley?"

"No." Lance hadn't even recognized their names, and he'd been close to Sharp for twenty-three years, ever since Sharp, then a police detective, had investigated the disappearance of Lance's father. When Vic Kruger's missing-persons case had gone cold, and Lance's mother had spiraled into mental illness, Sharp had recognized that young Lance had needed someone to look out for him and had stepped up.

Morgan tilted her head. "Her appearance seems to have shaken him."

"You noticed that too?" Lance glanced down the hall. Sharp had moved closer to Eliza, but his posture was stiff, as if he didn't know where he stood with her. "You talked to Haley. Do you think she could have killed that boy?"

Morgan rubbed the back of her neck. "I don't know. I don't want to think so. She's so young and frail-looking, but she was also distant . . . almost out of it. According to Colgate, she was found alone with the body, covered in blood. Her fingerprints were the only ones on the weapon, she'd been seen leaving the club with the victim the night before, and forensics recovered a used condom at the scene. The first thing she said to the responding deputy was 'What have I done?' None of these things make her look innocent."

"But they don't mean she wasn't drugged and/or sexually assaulted."

"No. They don't." Morgan frowned. "But that will be damned hard to prove without a positive drug screen or some physical evidence that she was raped, restrained, struck . . ." She paused, her fingertips squeezing the bridge of her nose. "It's hard enough to get a rape conviction *with* physical evidence."

"I know."

She checked her watch, then took two more Tylenol from the bottle in her bag.

Rape cases were notoriously hard to prosecute. Evidence might be insufficient or could be interpreted in multiple ways. The brain needed time to process a traumatic event. Victims often got confused and then were accused of lying.

The door down the hall opened, and a nurse stepped out. Morgan and Lance hurried back. Morgan went into the room with Eliza.

The deputy took a call on his cell phone, backing away from the group but keeping his eyes on them.

Sharp tapped a foot. The crow's feet around his eyes were more pronounced. Morgan was right. He was shaken, a rare occurrence.

"So how long has it been since you've seen Eliza?" Lance asked.

Sharp sighed. "Almost twenty-five years."

"How old is Haley?"

"Twenty-five." Lifting a hand, he added, "No. She's not mine. Her father was my best friend back in the day. Ted died when Haley was just a baby."

"Killed on the job?" Lance assumed.

Sharp looked away. "Yes."

The faraway pain in Sharp's eyes said there was much more to the story. "I'll tell you all about it later, OK?"

"OK," Lance agreed.

The door opened. Morgan and Eliza walked out. Haley followed, looking small and fragile as a baby bird. She could have passed for a teenager. Yoga pants, a loose sweater, and sneakers emphasized her slight frame. Her long red hair was pulled back into a pony tail. Morgan might have been the one with the bruised face, but Haley looked beaten. A true ginger, she had freckled skin so pale it seemed nearly translucent.

It might be sexist, but Lance had trouble picturing this slender young woman committing an act as violent as a stabbing.

Haley turned giant blue eyes on them. "What do I do now?" she asked in a timid voice.

The deputy stepped forward. He'd put his phone away. "Haley Powell, you are under arrest for the murder of Noah Carter."

Lance had expected Haley to be arrested, but to have her handcuffed moments after the rape kit had been collected was a tough break.

"Turn around and extend your arms out at your sides," the deputy instructed. "Turn your palms to me."

Haley stood stock-still for a minute, trembling. Then she complied, her movements slow and halting. A single tear rolled down her cheek as the deputy handcuffed her. The look in her eyes was complete devastation. Though the deputy was professional, even gentle, as he took her into official custody, Lance couldn't help but feel like the girl was being violated.

"It'll be OK," Morgan said. "You should be arraigned tomorrow morning. I'll be there. You just have to get through the night. Do not talk to anyone about your case, not the jail personnel or other inmates. Other prisoners might try to use anything you tell them as bargaining chips in their own cases."

Haley didn't respond. Her gaze was fixed straight ahead. The only movement on her face was the slight quiver of her lower lip. But she kept her chin up as the deputy clipped the cuffs on one wrist and then the other.

The deputy took Haley away.

Eliza stifled a sob. Sharp's face tightened.

Morgan turned to Eliza. "We need to talk. I need information to prepare for the arraignment tomorrow."

Eliza nodded, her eyes filling with moisture as she watched Haley and the deputy exit the ER.

"We'll go to the office," Sharp said.

"She has to spend the night in jail?" Eliza asked.

"Yes." Morgan took her phone from her tote. "But I'll see if I can get Haley assigned to the medical ward for the night."

"Let's get you out of here," Sharp said to Eliza.

Eliza looked lost.

"We'll meet at the office and review the case details," Morgan assured her.

Eliza nodded, then she and Sharp turned and walked away.

After they had disappeared down the hallway, Morgan said, "They found no evidence of sexual assault or drugs. I should have known too much time had passed to get positive results. The sheriff's department held on to her for too long. Club drugs are hard enough to nail with toxicology screening if the testing is done promptly. Now the prosecutor will use the lack of sexual assault evidence to thwart any self-defense case I present. All I've done is strengthen his case."

Chapter Eight

Morgan walked toward the hospital exit for the second time that day. Lance opened the door, and she phoned the sheriff's office as they crossed the parking lot. She climbed into the passenger seat as the line rang. To her surprise, the sheriff took her call.

"Your deputy just took my client to jail," she said.

"Yes. The warrant came down from the DA's office." To his credit, there was no arrogance or satisfaction in the sheriff's voice. Colgate was all business.

"My client has a serious medical condition," Morgan said. "She requires medication several times a day and has special dietary needs that must be met, or she will become very ill. When she arrived at the ER, her blood pressure was dangerously low. She was dehydrated and hypoglycemic. That's why she was so confused when she was in your custody."

"I cannot change the fact that she is under arrest for the most serious of charges. Noah Carter's murder was a heinous crime."

"One that Haley is innocent of until proven guilty," Morgan argued.

"The expedited DNA results came in," the sheriff continued. "The DNA taken from the condom contained both the victim's and Haley's DNA, and the blood on Haley's body and under her fingernails was Noah Carter's. In addition, the preliminary autopsy cited his stab wounds and resulting exsanguination as the main cause of death. The case is solid."

Disappointment twisted in Morgan's belly. If the evidence kept piling up, soon it would be so far over Haley's head, she wouldn't be able to see daylight.

"But you can put her in the medical wing, where her vital signs can be monitored. An Addison's disease crisis can be fatal." Morgan paused. "I'm not exaggerating, Sheriff. She could die."

Colgate's sigh was long and brimming with the kind of bone-deep exhaustion that took decades to accumulate. "I'll have her put in the medical wing tonight. But no promises on where she'll end up after that."

"Thank you, Sheriff."

"You are welcome." The sheriff ended the call.

Morgan lowered her phone to her lap, but the wave of relief was short-lived. "What is Haley going to do if the judge doesn't grant bail? Jail is tough enough without a difficult medical condition to manage."

"You can only handle one thing at a time," Lance said. "Focus on the hearing tomorrow."

"You're right." Morgan rubbed her non-swollen temple and willed the pain relievers to kick in. She needed a clear head. She needed to think. She gazed through the windshield, surprised that they'd left the parking lot already.

Morgan's phone vibrated. "It's my sister." Morgan's sister Stella was a detective with the Scarlet Falls PD.

She answered the call.

"How are you?" Stella asked. "I heard about what happened at the courthouse."

"I'm OK." Morgan closed her eyes.

"It's all over the news," Stella said. "Someone caught it on video on their cell phone and posted it everywhere. Esposito gave an interview outside the courthouse. He was puffed up like a male gorilla."

"I'll bet." Discouraged and frustrated, Morgan rested her elbow on an armrest and dropped her head into her hand.

"You're really OK?" Stella didn't sound convinced. "It looked like he really tagged you."

"Well, I've had better days, but other than the Rocky Balboa black eye, I'm fine." Morgan opened her eyes and raised her head. They were almost at the office. "I have to meet with a client. Can you call Grandpa and let him know I'm OK? If you saw it on the news, then he probably did too."

"Will do," Stella said. "I have a call coming in. Gotta go. Call me if you need anything," Stella said, and the line went dead.

Morgan lowered her phone and opened a local news media feed. She cringed as she read the headlines aloud to Lance. "'Female attorney punched in face.' 'ADA Esposito saves female attorney from own client.'"

"Why does he get a mention and you only get referred to as *female*?" Lance's tone was annoyed.

"Because damsels in distress are clickbait."

"You are hardly a helpless female."

"Drama sells."

"McFarland sucker punched you," Lance said. "No one would have seen that coming. I've seen you handle tougher situations, including saving my butt a time or two. You are a total badass."

She couldn't hold back the short snort of laughter. Her headache was making her punchy. There was nothing funny about the situation.

"Thank you." She scrolled through the articles. "I needed to hear that."

"Anytime. Unless you have a crystal ball, there will always be things you cannot predict."

"I know." She clicked through a link. A short article accompanied a video on the main page of the local news. "It seems the original video was taken on the cell phone of a reporter who was in the courthouse corridor when McFarland attacked me."

"And chose to film it rather than help you," Lance said in a harsh voice.

"To be fair, the only person close enough to help me in time was Esposito." She turned up the volume and watched the ADA give his interview.

"I only did what any man would do," Esposito said. "Being a defense attorney is a dangerous job. I don't know why anyone is surprised this happened. Ms. Dane represents criminals." His tone and expression implied *When you lie down with dogs, what do you expect?*

Someone called him a hero. Esposito denied it, but he preened like a rooster.

Morgan wanted to crawl under the vehicle seat.

"Turn that off," Lance said. "He's just being a jerk."

"Everything he's saying is true. He really did save me from my own client."

Lance scowled. "The deputies were on McFarland in seconds."

"His boot was one second away from my head." Morgan gingerly touched her face. Pain swelled from the point of contact. If one punch had done this much damage, she couldn't imagine what a full kick to the face from a man the size of McFarland would have done to her. "Is it shallow of me that I don't want to be in debt to Esposito?"

"Not at all. He will likely lord it over you every chance he gets." Lance reached over and turned the phone away. "There wasn't anything you could have done to prevent what happened."

"You're right." All Morgan could do was move forward and help Haley.

Lance parked at the curb in front of the office, and they went inside. Sharp and Eliza arrived right behind them. Sharp settled Eliza in his office.

Morgan went into her own office to hang up her coat and stow her tote. She brewed a cup of coffee in the small machine on her credenza. When she entered the kitchen, Sharp was busy at the blender.

"What are you thinking?" He reached for her cup. "Caffeine will only make you feel worse."

She curled her fingers protectively around her cup and held it closer.

Sharp raised his eyebrows. "Do you want to get better faster?"

Yes, but enough to give up my coffee?

"Fine." Morgan sulked and loosened her grip.

He turned to the blender. Its whir drowned out most of his short lecture on anti-inflammatory compounds and vitamins. He poured the pale-orange smoothie into four glasses and handed her one.

"What's in it?" She sniffed it.

"It's easiest just to drink it." Lance walked into the kitchen. He'd changed from his suit into his usual attire: tactical cargos and a plain black T-shirt. "You know there's no point trying to stop him once he goes into full mother mode."

They gathered in Sharp's office. Eliza paced. Sharp gestured for Morgan to sit behind his desk. She eased gratefully into the chair. Her head swam, her belly flip-flopped, and her efforts to concentrate just made her feel worse.

"Haley didn't do this," Eliza said. "She wouldn't hurt anyone."

"And we'll try to prove that. But tomorrow's hearing will strictly be about bail, though the strength of the prosecutor's case will impact the judge's decision on bail." Morgan sipped her shake. "I'll need to mitigate the strength of the evidence and heinous nature of the murder." She paused. "Tell me about Haley. Has she ever been in trouble with the law?"

"No." Eliza shook her head. "She's never even had a speeding ticket."

"Where does she live?" Morgan asked.

"With me." Eliza gave them a Grey's Hollow address.

Morgan wrote the address on her file. "Carranza Road. Why does that sound familiar?"

"It's off Route 47 in the foothills of the Adirondacks," Eliza said. "Haley had her own apartment, but after I moved to Grey's Hollow last summer, I convinced her to move in with me. I travel quite a bit, and Haley house-sits for me. There's plenty of room, and she gets to save the money she would pay in rent."

"That's good." With additional questions, Morgan filled in Haley's background with basic personal information. "One thing we haven't discussed is money. A solid defense will be expensive. We'll need expert witnesses and many investigative hours. I know it sounds intrusive, but what is your financial situation?"

"I have money," Eliza said. "I can pay."

"My hours are on the house." Sharp crossed his arms over his chest.

"No. I insist on paying your usual rate." Eliza lifted her chin. "I haven't contacted you once over the past twenty-five years."

"It doesn't matter." Sharp frowned at the reminder, and regret filled his eyes. No matter how much time had passed, he clearly had feelings for this woman.

"It does to me." Eliza opened her purse and pulled out a checkbook and pen. "I won't take advantage of Ted's death. Or our past. You'll need a retainer." She wrote a check.

"Thank you." Morgan accepted it and glanced at the amount. Ten thousand dollars.

"Is that enough to start?" Eliza asked.

"Yes." Morgan wouldn't have turned down the case if the check had been written for ten dollars. "But it won't be nearly enough for bail."

Eliza put her checkbook back in her purse, then hesitated. "I never liked wearing makeup. It always looked awful on my pale skin. Ten years ago, I started a line of all neutral-toned cosmetics called Wild."

"The stores in the mall?" Morgan was impressed. Wild kiosks and boutique-style stores seemed to be popping up everywhere.

"Yes. I started out selling online, but we branched into retail locations about eight years ago. There are currently forty-six stores. So far, we're only in the Northeast, but we're branching out into Seattle this year."

"I don't care how much money you have. I won't take any of it." Sharp stood square, his arms still folded over his chest, his posture determined.

"We'll see." Eliza sighed. She looked as stubborn as Sharp.

Morgan rubbed her forehead. "The last time I defended someone accused of murder, bail was set at a million dollars. This crime is just as violent. A million will be the lowest amount we should expect. It could go higher. You would have to produce ten percent of the bond. Can you do that?"

"Yes," Eliza said without hesitation.

"Good." In that case, all Morgan had to do was talk the judge into granting bail for a woman accused of a heinous murder.

She asked Eliza a few more questions to round out her knowledge of Haley's life. There was nothing in her background that would suggest she was dangerous or a flight risk. It was the murder itself—and the strength of the evidence—that would present the hardest hurdles to overcome.

Haley would be unavailable during the jail intake. The process would take the rest of the day. The next opportunity Morgan would have to speak with her would be just before the bail hearing, and that would only happen if Haley's place on the court docket allowed ample time. If they did get the opportunity, they would only be allowed a few minutes of relative privacy.

"Is there anything else I can do?" Eliza asked.

Morgan gave her the contact information for a bail bond service. "They'll tell you what paperwork you'll need to expedite the process tomorrow morning. If bail is set, it will take all day to get Haley released."

Eliza paled. "If?"

"Yes," Morgan said. "Unfortunately, there's a chance that the judge will insist she remain in custody."

Eliza's hands trembled. She'd lost her husband and raised her daughter alone. She was tough. Yet Morgan knew, one widowed single mother to another, that a conviction for Haley would break Eliza.

"Thank you for trying." Eliza stood.

"I'll see you out." Sharp followed her from the room.

Morgan leaned back in the chair and closed her eyes for a few seconds. Every beat of her heart felt like the strike of a tiny hammer to her temple on the spot where McFarland's fist had landed. She wanted to lay her head down and not lift it for a week.

"Are you OK?" Lance asked.

Opening her eyes, she shifted forward to rest her elbows on the desk. "Yes."

"Liar." He rounded the desk to gently knead her shoulders.

"That feels good." Morgan sighed. She could feel the impact of McFarland's punch through her entire neck. Rolling a shoulder, she used her phone to check her email.

"Anything from the prosecutor's office?" Lance's thumb pressed a tight knot at the base of her neck.

"No, but I have the arrest warrant and the initial police report from the sheriff's office. We can get started. The police interviewed eleven witnesses. Some employees of the club, a few random witnesses, three of Noah's friends, and the girl that Haley had gone out with that night." She turned her head to give him better access. "Esposito doesn't like to rush the discovery process. I don't expect to receive much from him until after the arraignment."

The ADA would comply with the legal requirement to provide Morgan with all evidence in the case, but he'd hold back as long as possible. The less she knew, the less prepared she'd be for the hearing tomorrow.

"He's such a jackass," Lance said.

Her phone vibrated with an incoming text from her sister.

Lance leaned over her shoulder and read the message out loud. "'Check social media.'"

She opened a social media app where she never posted but maintained an account simply to see what clients and others did. As soon as she logged on, a GIF appeared in her feed. She'd been tagged. "Morgan Dane gets what she deserves."

Someone had made a GIF from the video clip of McFarland's attack. She watched in horror as McFarland punched over and over on a continuous loop.

She checked a few other web pages. The video was going viral on social media.

Lance glanced over, his face reddening with anger. "Son of a—"

"It's OK. I should have expected it." But Morgan had been preoccupied with her client's troubles—and her own. "Everything ends up on social media these days."

"But the message is a threat."

"Not technically. I'll contact the social media site and report it, but when something goes viral like this, there will be no stopping it."

The clip would be posted everywhere.

Social media swayed public opinion, and part of Morgan's job was to use her own reputation to defend her client. It was nearly impossible to find an unbiased jury pool. The internet spread real and false news across the globe far too quickly. Changes of venue had become moot, at least in regard to big cases.

Morgan's colleagues considered her a tough lawyer. McFarland had damaged her reputation. She viewed the video again, stopping it just as McFarland raised his boot over her head. There she was, cowering on the floor. Her hands were in front of her head to block the blow, her face turned away.

She looked weak and helpless.

In her brain, she knew that wasn't the case. She hadn't had any time to react. But the video clip left her looking fragile and less than competent.

She ripped her eyes off the screen. "This isn't going to help the case."

"Did someone post this because they have a sick sense of humor?" Lance asked.

"Could be revenge on McFarland's part." Morgan watched the clip again. "Though he's in jail and didn't have access to a computer."

"And he doesn't have any friends that we could find. We tried for days to locate a single person who would testify in his behalf. Maybe someone wants to interfere with Haley's case," Lance suggested.

"But who would want to do that?" Morgan drummed her fingers on the desk. "Even if Noah's family is convinced that Haley killed him, would they want to jeopardize the trial? Biased pretrial media coverage provides grounds for mistrial and appeal."

"We won't know until we investigate." Lance shook his head. "Maybe my mom can trace the origin of that video or GIF."

Lance's mother was an online computer science teacher with her own business in website design, maintenance, and security. Unfortunately, she also suffered from agoraphobia and severe anxiety. She worked out of her home and sometimes helped with any computer forensics necessary in their investigations.

"Are you sure she's ready for the extra work?" Morgan asked.

Last fall, his mother had been attacked, and the incident had exacerbated her mental illness.

"I hope so," Lance said. "We managed without her over the winter because we didn't have any big cases. But we're stretched thin on Haley's investigation. Background checks take time, and my mother is the best."

Morgan sighed. "Maybe it's a friend or relation of the victim."

"Wonderful. There's nothing like vengeance for motivation."

Chapter Nine

Anger burned a slow path down to Lance's gut as he watched the clip of McFarland hitting Morgan. Taking her phone, he turned off the display. "You don't need to keep watching it."

She sighed.

Lance studied her face. If he could have changed anything about that day, he would have stayed next to her in the courthouse hallway. McFarland wouldn't have done what he'd done if Lance had been there. McFarland had surprised him too. "I didn't see it coming either."

But Lance should have been prepared for McFarland to lash out, especially if events weren't going his way. McFarland had demonstrated his violent nature in the bar. He'd attacked his ex's boyfriend in full view of dozens of witnesses too. He'd exhibited no remorse. No regret. No conscience.

And being a psychopath made him an excellent liar.

"I shouldn't have left you alone with him," Lance said.

Morgan shook her head. "I was hardly alone. I was in the middle of the courthouse. I should have been safe. You can't possibly stand next to me 24/7. I have a job to do."

But she hadn't been safe. McFarland's actions had been crazy and unpredictable.

Her small smile was lopsided. "I do appreciate the thought, though."

"You need some rest if you're going to be alert tomorrow for the hearing," he said. "Let me take you home."

"You're right." She rose, pushing off the desk with both hands. "I can review the paperwork again after the kids are in bed. I'll get my things."

She kept one palm flat on the blotter for a few seconds, as if she were testing her balance.

Sharp stuck his head into the office. "There's a crowd of reporters outside."

"Really?" Morgan asked. "Reporters here? That's unusual."

In previous cases, the press hadn't gathered outside the office. The courthouse provided a more dramatic backdrop.

Lance went to the window. Using one finger to separate the slats of the blinds, he peered out. News vans were unloading at the curb.

"I'll occupy the reporters," Morgan said to Sharp. "You can take Eliza out the back door, circle around the building, and get her to her car quietly."

"That should work," Sharp said. "I'm going to follow her home too. If Haley is released tomorrow, I want to address any security concerns in case the press decides to camp in front of the house." He stepped farther into the room and closed the door behind him. "I want to thank you for doing this, Morgan. I know you aren't feeling well. You should really be home in bed. I feel guilty for asking, but I don't trust anyone else." Sharp paused for a breath. "Ted and I went to the academy together. We started in patrol with the SFPD the same day. I was the best man at his wedding. I was at the hospital when Haley was born. One day, we were both on patrol when we stumbled into a convenience store robbery. Ted took a bullet in the neck." Sharp stopped, swallowing hard. When he continued speaking, his voice was harsh, barely recognizable. "The bullet severed Ted's carotid artery. Even if there had been a surgeon on-site, his chances of surviving that shot would have been slim. He bled out in minutes." Sharp looked up.

"Did the robber die?" Lance had been shot in the thigh in the line of duty. He'd nearly died. The injury had ended his police career, but he was very lucky that he'd survived. His memories of the event were as fragmented as a broken mirror. He occasionally had nightmares, but he wondered if it would have been even harder to watch your partner bleed out.

"No." Uncharacteristic bitterness tightened Sharp's lips, the resulting lines around his mouth aging him. "Ted took one unlucky bullet to the neck, while the meth head survived five bullet wounds. I shot him four times. I only remember pulling the trigger once." Sharp swallowed. "I promised Ted that I'd always look after his family."

Lance's heart bled for him. He could imagine the responsibility, regret, and grief all too well.

Morgan came out from behind the desk and put a hand on Sharp's arm. "You don't owe me any explanations, not after everything you have done for me over the past six months. I will do everything in my power to help Haley."

"Thank you." Sharp seemed to choke on the words.

"Now, get Eliza out of here." Morgan went to her own office to collect her coat and bag.

Lance grabbed his leather jacket and put it on. "Ready?"

She straightened her shoulders. "Yes."

Sharp and Eliza headed for the back of the office as Lance opened the door. Reporters swarmed them as soon as they hit the sidewalk. They were all yelling at once. Lance couldn't tell who was asking which question.

"Ms. Dane! Did Haley Powell kill Noah Carter?"

"How will your client plead tomorrow?"

Morgan stopped and scanned the reporters. "Please. It's too soon for specific questions. All I can say is that Haley is innocent, and we're going to prove it."

"Was Ms. Powell covered in Noah Carter's blood?" a reporter called.

Another shouted, "Is it true that she's claiming to have amnesia?"

Morgan spoke into a cluster of microphones. "I can't speak about details of the case."

But someone had. Important investigation details had been leaked to the press. Had it been an accident or an intentional attempt to taint the potential jury pool? Lance had no difficulty seeing Esposito orchestrating it. He didn't know why the ADA had come to Morgan's aid when McFarland had attacked her, but the act hadn't changed Lance's opinion of him.

A figure stepped out of the crowd. Lance expected a reporter getting aggressive, but instead it was a young man. Fury twisted his features. Lance's instincts went on alert. He moved closer to Morgan, ready to block her with his body if necessary. At just under six feet tall, she wasn't a small woman, and she was more than capable of defending herself under normal circumstances. But tonight, she was already injured.

And just because she *could* defend herself didn't mean Lance was going to step aside and let the man attack her.

The young man rushed at them.

Lance stepped between the approaching man and Morgan. The man shoved his hand under his jacket. Lance's hand went reflexively for his weapon. The teen pulled out a spray bottle.

Lance had no idea what was in the bottle, but he wasn't letting it anywhere near Morgan. But he didn't want to shoot the man. He blocked the attacker's path like a defensive lineman.

The man raised the bottle. Liquid streamed out and hit Lance smack in the center of his chest. He bent his knees and launched himself forward, catching the man around the waist and tackling him. They hit the ground hard. On the bottom, the attacker took the brunt of the impact. Plastic cracked, liquid splashed, and noxious fumes filled the air.

Lance's eyes teared. His lungs burned.

As he choked, he flipped the man over and pinned his arms behind his back. Eyes watering, Lance yelled, "What was in the bottle?"

"Fuck you," the man wheezed over his shoulder. His eyes were shut, the lids red and swelling. Had some of the liquid hit him in the face? Lance's skin burned, and the fumes alone were enough to blur his vision.

"Do you want to go blind?" Lance yelled, leaning some weight on the man's back and patting his pockets for weapons, drugs, or a wallet. He found nothing. "What was in the bottle?"

Morgan pulled on Lance's shoulder. "You need to wash that off right now, whatever it is."

She was right. A wet spot on the front of his shirt showed where the stream of liquid had hit him. He lifted his shirt off his chest. The fabric wasn't disintegrating. The liquid probably wasn't acid.

He rolled off the kid and got to his feet. Leaning on his thighs, he bent over, choking on fumes.

The young man sat up, his eyes still squeezed closed, tears and snot streaming down his face. The bottle had been crushed under their bodies. Some of the liquid had splashed in the kid's face and down the front of his sweatshirt and jacket. He coughed and gagged.

Lance searched the ground for the bottle. Stumbling over to it, he turned it over with his toe. It was the sort you bought empty and filled yourself. A copious amount of the liquid had dumped onto the ground. The fumes wafting up from the puddle irritated his lungs.

It felt like the time he'd been doused in pepper spray in the police academy.

"Is that some kind of pepper spray?" he asked the kid.

Unable to speak, the kid flipped him a middle finger. Then he reached for his face with both hands.

"Don't rub your eyes. It'll make it worse." Lance hauled the man to his feet and dragged him by the back of the collar toward the office like a badly behaved puppy.

"Put me down." The young man tried to pull away.

"Whatever is in your eyes needs to be washed off before it does permanent damage, dumbass," Lance said.

As he dragged the man toward the office, Lance blinked repeatedly. The crowd of reporters followed them to the front porch. Morgan opened the door. Lance pulled the man into the foyer and kicked the door shut in a cameraman's face. The attacker stumbled in the hall. Lance held him upright.

"Turn on the shower," he said to Morgan.

But she was way ahead of him, rushing down the hallway. She dropped her coat and bag on the floor. When Sharp had converted the apartment to office space, he'd left the kitchen and full bath intact. In the bathroom, spigots squeaked and water rushed as she turned on the shower and the faucet at the sink.

Lance put the man in the shower fully dressed and held his head under the spray. "Let the water flush your face." He looked over his shoulder for Morgan. "Try dish soap."

Morgan rushed from the room, returning in a few seconds with a bottle of blue liquid in her hand. "I've got it."

"Open your eyes and let the water flush them," Lance said. "Use soap everywhere else."

The man stopped protesting, his discomfort no doubt overpowering whatever emotion had caused his attack.

Lance peeled off his jacket and T-shirt. Dropping them on the floor, he put his head under the faucet and let the cool water flow over his face. After a thorough rinse, he washed with soap multiple times and then moved on to his chest. When he was finished, he grabbed towels from the narrow closet behind the door and dried off. His skin was pink and slightly irritated, but there didn't seem to be any damage.

He used his cell phone to call the Scarlet Falls PD and report the incident. Morgan was helping the creep. She held him by the back of

71

the collar and kept his face under the spray. A few minutes later, she turned off the water.

Lance handed him a towel.

The young man's eyes were bloodshot. He blinked over and over. Holding his eyes open clearly took effort. Tears still ran down his face.

"What was in the bottle?" Lance enunciated each word for emphasis.

The man's lips mashed flat.

"What's your name?" Lance asked.

He stared at the wall.

"Fine. Talk to the cops." Lance gave up. "They're on the way."

He dropped a towel to the floor to mop up the water. He used a fresh towel to dry his hair and clean up the sink area.

Five minutes later, someone banged on the front door. Tossing the towel around his neck, Lance walked down the hall to Sharp's office and peered out the window. A black-and-white Scarlet Falls police car sat at the curb, lights swirling. An unmarked sedan pulled up behind it. Morgan's sister Stella and her partner, Detective Brody McNamara, climbed out. Stella hurried up the sidewalk, parting the sea of reporters with her badge and pissy attitude.

Lance opened the door and let them in. "Morgan's OK."

"What happened?" Stella asked.

Lance gave her a quick rundown of the incident.

"Who is he?" Stella asked.

"I don't know yet. He didn't have any ID on him." Lance turned around and led her back to the bathroom. "We cleaned him up."

The man took a dry towel from Morgan. Then, blinking at her, he recoiled, as if he'd just realized who was helping him. "Get off me."

Bristling, Lance moved forward.

Stella stopped him with a hand on his arm. "We've got this."

Morgan retreated to the hall with Lance, letting Brody and Stella deal with the young man. Lance went into his office and grabbed a dry shirt from the closet. Morgan followed him.

"You were his target." Lance tugged the shirt over his head.

"I know. Thank you for stepping in." She walked closer, sliding her arms around his waist and pressing the uninjured side of her face into his chest.

He wrapped his arms around her and held her for a couple of seconds.

"You jumped right in front of me. What if he'd had a gun?" She shivered.

"He didn't." But the thought sent a wave of cold right through Lance's belly. He didn't want to let Morgan out of his sight. He couldn't imagine how a spray of Mace would have felt on her already sore face.

And if the man had had a gun . . .

Morgan usually carried a sidearm, but not on days she went to court.

Brody appeared in the doorway. "His name is Adam Carter, Noah Carter's brother. He is twenty-one years old and a local university student. What he sprayed on you was homemade pepper spray. He cooked it up in his garage. When he saw reporters doing sound bites outside Morgan's office, he knew she was here. He brought his pepper spray, intending to incapacitate her so she wouldn't be able to represent Haley at the bail hearing tomorrow. Apparently, Adam's parents are planning to attend."

"He's running on all emotion, not logic," Morgan said. "He just lost his brother."

"He was thinking straight enough to play amateur chemist and commit a planned assault." Lance pitied the man but not enough to justify his attempted attack on Morgan. "I wonder if he was also behind the nasty videos on social media."

"What videos?" Brody asked.

Lance went behind his desk and pulled up the video and GIF on his computer.

Brody frowned. "We'll look into it. Technically, this isn't a threat, but based on Adam's attack today, I'm going to get a search warrant for their house and computers. Who knows what other DIY projects he's been researching or planning? *Morgan Dane gets what she deserves* is not the same as *what I will do to Morgan Dane*, but if he made the video, I think we might be able to show it as an additional threat."

Brody, Lance, and Morgan went into the hallway. Stella had put the young man in handcuffs. Soaking wet, Adam shivered. His jeans and sweatshirt dripped on the hardwood. His face was still hardened with anger and insolence.

"Do you want to file a complaint?" Stella asked Lance. "Several cameramen filmed the attack."

"Yes." Lance studied Adam.

The face full of pepper should have been an immediate lesson. But despite the obvious pain he was still in, his chin was up, his back straight, and his jaw set. He'd dialed back his rage from boil to simmer, but it was still there.

He wasn't sorry. Not one bit.

But then, grief and self-righteousness were long-burning sources of fuel. Adam wasn't going to abandon his cause anytime soon. Hopefully, the police and his parents would be able to keep him out of trouble.

"In that case, we'll take him in." Stella guided Adam toward the door. "You should think about how your behavior will affect your parents. They're already going through hell. They don't need this."

"You want to help Haley Powell." He glared at Morgan, then at Lance through bloodshot eyes. "She should pay for what she did. She killed Noah." The insolent mask melted off his face. His shoulders shook. Grief twisted his features.

Lance empathized, but if Adam didn't learn to control his anger, he'd end up like McFarland. On the other hand, Stella was right.

Mr. and Mrs. Carter did not need to bail their younger son out of jail so soon after losing their oldest.

"Let's go." Brody took Adam's other arm. With the boy sandwiched between them, he and Stella marched him out the front door.

Lance closed and locked the door. "Let's give the reporters a little time to leave." He followed Morgan back toward her office.

She picked up her coat and big bag from the floor.

His phone rang. "It's my mom."

Guilt turned inside Lance. Had she seen the news? He should have called her.

He answered the call. "Hey, Mom."

"Are you and Morgan all right?" she asked in a shaky voice.

"Yes," he assured her.

"Because I saw a video of Morgan's client hitting her," she continued as if he hadn't spoken.

"Mom." Lance raised his voice. "Morgan is OK."

But she didn't seem to hear him. "And then just now, there was a breaking news report. I saw a man attack you right outside your office. The reporters said it was some sort of caustic—"

Lance needed to change the subject before her anxiety snowballed.

"Mom," he interrupted her. "I'll stop by on my way home. I have to ask you for a favor anyway."

"You do?" She sounded cheered.

"We need help with an investigation. Are you up to it?"

"Yes. Definitely." Her voice was almost perky.

"I'll see you later." Lance disconnected. They hadn't given his mom any work since her attack the previous fall. He'd been afraid the added stress would slow her recovery. But now he wondered if he'd made the wrong call. Maybe she missed the work.

He grabbed his T-shirt and leather jacket from the floor. Pepper fumes wafted from them. He held them at arm's length and went to the kitchen for a garbage bag.

The shirt wasn't worth the effort of saving it. His jacket had taken a direct hit. There was no way to clean leather without ruining it. He shoved both items in the plastic bag and tied it closed. Grabbing a zip-up sweatshirt from his office, he tossed the bag in the garbage can on the way out of the building.

He hoped this was the worst thing that happened in this case, but experience told him it was just the beginning.

Chapter Ten

Grateful to be home, Morgan pushed open her front door. Lance followed her through the opening. Three pajama-clad little girls and two dogs bolted toward them. She braced herself for the impact of their enthusiastic greeting. Lance stepped in front of her.

"Stop!" her grandfather's voice boomed from the next room. "Easy on your mom."

The girls slid to a halt. Lance dropped to one knee and intercepted the dogs. Morgan's Frenchie, Snoozer, snuffled his face, and Rocket the bulldog mix wagged her stump of a tail.

"That's not necessary," Morgan protested.

"Mommy!" Three-year-old Sophie's eyes were wide as she stared at Morgan's face.

Morgan knelt on the floor. "It's just a bruise, honey. It's no worse than that one you had on your knee last week."

Her daughter leaned in and kissed Morgan softly on the goose egg. Typically, greetings from Sophie were like catching a cannonball. Morgan's face must be truly intimidating.

Five-year-old Mia was quieter by nature. She slid into Morgan's embrace and gave her a gentle squeeze.

"Don't hurt Mommy," Ava said. At six, Morgan's oldest tried hard to be more mature than her sisters. Sometimes too hard.

Morgan shifted to free up one arm. She waggled her fingers at Ava. "I need one more hug."

Ava rushed in. Holding her girls, Morgan closed her eyes and inhaled the sweetness of bubblegum-scented conditioner in their still-damp hair. Sophie was the first one to wiggle free.

The little girl looked up at Lance. "Are *you* hurt?"

"Not at all," he said.

With a happy grin, she launched herself into his arms. He caught her, and she wrapped all four limbs around him and smacked a kiss on his cheek. Leaning back, she squished his face between her hands. "Will you put us to bed?"

"You betcha." Lance shifted her to his hip and turned to the other girls. "Who's ready for a story?" He knelt down and opened his arms. Sophie scrambled around to his back. He gagged as her forearm wrapped around his windpipe. Mia and Ava abandoned Morgan. Lance scooped the two older girls into his arms and carried the three giggling children down the hall toward the room they shared.

After the girls and Lance disappeared, Morgan shed her coat and set her tote on a chair. She removed her phone from a side pocket and went into the family room, where her grandfather, Art Dane, sat in his recliner. The smile that tugged at her face ached, but she didn't care. Watching Lance with her kids always made her happy. She'd been dealt terrible tragedies in her life. She'd learned to appreciate the good moments, and tonight she felt very lucky.

She'd found love a second time. Her line of work showed her how rare truly good men were. Yet she'd been blessed with two of them in her life.

She plugged her phone into a charging cord on the end table and leaned down to kiss her grandfather on the cheek.

Make that three good men.

She wouldn't have gotten through John's death without her grandfather.

Grandpa set down his iPad and swore under his breath. Before he'd broken his leg the previous autumn, he'd have been on his feet to greet her. Extensive physical therapy had enabled him to walk with a cane, but he was never going to recover 100 percent.

"I'd like to get my hands on that creep that hit you." He used the electric control to lower the footrest of his chair and sit upright. "My much younger hands."

"I'm OK." She tried to sound chipper to reassure him.

"You have never been able to snow me." There was no fooling the retired NYPD homicide detective. He saw through her game face, just as he'd seen through every lie she'd attempted to tell in high school.

He shook his head. "I don't know how you can look so happy with that black eye."

"The man who gave it to me will serve time."

"Small favors." Grandpa huffed.

Morgan's cell phone buzzed. Straightening, she went to the table and glanced at the phone. She didn't recognize the number. Disconnecting the charger, she answered warily. Good news didn't generally come at nine o'clock at night. The call would be harassment—or worse.

"Morgan Dane," she said.

"Hello, Ms. Dane. I apologize for the late hour. My name is Max Garcia. I'm the district attorney of Eastbridge County in New Jersey."

"How can I help you?" Morgan eased onto the couch.

"I won't waste your time. I have two openings for assistant district attorneys. Bryce Walters and I are good friends. We went to law school together. He mentioned your name. Your recent work has been very impressive, even if it has been on the wrong side of the law." Max laughed.

"Bryce Walters, the Randolph County DA, recommended me?" Morgan asked, floored.

"He did. He thought you might miss working on the state's side of the courtroom." Max paused. "I know my call is a surprise, but I'd

79

like to interview you for the job. Eastbridge is a midsize county. We're actually a suburb of Philadelphia. You'd be challenged here. I understand you have a family. Our schools are top rated, and"—he paused for effect—"we're only a twenty-minute drive from the beach."

"I'm in the middle of a big case right now," Morgan said. "I'm not sure when I would be able to get down there."

Although, at the moment, nothing sounded more appealing than scrapping her whole practice and becoming a beach bum.

"I understand. I have a decent list of first-round applicants to interview. You have some time. With your level of experience, I could move you directly to round two. We're only two hours south of New York City. If you took an early-morning train, you could do the interview at lunchtime and be home for dinner."

"Your offer is very flattering." Temptation whirled through Morgan. What would it feel like to be back behind the prosecutor's desk? No more worries about billable hours or paying her office rent.

Or having clients punch her in the face. Her client would be the state.

But her life, her new practice, her family—and Lance—were all here, in Scarlet Falls. This was her home. "But my plate is more than full right now."

"Come for an interview, then think about it." Max had a persuasive voice. "You only need to spare one day. You have nothing to lose. I'll even buy you lunch."

"Thank you for the offer, but I'm not interested in relocating."

Lance walked into the room. His amused expression shifted to concern as he scanned her face.

"I'm not taking no for an answer until you meet with me," Max said. "Just think about it. I'll call you again in a few weeks."

Morgan tapped "End" and lowered the phone to her lap.

"Is something wrong?" Lance asked. Despite his curiosity, he clearly wanted to respect her privacy.

Grandpa had no such concerns. "Who was that?"

"A DA in New Jersey." Morgan summed up the call.

"Maybe you should think about it," Lance said. His mouth had tightened, and the amusement had faded from his face.

Morgan shook her head. "I don't want to move to New Jersey. I'm just getting my life on track. I don't want to move anywhere."

"Bryce will never hire you after you turned on him," Lance said in a serious voice. "If you want to be a prosecutor again, you'll have to move."

"I didn't say I wanted to be a prosecutor again," Morgan protested.

"You didn't say you didn't either." Lance pulled his keys from his pocket.

Grandpa snorted. "Walters just wants you out of the way. You keep making him and Esposito look like chumps."

"Not on my last case, I didn't." Morgan let out a breath. "Esposito looked like a hero."

"He's a grandstander." Grandpa rolled his eyes. "In my day, a man did his duty without gloating about it to the press."

"Still, it might be a good opportunity." Lance's gaze lingered on Morgan's eye for a second, then he backed toward the door and opened it. "You shouldn't blow it off without talking to him."

Morgan stood and followed him outside to the front stoop. "I don't want to move."

Though she had to admit, the offer was attractive.

Lance nodded. "I love you, and I want you to be happy more than anything else. Just promise me you'll think about the job before turning Garcia down."

"It won't change my decision." Morgan rose onto her toes and kissed him on the mouth. So why did the offer still feel tempting?

He kissed her back, then his hands went to her arms, rubbing them. "It's cold. You shouldn't be out here without a coat. I'll see you in the morning." He nodded toward the house. "Get some rest. Big day tomorrow."

"Goodnight." Morgan kissed him again, then walked inside. She went to the kitchen and took an ice pack from the freezer. She wanted to prevent as much swelling as possible. The hearing would be difficult enough without her looking wounded.

She went to bed with her computer and notes and spent the next few hours researching case precedent, reviewing her arguments for Haley's bail, and praying she could convince the judge. Come morning, Haley's fate was entirely in the hands of Hard-Ass Judge Marlow.

Chapter Eleven

Morgan set her tote on the defense counsel table and removed her legal pad. Her private case notes were written in her personal shorthand on the second page, covered by the blank top sheet.

Not that she was paranoid or anything.

She didn't bother to sit. The hearing would be over in minutes. The courtroom hummed with low voices as she waited for her client. Judge Marlow set a pair of black-rimmed reading glasses on his nose and lifted a sheet of paper. He was reading the charges, no doubt.

The rattle of metal signaled Haley's arrival. A bailiff led her into the room. Her stunned gaze flitted around the courtroom, as if looking for a safe place to land. Haley seemed to decide the floor was her only option and dropped her head. She shuffled as she walked. The shackles around her ankles seemed to weigh her down, and her orange jail uniform hung loose on her tiny frame. She could have been a child dressed as an inmate for Halloween.

Her hair fell in a disheveled curtain around her face, and Morgan wanted to smooth it. The young woman looked wild. This was not the steady, stable impression Morgan had wanted to make on the judge. But then, the jail intake process was humiliating and dehumanizing. For Haley, it must have been even more traumatic.

The bailiff steered her to the table. Haley lifted her gaze to Morgan's. The girl's face was pale and freckled. She looked unbearably young and vulnerable.

Victimized.

Morgan's heart clenched, and she hoped that's what the judge would see.

She glanced at Esposito, standing at the prosecutor's table across the aisle. So arrogant. So sure of his role. Of Haley's guilt.

Morgan thought of all the defendants she'd prosecuted. Had she ever taken the time to really look at them? Had any of *them* been innocent?

Behind Morgan, the courtroom door opened. Bryce Walters slipped in and joined his ADA. Only the highest-profile cases warranted the DA's personal attention.

The judge coughed, drawing Morgan's attention back to him. He scrutinized Morgan's face; sympathy softened his expression for a brief moment before he got back to business. Morgan mentally cursed McFarland. Her diligent use of ice overnight had kept the swelling to a minimum, but her black eye was visible through two layers of concealer.

She supposed she should be grateful McFarland hadn't punched her in the mouth. At least her voice was clear.

Judge Marlow officially called the case and identified the parties present for prosecution and defense. "Does the defense waive the formal reading of the charges?"

"Yes, Your Honor." She saw no benefit in dragging out the process, especially with Judge Marlow. He liked cases in his courtroom to move along at a brisk clip.

"Mr. Walters." The judge shifted his gaze to the prosecutor's table. "You may proceed."

"The state strongly feels that Ms. Powell should remain in custody." Bryce's voice rang out, clear and confident. "The crime is particularly heinous in nature, and the evidence is solid. The defendant is clearly a danger to the public."

"Ms. Dane." The judge looked to Morgan.

"Your Honor, Ms. Powell has never been in trouble with the law," Morgan argued. "She has lived in the area for seven years and was also born here. Her father was a Scarlet Falls police officer who lost his life in the line of duty. She has worked for the same employer since graduating from the local university three years ago. Her mother lives in Grey's Hollow, and Haley lives with her. There is nothing in her background that suggests she is a flight risk or dangerous."

Judge Marlow lowered his black-framed reading glasses to the very edge of his nose and squinted at the prosecutor, waiting for his rebuttal.

Bryce's face hardened with disapproval. "Ms. Powell stabbed Noah Carter in the abdomen three times. She then went to sleep, covered in his blood, leaving him to bleed to death. Her fingerprints were found on the knife, and the expedited DNA report shows that Mr. Carter's blood was literally on her hands."

In the back of the courtroom, a woman sobbed. Morgan knew without looking that the woman was Noah Carter's mother.

Ignoring the empathy in her heart, Morgan argued, "Ms. Powell has strong ties to the community. Her record is as clean as it can be. She's never even received a parking ticket. In addition, she has a serious health condition." Morgan defined Addison's disease for the judge. "She became seriously ill over the weekend in the sheriff's custody and required treatment in the hospital. Jail could be deadly for her."

Judge Marlow set his glasses down and scrubbed both hands across his face. Dropping his hands, he stared at Haley for a few seconds. She trembled, her shoulders caved inward and her small body curled protectively around itself.

Morgan prayed the judge interpreted her unfocused eyes as desperation, illness, and fear, not insanity.

The judge rubbed his jaw, his expression thoughtful. "Ms. Powell, the district attorney has indicated he will be charging you with first-degree murder, a very serious charge with significant penalties. While I will not insist you remain in custody, I agree that a high bond is warranted in this matter. I am going set a one-million-dollar cash bond in this case, with an additional condition of electronic monitoring, at the defendant's expense."

Cash?

Instead of putting up 10 percent of the total bond and using a professional bail bond service for the remainder, Eliza would have to secure Haley's release with $1 million in cash.

Judge Marlow set his jaw and leveled his gaze at Morgan. He was not going to yield, but she had to try. "Your Honor, we feel a million-dollar cash bond is excessive and ask for a professional bond option."

"Denied. Bail is set at one million dollars cash." Marlow's tone and gavel announced that his word was final.

At the prosecutor's table, Bryce looked irritated, but Esposito's glare could have sliced Morgan in two. What was wrong with him? Why did he act as if every small win for her was a personal affront? Besides, with the judge requiring the entire bond to be produced in cash, there was a chance that Haley would have to remain in custody anyway.

Morgan turned away from his glower. She had no time for his ego issues. Sinking into her chair, she slid her legal pad into her tote. Next to her, Haley sat, pale and silent and shaking.

"A million dollars in cash?" she asked in a small voice.

"We'll figure this out." Morgan hoped. With a business the size of Wild, Eliza must have assets. Right? She must have something she could liquidate or borrow against. If not, they could appeal. The judge was supposed to set two forms of bail.

The bailiff led Haley away.

Esposito nodded toward the hallway. Morgan collected her tote and followed him. He'd reined in his temper, but cold anger still glittered in his eyes. "Once the grand jury and judge see the overwhelming amount of evidence, her bail will be revoked."

Bail could be revisited after the grand jury issued an indictment. Because that wasn't an *if*. It was a *when*. Grand juries met behind closed doors. Only the prosecutor presented evidence. Unless Haley wanted to testify—which Morgan wouldn't allow—defense counsel wouldn't even be present. After the grand jury handed Bryce his indictment, he would no doubt petition the court to revoke bail and remand Haley into custody until the trial.

Morgan's head felt like a monkey was clanging cymbals behind her eyes, but she lifted her chin and looked Esposito squarely in the eyes. "We'll see about that."

His nostrils flared as he exhaled. "How is your head?"

The question surprised Morgan and made her wary. "It looks much worse than it is."

"I hope so, because it looks terrible."

Ass.

She waited for his going-out-of-business-limited-time-only plea offer.

"Ms. Powell is just as guilty as your last client," he began. "But in the interests of the taxpayers, I'll make you an offer. If she pleads guilty to the murder charge, we'll settle on twenty-five years and won't pursue a life sentence. She's young. She could still have a life after she's released."

"I'll relay your offer to my client." Morgan didn't even want to counter. Haley's life would be over if she took the plea. This was an all-or-nothing case. Morgan had to win it. But could she?

"My offer expires when the grand jury issues the indictment." Esposito smoothed his tie.

Of course it does.

"Understood."

"If you refuse my offer, your client will go to prison for the rest of her life." Esposito's mouth twisted in a smug smile. "One other thing—your client's blood tests show no evidence that she ingested any of the common club drugs. Thanks for insisting that she be tested. You just filled a nice hole in my case."

Chapter Twelve

"I can't believe Eliza produced a million dollars in cash that fast." Anxious to get to work, Lance paced Morgan's office. It could take all day for the county corrections department to process the paperwork to release Haley. There was no reason for him and Morgan to waste the day waiting. Sharp and Eliza could handle that on their own.

He'd missed working closely with Morgan on a case. Their offices were side by side, but over the winter, they'd been busy with their own caseloads.

What would he do if she took that job offer in New Jersey? She claimed to have no interest, but he'd seen the temptation in her eyes. Did she really want to work criminal defense? If she accepted the job, she'd have to relocate, something he'd never considered. His mother's mental illness kept her housebound. She had no other family. What would happen to her if Lance moved away?

Behind her desk, Morgan opened her laptop. "We're in business. Discovery evidence is coming in from the prosecutor's office. I'm downloading documents."

Lance picked up a dry-erase marker. "Let's get some basics down before we start theorizing. Let's start with the victim."

Morgan scrolled on her computer. "Noah Carter was twenty-six years old, and he rented the house he was killed in."

"The landlord would have a key to the house." Lance tapped the closed marker on his palm.

"The owner of the property lives in Colorado. A sheriff's deputy phoned him on Saturday and verified that he was in Colorado."

Lance listed the landlord at the bottom of his list. "Employer?"

"Excite Site, a small web design firm. Noah worked remotely from home, as do all the company's employees. According to the phone interview with the boss in Austin, Texas, Noah was working on a bid to design a new website for Randolph Savings and Loan."

"Where Haley works as a social media coordinator."

"Yes," Morgan confirmed. "Multiple witnesses stated that's where they met."

"We'll put Noah's boss and his company on the background-check list I gave my mother last night." Lance added them to the bottom of the board. "What do we have on Noah's parents?"

"A few basics. They live in a nice neighborhood. Mr. Carter is a project manager for a construction company. Noah's mother is a dental hygienist. No obvious financial problems. In addition to Adam, the Carters have a daughter, Penelope, age twenty-two. She is on her way home from college in Oregon. On the surface they appear to be a typical middle-class family."

Lance listed Mr. and Mrs. Carter on the board. "Who did Haley go out with on the night of Noah's murder?"

Morgan scrolled. "Her name is Piper Allen. She's an IT tech for the bank. According to her statement, last Friday was her birthday. She and Haley went out to celebrate. Piper left the club at eleven. She doesn't know what time Haley left." Morgan looked up from the screen.

"She goes to the top of our interview list." Lance wrote her name down. "What about Noah? Did he go to the club alone that night?"

"No. He was out with three friends. Justin O'Brien is a freelance graphic artist. Isaac McGee is a software engineer, and Chase Baker works in the accounting department of a local credit union. All three confirm that they left the club around one a.m. Haley and Noah left at the same time, together. The police have a copy of the surveillance video that confirms this. They also interviewed club employees and patrons. So far, all the statements match in basics. We do not have a copy of the surveillance tape yet."

"We'll need to talk to all three of Noah's pals and visit the club." Lance wrote the young men's names on the list. He stepped back and scanned the board. They were off to a good start. "Now, what about Haley? I'm having a hard time picturing her overpowering a healthy young man. She's small. Noah had a generous size advantage."

"Maybe she took him by surprise," Morgan suggested.

"That plays right into the prosecutor's murder charge," Lance pointed out. "Self-defense doesn't allow for sneaking."

"Damn it." Clearly frustrated, Morgan blew a hair off her face. "Could he have attacked her in the kitchen, and she grabbed whatever was handy to defend herself?"

"A knife isn't a good weapon for an untrained woman. It's too easily taken away and used against her."

"But maybe he didn't expect her to fight back. Or maybe he didn't see her grab the knife." Morgan rubbed her forehead.

"Good possibilities." Lance added the questions to the board.

Behind him, Morgan was quiet. He glanced over his shoulder. Her face was grim.

"What's wrong?" He turned around.

"I'm reading the sheriff's initial interview with Haley."

"And?"

"It's disturbing."

"Is Haley disturbing or Colgate?"

"It's all disturbing, actually." Morgan nodded toward the printer, which started to hum and spit out papers. "I printed you a copy of the interview and the police reports."

"Colgate has been in law enforcement a long time. I've never heard of any scandals associated with him." Lance collected the papers, then he perched on the corner of her desk and began to skim through the pages. "When did the call come in?"

"At eleven fifteen a.m. on Saturday, one of Noah's neighbors heard a woman screaming outside and called 911. The deputy arrived ten minutes later and found Haley kneeling over the body. He confirmed that Noah was dead and called for backup. Haley was rocking back and forth on the grass, asking, 'What have I done?' over and over. He asked her for her name and address, but she did not respond to his questions. She was compliant but, in his words, 'out of it.' He asked her if she was injured, and she shook her head, indicating that she was not." Morgan huffed. "Considering her mental state, she could have been seriously injured and not known it."

Lance found the correct page on the police report. "The deputy also stated that he looked her over for injuries and found none."

"He is not a doctor." Morgan frowned. "He should have called an ambulance. She could have had a head injury or been under the influence of drugs. She could have been raped."

"I agree." Lance moved to the next page. "But he didn't. And when she finally *was* examined, there was no evidence that any of those things occurred." He held up a hand before she could protest. "*We* know too much time had passed for some of those tests."

"But I'll never be able to convince a jury the deputy didn't make the right call." Morgan rubbed the back of her neck and then went back to reading her computer screen. "At that point, the deputy gave up on getting any information out of her. She was wearing only the thin black dress. Her lips were tinted blue, and she was shivering. Not knowing what had happened inside the house, he didn't want to enter the building without backup. The temperature was below freezing that morning. Concerned for her welfare, but also worried that she could be the killer, he handcuffed Haley and put her in the back of his car with the heater running to wait for the sheriff, who was on his way."

Lance skimmed the next page. "Once backup arrived, the deputies cleared the house to make sure no one else was inside, dead or alive. The crime scene was secured, and the medical examiner and forensic team were called in forty-five minutes after the initial 911 call. The sheriff interviewed Haley in the back of the patrol car. The inside of the car was warm, but she still appeared to be cold, so he got her a blanket. During this very brief interview, Haley repeated her initial statement of 'What have I done?' Then she turned away and refused to speak anymore." Lance lowered the papers.

"Colgate didn't push very hard." Morgan leaned back in her chair, picked up a pen, and drew circles on the bottom of her legal pad.

"At that point, he didn't know about the fingerprints on the knife. He was covering his bases and not making assumptions."

"Good point." Morgan pointed her pen at her computer screen. "The deputies found her purse inside the house and identified her via her driver's license. The sheriff decided to bring her into the station for further questioning."

"He hoped the trip to the sheriff's station would get her talking." That's exactly what Lance would have done.

"No doubt." Morgan nodded. "That's the end of the on-scene interview."

"That's a good start." Except that Morgan's new client looked pretty damned guilty.

Lance's stomach rumbled. He glanced at his watched. It was two p.m. "We should eat. We missed lunch."

Engrossed in her reading, Morgan waved a hand. "You go ahead. I'm going to watch Haley's video interviews at the sheriff's station."

"You need to eat." Lance sighed. "Do you want me to make you one of Sharp's protein shakes or order pizza?"

Morgan's head snapped up. "Did you say pizza?"

He pulled out his phone. "Extra cheese and mushrooms?"

"Yes, please." She turned back to her computer.

"Don't start that video without me." Lance placed the order and requested delivery.

Morgan wrote on her legal pad. "The sheriff began questioning her at 1:53 p.m. The forensics team had taken her fingerprints and swabbed her cheek for DNA at the scene. They also sampled the dried blood on her body from multiple locations and scraped under her nails. I'm surprised they didn't request her dress as evidence."

Lance rounded Morgan's desk and perched on her credenza to watch the computer screen over her shoulder. The video was frozen on the first frame. Haley huddled in the metal chair in the sheriff's station interview room. The sheriff and a young deputy sat on the other side of the table. Haley was no longer handcuffed, and she clutched a blanket around her shoulders. Her face was smeared with makeup.

"The dress is tight and skimpy," Lance said. "She looks uncomfortable in it. I suspect the sheriff wanted her to remain that way. Besides, the dress wasn't going anywhere. It's not torn or damaged. She had no way to dispose of it. She's already complied with their requests for physical evidence, and she wasn't claiming to have been raped. Plus, he'd have to find something for her to wear or let her use the phone to make a call. If he offered her the phone, she might have called an attorney. Once suspects lawyer up, they stop talking."

"She's clearly not trying to hide anything," Morgan noted.

"No. She doesn't look like she's formulating any grand plan to exonerate herself, but she isn't answering questions either."

"She looks traumatized." Morgan drew more overlapping circles on the yellow notepad.

"But from what?" Lance reached forward and clicked the "Play" button to start the video.

On the screen, Sheriff Colgate identified himself, Deputy York, and Haley. He noted her address for the official record. Then Colgate read

Haley her Miranda rights, slid a paper and a pen across the desk, and asked her to sign to acknowledge that she understood her rights. She ignored his request. Colgate didn't press the issue. Instead, he spoke to the camera in the corner of the ceiling. "Let the record show that Ms. Powell has been verbally apprised of her rights."

Haley blinked, her gaze resting on the sheriff for a few seconds, then drifting away.

Colgate's shoulders were planted against the back of the chair. He was giving her space, feeling her out at this early stage of the interview. "Ms. Powell, how did you come to be at the residence of Noah Carter this morning?"

Haley's breath hitched, and one shoulder lifted and dropped, the movement almost imperceptible.

"You were at the nightclub Beats last night." The sheriff shifted forward slightly, resting his forearms on the edge of the table. "What time did you leave the club?"

"I don't know," Haley mumbled and stared down at her fists, which were clenching the blanket edges together in front of her belly.

"You were covered in blood this morning." The sheriff's tone was firm but gentle, as if he were talking to a teenager who'd wrecked her dad's car. "How did that happen?"

"I don't know."

"Did you go home with Noah last night?"

"I don't know." Haley's voice rose both in volume and pitch, then dropped to a whisper. "I want to call my mother."

The sheriff stood, walked around the table, and perched on the corner next to her. He was getting in her personal space now, applying pressure through body language. "Did you kill Noah Carter?"

"I don't know I don't know I don't know." Haley's words ran into one sentence. She stifled a sob. A tear rolled down her cheek. She folded her arms on the table, laid her head down, and wept. The sound of her sobbing ripped at Lance's heart.

On the video, compassion flickered briefly over the sheriff's face.

For the next fifteen minutes, the sheriff asked her multiple times and in multiple ways if she had killed Noah Carter. But Haley had shut down. She wouldn't even lift her head. A knock sounded on the door. A deputy stuck his head in and waved frantically for the sheriff.

"The first interview ended at 2:12 p.m. Saturday," Morgan said.

"That's right about the time Shannon Yates's car was found."

Morgan sat back in her chair, twirling her pen in her fingertips. "Haley sat in the holding cell until Monday morning, when the sheriff realized he was running out of time and needed to either charge her or let her go."

"But they weren't entirely ignoring the case. In the meantime, they matched her fingerprints with those found on the weapon and expedited a DNA test of the blood that was all over Haley, confirming that it was Noah's." Lance thought the sheriff had handled the situation well, except for not taking Haley to the ER. "Haley never specifically told the sheriff that she didn't remember the night before."

"She wasn't thinking straight." Morgan tipped her head back and closed her eyes. "She was clearly confused, or 'out of it,' as the responding officer noted."

"The prosecutor will spin it that she was merely avoiding questions and took that time to come up with a story."

"Or that I suggested it when I met with her on Monday morning." Morgan sighed. "That's exactly how I would have spun it when I was an ADA." She leaned forward and wrote on her legal pad. "I'll prepare a motion to get her initial statements to the sheriff's department disqualified due to her confused mental state brought about by her untreated Addison's disease. I'll need to get Haley's doctor to testify that her medical condition made her disoriented and confused."

The doorbell chimed.

"That'll be the pizza." Lance went to the front door, handed the delivery kid some cash, and brought the pizza back to Morgan's office.

He opened it on her desk. She ripped her attention from her notes long enough to inhale two slices. Lance ate four, then stowed the rest of the pizza in the refrigerator in the kitchen.

He returned to Morgan's office. They watched the second video. Colgate read Haley's Miranda rights a second time. Then he confronted her with the results of the DNA test and the fingerprint analysis.

Haley's eyes were sunken, her posture exhausted, and her skin paler. She replied to every question with a small voice. "I want to call my mother."

"I'll arrange it." Colgate gave up, and the video ended.

Morgan stood, crossed the room, and brewed a cup of coffee. When she turned around, a deep-in-thought line divided her eyebrows. "We need to start interviewing people."

"It's three o'clock." Lance returned to his place in front of the whiteboard. He studied the list of names.

Morgan went back to her desk, sipped her coffee, and tapped on her keyboard. "Let's start with Haley's girlfriend Piper. She'll be the least hostile. We can go to Beats tonight and interview employees, but the club doesn't open until later. We also have to talk to Noah's three friends: Isaac McGee, Chase Baker, and Justin O'Brien."

The police reports included driver's license photos of all the witnesses. Morgan printed them out, including pictures of Noah and Haley. She made multiple copies of each, one for the whiteboard and another for her own file. She also liked to have pictures on hand when doing interviews. A photo could jog the memory of a waitress or bartender.

"We'll walk the crime scene tomorrow," Lance added.

"I'll email the prosecutor's office now and request entry to Noah's house. Then I'll call Piper and see when she'll be available." Morgan typed a quick email. She pressed the "Enter" key and froze.

"What is it?" Lance asked.

"An email." She turned the computer, so he could read the screen.

Counselor Dane,

Haley Powell brutally murdered Noah Carter. If you continue to represent her, you will be complicit in her crime, and you will be punished for your wickedness. Consider this your only warning.

"You've been carrying your handgun, right?" Lance asked.

Both sides of a criminal case often received nasty emails. Most of the time nothing came of them, but the tone of this one set off his creep meter. Morgan could handle herself, but Lance still wanted to play bodyguard.

"Yes," Morgan said. "Except at court appearances, like today."

"Until this is over, don't leave home without it."

Chapter Thirteen

Morgan reached for the doorbell of Piper Allen's second-floor apartment door. Gray siding and neat white trim gave the newer complex a crisp, clean appearance.

The young woman who opened the door wore slim jeans and a body-hugging top with the shoulders cut out. Thick gray socks covered her feet. Royal-blue highlights in her jet-black hair made her pale skin and blue eyes pop. Whether she intended it or not, the effect was elfin.

"Piper Allen?" When the young woman nodded, Morgan handed over a business card and introduced herself. "This is my investigator, Lance Kruger. \Thank you for seeing us."

"Come in." Piper stepped back and opened the door wider. "I'll do whatever I can to help Haley."

They went into a tiny tiled foyer. Piper closed the door and led them back to a living room, which was open to a bright kitchen and eating area. Her modern furnishings looked like the type that came in a flat box to be assembled with a hex key.

"How is Haley?" Piper walked into the kitchen.

Morgan followed her. "She should be home soon."

Lance crossed his arms and leaned against the wall.

"I can't believe that she killed Noah, no matter what the police say." Piper stopped in front of a cutting board loaded with onions, carrots, and celery. The rest of the apartment might have been furnished on a budget, but the kitchen appliances were all high-end. "You don't mind if I continue chopping? I need to keep busy."

"Chop away." Morgan waved toward the cutting board. "You and Haley went out together Friday night? Whose idea was it to go to the club?"

Regret troubled Piper's face, and her fingers trembled. She squeezed them into tight fists and then opened her hands. A little steadier, she picked up a large, fat-bladed knife and began to chop carrots. "It was mine. Haley doesn't really like clubs. She'd rather stay home and game."

"She plays video games?" Morgan asked.

"Online games. Haley's a geek. She likes *League of Legends*, *Call of Duty*, and *World of Warcraft*." Piper lifted the cutting board and used the back of the knife to scrape the chopped carrots into a large bowl. "She didn't want to go out Friday night, but it was my birthday. She did it to make me happy."

"Have you and Haley been friends long?" Lance's gaze was fixed on Piper's knife.

With practiced hands, she worked the blade through a row of celery stalks. "Since I took the job with the bank three years ago."

"Would you say Haley is your best friend?" Lance asked.

"Yes." Piper pushed the celery into the bowl and moved an onion to the center of the board.

"How closely do you work together?" Lance frowned as Piper sliced the onion in half in one deft motion.

"We don't work in the same department." She turned the cut sides down and chopped the onion into even pieces. "She's in marketing, and I'm in tech support. But the bank isn't that big. We see each other during the day."

"What time did you get to the club Friday night?" Morgan eyed the wooden knife block on the counter. Piper had clearly not purchased her knives at Target.

"Around nine, I think." Piper transferred the onion to the bowl, turned to the refrigerator, and took out a whole chicken. Despite her mad knife skills, her hands still shook as she removed the packaging and exchanged her fat knife for a skinny-bladed one.

"What are you making?" Morgan's kitchen skills leaned more toward short-order than fancy fare.

"A chicken roll." Piper set the knife down on the board. "My mom used to own a restaurant. I've been cooking since before I could reach the counter." She paused for a deep breath. "I have problems with anxiety sometimes. Cooking helps me relax."

Morgan watched, both impressed and slightly horrified as Piper snapped the chicken wing joints and slid the bones out whole. Piper picked up her knife, chopped off the tips of the wings, and added them to her bone pile. Then, in one stroke, she cut right through the center of the chicken breast.

"Does it work?" Morgan couldn't take her eyes off the chicken. It was on its back, the breasts and wings splayed out in a position that reminded her of an autopsy.

Piper worked the knife through the shoulders and around the chest cavity, separating the carcass from the skin. She lifted one pale shoulder in a quick shrug. Her voice quivered. "Sometimes. At least I have a nice meal at the end."

Had she been this nervous with the police?

"What time did you leave the club?" Morgan asked.

"Around eleven." Piper shifted her attention to the chicken's legs.

"You only stayed two hours?" Lance raised an eyebrow. "It was *your* birthday."

Piper fumbled. "Damn."

She shook her hand. Blood welled from a slice across her thumb. She went to the sink and washed her hands with soap and water.

"Are you all right?" Morgan stepped closer and peered over the girl's shoulder. The cut appeared superficial.

"It's not deep." Piper dried her hands with paper towels and wrapped a Band-Aid around her thumb. She reached into the cabinet under the sink and removed a clear vinyl glove from a box. Tugging it onto the hand with the Band-Aid, she picked up her knife again.

"You left early," Morgan reminded her.

With a combination of slicing and joint cracking, Piper removed the bones from the drumsticks and thighs. "Haley was talking to Noah. She kind of ditched me. I shouldn't have left her." Guilt quivered in Piper's words. "I feel like this is my fault. We have a code. 'No woman left behind.' No matter what, we don't let each other drink too much, and we don't let each other go home with strange guys. Girls have to watch each other's backs."

"That's a good policy." Morgan couldn't decide if the girl was nervous or hiding something.

"But I broke it because I was mad. It was my birthday, and Haley ignored me to spend time with Noah." Piper's eyes brightened with anger. She blinked away the moisture.

"Did Haley have her car at the club?" Lance shifted his weight back.

Piper shook her head. "No. We took an Uber. But I figured she'd be going home with Noah. They were into each other in a big way. If she changed her mind, she could always get a ride." Piper's voice broke. "But I didn't even say goodbye. I didn't even let her know I was going." She took two quick, steadying breaths, set her jaw, and resumed deboning the chicken. "But Noah and Haley knew each other, so I convinced myself that I wasn't really breaking our code. I wasn't letting her go with a stranger."

Morgan sensed there was more. "But?"

"But that was just a rationalization. I know I couldn't *make* her leave with me, but we should have had a good fight about it before I gave in. She's my friend, and I let her down." Piper stared at her pile of bones. "It's funny. Our code is designed to protect *us*. I never thought it would be a man who'd need protecting. Or that Haley would have been capable of . . ."

A tear rolled down her cheek. She wiped it away on her shoulder.

"What did you do when you left the club?" Morgan asked.

"I didn't really want to see anyone." Piper shook herself. "I came back here and went to bed."

Piper had no alibi.

"Has Haley ever demonstrated that she has a temper?" Lance studied the girl's face.

"No." Piper shook her head. The afternoon sun filtered through the blinds and gleamed on her blue highlights.

Morgan flipped the page on her notepad. "Have you ever seen her in a heated argument with anyone?"

Piper's shoulders drooped. "Haley's a geek. She likes to be alone. She's nonconfrontational to a fault. She lets people take advantage of her. Honestly, I was super surprised to see her being so flirty with Noah. She isn't normally so outgoing."

"Her behavior on Friday night was out of character?" Morgan probed.

Piper nodded, her face thoughtful. "Now that you mention it, she was louder than usual too."

"She'd been drinking," Morgan suggested. "Maybe the alcohol loosened her up."

"Haley isn't a big drinker." Piper's head tilted. "She's usually the designated driver. She tries to downplay it, but she has to take care of herself or she gets sick. She usually limits her alcohol intake to a drink or two."

Morgan circled back around to the night of the murder. "Did anything else unusual happen at the club?"

"Unusual?" Piper looked up from the chicken, the knife poised over the bit of flesh that connected the carcass to the meat.

Morgan rolled her hand in the air. "Fights, arguments, weird behavior from someone besides Haley . . ."

Piper looked to the ceiling, as if replaying the night in her mind. "I don't remember anything specific."

"Did you know anyone else who was there that night?" Lance asked.

"A couple of people. Noah and his friends. I've seen them around before. There aren't many clubs in this area. Beats is the newest and most popular. You run into the same people every weekend." Piper's chin lifted. "Wait. Haley's ex was there. That was unusual."

"Haley has an ex?" Morgan's interest piqued.

Piper nodded. "His name is Kieran Hart. I forgot he was there. The police only asked me if I'd seen anyone angry with Noah. Kieran didn't even talk to him."

"Was their breakup volatile? Who broke up with whom?" Morgan noted the ex's name in her phone.

"Haley broke up with Kieran." Piper used the point of the knife to sever the whole rib cage from the rest of the flesh. "I don't know why. He treated her so good. He opened doors. He sent her flowers all the time and took her to really nice events, but then Haley is rich too. I guess those things don't mean as much to her."

As they would to someone like Piper . . . Did she have a crush on Haley's ex? Was she jealous?

Piper set the carcass next to the rest of the bones. "He called Haley for weeks afterward. But all that was over more than six months ago. She hasn't heard from him recently."

Or if she did, she didn't mention it to Piper.

"Did they talk at the club?" Morgan wondered if Kieran was really over Haley.

"He said hi, but Haley ignored him. She didn't want to lead him on, considering how hard he'd been to get rid of." Piper shrugged, but her face pinched in disapproval. "But when he saw her hanging out with Noah, he got all annoyed and left. I felt bad for him. I was pretty irritated at Haley too."

"You thought Haley treated Kieran badly?" Morgan asked.

"She was kinda rude, just walking past him with her nose in the air." Piper's sniff was more judgmental than sad.

"What time did Kieran leave?" Morgan asked.

"Maybe a half hour before I left." Piper used her hands to pull out a few remaining bones.

Morgan noted the time that Kieran left Beats as approximately ten thirty. "By any chance, do you have Kieran's contact information?"

"Kieran didn't even interact with Noah," Piper protested, her back straightening and her tone becoming defensive, almost as if she were protecting Kieran.

"We're trying to talk to everyone who was at the club that night." Morgan waved a hand in the air. "You never know what someone might have seen."

"Oh, OK." Piper washed her hands thoroughly. Then she removed her vinyl glove, opened her phone, and read Kieran's full name, address, and mobile number.

"Thanks for talking to us." Morgan entered the information into her own phone. "We might have more questions."

"OK. Just call me. I'll do anything to help Haley." Piper gave Morgan her cell phone number, then walked them to the door.

Back in the Jeep, Lance said, "Piper was very nervous."

"She said she suffered from anxiety." Morgan lowered her window an inch.

Lance tapped a finger on the steering wheel.

"You don't believe her?" Morgan removed her legal pad from her tote.

"I don't know. She was so anxious during the whole interview that I can't pinpoint what she seemed most uncomfortable discussing."

"I found it hard to read her as well." She began making notes on the interview while it was still fresh in her mind. "But we did learn several things. One, she was mad at Haley for ignoring her on her birthday. Two, Haley has an ex who might also have been angry that night. Three, Piper has feelings for the ex, and four, Haley was behaving out of character that night, less reserved than usual, more social."

"Alcohol lowers inhibitions, especially for those who can't handle it."

"True." Morgan had no tolerance for alcohol. Since she preferred not to be stupid in public, one drink was her limit. "Date-rape drugs also lower inhibitions."

"We can't prove someone drugged Haley."

"I know." Morgan drummed her fingers on her notepad. "Let's get background info on Haley's ex."

"I'll call my mom and get her to add him to the top of her list."

"And I'll go through the police reports again, but I don't remember any mention of Haley's ex-boyfriend."

"Me either." Lance put the Jeep in gear. "We learned one other thing in Piper's interview. She has crazy knife skills."

"She certainly does."

His phone vibrated with a text. He picked it up and read the screen. "Sharp says they're leaving the jail with Haley, and the place is crawling with reporters and protesters. He wants me at Eliza's house to play bodyguard in case there's trouble."

"Protesters are there already?" Morgan used her phone to access a network news station's website. "Oh, no. The case made the national news." She turned up the volume.

"We're outside the county jail, where a crowd has gathered to protest the release of Haley Powell on bail. Ms. Powell is being charged with first-degree murder in the stabbing death of Noah Carter." The reporter went on to relay the gory facts of the case. "Haley is the daughter of Eliza Powell, the owner of Wild, a hugely successful cosmetic company."

The reporter detailed the evidence the police claimed to have and the wealth of Haley's mother. He then approached a young man carrying an enlarged photo of Noah Carter. "Why are you here today?"

The young man shook his sign. "That crazy bitch butchered Noah. She shouldn't be out on bail. We want justice."

The feed went to a commercial. When the news returned, a different reporter stood on a rural street. The picture panned away from the reporter to an upshot of a house. Eliza's house was a mansion, and the camera angle made the structure look even bigger and more imposing that it was. All glass and cedar, it perched on top of a foothill, no doubt commanding multimillion-dollar views.

The reporter said, "This is the Powell residence, where Haley Powell will be on house arrest until her trial for the murder of Noah Carter."

When the segment ended, Morgan closed her laptop. "I don't like the attention. Not one bit. They're treating her like some sort of spoiled celebrity. We won't be able to find a single juror who won't walk into that courtroom with a predisposed opinion of Haley as a privileged rich girl who thinks she can get away with anything—even murder."

"What do we do?" Lance asked.

"I don't know yet. But I'd better think of something fast, or Haley will be found guilty before her case ever makes it to court."

Lance's phone buzzed again. "Let's go. Sharp says Haley just received her first death threat."

"With this amount of publicity, she'll receive more of those before this is over." Angry, Morgan jammed her notepad into her tote. "And thanks to the media, everyone now knows exactly where she lives."

Chapter Fourteen

Peering out the front window of Eliza's house, Sharp swallowed a curse. A throng of reporters gathered at the base of the long, steep driveway. News vans lined the gravel shoulder of the road. A tall wrought-iron fence enclosed the property, and an electronic gate barred the driveway entrance. Across the road from the media, protesters shouted and waved signs.

JUSTICE FOR NOAH.

KEEP KILLERS BEHIND BARS.

JUSTICE SHOULDN'T BE FOR SALE.

Eliza stepped up next to him. "I can't believe there are so many people out there."

"I was hoping they wouldn't find your house so fast." Sharp closed the blinds, blocking out the setting sun.

Eliza hugged her waist. "Will the gate keep them out?"

"Most of them will respect the gate."

"Most?" She pivoted to face him.

"There's always one." He searched her face. "How are you holding up?"

She was strong, but Haley was her weakness.

"I'm trying not to think too far ahead. There are just too many horrible possibilities." She shivered. "Part of me cannot believe the situation Haley is in. She was an easy baby and an easy kid. When other parents complained about their teenagers getting into trouble and being difficult, I counted my blessings." Eliza pressed a fist to her mouth. "Someone must have framed her for this crime. She would never do anything so terrible. She simply isn't capable."

Sharp didn't know Haley well, but he couldn't believe any child of Ted's would turn out to be a killer. He squeezed Eliza's arm. "We're going to see her through this."

"Thank you." Tears welled in Eliza's eyes. "I don't know what I'd do without you right now."

"That's something you don't have to waste a second thinking about. I'll stick with Haley, no matter what."

Eliza reached up to cup his jaw. "You were always such a good friend."

Sharp covered her hand with his. "I wish I'd been there for you more over the years."

"It was *my* choice to leave, Lincoln. You can't blame yourself. I had to go. I couldn't heal with reminders of Ted everywhere."

"I was one of those reminders."

Her sigh was long and deep, and she seemed to exhale sorrow. "Yes. I'm sorry."

"Don't be. You did what you had to do to survive. Haley was the most important consideration then. She still is." Sharp meant every word, but sadness flared in his chest. He and Eliza shared a past and emotions only they could understand. Unfortunately, not all those feelings were healthy. Whatever remained between him and Eliza could be sorted out later. Today, he needed to focus on Haley. He dropped his hand and stepped out of her reach.

"I'm going to make coffee." Eliza headed toward the back of the house.

Sharp followed her to the great room. The center island, a cream-colored slab of granite the size of an Escalade, divided the family room from the kitchen area. The floors were dark wood, the view spectacular.

Haley stood in the middle of the room, looking lost.

Sharp didn't know how to comfort her any better than he did Eliza. He turned to the glass wall that faced the gorge behind the house. Below, a small patch of grass was enclosed with more wrought-iron fencing. At the rear of the yard, a bike lock secured a gate that opened to a hiking trail.

"What made you move out to the woods?"

"I was tired of the city." Eliza scooped coffee grounds into a filter. "I love the clean air and the quiet. Being in the middle of nowhere was disconcerting at first, but the house was built with security in mind, and I had the alarm system upgraded. Now I can enjoy the solitude."

"Do you like being alone?" Sharp asked.

"Very much so." Eliza nodded. "I can be back in New York in a few hours, and I'm fond of traveling, but this has become home."

She cast a worried frown at her daughter. "Haley, I'm going to make some dinner. Mac and cheese?"

"OK." Haley hadn't moved.

Eliza turned on the coffee machine and opened the refrigerator.

Haley lifted her foot and stared at the black monitor strapped around her ankle. "It's heavier than I expected."

"Whoever called it a bracelet obviously never wore one," Sharp said.

Haley blinked at him as if coming out of a daze, and Sharp pictured a smiling infant, cooing and squealing, unaware that the people around her were mourning her father.

Eliza's voice brought him back. "Would you like coffee?"

"No, thank you." Sharp shook off the melancholy. He needed to be on his game. He'd promised Ted he'd look out for his family. The passage of years did not diminish his responsibility. "Do you have green tea?"

"I do. That's what Haley drinks." Eliza put a tea kettle on the stove, then took a foil pan from the freezer and slid it into the oven. "Do you want a cup, honey?"

The conversation seemed to pull Haley out of her daze.

Eliza gestured to an island stool. "Maybe you should drink some Gatorade?"

"You're right." Haley's brow crinkled. "I'm probably dehydrated. I couldn't drink out of that sink in the jail. The spigots were too low, and the water barely trickled out."

How would she cope if she were sentenced to twenty-five years in prison? Sharp thought about the overwhelming amount of physical evidence against her, and his gut twisted.

Stop!

His job as Morgan's agent was to find the cracks in the prosecutor's case, not to determine Haley's guilt or innocence.

Sharp's phone buzzed with a text. "It's Morgan. They're here." He and Eliza went to the front window. Sharp separated the blind slats and spotted Lance's Jeep crawling up the road toward the gate, its slow and steady motion forcing the reporters and protesters to move out of the way. He pressed a button mounted near the front door, and the gate swung open. Lance drove up the driveway and parked in front of the house. Sharp let them inside.

Morgan was moving gingerly, and Lance was hovering, clearly worried about her.

Her head came up. "Do I smell coffee?"

"Yes. Would you like some?" Eliza asked, turning back toward the kitchen.

"Definitely," Morgan said.

Sharp opened his mouth to comment.

Morgan blew past him. "Not today, Sharp."

Shaking his head, Sharp returned to the two-story great room.

"Tell me about the threat," Morgan said.

Sharp opened a laptop on the island and turned it to face Morgan. He'd read the email enough times to memorize it.

Ms. Powell,

You have shed innocent blood. You are a murderess. Give up your folly of innocence. Cease your
lying. You must repent, or you will be destroyed.
The wicked cannot escape their punishment.

Lance frowned at the computer. "Morgan received a similar email this afternoon."

Morgan removed her computer from her tote, opened it, and read the email she'd received to Sharp.

He ran a hand through his hair. "Shit."

"The case could drag on for months or even years." Morgan closed the laptop and turned to Haley. "As much as I hate to tell you, this is not the last threat you will receive. I'd like to give our computer expert access to your email. She can monitor and track any threats that come in."

Haley's shoulders rounded with defeat. "OK."

Lance frowned at the floor-to-ceiling glass. "I don't like this much exposure."

"I know," Sharp said. "When I came last night to inspect the security system, Eliza and I discussed covering these windows."

The backyard dropped off into a deep ravine just beyond the black safety fence.

Eliza stood next to him, rubbing her arms. "I have blinds in all the other rooms, but I've never needed them out here. We always wanted the view to be unobstructed. But last night, I dug out all my spare sheets."

Haley hadn't moved, but she was now staring at the wide expanse of windows. "I always loved these windows, but now I feel like someone is watching me."

Lance scanned the vista. "What's on the other side of that gate?"

"A hiking trail that leads to an overlook." Haley's voice was wistful. "The view is spectacular. Mom and I go down there a few times a week." She frowned at her ankle monitor. Who knew how long it would be before she could hike again?

"The overlook trail gets popular in the summer," Eliza added, "which is why we have the lock on the gate."

"Have you hiked down there?" Lance asked Sharp.

"Yes, last night," Sharp said. "On the other side of the overlook, the trail picks up again and leads up to a small parking area on the road about a half mile from here. It's not a difficult hike. I walked it in the dark with a flashlight. The terrain will not be a deterrent for a determined photographer."

A strong telephoto lens could even capture a decent shot from the other side of the ravine.

"I'll check the trail when I leave tonight." Lance rubbed his palms together. "Let's get these windows covered."

"I'll get the sheets." Eliza left the room.

Sharp fetched a ladder from the garage. They hung the sheets with duct tape. When all the glass—and the view—was covered, the stunning room with its million-dollar vistas became claustrophobic and depressing.

Haley might not be in jail, but she definitely wasn't free. Her beautiful house had become an expensive prison.

Chapter Fifteen

Watching Eliza pour coffee, Morgan perked up. Her own Pavlovian response?

Haley drank pale-purple liquid at the island, but her gaze kept straying to the sheet-covered windows.

"I need to ask you some questions today," Morgan said.

"I know." Haley sipped her drink. "I'm sorry I was so stupid when we talked before. My head gets foggy when I'm off my meds."

"Don't worry about it." Morgan scanned her. Haley wore the sweater Eliza had brought to the hospital the day before. She obviously hadn't been home long enough to shower or change clothes. "Have you eaten anything?"

"Not yet." Haley shook her head. "Mom is making me dinner. But I desperately want to shower." She lifted her foot and shook it. A black band encircled her ankle. "They said this was waterproof, right?"

"Yes," Sharp answered. "You can shower, but don't submerge it."

"OK." Haley sighed, her posture sagging. "I feel like a zombie. I don't know how to feel. It's all . . . too much. I can't take it all in."

"I know, but I need to ask you some questions," Morgan said gently. "Get your shower first."

The poor girl.

Morgan couldn't imagine sitting in a holding cell for days, barely dressed, in bare feet, and then spending the night in jail. Neither could she imagine the quiet, slender girl stabbing a young man to death.

"OK." Haley exhaled, a long and depressed sound, as she turned and left the room.

"Is her room safe?" Lance asked.

"Eliza has a top-notch security system," Sharp said. "The house has steel doors, reinforced doorframes, and heavy-duty dead bolts. No one is getting in easily."

"Good. I'm sure she needs a little alone time to process the last few days." Morgan perched on a stool.

Eliza handed her a cup of coffee and sat next to her. "I feel so helpless. What do we do now?"

"We investigate." Morgan drank her coffee. "Do you need to travel any time soon?"

"No." Eliza jumped off her stool to pace. "Haley is my number-one priority. I have very good employees in my Manhattan location and a full office in the house. I can run the company from here."

"Good. Here's the plan." Morgan set down her cup and checked her phone. "The evidence is starting to come in from the DA's office. We'll spend tomorrow reviewing it. We've already ordered some background checks. We'll add more as the investigation progresses. Lance, Sharp, and I will interview witnesses and hire experts to go over all of the state's evidence. We will review every report word by word looking for weaknesses. Our goal is to poke as many holes in the case as possible."

"It sounds like you believe Haley is guilty and just want to destroy the prosecutor's case," Eliza said. "My daughter is innocent. I want to prove that."

Morgan nodded. "That's our ultimate goal, but we don't have to adhere to such a high standard. We only need to show that the prosecutor hasn't proven her guilt."

"I don't want her to get off on a technicality," Eliza argued. "Her life will be ruined. We need to find out who really killed that young man. I know the law says she's innocent until proven guilty, but we all know that's bullshit. We need to find the real killer."

"That would be optimal," Morgan agreed. "And we will do everything in our power to do just that."

Haley returned to the kitchen in flannel pajama bottoms and a sweatshirt.

"Is there somewhere quiet we can go to talk?" Morgan reached into her tote for her notepad and a pen. She wanted Haley to speak freely, and Morgan thought her best chances for honesty would be if she and Haley were alone. There were things a woman might not want to say with her mother or men she didn't know well in the room.

"My bedroom." Turning away, Haley led her up the steps to the upstairs hall. "My mom's room is downstairs. I have my own space up here."

Her bedroom was a suite, with a large private bath and sitting room, complete with desk, big-screen TV, and a small sectional couch.

Haley flopped onto the sofa.

Morgan sat on the other leg of the *L*. "First, I want you to relax and tell me everything you remember about last Friday night. Start from when you left the house. No detail is too small. Just picture it in your mind and tell me what you remember."

"I'll try." She took a deep breath as if preparing herself. "Piper and I took an Uber to Beats. It was her birthday, otherwise I would have stayed home. I don't like clubs much." Her story didn't waver as she described having an alcohol-free cocktail and dancing with Piper. "Then I ran into Noah. He consulted on a new website for the bank. I'd met him a couple of times." She paused, plucking a tissue from a box on the end table. "I liked him—too much, I guess, because I let him buy me a drink, then I totally blew off Piper to dance with him. I shouldn't have done that."

"Do you know what time that was?"

"Maybe ten?" Haley didn't sound sure. "I wasn't paying attention to the time."

Piper had remained at the bar for about an hour after Haley deserted her.

"Then what happened?" Morgan asked.

"He bought me another drink. We ate nachos. We danced some more. Then it all starts to get fuzzy." Haley frowned. "Yesterday and today, I've been remembering pieces of the evening, but I still have significant blank spots." Haley closed her eyes. "I tripped on my way out of the club and banged my leg. It hurt, so when we got to his place, I asked him for an aspirin and ice." She opened her eyes. Her expression turned bittersweet, then confused, then devastated. "He was really nice. I don't understand what happened."

"Is that the whole memory?" Disappointment filled Morgan as she noted the explanation for the bruises on Haley's leg. She'd been hoping Noah had gotten violent, not that he'd been sweet.

"No. He took me to his house, put me on the couch, and got me an ice pack. Then I wanted something salty. I took extra medication because salt cravings are a warning sign that I need it. Noah brought me water and some chips. We went into the family room. Noah turned on the TV. But I don't remember what was playing. We were kissing . . ." Her face darkened. She shuddered. "Then I have a big blank space until I woke up."

Shivering, Haley pulled a fleece blanket bearing a university logo across her legs. "The rest of the weekend is fuzzy. Even finding Noah doesn't feel like it was real. Everything until I was treated at the hospital is hazy. I haven't felt that Addison's brain fog in a long time. I never let myself get that sick."

"Have you ever passed out from drinking alcohol before?" As much as Morgan hated it, Haley's entire life and lifestyle would be under scrutiny.

"Yes. Once." Haley sniffed. "After a frat party freshman year. There were tequila shots and beer and something the fraternity called jungle juice, which tasted like spiked fruit punch. I blacked out. But I had a lot more than two drinks, and I vomited for an entire day afterward. When I woke up at Noah's, I was confused and foggy, but I wasn't hangover-sick like that." Haley's posture stiffened with resolve. "I couldn't have passed out drunk and not been violently ill the next day."

"I agree."

But was Haley being truthful? Her story was bizarre, and she wouldn't be the first defendant to lie to her attorney. She wouldn't even be the first client to lie to Morgan this week.

Morgan moved on. "Do you have an ex-boyfriend?"

Haley cocked her head. "Yes. Kieran Hart." She spelled the name for Morgan. "And now that you mention it, he was at Beats Friday night."

"Did you argue?"

"No. He said hi. I ignored him, and that was the end of it. We haven't talked in more than six months, but there was no way I was opening up any line of communication with Kieran. When we were going out, he would text me constantly. He always had to know who I was with and when I was going to be home. I asked him to stop. When he wouldn't, I shut that relationship down."

"Was he ever violent or abusive?"

"Not exactly, but he was very controlling, and he lost his temper really quickly." Haley twisted the tissue. She clearly had something to say that she was uncomfortable discussing. "This is really embarrassing."

"Everything you say to me is in confidence. I won't repeat it to anyone unless it's essential for your defense. That said, it's best I know everything that someone else might bring up against you. The more honest you are with me, the better I can defend you."

Haley nodded. "I'd spent the night with Kieran. When I got up in the morning, he'd already left for the office. That wasn't uncommon. He works long hours." She looked away. "He left a rose, a croissant, and a thermal pot of coffee for me on the nightstand. I wanted to thank him. I went to his study, intending to write him a note. Kieran is very meticulous. When he comes home at night, he heads right into his study to stow his briefcase. I was looking for a Post-it when I found a photograph of me in his pencil drawer. He'd recently bought one of those retro Polaroid cameras. I was asleep in his bed. Naked." Her face flushed.

"Did you confront him about the picture?" Morgan asked.

"I did. I called him immediately. He said he took the picture because he thought I was beautiful and didn't think I'd mind. It wasn't like he was posting it online. The photo was for his eyes only. We were lovers, so why did it matter if he had a nude picture of me?" Haley's eyes flashed with anger. "When I said I didn't appreciate him photographing me naked without my consent, he said I was a prude. I broke up with him right there and then, over the phone."

"How did he take it?"

"Not well," Haley said. "He texted and called me for a long time. But I don't need a man I can't trust in my life." Haley tossed her crumpled tissue in a trash can next to the couch. "He didn't understand why I felt violated."

Morgan drew a box around Kieran Hart's name. Was Haley's ex at Beats by coincidence or had he followed her? "Do you have a picture of Kieran?"

Haley shook her head. "The police took my phone . . . Oh, wait. I have a cloud backup account." She got up and went to a sleek computer on the desk and opened it.

"Didn't the police take your computer?" Morgan asked.

"Yes. My mom bought me a new one. She knew I'd go nuts if I was totally cut off from the outside world. It's bad enough that I'm trapped here." Haley worked her keyboard like a pro. "Not that I'm not grateful to you for getting me out of jail. I am. So grateful. That place was . . ." Her eyes showed the disgust and fear she couldn't seem to vocalize.

"I understand. House arrest is better than the county jail, but it's not the vacation everyone thinks it is."

A dozen keystrokes later, Haley emailed a photo to Morgan.

"Is there anyone else I should talk to?" Morgan asked. When Haley didn't answer, Morgan prompted her with questions. "Did you notice anyone following you at the club?"

"No."

"Is there anyone at your job who could be a threat?"

"No."

"What is your boss like?"

"My boss is nice. She gives me space to do my job. I can't think of anyone at work that's a problem." Haley yawned, and exhaustion dragged at her face. "I'm really tired, but I'm also wired."

"I have one more question. Do you usually wear a medical alert bracelet?"

Haley nodded. "I do, but I can't find it."

"Were you wearing it Friday night?"

"I always wear it," Haley said adamantly. "Always."

"OK. Then that's enough for now." Morgan flipped the blank top sheet of paper over her notes. "Try not to think about the case any more tonight. Sometimes memories come back when you aren't pressuring yourself to recall them. Do something that makes you relax and clears your head. Do not check your email or go on social media. In fact, I want you to deactivate your social media accounts for now."

Haley seemed to deflate even more. "You realize social media is my whole job."

"I'm sorry." Morgan commiserated with her. "It's just temporary. Social media is not a place you want to go right now. Trust me. Have you talked to your employer?"

"Not yet," Haley said in a soft voice. "I'll call tomorrow. Though I can't go to work, so I might not even have a job anymore." Even if she was ultimately found innocent, Haley's life would be forever changed by the murder charge.

"Yes. That's very likely."

"You're going to find out what happened to me, right?"

"We're going to do everything we can," Morgan said. "I want you to see a psychiatrist. If you experienced some sort of trauma, the right doctor can help with the aftereffects and perhaps help you recover the missing pieces of your memory."

"I'm not sure I want to remember."

Morgan thought not knowing would be worse, but maybe Haley's mind had blocked the event because she couldn't handle the truth.

"OK." Haley reached for a game controller on the table. "I'm going to play some *Call of Duty*."

Morgan would have thought a good book or favorite movie would have been better, but to each her own.

"Make sure you eat and get some rest." Morgan stood and returned to the kitchen.

Sharp and Lance sat at the island drinking steaming liquid from white mugs.

Standing at the stove, Eliza lowered the flame under a pot. "How is she?"

"She needs some time to decompress." Morgan gathered her notepad and tote.

"I know." Eliza stirred the contents of her pot. "I just don't know what to do to help her."

"You're doing everything you can." Sharp lifted his mug.

"Morgan and I had planned to visit the club tonight." Lance stood and carried his cup to the sink. "It opens soon."

"I'll stay with Eliza and Haley," Sharp volunteered.

Eliza shook her head. "I called the security firm who handles Wild's New York office. They're sending a bodyguard this evening. He should be here within the hour."

"That wasn't necessary." Sharp sounded irritated.

"It is," Eliza said. "I've already told you that I won't take advantage of you, Lincoln. Besides, you're only one man. The agency will rotate bodyguards every twelve hours so one will always be on guard. And this leaves you free to investigate."

All sounded like rational reasons, but Sharp did not look pleased.

"Please have Haley call me if she remembers anything else." Morgan donned her coat. Then she and Lance walked toward the front door.

"I'll stay here until the bodyguard arrives." Sharp followed them to the foyer. He gave Lance the combination to the rear gate and a clicker to operate the gate at the bottom of the driveway.

Outside, Lance took a flashlight from the Jeep's glove compartment. Morgan followed him around the back of the house to the rear gate.

Lance opened the combination lock, and they walked through. "Are you sure you're up to this?"

"No, but the fresh air is clearing my head."

The trail was wide, and although it sloped downward, the descent was gradual. But fifty feet into the walk, Morgan's head began to ache. Taxing herself was not the smartest decision.

She paused. "I'm going to head back. I'll meet you on the road at the other end of the trail."

Lance walked her back to the gate and watched her go through.

She slid behind the wheel of the Jeep, drove through the main gate, and stopped at the base of the driveway. Protesters shouted and waved signs but moved out of the way. A dark-gray sedan approached.

The sedan slowed as it neared, stopping as a few protesters cleared the road. The light from the gate shone into the vehicle. Morgan stared through the windshield, not believing what she was seeing. The driver of the sedan was Esposito.

What was the ADA doing near Eliza's house?

Chapter Sixteen

Lance shone his light over the edge of the overlook's metal barrier. The light didn't reach the bottom of the ravine. How deep was the drop?

He tossed a pebble over the side and listened for the sound of it hitting the bottom.

Deep enough that a fall would be deadly.

He backed away from the curved metal barrier and crossed the twenty-five-foot-wide clearing to the path on the other side. The trail that led up to the road was steeper but shorter. He emerged on a small gravel parking area. His Jeep was the only vehicle in the lot.

Morgan got out and went around to the passenger door.

"You OK?" he asked.

"Yes, but oncoming headlights are rough on my headache." They climbed into the vehicle.

Lance put the Jeep into gear. "The hike isn't hard, but the overlook could be dangerous in the dark. The barrier isn't very high."

"Good to know. Guess who I just saw?" She didn't wait for him to answer. "Esposito."

"The ADA?" Lance steered the Jeep onto the road.

"I looked up his address while I was waiting for you." Morgan pointed. "He lives right down the road, which explains why he was so angry when the judge granted Haley's bail."

"I'm sure he's not happy about the protesters and media in the neighborhood."

While Lance drove to the nightclub, Morgan filled him in on her interview with Haley.

"I'm hoping more of her memories return," she said.

"It's possible." Lance turned onto the street that led to Beats. The nightclub was located in a renovated warehouse. The buildings on either side were vacant, and the parking lot was nearly empty.

Morgan scanned the area. "I'll bet this area is deserted late at night."

"No other businesses to borrow surveillance videos from." Lance parked, and they went inside.

Expecting a blast of dance music, he was relieved that the club was relatively quiet.

"Thankfully, the music isn't on full blast yet," he said. "My ears are too old for that."

"Clubbing never appealed to me either," she agreed. "At least, not since the girls were born. In college, it was fun."

At almost eight o'clock, the club was mostly empty. Three young women drank wine in a booth just behind the bar. In front of a big-screen TV, a small group of young men, probably college students, drank beer and watched a basketball game.

Morgan led the way toward the bar. She flashed a smile at the blond bartender. He wore jeans and a T-shirt bearing the club's logo, a red EKG line of heartbeats with Beats scripted into the spiky lines. Usually, men of all ages straightened up and paid attention when she approached. But tonight, the baby-faced bartender actually winced as he looked at her eye.

"Man, that looks like it hurts." He tilted a tall glass under the tap of a craft beer.

"It does." Morgan sighed. Her fingertips went automatically to the bruise on her temple.

Lance read the bartender's name tag. Bingo. Todd was the bartender they were looking for.

"Do you have a few minutes to answer a couple of questions about last Friday night?" Morgan asked.

"The night of the murder?" Todd frowned at her, then at Lance. "I already gave the police a statement."

"We're not cops. I'm a PI. I'm investigating the murder." Lance slid his business card across the bar, along with a folded twenty-dollar bill. He left out the defense attorney part. Without knowing how a witness stood on the murder, it was best to avoid giving away which side they were on.

"Seriously? Cool. I never met a PI before." The bartender pocketed the cash. "I guess I can talk as long as I can keep filling orders. Weeknights are usually slow."

Morgan took a stack of photos from her tote and lined them up on the bar as if she were dealing cards. Noah. Haley. Piper. Noah's three friends. "Do you recognize any of these people?"

The bartender glanced over, then pointed at Haley's photo. "This is the crazy chick who killed this dude last Friday night." He shifted his finger to Noah's picture.

Not the answer they were hoping for.

Then he pointed at Piper. "She came in with the crazy chick." He waved a hand over Noah's three friends' faces. "They look familiar, but I don't remember them specifically."

Lance tapped on Haley's photo. "Have you seen her in here before Friday night?"

Todd shook his head. "I don't think so. I've only been working here a few weeks."

"Did you serve her Friday night?" Morgan asked.

"I made her a drink when she first came in." Todd set the full beer on the bar and picked up another glass. "I remember because she asked for a virgin cosmo, which is basically cranberry juice. Anyway, I thought it was cute. She was buying for her girlfriend too."

"What did the girlfriend order?" Lance leaned both forearms on the bar. Next to him, Morgan perched a hip on a stool.

"A shot of tequila and a margarita on the rocks." Todd filled the second glass.

"You have a good memory for drinks," Lance noted.

Todd grinned. "I have a better memory for hot girls."

"I hear ya." Lance faked a male-bonding tone. "You only made her one drink?"

"She only *paid* for one drink," Todd clarified. "Hot girls don't have to buy their own alcohol. Dudes could have been buying her drinks later."

"Did you see this man?" Morgan showed the bartender the photo of Kieran on her cell phone.

The bartender shook his head. "He doesn't look familiar. Sorry."

Morgan collected the stack of pictures, and Lance led the way toward the exit. Since they'd arrived, a bouncer had taken up a position by the door. Short and stocky, with black hair and eyes, he wore a black polo shirt with a smaller version of the club's logo on the chest. His nose looked as if it had been shaped with a hammer.

He glared at them. "I already talked to the cops."

"We're not cops." Lance offered him a business card.

The bouncer ignored it.

Morgan stepped forward and fanned the pictures in front of him. "Do you remember seeing these people last Friday night?"

The bouncer's nod was tight. "I told the cops everything."

"I'm sure you did," she said. "We're just verifying and making sure they didn't miss anything."

He tapped the photos of Haley and Noah. "These two left together, but I couldn't swear on a Bible what time that was. I only noticed the girl because she tripped."

Morgan separated Haley's and Noah's pictures and returned the other photos to her bag. "Did she trip because she was drunk?"

"I don't think so. It looked like her heel got caught in the sidewalk. The guy looked OK. He helped her up, and they kept walking." The bouncer leaned back. "That's all I can tell you."

"Thank you for your time," Morgan said.

Lance followed Morgan out the door. Outside, the cool night air felt damp on his face. "Everything the bartender and bouncer said agreed with Haley's statements."

"Yes, but no one has given us a single lead. Basically, we've verified information that either means nothing or supports the prosecutor's case." Morgan buttoned her coat, her movements jerky and frustrated. "What if we never find anything? Haley is too fragile to survive prison."

"It's early in the investigation yet." Lance took her elbow in a firm grip. "We'll keep digging." He turned toward the spot at the curb where they'd parked.

"I know." She blew a stray hair out of her eyes. "We'll need to watch the surveillance videos from the club as soon as they come in." Morgan took out her phone. "And I want to talk to some of Noah's former girlfriends and see if they have any complaints about him."

"You're thinking maybe he got rough with her?" Lance asked. "Haley's interview seems to suggest he did not."

"Honestly, I'm stretching for possible theories. We have no evidence to suggest Noah did anything wrong. So far, we've found nothing at all to formulate a defense except Haley's amnesia."

A raw wind sent a pile of dead leaves scurrying down the asphalt. Morgan shoved her hands in her pockets. "And we don't know what caused her memory lapse."

Lance wrapped an arm around her shoulders to block the wind. "Or if she's telling the truth."

Haley could simply be lying.

Chapter Seventeen

"What have you done to me, Haley?" The whisper surrounds her. Its low tone and slow cadence slides along her skin, raising goose bumps. She can't escape it.

No. That's not the voice. It's a physical substance. Liquid. Slippery and thick.

She startles, her stomach rolling.

Blood. It's everywhere. On her. Around her.

Panic bubbles into her throat, burning like a carbonated drink. She gags, her stomach heaving. Her breaths wheeze in and out of her lungs. Not enough air. Not enough oxygen. She can't breathe. Fear closes around her throat, choking her.

She tries to wipe her hand on her leg, but she is naked, and it simply smears across the skin of her thigh.

She looks down. A huge knife juts from her grip. Not a hunting or fishing knife. This one comes from a kitchen. It's long and sharp, with a rounded blade.

A carving knife, she thinks.

Blood drips from the blade. How did the knife get in her hand? She doesn't remember picking it up. Doesn't want it in her hand now. Yet she can't open her fingers to drop it.

Terror lurches through her. The room spins. Her legs weaken.

No!

I didn't stab Noah. I didn't.

I like him.

A groan vibrates through her lips. She wants to run away. To get help.

She turns, but she has no traction. Her bare feet slip and slide in the blood on the floor.

No!

She wants to scream, but the sound is trapped in her constricted throat. Blood. Warm and wet, it coats her hands, drips from her fingers. She begins to cry.

I don't want to do this.

But it's happening, and she can't stop it.

It feels as if she is a character in a role-playing game and someone is controlling all her movements from a faraway keyboard. She could watch herself on the screen, helpless to change her course of action.

She shakes the knife from her grip. It hits the floor and bounces twice, landing in an expanding puddle of blood.

"You killed me." The whisper slithers through the dark toward her like a snake. "My blood is on your hands."

Noah . . .

Haley woke and jerked upright. Her throat opened. Air flooded her lungs. Her pulse thundered in her ears, the echo of her own heartbeats drowning out the voice.

She blinked in the darkness. A line of light glowed under her closed door. A shiver passed through her. She was soaking wet.

Blood?

Terror obliterated her senses. She sucked air into her lungs and released it with a scream that sounded nothing like her own voice. It was as foreign as the whispers from her dream.

The door burst open, and her mother rushed into the room. She slapped a light switch on the wall, and the room brightened. Fear opened her eyes wide.

Haley scrambled out of bed, the sheets twisting around her feet, tripping her. "There's blood on me. Get it off."

She fell to the floor, not feeling the impact with the hardwood as she kicked her feet to free herself. She had to get away. To get it off her.

"Haley!" her mother yelled.

"Get it off!" Haley tore at her pajamas.

"Stop." Her mother crouched in front of her and took Haley's face in both hands. "You had a nightmare. There's no blood."

The warmth of her mother's palms on her cheeks seeped through the cold terror. Haley froze, staring down at her hands. They were clean. "But I'm all wet."

"Sweat," her mother said in a firm voice. "Your pajamas are soaked through."

Haley touched her T-shirt. The wet cotton stuck to her chest and stomach. "Sweat?"

Her mom nodded.

A shiver racked Haley's bones. She'd had a nightmare.

"It seemed so real." She shoved damp hair off her forehead.

"Let's get you in dry pajamas." Her mom went to the dresser and rummaged through a drawer. She set a folded T-shirt and flannel pajama bottoms on the nightstand. Then she helped Haley tug off her wet shirt and pull a fresh one over her head. Once she was dressed in dry pajamas, her mom helped her off the floor. But despite the firmness of her tone and actions, her hands trembled.

Haley wobbled, her legs muscles as weak as cooked ramen.

Her mom steered her toward a chair in the corner. "Sit here. I'll get clean sheets. You'll need a pill and some water too."

Haley curled in the chair. She brought her knees to her chest and hugged her legs. A shiver started in her bones and shook her body. Her mom covered her with a soft blanket.

Mom bustled from the room, all efficiency and purpose. She returned in a few minutes, sheets tucked under one arm, carrying a tray loaded with medication, a bottle of water, and a bag of pretzels. "Try to eat some of these. You need the salt."

Her mom changed the bedding. Haley took her pill and tried to sip the water, but her stomach rebelled. The dream had felt so real. Exhaustion swept over her in a cold shudder. She felt as if she'd just gone to sleep.

She checked the time on her computer. "It's only four? I didn't fall asleep until at least two."

"I'm sorry. Is there anything I can do? Do you want some chamomile tea? It might make you sleepy."

"No." Haley shuddered. "I don't really want to sleep after that nightmare."

"I'll bet." Worry filled her mom's eyes. "Want to watch TV?"

"OK." Anything except lying alone in the dark sounded good to Haley.

Her mom handed her the remote control to the TV on the wall.

"All ready." Her mom led her back to bed and tucked her in as if she were five instead of twenty-five. Haley didn't mind. She lay back against the pillows.

Her mom fluffed the pillows and climbed into the other side of the queen-size bed. "What do you want to watch?"

"I don't know." Haley handed the remote over. "You pick."

"*Friends* is binge-worthy." Her mom changed the channel and dropped the remote between them.

Two episodes later, her mom's breathing deepened into sleep. But Haley resisted. Rationally, she knew she'd had a bad dream. But the memory of it still lifted the hair along her arms in a chilling rush. She drank more water and sat up straighter. She did not want to sleep.

Over the past few days, she'd been in a daze. Her time in the police station didn't seem real. But the nightmare had.

Was she going crazy?

What was real?

Chapter Eighteen

"That eye looks painful," Grandpa said from the doorway early Wednesday morning.

"It's that bad?" Morgan sighed over her empty coffee cup. Her head pounded, and her eyes ached. But she'd been hoping she didn't look as bad as she felt.

Morgan had already showered and put on makeup, including an extra layer of concealer around her black eye and on the bruise that had replaced the goose egg on her temple. But all these years after retirement, Grandpa was still cop-blunt, and he had X-ray vision that could see through industrial-strength cover-up, as she'd learned in high school when she'd tried to hide a hickey or two.

Leaning heavily on his cane, Grandpa shuffled into the kitchen. As he passed, he patted her on the arm. "It'll start to fade in a few days. In a week or two, you won't even know it was there."

"I know. But that doesn't help me today." Morgan poured a second cup for herself and one for Grandpa. She set his on the kitchen table.

"But seriously, you have a concussion, and you worked late last night. You really could use some rest. There's no way you can take the day off?" he asked, easing into the chair and propping his cane against the wall.

"No." She sat across from him. "I'll be able to manage as long as I get this second cup down before the kids wake up."

She'd already taken extra-strength pain relievers, which were not living up to their promise. She'd slept poorly and woken at dark o'clock, achy and grumpy.

"Have the dogs been out?" Grandpa glanced in the corner, where Rocket and Snoozer were curled in their dog beds.

"Yes. They've been fed and walked." Morgan had hoped the cold, fresh air would help clear her head. No such luck. "Neither of them complained about the early breakfast."

"I'll bet." Grandpa placed both palms on the table and pushed to his feet. "I'll make *us* some breakfast."

Morgan started to stand. "I can do that."

"Sit." Her grandfather pinned her in place with a look. "I may not be able to fill my dance card, but I can make a couple of eggs. You've been babying me since I broke my leg. I know you mean well, but I have to be useful or I'll go crazy. It's time I got moving."

"OK." She sank back into her seat. "But I can think of better ways you can help."

"With your case?" Grandpa's voice perked up as he lit a burner under a frying pan and plunked an overly generous pat of butter into it.

"Olive oil is better for your heart," she said automatically.

"But it doesn't taste the same." He cracked eggs into the pan and added more salt than he should have. "Life is short. Live a little."

Morgan didn't nag, even though she worried about his heart and high blood pressure. He wouldn't listen anyway. He put bread in the toaster and flipped the eggs.

Outside, daylight began to filter through the blinds.

Morgan booted up her laptop. "I could use your help with the case, if you have the time. I received hours and hours of surveillance video from a nightclub. Someone needs to watch them. Someone who knows what to look for."

With decades of experience as an NYPD homicide detective, Grandpa had already proven that he hadn't lost his mental edge when she'd asked him for help in other cases.

"It'll be boring," she added. "A whole evening of coverage from multiple cameras, and I'm not even sure what you'd be looking for."

"Sounds perfect." Grandpa loaded two plates with food.

Morgan summed up the case. "I'll give you the videos and photos of the main players."

"You want to look for someone spiking your client's drink?" As usual, Grandpa cut to the chase.

"Yes. And any other interesting interactions. Arguments, who was chatting up whom, that sort of thing. I trust your judgment and your eye."

"I'll start on it after breakfast." Grandpa attacked his eggs and toast with renewed zeal.

Morgan finished her food, feeling better after having delegated a monumental task. She fetched her grandfather's laptop and the thumb drive containing the videos. He settled in the living room in his recliner just as the girls appeared in the doorway. In a few heartbeats, the house went from quiet haven to complete zoo. Morgan's nanny, Gianna, fed the girls pancakes. While Gianna cleaned up the kitchen, Morgan herded them into their room to get dressed. Mia and Ava liked to coordinate outfits, but Sophie . . .

"Don't I look colorful, Mommy?" Sophie twirled in the center of a giant pile of clothes she'd pulled from her drawers. She wore plaid leggings under a flowered dress. One sock was purple, the other red.

"Yes, you certainly do," Morgan said. "Let's get that hair combed." Her youngest looked as if her hair had been styled with a leaf blower.

"No," Sophie wailed, covering her head with both hands. "Gianna pwomised to make kitten ears."

"OK. I'd be excited for that too." Smiling, Morgan lifted her hands in surrender.

"Mommy, there's something sticky in my hair," Ava cried.

Morgan sniffed Ava's hair. "It's just a little syrup. Into the bathroom."

She led the way into the next room. Kicking the step stool into place for Ava, Morgan rinsed most of the syrup out. "There. All gone."

"Now my shirt is wet," Ava said, near tears.

"It'll dry before you get to school." Morgan's headache rapped on the backs of her eyes. "The bus will be here soon. Go get your shoes."

Sniffing, Ava left the room, and Morgan mopped up the sink.

The dogs barked in the other room. Each yap felt like a gong between her temples.

"Is that the bus?" Morgan shouted.

"No. Just me." Lance popped his head in the doorway. Sophie was riding him piggyback. "Rough morning?"

"Just a little." She hung the wet towel over the shower-curtain rod. "I have to get the girls on the bus. Why are we always running late?"

He glanced down at her yoga pants and water-splotched sweatshirt.

"Why don't you change? I've got this." He called over his shoulder to Mia and Ava. "Grab your gear, girls. I'll take you to the bus." He leaned in to give Morgan a quick kiss. "Remember, after we interview Noah's friend Isaac this morning, we're visiting the crime scene. I wouldn't wear anything fancy."

Instead of heading to her room to change, Morgan walked out of the bathroom, leaned on the wall, and watched him contain the chaos. He handed Sophie off to Gianna, then gathered kids, coats, and school gear like a pro before herding her two older girls to the bus.

When the door closed behind him, Morgan changed into dark jeans, boots, and a sweater.

He was waiting in the foyer when she came out of her room.

"Ready?"

"Thank you for that." Morgan couldn't help but think how much easier mornings would be if he were always here.

Lance held her coat open for her. "I love the girls, and you are not feeling your best."

"No, I am not." She slid her arms into the coat sleeves.

"Morgan!" her grandfather called from the living room.

She poked her head into the room. "Yes?"

"One of these camera feeds is blank." He looked up from his laptop. "And I don't see one for the restroom hallway at all. I'm sure they have a camera in that area."

She crossed the floor to stand at his side. "Which one is blank?"

"One that covers the tables alongside the dance floor"—he pointed to static on his computer screen—"which is where most of the patrons are drinking."

"And the one that would have shown if someone slipped a substance into Haley's drink." The ache in Morgan's head echoed. "We cannot get a break in this case."

Chapter Nineteen

Lance followed the GPS directions to Isaac's neighborhood. Worried, he glanced at Morgan, who was talking on her phone and rubbing her temple. It was only nine thirty in the morning, and she was already in pain.

She lowered her phone, irritation brightening her eyes. "The sheriff's secretary says he's too busy to speak with me. She suggested I set up an appointment to meet with him in a few weeks. If I need to discuss the case sooner than that, I should contact the prosecutor." Morgan shoved her phone into her bag. "She implied that he's prioritizing the Shannon Yates investigation."

"I'm not surprised." If Lance were in the sheriff's big ugly cop shoes, he would also want to focus on the unsolved case. "Colgate thinks he's caught Noah's killer and wants to focus on the active investigation."

"I'm not surprised either. But I suspect he won't meet with me because he doesn't want to discuss any potential weakness in his investigation. He's overextended."

Lance said, "It's safer to pass you off to the DA."

"Who is even less cooperative." Morgan swiped both hands down her face. "The police were much more helpful when I was a prosecutor."

"You're on the other side now." Lance wondered again if she was happy with her new career.

They turned into the development and passed two homes still under construction. Isaac's white colonial-style house was brand spanking new. The landscaping consisted of mud and weeds, and the front window still sported a sticker.

He spotted two security cameras under the eaves. "This place looks expensive. What does he do for a living?"

"He's a software engineer." Morgan washed two pills down with a bottle of water. Then she gathered her tote and climbed out of the car.

Lance joined her on the sidewalk.

"According to his police statement, Isaac has been friends with Noah since college. I doubt he'll be very cooperative."

"I'm surprised he agreed to the interview." Lance started up the driveway.

"Yes. Me too."

"Give Esposito another week," Lance said, "and he'll make sure he tells everyone they are under no obligation to speak with us."

They walked to the door and knocked. The door swung open, and a young man stared down at them. Isaac McGee was a gawky six feet, two inches tall with a goatee and black hair pulled back into a ponytail.

"I'm Morgan Dane." She handed him her card. "Thank you for agreeing to speak with us."

Isaac nodded curtly. "You might as well come in."

Morgan stepped over the threshold. Lance stuck close. Isaac's face pinched. He was clearly not happy to be speaking with them, not that Lance could blame him. Who would want to talk to the lawyer representing your friend's alleged murderer?

"Nice house." Lance took in the dark hardwood floors and high ceilings. "When did you move in?"

"January." Isaac led them down a wide hallway. The corridor opened into a large kitchen with an attached living area. An L-shaped sectional sofa faced a giant TV. A set of triple sliders overlooked the backyard.

The property backed to woods. Even without proper landscaping, the view wasn't bad.

Lance stopped short. He'd expected Isaac to be alone, but two young men sat at a rectangular dining table. A bottle of whiskey and three empty shot glasses served as the centerpiece. The glasses looked clean. They hadn't started drinking yet. Maybe they were saving the whiskey for after the interview.

Lance knew the men from their photos. They were Noah's friends who had gone to the club with him. Justin O'Brien was the skinny redhead. A graphic artist, his eyes were red-rimmed and watery. The short, pudgy guy was Chase Baker, a programmer.

Isaac took his place at the head of the table and nodded toward two empty chairs at the opposite end. Morgan and Lance eased into seats. The tension in the room was palpable. It would have been preferable to meet with the young men individually, but technically, they weren't required to speak to the defense counsel until the trial. Lance and Morgan would have to take whatever interviews they could get.

Justin's fingers curled into fists on the table. "My lawyer said we don't have to talk to you at all."

"This is true." Morgan set her bag at her feet and removed her notebook and pen. "You are under no obligation to meet with us now. But you will eventually have to answer my questions in court."

"Look, we're just doing our jobs." Lance splayed his palms toward the men. "We need to verify the facts you already gave the police, and we'll be out of your way."

"Wouldn't you like to be absolutely sure the right person is held responsible for Noah's death?" Morgan added.

Isaac shot her a look. "Seriously? I watched the news. She was there with Noah. Her fingerprints were on the knife." He ticked off his points on his fingers. "And his blood was . . ." He swallowed and looked away, as if unable to continue.

All over her.

Isaac swallowed. "I heard on the news that she *says* she doesn't remember anything. Is that true?"

"You can't believe everything you hear on the news," Lance said.

Without medical tests proving she'd been drugged, Haley's memory loss sounded fabricated. They *needed* a better defense, something a jury might actually buy.

"So it's not true?" Isaac's jaw stiffened.

"She remembered some things," Lance answered vaguely.

"At this point, we have more questions than answers," Morgan chimed in, "which is why we're conducting a full investigation."

Chase's eyes hardened with anger. "Don't bullshit us. Are you going to try and get her off on an insanity plea? Because that's not right. She should pay for what she did."

Morgan let Chase's statement fade without comment. Noah's friends were venting, which was totally understandable. She let a few seconds pass, hoping everyone had settled enough to get the interview back on track. "Tell me about Noah. How long have you known him?"

Isaac exhaled audibly through his nose. "We all met at the university."

Chase nodded, his jaw clenching.

Morgan continued. "Did he have hobbies?"

"Video games," Isaac said. "That's about it."

"No outdoor sports or physical activities?" Morgan asked.

Judging from their pale complexions, Lance thought they spent most of their time inside.

"My dad is a hunter. He took all four of us on a big trip last year." Chase shook his head. "Noah was traumatized by seeing his first dead deer. So no, he wasn't an outdoor guy."

Morgan made a notation. "Before Friday night, when did you last see him?"

"He had a gaming party at his house the night before. We were all there, plus maybe a dozen other players. A couple of guys brought their girlfriends. People came and went all evening."

Morgan tapped her pen. "Can you make a list of people you know were there?"

"I already gave it to the cops." Isaac shrugged. "You can get it from them."

But the fact remained that there would be numerous unidentified fingerprints at the crime scene, which was actually typical. The sheriff's department would eliminate the prints of close family and friends and run the leftover prints through the Automated Fingerprint Identification System. If any of the prints were those of a known felon, they would turn up in AFIS. Otherwise, the leftover prints were simply kept on file in case another suspect was identified.

"Noah shouldn't be dead," Justin blurted out. He sniffed and swiped a hand over his eyes. His face looked strained, as if he were holding back tears.

Had Justin been closer to Noah than Isaac or Chase? Or was he simply more sad than angry? Everyone grieved differently.

Lance unzipped his jacket. "Before Friday night, had any of you ever been to Beats?"

"Yes." Isaac interlaced his fingers on the placemat in front of him. "Since it opened, we've gone most weekends. Grey's Hollow isn't Manhattan. Beats is the best club around. Everybody goes there."

"Did you all go to the club together last Friday night?" Morgan noted the date and people present.

"The three of us drove together." Isaac motioned between them. "Noah was running late, so he met us there."

Morgan held her pen over her notebook. "When did Noah notice Haley?"

"Right away. She was all over him." Justin's lips pressed into a flat line. "We had a beer together, but he was more interested in her."

"Did it bother you that he was spending all his time with her?" Morgan asked.

"Why would that be a problem? He wanted to hook up with her." Isaac shot Justin a look. "Noah didn't usually go for the slutty type, but he was really into her. We all let him do his thing." He frowned. "But I don't get it. She definitely wanted to go home with him. Did she plan to kill him all along? Is she some kind of psycho-killer bitch? The whole thing is totally fucked."

Lance couldn't agree more with the last sentiment. "Was anyone else paying attention to Haley?"

Isaac shook his head. "Noah had it wrapped up."

"Did you all leave together?" Morgan asked.

"We walked out together," Isaac said. "Then Haley and Noah left in his car."

"What did you three do?" Lance scanned their faces.

Isaac shrugged. "Not much. We came back here and played video games."

"Do you remember what time your party broke up?" Lance wanted specific times to establish alibis.

Isaac gestured to the adjoining living room. "Justin and Chase ended up crashing on my couches."

Lance leaned forward and rested his forearms on the table. "The three of you were together all night?"

"Yes." Isaac blinked and looked away, his eyes misting. "We were hanging out and chilling, while she was killing Noah."

Eyes tearing, Justin abruptly stood, turned, and punched the wall. For a skinny guy, he was either stronger than he looked, or his emotions lent him some power, because he left a decent dent in the wallboard. He spun around and stared at Morgan and Lance, his chest heaving, his face red. He opened his mouth to speak, then closed it again. The fist he'd hammered into the wall opened and closed as if he were testing his fingers for damage.

"You should put some ice on that hand," Lance said. "Could be broken."

Justin flinched at the words. Then his shoulders caved in. He grabbed his keys from the kitchen counter and fled the house. The front door slammed behind him.

"He's taking it hard." Isaac stared out the window, but his gaze didn't seem to be focused on the wooded view. "We all are."

"We understand." Lance did commiserate with them. They hadn't even buried their friend yet. But there was no way to investigate Noah's murder without digging into everyone's background, including the victim's.

Especially the victim's.

"Did Noah have a temper?" Morgan asked.

"No." Isaac picked up the whiskey and poured two shots. He slid one across the table to Chase. "He was a quiet guy."

Morgan wrote something in her personal shorthand. "Did he have a recent girlfriend?"

Isaac spun his shot glass on the table. "He broke up with a girl last summer."

"Do you know her name?" she asked.

"Sorry." Isaac ran a finger around the rim of the small glass. "I don't remember. They didn't go out for long. Noah wasn't ready to be a one-woman guy."

"Her name is Callie Fisher." Chase tossed his shot down. "But Isaac is right. They weren't together more than a month or two. Noah lost interest in her pretty fast."

"If Noah didn't have a steady girl"—Morgan lifted her pen and looked up at the two men—"did he hook up often?"

Chase banged a fist on the table. If he was trying to intimidate Morgan, he was going to have to try much harder. She ignored his display of temper. Lance had seen her up against hardened criminals. These two geeks were hardly menacing.

"Stop it!" Chase leaned away from the table, his body tense as he jabbed a finger toward Morgan. "I know what you're trying to do here, but I won't let you say anything bad about Noah. He was a great guy." Anger glittered in his eyes. "He didn't deserve to die like that." He turned away and crossed his arms over his chest.

"We're just trying to get a sense of who he was." Lance tried to defuse the men's anger.

Isaac got to his feet. "I think we've answered enough of your questions. We aren't going to drag Noah's reputation down. Attacking the victim is not OK just because Noah is a man."

"Thank you for meeting with us." Morgan slid her notepad into her tote and stood. She was doing her best to school her expression, but Lance could see the subtle signs of pain on her face. Her mouth was tight and her voice slightly higher than normal. "I know this was difficult for you." Morgan lifted her coat from the back of the chair, but she didn't pause to put it on. She headed for the door with it draped over her arm.

"We can see ourselves out." Lance followed Morgan outside. In the cool air, she exhaled hard, clearly stressed.

"How do you feel?" He took her bag while she donned her coat.

She nodded. "I'm fine."

"You don't look fine."

Lines fanned from her eyes, and her color had gone gray.

"Do you need to go home?" Worried, Lance scanned her face. As much as he would respect her decision, he also wanted to sweep her off her feet and tuck her into bed until she was fully healed. He followed her as she walked to the Jeep.

"I can work through tired, and I can work through a headache." She turned to meet his gaze. "What I need is coffee."

"Back to the office?" he asked.

"Yes." Once inside the vehicle, she checked her phone.

Lance gestured out the window. "What did you think of Noah's friends' reactions?"

"I think they're grieving, and it's natural for them to defend their friend's reputation." She glanced back at the house. "But I also felt as if there was something specific they didn't want to tell us about Noah."

"I agree. You didn't ask for any dirt on Noah. You asked if he hooked up with girls. That's nothing incriminating. That's a normal activity for twenty-something men."

"So what are they trying to hide about Noah?"

Chapter Twenty

Forcing her brain to work felt like wading through snowdrifts. Craving sugar, Morgan checked her desk drawer for candy. Nothing. She picked up the cup of coffee at her elbow. As she brought it to her lips, her stomach rolled over. She carried her coffee into the kitchen and poured it in the sink.

Sharp was in the doorway. He held a reusable nylon bag from the local organic grocery store. "If you're dumping your *coffee*, you must feel pretty bad."

"When did you get here?" Morgan took a glass from the cabinet, then opened the refrigerator and reached for a pitcher of filtered water.

"Just now," he said. "I stopped to see how Haley and Eliza were doing this morning."

Morgan filled her glass. "How was Haley?"

"Not good." Sharp gave his head a worried shake. "She looks worse than you, like she didn't sleep at all. Eliza said she had trouble sleeping, and when she finally fell asleep, she had a terrible nightmare."

Morgan sipped her water. "Did she make an appointment to see the psychiatrist?"

"Yes. The doctor is squeezing her in tomorrow morning." Sharp opened the fridge, then looked over his shoulder, his gaze critical, as if he were assessing her. "How do *you* feel?"

"I'm all right." Morgan sipped her water.

But Sharp wasn't buying it. "Don't bullshit me."

She sighed. He was just like her grandfather. "I feel hangover-ish. My head hurts, and I'm a little nauseated. But it's not debilitating."

"Did you eat this morning?"

"I had eggs."

"Eggs are good." Sharp set the bag on the counter. "I'll make you lunch."

"I'm not very hungry," she protested.

He gave her a look.

She gave up. "What am I having?"

"You like salads, right?"

"Yes." Morgan hesitated, picturing the last meal she'd watched him eat. "But I don't like those sprouty things you've been eating."

Sharp rolled his eyes. "I bought free-range chicken, avocado, spinach, and berries."

"I like those."

"I know. I'm trying to balance food that will help your brain heal with what you'll agree to eat. It isn't easy. Except for your coffee addiction, you have the taste buds of a toddler."

Morgan smiled. "Thank you."

"Get out of the kitchen." Sharp shooed her from the room with a package of chicken. "Go lie on the couch in my office while I cook."

"I've only gotten through a portion of the evidence the DA sent over."

"And a break will help you focus to get through the rest." Sharp used his bossiest, know-it-all voice. "Where's Lance?"

"In his office, reviewing social media accounts and phone records."

"OK. Go rest," Sharp ordered.

"I don't have time for a nap." Still grumbling, Morgan dragged herself into Sharp's office and stretched out on the couch.

She closed her eyes. When she opened them, it felt as if a few seconds had passed, but a glance at the clock told her she'd slept for forty-five minutes. Her head felt clearer, her nausea had faded, and her stomach rumbled with hunger.

Following the sound of voices, she went to her office. Sharp was behind her desk, reviewing papers. Lance was writing on the whiteboard.

Sharp scanned her face and nodded. "You slept."

"Yes. Now what did I miss?" Morgan surveyed the board. They'd been busy. Lance had written notes from their interviews under each subject's picture. He'd also added a photo of Kieran Hart to the board. He'd labeled Isaac, Chase, and Justin's pictures with *at Beats Friday night* and *hiding something about Noah?*

"You need lunch." Sharp got up and passed her on his way out of the office. "Sit."

Morgan sat behind her desk, and he brought her a salad. "Did you find anything interesting?"

"I dug through social media accounts," Lance said. "Their pages are all pretty boring. Occasional party pics. Family. Pets. Nothing outrageous, but I did spot Noah's ex-girlfriend Callie on his page."

"I can track her down." Sharp perched on the corner of Morgan's desk. "No one dishes dirt like an ex. If Noah behaved badly, she will talk."

Lance pointed toward Kieran Hart's photo on the whiteboard. "Kieran Hart follows Haley on social media. But he's never posted or interacted with her."

"Interesting. I called Kieran this morning to request an interview. I'm meeting him at his house later today." Morgan speared a blueberry and pointed toward the board with it. "What did Haley's phone records show about their breakup?"

"He texted her daily for six weeks." Lance indicated the photo of Kieran on the board. "At night, he called instead of texting."

"When he knew she'd be home from work," Sharp added.

"Right," Lance agreed. "But Haley stopped answering his calls. After a couple of weeks, she blocked him."

"Were the messages threatening?" Morgan asked.

"No." Lance shook his head. "But he constantly wanted to know where she was and who she was with, even before they broke up, and he completely ignored her requests for him to stop contacting her."

"Haley's claim that he was controlling is true." Morgan chewed a piece of chicken. "And we don't know if he has an alibi. The sheriff didn't interview him. In fact, I found no mention of him in the prosecutor's files."

Lance tapped on Kieran's photo. "Why didn't he interact with her on social media? In fact, it doesn't appear that he uses his account at all. His profile is mostly blank."

"He probably uses his account the same way I use mine and you use yours—to see what other people are up to." Morgan had accounts on all the main social media platforms. She never added personal information or posted, but she needed to be able to keep tabs on what her clients and witnesses posted.

She pushed the last piece of chicken around the bottom of the bowl, gathering up the remaining dressing. She stopped and looked up at Lance. "He didn't want her to know he was watching her. He didn't want her to block him. What a creeper. I assume Haley posted about going to Beats."

Lance sighed. "She did."

"That explains how he knew she was going to be there." She ate the chicken and pushed the plate away. "Thank you, Sharp. I do feel better."

"I'm glad," Sharp said.

Morgan glanced at her coffee machine.

"Don't even think about it." Sharp stood. "I'll make green tea, and before you go digging through your desk for candy, I bought organic oatmeal cookies." Sharp collected her salad bowl and carried it from the room, muttering, "Sugar addict."

"What about the background checks?" Morgan asked Lance.

"Haley and Noah are both clean, so is Piper. Mom didn't find any dirt on Noah's employer either," Lance said. "She's still working on Noah's friends, and I just gave her Kieran Hart's name last night."

"We still have a big mess." Morgan flattened a hand on her forehead.

"Sharp and I are trying to focus the case." Lance pointed at the board with a dry-erase marker. "We have two main options. One: Haley killed Noah, in which case, she is either lying to us or suffering from a mental illness."

"She meets with the psychiatrist tomorrow," Morgan said.

Sharp carried a mug into the room and set it on Morgan's desk. "But she has no history of mental illness."

"Can we make a case for self-defense?" Morgan picked up the cup of green tea and tasted it. Sharp had added sugar. He really *was* babying her. Normally, he equated sugar with the devil.

"Not yet," Lance said. "If she was defending herself, why wouldn't she remember?"

"Trauma?" Morgan suggested. "Maybe she blocked it out."

Lance turned to face her. "She had none of the typical defensive injuries I would expect to see. No torn fingernails, no skin under her nails, no bruises on her forearms, no signs of being restrained. The prosecutor is going to point to all the evidence that shows she went home with Noah and slept with him willingly. He even used a condom and tossed it in the trash. He didn't try to hide their sexual activity."

"Unless the psychiatrist works some serious magic, self-defense isn't going to fly with any jury without physical evidence," Morgan agreed.

"Option number two: Haley didn't kill Noah," Lance said, "which means someone else did. Ideally, we want to prove her innocence. But our backup plan is to provide additional suspects with means and motive and poke as many holes in the DA's case as possible."

"The physical evidence is strong," Morgan said, worried. "If we can discredit any of it, we'll be in a better position. We need to review the forensics and DNA reports line by line and look for a chain of evidence lapses. The sheriff expedited the DNA test of the blood on Haley. Let's find out if the lab has made any mistakes in the past."

"We haven't ruled out the possibility that she was drugged." Sharp paced in front of the board. "What if someone slipped something in her drink at Beats? She went home with Noah and had sex with him, which she doesn't remember. While she was passed out, someone else killed Noah and framed Haley for the crime. We make the overwhelming amount of physical evidence work for us. Haley had no reason to kill Noah. But if she did, why would she not make any attempt to clean up or at least cover her own tracks?"

"Let's look at the crime scene photos." Morgan opened the laptop on her desk and pulled up the file. Sharp and Lance gathered around her.

The first set were of Noah's body in the grass. He was on his side, his arms stretched out.

"He's dressed but barefoot." Morgan pulled out the preliminary autopsy report. "He wasn't wearing underwear, as if he got out of bed for some reason and stepped into jeans and a T-shirt."

Lance rubbed his chin. "He was killed in the kitchen."

Morgan scrolled slowly through the pictures. The images followed a bloody trail through the front door and living room to the kitchen, where blood had puddled.

"That's where he was stabbed," Sharp said. "Not a lot of blood spatter, considering he had three wounds."

Morgan scrolled slowly through more photos. "No. The ME says the first two wounds bled mostly internally. It was the third that nicked an artery and caused most of the external bleeding."

"And this spray of blood over here." Sharp indicated a red streak on the wall.

Lance said, "The size of the bloodstain on the floor tells me Noah lay there for a while, bleeding, before he tried to crawl away."

Sharp tilted his head at the photo. "The blood on the floor is all smeared."

"Noah did crawl through it." Lance leaned closer to the screen. "But how did it get all over Haley? Did someone carry her unconscious body into the kitchen and slide her around in the blood?"

Morgan checked the crime scene fingerprint report. "The fingerprint tech says all the bloody toe and footprints they found belong to Haley or Noah."

Like fingerprints, toe prints had unique ridges and whorls that could be used for identification.

"The only prints on the knife belonged to Haley. Noah had had a gaming party the night before with a dozen friends attending, including Isaac, Justin, and Chase, along with Noah's brother, Adam. There were a number of unidentified prints on scene, which wasn't unexpected."

Sharp scratched his chin. "But any fingerprints not on the weapon or made in blood are basically useless unless we identify another suspect who has never been to Noah's house for a legitimate reason."

"Like Kieran Hart," Lance suggested.

"Right," Morgan agreed. "But unless he has a prior felony conviction, his prints won't be on file anywhere. We can't force him to submit his fingerprints without probable cause."

Sharp leaned back. "We definitely need a blood spatter expert. That kitchen floor looks like Jack the Ripper channeled Jackson Pollock. I have the perfect guy. I'll call him today."

Morgan moved on to study the rest of the kitchen photos.

A bag of potato chips, the open end rolled up and fastened with a paper clip, sat on the kitchen counter. A close-up shot of the kitchen sink showed a Ziploc bag of water and two glasses sitting in the bottom. An empty plate and a jar of peanut butter sat on the counter. Every piece of evidence was marked with a yellow evidence tag.

"The Ziploc bag was probably the ice pack he made for her. She also said he gave her water and potato chips." Morgan pointed at the screen.

"He took out an empty plate and peanut butter." Lance leaned over her shoulder. "Did someone come to the door before he finished putting his snack together?"

"Kieran?" Morgan asked. "Maybe he followed them from the bar."

"Possible, but why would Noah let him in?" Sharp's brows knitted. "Do they know each other?"

"We'll have to ask Kieran when we see him." Morgan wrote the question down.

Sharp continued. "If someone else killed Noah, he didn't get out of the house without blood on his clothes and shoes. He could have tracked it into his car."

Morgan followed Sharp's train of thought. "If we find a suspect, a search of his car and house might turn up physical evidence. The problem is that we'd have to find enough probable cause to convince the sheriff a search is necessary and a judge to issue a warrant."

"Yes," Sharp said. "But I've worked with Colgate over the years. He's a veteran cop, not a politician. He thinks Haley is guilty right now, but unlike the last DHIC, he won't suppress evidence to get her convicted."

Morgan gave Lance a questioning look. "DHIC?"

"Dickhead in charge," Lance translated.

Sharp nodded. "If we get real evidence on a plausible suspect, Colgate will ask for a search warrant to look for bloody shoes and clothing."

"Unfortunately, our theories don't demonstrate probable cause." Morgan closed her laptop. "It's time to head to the crime scene. Let's go find some evidence."

Chapter Twenty-One

Lance parked his Jeep outside Noah Carter's rented house. Crime scene tape fluttered from the doorway. He dug in his glove compartment for shoe covers and gloves. Sharp parked his Prius next to them. Lance took a camera from the center console. They would take their own pictures.

A sheriff's deputy pulled in next to them. He got out and unlocked the door. Though forensics had finished collecting evidence, the sheriff had not yet released the scene. Booties and gloves were no longer required. Lance handed them out anyway. They had all seen the crime scene photos of the kitchen. No one wanted to step in blood, even if it was dry.

The deputy unlocked the door, then stepped back. "I'll be in my vehicle. Let me know when you're ready for me to lock up."

Clearly, he had no burning desire to see the kitchen again. Lance couldn't blame him. Lance followed Morgan and Sharp into the house. He was glad the cop stayed outside so they could speak freely without worrying about him overhearing.

The front door opened into a foyer with a small formal living room on the right. They walked down a short hallway to the family room. A couch faced a flat-screen TV. The room was neat and uncluttered, with no knickknacks aside from a few framed photos—about what Lance would expect from a young bachelor.

Morgan reviewed Haley's memory of leaving the club, tripping, the ride home. "After Noah brought her chips, water, and an ice pack, Haley remembered kissing him on the sofa. Then she blanks out. She assumes they had sex but has no memory of it. But in the morning, she found her dress on the floor in here."

They moved on to the kitchen. Lance went through the doorway and stepped to the side to make room for Morgan and Sharp. They stood in silence several minutes, taking in the scene.

"I can't believe Haley was strong enough to overpower a healthy young man," Lance said. "She barely weighs a hundred pounds. Noah had at least a fifty-pound weight advantage and six inches of reach on her."

"Haley isn't any kind of athlete either," Morgan said. "If anything, she's fragile."

"He was stabbed in the front of the body." Lance studied the space. "He must have been facing his killer at the time. Did he not see the knife coming? The dress wasn't covered in blood, so she was naked when she supposedly stabbed him. She wasn't hiding the weapon in her clothes."

"Let's run the mechanics of the prosecutor's case," Sharp suggested. "Noah was at the counter preparing a snack. Haley came in and grabbed the knife from the block without him seeing. He turned around and she stabbed him before he realized what was happening."

"That's the only way I see this occurring." Lance realized with a sinking feeling that Sharp's explanation was *too* plausible and would not help their defense.

From the expression in Sharp's eyes, he knew it as well.

Sharp examined the spray of blood on the wall, then pointed to a spot on the floor in the middle of the largest bloodstain. "He would have been standing there. These spatters of blood"—he pointed to two groups of small blood spatters on the cabinets—"were the first two stabs. They didn't cause much external bleeding, but a few drops would have flicked off the blade as it was pulled out of his body. The larger spray was from the last and fatal stab wound."

"He never tried to run or evade the attack, so the wounds must have been delivered in quick succession." To demonstrate, Lance moved his arm in three quick jabs.

"Yes." Morgan turned her attention to the largest blood smear. "And once the artery was nicked, he went down and bled heavily. Then he lay there for a few seconds, in shock, processing what had just happened, before he dragged himself out the back door."

In unison, they followed the long dark-brown smear. Lance opened the door, and they stepped out onto the back porch.

Morgan pointed ahead. "He was found right there, at the base of the porch."

"Why did he try to crawl away?" Lance asked. "Calling 911 would have given him a better chance at survival."

"He doesn't have a landline," Morgan said. "The police found his cell phone in his car. He must have left it there. They found Haley's phone buried in the sofa cushions."

They walked back into the kitchen.

Lance examined the back door. "This is where Noah crawled out of the house. There's blood on the doorknob but not on the dead bolt. Haley and Noah probably came in through the front door when they entered the house. That's where Noah's car is parked. When Haley found Noah, she said the back door was open. If Noah had to unlock the dead bolt, it would have some blood on it, like the knob. Was Noah in the habit of leaving his house unlocked?"

Sharp crowded him.

"No." Morgan shook her head. "The responding officer's report said the front door was locked when he arrived."

Sharp leaned closer to the door. "The knob itself has no lock. The dead bolt is the only way to secure the back door."

Morgan closed her eyes for two seconds, then opened them again. "I don't remember seeing pictures of the back door dead bolt in the crime scene photos, but then there are hundreds of them. I'll check when I get home."

"I can't imagine Sheriff Colgate missed the absence of blood on the back door dead bolt," Sharp said.

Morgan frowned. "But even if he saw it, neither the sheriff nor the prosecutor is going to point out anything that weakens their case."

"You cannot always explain every single thing at a crime scene. It's possible that Noah simply forgot to lock the back door that night. But it's also possible that the real killer used the back door to get into the house. If that is true, then he would have needed a key." Sharp brightened. "What if, instead of Haley surprising Noah in the kitchen, someone else did? Someone who let himself in through the back door while Noah was occupied with Haley in the bedroom." He led them back into the kitchen. "Maybe the killer waited for Noah in the family room." Sharp moved from room to room, his gaze roving. "When Noah went into the kitchen for food, the killer surprised him. The stabbing happened just the way we imagined it earlier but with a killer who was not Haley."

Lance pictured the scenario. "Then how did Haley end up covered in blood?"

Sharp rubbed his clean-shaven chin. "The killer went into the bedroom and carried Haley into the kitchen. She was unconscious. He laid her in the blood, then carried her back to the bed, dripping blood all the way."

"He would have had to have watched every step to make sure he wasn't leaving footprints." Lance couldn't see it. "The toe and footprints in the blood belonged to Haley and Noah. She walked in the blood in the kitchen while it was wet."

"Damn." Sharp propped a fist on his hip. "You're right."

"Assume the real killer was able to keep his feet out of the blood and somehow set Haley's feet down. For this to make sense, the killer would have had to know she was drugged," Morgan pointed out. "We've been assuming if Haley was drugged, then Noah drugged her. But maybe the killer did it. Maybe it was part of *his* plan."

"Haley is small and light. All of our potential suspects are young men capable of carrying her."

Sharp gestured toward smears in the blood on the floor. "When I first looked at the photo of this area, I hypothesized that Haley might have slipped in the blood. But maybe not."

"It's the best working theory we have at the moment." Morgan blew out a long breath.

It was also their only theory.

They returned to the kitchen, then walked through the rest of the house again. Morgan took out her legal pad and began to make sketches and write notes. They might not get another chance back inside before the house was cleaned. No doubt the landlord wanted the scene released. As a murder scene, the property would be hard enough to rent or sell. Lance took pictures of everything, finishing with the back door and dead bolt.

"I want to know how many people have keys to Noah's house." Morgan returned her notebook to her bag.

"The lock is old and weathered." Sharp gave the doorknob a jiggle. "It wouldn't be that hard to pick."

When they were finished, Lance led the way out the front door. The sunshine on his face was welcome after the bleakness of the murder scene.

"At least we have a new lead to follow." He slid behind the wheel and started the engine.

Morgan's phone rang as she got into the passenger seat. "It's my grandfather."

She answered the call, listening for a few seconds. "Hold on. I'm going to put you on speaker. Lance is here too." She held the phone over the Jeep's center console. "Go ahead, Grandpa."

"I haven't finished watching all the tapes yet, but I wanted to call you with one bit of information," Grandpa said. "Noah went to the bar twice. Each time he bought himself a beer and another drink made with cranberry juice, triple sec, and vodka. At one point, he also ordered nachos. I'm assuming the froufrou drinks were for the young lady. Anyway, they were doubles."

"You're sure?" Morgan asked.

"Yes," Grandpa answered. "Two generous shots of vodka and one full shot of triple sec in each drink. They were ordered almost two hours apart. That's the only interesting thing I've seen so far. But then, I can only see the bar and the dance floor. Mostly, people are dancing and having fun. Nothing unusual."

"Thanks, Grandpa. Let me know if you notice anything else."

"Will do." Grandpa ended the call.

Lance pulled away from the curb. "I don't even know what's in a cosmo."

"I drank them in college when I went out, but I don't know exactly how they're made. I'll Google it." Morgan searched for the drink recipe. "One shot of vodka and a half shot of triple sec shaken with ice and cranberry juice."

"That sounds disgusting," Lance said.

"They're delicious, which is why they are dangerous. You can't taste the alcohol. I haven't had a cosmo in many years. One was always more than enough for me. But then most people have better alcohol tolerance than I do."

"Kittens handle alcohol better than you," Lance agreed.

"Haley thought she'd had two drinks, when she'd actually consumed four. That's a total of six shots of alcohol. I'd have had a hangover, but even with my sad tolerance for alcohol, I doubt it would be enough to make me pass out, especially not if they were spread out over an entire evening and consumed with food."

Lance's fingers tightened on the wheel. Alcohol was the original date-rape drug. "But it's enough to say that Noah was no choirboy."

Chapter Twenty-Two

Sharp sat at his desk, typing his notes from their visit to the crime scene while the images were fresh in his head. He was trying to be positive, but the theory they'd come up with at the scene felt thin. He could see someone breaking into the house and stabbing Noah. But carrying Haley to the kitchen and standing her in the blood? That felt sick and depraved and, frankly, physically challenging. She might be small and light, but dead weight was difficult to manage. Haley had been naked and would have been slippery.

The longer he thought about it, the *less* likely the theory seemed. Morgan and Lance hadn't shot his idea down completely, but he'd seen the skepticism on their faces.

What if the killer had simply taken blood from the scene and put it on Haley's body? That would be another way to explain the smears on the floor. Nope. Still didn't explain her footprints in the blood. By the time she wandered into the kitchen the following morning, the blood would have been dry. The cold air coming through the open door would have slowed drying time, but her footprints were left sometime during the night, likely within an hour or so of Noah's death.

Morgan popped her head into his office. "I found no photos of the back door dead bolt in the files from the DA's office. I have calls in to both the sheriff and prosecutor to see if they have pictures that were somehow left out of the evidence they sent. Neither the DA nor the sheriff will take my calls, so I doubt they'll rush to respond. We don't know if the sheriff overlooked the absence of blood on the dead bolt or not."

"Bastards," Sharp said. "Let's—"

A knock on the door interrupted him.

"I'll get it." Sharp went to the window and peered through the blinds. On the front stoop, he saw a familiar brunette in a khaki trench coat. Olivia Cruz.

He could ignore her. Morgan didn't need the distraction.

Ms. Cruz knocked again.

He gave her points for persistence.

She knocked a third time, and he opened the door. "Ms. Cruz."

"Mr. Sharp." She tilted her head. "Did you give Ms. Dane my message?"

"It must have slipped my mind." Sharp leaned on the doorjamb, hooked his thumbs in his front pockets, and gave her his best *do you know how fast you were going?* cop glare.

Seemingly unperturbed, she glanced behind her. "It might be best if we didn't conduct this conversation in the open."

Sharp scanned the street. He didn't see any other reporters in sight, but she was right. Still, he didn't really want to let her in. "Why don't you call for an appointment?"

"I'm not here to see you." Her voice was flat and stubborn. "I want to talk to Ms. Dane."

"She's busy." Sharp moved to close the door.

"Yes. I know. She's working another big case. Haley Powell is her client."

Damned reporters. Always sticking their noses—

"Sharp?" Morgan called.

He looked over his shoulder.

Morgan was standing in the hall. "Did I hear my name?"

"Yes." Sharp exhaled through his nose. He stepped back, making room for the reporter to enter. She didn't thank him.

Morgan walked down the hall and extended a hand. "I'm Morgan Dane."

Sharp closed the door.

"My name is Olivia Cruz." She handed Morgan a card and untied her coat. She was wearing a copper sweater, jeans, and boots with impractical, skinny heels. "Before you say that you don't talk to reporters, please listen. Remember the information I delivered on Mr. McFarland?"

Morgan turned to Sharp with a confused look.

He sighed. "Ms. Cruz is the one who told me about McFarland's prior conviction."

With suspicious eyes, Morgan refocused on the reporter. "And now you want . . . ?"

"I'm sorry you didn't get my message." Ms. Cruz speared Sharp with a glare. "I did you that favor to show my good faith. There were no strings attached."

"Then why are you here?" Morgan folded her arms, her cross-examination face firmly in place.

Behind Morgan, Lance came out of the office and leaned on the wall, listening.

"I've been trying to reach you for some time," Olivia said. "I'm working on a true crime novel about the Chelsea Clark kidnapping. The Clark family is cooperating, and they will receive a portion of the book's proceeds. You know they moved back to Colorado? Can't blame them for wanting to leave a place with such terrible memories. Unfortunately, they haven't been able to sell their New York house. They could use the money."

Morgan didn't respond, but Sharp could see her brain processing the information.

"Here's my offer." Ms. Cruz was persistent. "I have some information you could use in Haley Powell's case. You will probably find it on your own, but I can save you time. You've precious little of that. The public will have found Haley guilty long before she is actually tried. You need traction with this case, and you need it quickly."

"Where did you get this information?" Wariness tingled in Sharp's skin. But he was also curious. What did she know?

Ms. Cruz's left brow rose in an arrogant arch. "If I divulged my sources, I would lose all my leverage."

"What do you want in exchange?" Morgan proceeded with her usual care. She was no fool.

"An interview with you," Olivia said. "Not now. I know you're tied up with this case. But when you have a free afternoon, I'd like to talk."

Morgan's eyes narrowed. "I'll have to call the Clarks before I agree."

Sensing success, Ms. Cruz's eyes brightened. "I wouldn't expect anything else. But after you speak with them, you'll answer some of my questions?"

"After I get permission from my client, I will entertain your questions," Morgan answered carefully.

Ms. Cruz laughed. "Interesting choice of words."

Morgan waited, her face expectant.

"I assume you've already discovered that Kieran Hart was Haley Powell's ex-boyfriend." Once again, Ms. Cruz knew too much about their case. "But you probably don't know that he has an arrest record." She paused for impact, her dark eyes glittering. She was enjoying this. "For stalking his ex-wife."

If Sharp didn't know Morgan so well, he would have missed the flash of excitement in her eyes.

But Ms. Cruz didn't miss it either. She smiled. "Kieran was arrested eight years ago in Connecticut. He followed his ex-wife and, according to witnesses, slapped her across the face. The ex-wife refused to sign a complaint, and the charges were dropped. But a little bird told me that he'd been following her for months. He called and texted her. He showed up in the parking lot where she worked and parked next to her car. At one point, his ex-wife had a restraining order against him, but obviously that wasn't much of a deterrent."

"A slap in the face is a far cry from stabbing a man to death." A deep-in-thought crease formed above the bridge of Morgan's nose.

"But it shows the predisposition for violence and the inability to accept rejection," Ms. Cruz said.

Morgan didn't respond, but she uncrossed her arms, her attitude and posture opening. "Thank you for the information."

Ms. Cruz belted her coat. "Thank you for your time."

"As soon as this case is settled," Morgan said, "I will check with the Clark family and call you."

"I look forward to hearing from you." Ms. Cruz turned to the door. Sharp opened it for her.

"I have excellent sources." Ms. Cruz smiled at him, which was irritating. "There's no reason we can't help each other."

Except she was a *reporter*.

Yet he had to admit she had presented herself openly and with integrity.

So far.

She sought and held his gaze. "I know what you think of me. But I'm not trying to screw anyone. Not all reporters are the devil incarnate."

Sharp wasn't sure about that. But as he studied her dark eyes, his bullshit meter remained quiet. He gestured toward the front stoop. "Next time, you should call first."

"So you can avoid me?" She laughed. "I don't think so. What would you do?"

The same as her, he thought. "Have a good day, Ms. Cruz."

"Olivia!" she called back as she walked away.

Shaking his head, Sharp closed the door. "I'm sorry about that, Morgan. I wouldn't have let her in, but she did prove herself useful in the McFarland case."

"We got a good piece of information." Morgan turned and walked down the hallway. "Can we verify it? A prior stalking arrest makes Kieran Hart look even better as a suspect."

"I'll call my mother and have her work on verifying Kieran's criminal background." Lance stopped at his office doorway. "We should know the answer before we question him in the morning."

But Sharp knew that the arrest charge would be valid. Ms. Cruz would expect them to double-check the information.

Morgan said, "Tomorrow's interview with Kieran Hart just became much more interesting."

Chapter Twenty-Three

Hands. Hands on her body. She pushes at them. Stop! Stop touching me!

"Haley."

"Hal-eeeey." The whisper draws her name into long syllables.

She whimpers. No. Stop. Please.

"You killed me," the whisper says.

I didn't.

I like him. I couldn't . . . I wouldn't hurt anyone like that.

But the whisper is adamant. I'm dead, and it's your fault.

No, *she cries.*

Blood pools at her feet. She looks down. Noah is on the floor, writhing. She is surprised. She thought he was dead.

He reaches one arm toward the door, toward help. She watches, helpless, unable to move as he wiggles on the tile. His chest heaves. His breath gurgles. He reaches a bit farther, his hand splaying on the floor. He leans on his elbow and inches forward, his movements simultaneously determined and futile.

Like a spectator, she stares as Noah slithers away like a snail. He makes it to the door. It seems to take forever for him to lift his shoulders high enough to reach the doorknob. But he makes it. The door opens. Cold air rushes in. Haley shivers as Noah heaves himself over the threshold, dragging his limp legs behind him. His feet disappear into the dark. But the door is open, and she hears him scraping along the boards of the back porch.

And then she doesn't.

Silence fills her ears. She strains for the sound of movement. From the open doorway, cold night air blows in. But there is no sound.

The whisper calls again, and she startles. Nausea swirls in her belly, acid rising and burning the back of her throat.

"Haley. What did you do to me?"

The scream ripped from her throat, and Haley jolted awake. Someone was touching her. She recoiled from the hand, cringing into the bedding. Her clothes were soaked.

Please let it be sweat.

She opened her eyes. The familiar furnishings of her bedroom came into focus. But in her mind, all she could see was red. Blood. It was on her hands, slippery and warm. She couldn't wipe it away.

"Haley, it's another nightmare." Her mom's voice pierced the confusion.

Haley blinked, her bedroom fixtures sharpening. Her mom was sitting on the edge of her bed, her hands hovering above Haley's shoulders, as if she'd been shaking her before she'd woken.

"Are you awake now?" Mom asked, her eyes mirroring Haley's own exhaustion and fear.

Haley nodded.

"I'll get you something to drink." Mom stood. Turning to the dresser, she took pajamas from a drawer. "Put these on. I'll bring fresh sheets."

Haley crawled out of bed. "I'm going to take a quick shower."

She couldn't get rid of the feeling of blood on her skin.

Her mom left the room. Haley took the clean pajamas into the attached bath, turned on the water, and peeled off the wet flannel. She tested the temperature of the spray and stepped under it. She lathered up and scrubbed her skin over and over, but there seemed to be no way to wash away the blood in her mind. She turned off the water, toweled her body dry, and put on the clean pajamas. Even dressed and warm from the shower, she continued to shiver.

Her mom was waiting in the bedroom with her medication and a glass of purple Gatorade.

Haley took the pill and washed it down, draining the glass.

"You should try to get more sleep." Her mother took the empty glass from her hand and set it on the nightstand.

"I don't want to sleep anymore." Haley climbed into bed and fluffed her pillows to support her back. "That was horrible."

"Want to tell me about it?" Her mom perched on the edge of the mattress.

Haley shook her head. She didn't even want to think about it.

"Do you want to watch another episode of *Friends*?" Anxiety clouded her mother's eyes. Her mom must think she was crazy.

She thought she was crazy.

"OK." Trembling, Haley pulled the covers up to her chin, feeling as vulnerable, out of control, and helpless as a child. "I feel like I'm five."

"Maybe the psychiatrist will be able to help." Her mom climbed into the other side of the bed and turned on the television. "Which episode are we on?"

"Five." Haley settled back as the opening theme for *Friends* played. Haley's eyes stayed wide open. The thought of closing them was terrifying, and her brain refused to let go.

She stared at the television. How long could this nightmare go on?

Chapter Twenty-Four

"Kieran Hart comes from serious money." In the passenger seat of the Jeep, Morgan consulted her file folder. "He has a master's degree from Wharton, and he works as the managing director of The Hart Family Trust. The offices are located in that four-story, green-glass building on Route 32."

Lance stopped at a traffic light. "My mother found no criminal convictions associated with his previous addresses. His Connecticut record was erased due to the dropped charges, but she found and verified the arrest through the township newspaper online archives. They publish a weekly police incident report."

"Kieran was married ten years ago. The marriage lasted less than two years."

"The timing of the arrest for stalking his ex fits."

"Yes." Morgan closed her file. "Let's see what he has to say."

And how jealous he was.

Kieran Hart lived several miles outside of town. Lance pulled up to a set of wrought-iron gates, lowered the Jeep window, and pressed the intercom call button.

Cameras watched from either side of the gate. Infrared beams monitored the top of the gate and fence. Eliza had an excellent alarm system, but Kieran took home security to a whole different level.

"Yes?" a voice said from the speaker.

"Mr. Kruger and Ms. Dane to see Mr. Hart," Lance said. "We have an appointment."

The voice didn't answer, but the gates rolled open and Lance drove through.

Kieran's property was the type a great-grandfather left in trust for future generations. Mature trees dotted a parklike lawn. The long driveway ended in a circle like the upstate New York edition of Downton Abbey. Lance pulled up in front of the house. They got out of the car, and Morgan led the way up the walk. Cameras mounted under the eaves swiveled to follow them. More infrared beams winked from subtle locations.

"I feel like I'm being watched from every angle," Morgan said.

"That's because you are being watched." Lance frowned. "This is not the kind of property we can slip into unnoticed at a later date."

"What does that mean?"

Lance was suspiciously silent.

"You aren't going to snoop around." Even as she spoke, she knew that's exactly what he wanted to do.

"I might not get another chance, and I suspect that photo of Haley was the equivalent of seeing a bug in your kitchen. With sex crimes, there's never just one."

"But this place is monitored," Morgan protested. "I know you get impatient, but taking legal risks could jeopardize Haley's defense. She doesn't have that many people on her side. Kieran Hart could be a valuable asset."

Lance didn't mind cutting legal corners to speed up an investigation, but Morgan was desperately short on witnesses who would testify on Haley's behalf.

"He's her ex, so how can we be sure he's on her side of this case?" Lance asked.

"If he still has feelings for her, we can play on those." Morgan cringed. "That sounds terribly exploitative."

"Worrying about exploiting Kieran Hart won't keep me up at night." Lance rolled a shoulder. "If he was taking naked pictures of girls without their knowledge, what else was he doing without their consent? His behavior fits the profile of a serial sex offender."

Morgan couldn't argue with his logic. "Let's see what he has to say before we make any important decisions. We have only Haley's word that he took the picture without her knowledge."

"We need to find that photo."

Morgan reached for the doorbell. Before she could press it, the front door was opened by a man in a slim gray suit.

"I'm David." He stepped back to admit them. "I'll take you to Mr. Hart."

Morgan stepped over the threshold and handed him her business card. The foyer, tiled in black and white like a chessboard, was large enough to dance in. A sweeping staircase curved up one wall. Elegant dark-wood molding trimmed the walls. In the center, a round pedestal table held an arrangement of white roses. The scent of fresh flowers and beeswax filled the room. The muffled bark of a dog echoed in the two-story space.

"The house is beautiful." She followed him down a hallway. An Oriental carpet runner ran the length of the corridor. "It must be difficult to maintain a home of this size."

"He has me." David chuckled. "And some additional staff. As a bachelor, Mr. Hart's needs are simple." At the end of the corridor, David opened a door and exposed a stairwell that led downward. "After you."

Morgan and Lance descended into the basement. But it was no ordinary cellar. Kieran's basement contained a professional-quality indoor gun range with a single target on a ceiling-mounted electronic pulley system. They stepped onto a concrete floor.

"Mr. Hart," David called out. "Ms. Dane and Mr. Kruger to see you."

Kieran Hart stood behind a table loaded with a handgun, a box of bullets, and a silver coffee service. Next to the coffeepot, three delicate white china cups sat on saucers.

"Thank you, David. You can leave us." Kieran Hart looked younger than thirty-five. He wore tailored slacks, a black cashmere sweater, and Italian loafers the way a regular person wore sweats. Protective earmuffs were looped around his neck.

Morgan introduced herself, and she and Lance shook Kieran's hand. "As I mentioned in our phone call, I'm representing Haley Powell, and I'd like to ask you a few questions that might help with her defense."

"I'm glad to help Haley, but I'm not sure what I can do for you." Kieran's gaze narrowed on Lance and then brushed over Morgan's bruise. Frowning, he turned to the table and picked up a heavily engraved weapon with a rosewood stock. He gestured to several pairs of sport earmuffs. "Please help yourself to the coffee as well. My new toy was just delivered. Forgive me if I indulge myself."

Lance and Morgan donned ear protection. Morgan gratefully filled a cup. The ache that cradled the back of her head felt semipermanent.

Kieran raised his earmuffs. He pointed the gun down range and pulled the trigger two times. He paused, sized up the target again, and fired twice more. He set the gun on the table and lowered his earmuffs around his neck.

"Ed Brown Signature Edition 1911." Lance whistled.

Kieran pushed a button, and the paper target moved toward them. He'd hit the human outline twice in the chest, once in the forehead, and once in the neck.

"Care to try it?" Kieran gestured to the weapon. He loaded a new target and sent it back about thirty feet.

They all raised their earmuffs. Lance walked to the table, took the gun, and moved into position. He fired three shots at the target, then lowered the pistol. "Nice weapon."

Kieran brought the target in. Lance's shots had all pierced the target's center mass.

"Ms. Dane?" Kieran gestured toward the weapon.

"No, thank you." Morgan finished her coffee and set the cup on the table.

"Are you sure?" Kieran asked. "It doesn't have a strong kick, if that's what you're worried about."

"That's not what I'm concerned about." Morgan sighed. She wasn't into gun porn. Her handgun was a tool, not a fashion accessory.

"I assure you, the weapon's performance is even more impressive than its appearance." Kieran refreshed the target. "I insist."

Morgan just wanted to ask him questions, but apparently, he was going to make her shoot the gun first. What the hell? She took the pistol, secured her earmuffs, and fired three shots at the target.

Kieran brought her target in and frowned at it. "Well done."

But his tone belied his words. Was he annoyed that her cluster of shots was grouped slightly tighter than his? She'd been shooting since she was a child. Her father was a cop and insisted all his children learn to handle and respect guns. She practiced several times a month, not because she loved guns but because her father and grandfather had drilled the necessity into her head. Like self-defense, shooting was a perishable skill. A person had no business carrying a gun if he or she wasn't proficient in handling it.

Clearly, he expected some sort of gun-praise. "It's a lovely weapon." Morgan set it on the table. "What do you do for a living, Mr. Hart?"

Kieran ejected the magazine from the pistol. "My great-grandfather secured a patent for a lubricating oil. Small families have kept the fortune relatively intact. I don't have to *do* anything, but my father thinks that humans need purpose. I am therefore employed by the family trust. My main task is managing charitable contributions. One of the benefits of being disgracefully wealthy is having the ability to actually make a difference. Last year, the Hart family funded a pediatric emergency wing at the hospital in Scarlet Falls."

"That must feel wonderful," Morgan said.

"It's satisfying." Kieran opened the box of bullets. "I suppose my father is right. Even *I* need a purpose. In addition to donating money to charity, I host outlandish events and talk other wealthy people into opening their wallets for the less fortunate."

"That sounds easier than it probably is," Lance said.

"You know it." Kieran grinned. "It's easier to get donations from the homeless. The rich are notoriously tight with their pennies. That's why they're rich."

"I'll remember that." Lance folded his arms.

Kieran turned from Lance to Morgan. "Now, why all the questions about me? I thought you came here to discuss Haley."

Morgan waved a hand. "I was just trying to get a sense of who you are."

Kieran leveled a gaze at her. "If it comes down to testifying in a courtroom, I can assure you that I show well, Ms. Dane."

Kieran was articulate, handsome, and successful—all qualities that impressed juries.

Morgan moved on. "How long did you date Haley?"

"A few months." He tried to cover his irritation, but it showed in the tension around his mouth and the force he used to insert a bullet into the magazine.

"When did you break up?" Morgan asked.

"About eight months ago?" His questioning tone suggested he couldn't quite remember the exact date. "I'm happy to help her, but I can't imagine what I can tell you."

"How did you meet?" she asked.

"At a charity event I hosted for the hospital. Haley's mother made a sizable donation." He pushed another bullet into the magazine.

"Do you know why Haley broke up with you?" Morgan asked.

Kieran sighed. He was trying to look casual, but Morgan caught a flicker of anger in his eyes. He quickly suppressed it. "I'm ready for a family. Haley isn't. It wasn't her fault or mine. We're just not at the same place in our lives."

A little different from Haley's story, but it sounded good, she'd give him that. "Have you been to the new nightclub, Beats?"

"I have." His eyes closed to half-mast.

"Did you see Haley there on Friday night?" she asked.

A muscle in the side of Kieran's jaw twitched. "I did."

His hesitation told her if he could have lied, he would have. Kieran might be a jerk, but he was smart. There was no benefit in lying about a fact that could be easily verified.

"Why were you at the club?" Morgan asked.

"I just wanted to check out the scene." He shoved another bullet into the magazine, his movement more forceful.

"May I use your restroom?" Lance asked.

Kieran gestured toward the stairwell. "Yes. Second door on the right."

"Thanks." Lance jogged up the steps.

Morgan could only hope he didn't snoop anywhere he'd be caught. She knew from experience that there was no point trying to stop him. All she could do was keep Kieran occupied until Lance returned.

"Tell me about what happened Friday night," she said.

Kieran's free hand clenched. "You need to understand that I was saddened by the breakup with Haley. I haven't been out much. I was home, alone, bored, restless. I went to the club to break out of the rut. But when I saw Haley there . . . with that other man. Dressed the way she was dressed." A slide show of emotions passed across Kieran's face. Disappointment. Sadness. Resignation.

"How was she dressed?"

"Her dress didn't leave anything to the imagination." His sniff was oddly prudish. "This is going to sound arrogant, but I'd thought she

176

slept with me on our first date because we had some special chemistry. Now I know she was just a slut like most other young women today. They have no interest in commitments or relationships. They just want to *hook up*." He used air quotes around the term.

Kieran had a narrow, negative opinion of women. He stopped talking and stared over Morgan's shoulder. She glanced back, but there was nothing there but a cinder block wall.

Morgan steered him back on topic. "What time did you leave the club?"

Kieran's gaze dropped to the magazine in his hand. When his gaze lifted, his eyes were shuttered, and his emotions seemed to be back under control. "I don't remember exactly what time I left, but I didn't stay that long. If I had to guess, I'd say I left around ten thirty. But I wouldn't be able to swear to that time."

"What time did you get home?" she asked.

"I already said I'm not sure." His tone turned defensive. "I went for a long drive in the country."

"You must have been upset."

His gaze lifted to hers. "Why would I have been upset? I already said Haley and I haven't dated in a long time."

Morgan paused. "You were not upset to see her with Noah Carter?"

"Not at all. I was merely disappointed in her behavior. Do not put words in my mouth, Ms. Dane." His voice dropped to a threatening tone. "Are you trying to trap me?"

"Into what?" she asked.

Without the gun, Kieran wasn't especially physically threatening, and Morgan refused to be bullied by his wealth and position. Did he think they were living in feudal England?

His mouth snapped shut, and his eyes narrowed to mean slits. "Typical lawyer. Talking in circles. Trying to twist my words around. I won't play your legal games."

"I assure you, I'm not playing." Morgan's head pounded, and she lacked the patience to deal with his bull.

Kieran's personality had done an about-face after Lance had left the basement. Did he have such little respect for women, or was it because there wasn't a witness present? Either way, Kieran was either trying to intimidate her or he was unstable. Maybe both.

"I think we're done here." Kieran closed the box of bullets and picked up the pistol. "Where is your partner?"

Coffee sloshed uneasily in Morgan's belly. That was a very good question. She could think of only one topic that might distract Kieran from Lance's absence. It was time to poke the badger.

She leaned forward a few inches. "Eight years ago, you were arrested in Connecticut for stalking your ex-wife. Can you explain?"

Except for a twitch next to his left eye, Kieran's face froze.

"Did you text her multiple times a day, demanding to know where she was and who she was with?" Morgan propped her hand on her hip, closer to her own weapon. "Like you did with Haley."

"My ex-wife has mental health issues. The charges were dropped." Despite his explanation, livid red crept up his neck, and his gaze hardened. "My attorney made sure that the arrest record was erased. How did you get a copy?"

Morgan met his gaze head-on. "You can erase official records, but an article in the newspaper lives forever."

Glaring, Kieran shoved the magazine into the handgrip.

Where is Lance?

Chapter Twenty-Five

Lance hurried down the hallway. He didn't have much time. The house was large, but Haley had said the study was near the master bedroom. He took the stairs two at a time, keeping an eye out for the butler. On the left, a set of double doors stood open to reveal a library. He turned right and went through another set of double doors to another hallway. A long carpet runner silenced his steps. He glanced in open doorways as he walked. He passed several bedrooms, impersonally decorated. How many guest rooms could a house have?

He stopped in front of another set of double doors. He listened at the door but heard no sounds. Cracking the door open a few inches, he peeked inside. It was the only room that looked even remotely lived in. He peered in the closet at perfectly neat rows of men's clothes and shoes. This must be the master bedroom. It was the size of Lance's whole house.

What did one person do with all this space?

Lance continued down the hall. Two doors from the master suite, he found the study. It was exactly as he'd imagined it: an entire wall of bookshelves, a leather executive chair, and a desk the size of a barge with a matching credenza.

He slipped inside and closed the door behind him. The butler was on the first floor of the house, but Lance didn't want anyone to see him snooping. He pulled a pair of gloves from his pocket and put them on.

Then he went behind the desk and started opening drawers. Haley had found her photo in the pencil drawer, but if Lance were going to hide illegal photographs, he'd lock them up.

Lance opened the desk drawers one by one. In the top right drawer, he found the Polaroid camera. It was a new model that produced an instant photo the size of a credit card. He spun the chair toward the credenza. The drawers were locked. Fortunately, he'd come prepared. He took his lock-picking tools from his pocket and went to work. The locks were simple, and he popped them in a couple of seconds. But the drawers held contracts and other paperwork that Lance didn't have time to peruse. He closed and locked them again.

He turned back to the desk. Had Kieran moved his stash to a different room? The photo of Haley indicated more than the desire to look at a woman naked. Kieran had the real thing in his bed when he'd taken her picture. The lack of consent was part of the thrill. He'd gotten off on breaking her trust. If he had more pictures, he'd want to look at them often, to relive the excitement. He'd want to keep them close at hand.

Lance reached under the desk. His fingers hit something. He examined the underside of the desk. A yellow envelope was tucked under the rear-drawer support. He slid the envelope out and opened it.

Bingo.

Polaroids of naked, sleeping women, and Lance would bet all had been unaware they were being photographed.

Movement in the hall caught his attention. He slid the pictures back into the envelope and stuck it under his shirt at the small of his back, tucking it into the waistband of his pants. Something jingled in the hallway. Keys?

He stood and went to the door. Opening it two inches, he scanned the hall but saw no one. Lance listened for a few seconds, but the hallway remained quiet. He slipped out of the office, stuffing the gloves in his pocket.

The jingle sounded again, followed by heavy breathing. Lance turned and stopped dead. A Rottweiler stared at him from the other end of the hall. The jingle hadn't been keys but dog tags.

Lance considered the distance between him and the double doors that led to the second-floor landing. Twenty feet never seemed so far.

He took a step backward. The dog moved forward an equal distance. It emitted a low growl, the hair on its back rising.

Shit.

"Good boy." Lance eased backward another foot.

The growling intensified. But the dog did not bark.

Lance slid his foot backward on the carpet. His heart slammed in double time, and sweat dripped between his shoulder blades.

The dog bristled and took a stiff-legged step forward.

Lance glanced behind him. Could he make it?

Did he have another option?

No. He couldn't call for help without revealing his unauthorized search. That would be awkward. He'd have to make a break for it. But he'd rather face ten angry men than one large dog.

Lance spun and sprinted for the door. He heard the dog's feet dig into the carpet as it charged, but he didn't dare look back. He focused all his attention on the door. Fifteen feet. Ten. The jingling rushed up behind him. Almost there. Was that the dog's breath on his ankle?

Lance grabbed for the knob, opened the door, and slipped through the opening. His leg jerked, pulling him backward.

The dog's mouth was clamped around his boot at the ankle. The dog gave his leg a death shake, yanking Lance's whole leg back and forth. He kicked at the dog's head with his other foot. He caught the dog's jaw with his heel. The giant jaws opened, and Lance pulled his foot free.

Undaunted, the dog lunged for his leg again. But Lance dove through the opening, shutting the door just as the Rottie hit the wood on the other side.

Leaning on the door, Lance breathed, his pulse slamming, sweat gathering under his arms. On the other side of the door, the dog sniffed deeply at the half inch of space between the door and floor. It did not bark, and it did not scratch at the door. Lance pictured it staring.

And maybe plotting revenge.

Lance examined his boot. The dog's teeth had punctured the leather. Better to replace his footwear than his foot.

The dog hadn't been there before Lance went into the office. Had it simply been in a different room and heard him? Or had someone let the beast into the hallway because that person knew Lance was in there?

He walked quickly down the hall and peered over the balcony to make sure no one was in sight before he jogged down the stairs. He hurried down the corridor and stopped in the powder room to wash his hands. By the time he returned to the basement, his heart was no longer trying to race right out of his body.

"We were just wondering what had happened to you." Angry red stained Kieran from the neck up.

The strain on Morgan's face told Lance that something had happened while he'd been gone. He gave her a questioning look, but a small shake of her head convinced him not to ask.

"I don't have any more questions for now." Morgan's posture was stiff. "Thank you for speaking with us. You've been very helpful."

"You're welcome." As Kieran made eye contact with Morgan, something nasty flashed in his eyes. His protective instincts on alert, Lance automatically moved closer to her.

This creeper is going on the short list of suspects for so many reasons.

Kieran turned back to his new gun, his body language dismissing them.

Asshat.

Morgan led the way out of the basement. David showed them to the door, and they walked back to the Jeep.

Lance climbed behind the wheel and started the engine. "What happened?"

"His personality changed while you were out of the room." She told him about Kieran's Jekyll-and-Hyde attitude shift. "We definitely need more information about Kieran Hart."

Lance steered the Jeep down the driveway and through the gate. He paused at the road to check for oncoming traffic and squinted up through the windshield. "I wonder if the house across the street has a security camera."

"We should try," she said. "Maybe we can see what time Kieran came home. Underneath his inherited sophistication, Kieran gives out a nasty personal vibe. And he was probably lying. I seriously doubt it was a coincidence that he was at the club the same night as Haley. He couldn't cover his anger when he talked about her and Noah, though he tried. I think he followed her there. Or knew she would be there from her social media page and went there to try and talk her into getting back together. Men like Kieran don't take being dumped well. They prefer to be the dumpers rather than the dumpees."

"I agree. It was not a coincidence that he was trying out his new handgun during our interview either. Also, I found these." Lance reached behind him and pulled out the envelope of photos from under the back of his jacket and shirt.

Morgan opened the envelope and used the light on her phone to look at the pictures. "Where did you find these?"

"Stuck under his desk drawer."

"These are pictures of a dozen naked women. Not just Haley."

"Yes," Lance said. "I told you sex crimes are like roaches. When you find one, you know there are hundreds more you haven't yet discovered."

She stuffed the pictures back in the envelope quickly. "What should we do with them? Possessing photos of women you've slept with isn't a crime. We'd have to prove he took them without their consent and that they had an expectation of privacy, which might be difficult. I'm sure Kieran's attorneys will argue that the women were willingly naked in *his* bed, in *his* house, and that they were willingly nude with him. I doubt the prosecutor would bring charges, and in order to sue him in civil court, the women would have to prove damages. He hasn't used the photos in any way to harm them."

"We'd also have to track down all these women, tell them about the photos, and persuade them to file complaints."

"Most would probably be too embarrassed." Morgan propped an elbow on the vehicle door and rested her head in her hand. "Normally, cases of privacy violations involve revenge porn or the sharing or posting of intimate images. Not only did Kieran not do either of those things, but he also used an instant camera that does not record a digital image."

"We'll hold on to them for now. If we don't need them later, we'll burn them."

Morgan lifted her head. "He'll know you took them."

"Probably." Lance was counting on it. "But he's not going to call the police, is he?"

"No," Morgan agreed. "He can hardly report the photographs as stolen property. But when he sees that his images are gone and makes the connection that you stole them, he's going to be very angry."

"This is true." Lance thought it would be interesting to see Kieran's reaction. Would he pick on someone his own size? Or did he only bully women? Lance suspected the latter was true.

The Tudor-style home on the other side of the road was smaller than Kieran's family estate but still generously proportioned with at least two acres of green lawn surrounding it. There was no gate blocking access, and Lance turned into the long driveway. He pulled up to the walkway and parked.

"The family that lives here hasn't fared as well as their neighbors." Morgan studied the house through the passenger window. "The roof needs replacing, the landscaping is overgrown, and there's rot under the eaves."

"Must cost a fortune to maintain this place." Lance climbed out of the car.

"What happened to your pant leg?" Morgan stared down at his foot. The hem of his pants was ripped.

"Kieran has a dog. A big dog. I'm grateful only my pants and my pride were damaged."

"I didn't hear any barking." Morgan followed him up the front walkway.

"I guess he was taught not to bark with his mouth full."

They climbed four steps to a brick stoop. Lance rapped on the red arched door. A fiftyish man in jeans and boots answered his knock. Sunlight shone on his shiny, shaved head, and the smell of marijuana clung to him like Pigpen's dust cloud.

Lance had not expected a pothead in this neighborhood, which only reinforced the idea that assumptions were inherently flawed.

"Can I help you?" he crossed his arms over a Rush concert tee from 1983.

"Are you the homeowner?" Lance handed him a business card.

"Yeah, I'm Dexter Montgomery." He coughed, then expelled air smelling intensely of pot. "You can call me Dex."

"Nice to meet you, Dex," Lance introduced himself. Then he motioned toward Morgan. "This is my associate, Ms. Dane. We're investigating possible suspicious activity in the neighborhood last Friday night. We were hoping to get a copy of the video feed from your security camera that faces the street."

"What kind of suspicious activity?" Dex asked.

"The kind that suggests someone might be casing the neighborhood," Lance lied. "We're trying to verify the report now, which is why we're here. Your camera feed would be most helpful."

"You can't be too careful these days," Dex said. "I'll cooperate."

"Thank you." Lance nodded. "I'll need the name and number for your security company, and they'll need your permission to release the video."

Dex waved. "I handle the cameras myself. They don't require monitoring. The video feeds automatically upload to the cloud, where they're digitally stored for thirty days." He blinked from Lance to Morgan, his brows lifting. "Are you a PI too?"

Morgan smiled. "No. I'm an attorney."

"Are you a criminal attorney?" he asked in a hopeful voice that suggested he might need one of those.

"I am," Morgan answered.

"Could I have your card?" Dex's eyes brightened. "My younger cousin got himself into a jam. He's a nice kid, but he isn't the sharpest knife in the block. He needs a good lawyer."

Morgan dug a card out of her huge bag.

"Maybe you can give him a discount?" Dex asked.

The wind kicked up some dead leaves next to the door. Morgan shoved her hands into the pockets of her coat. "Sure. Have him call me."

"Where are my manners? It's cold. Please, come in." Cheered, Dex backed up and waved them into the house.

Lance and Morgan stepped inside. The door opened into a parquet-floored foyer. With a pronounced limp, Dex led them down a wood paneled hallway into a huge farmhouse kitchen. The slate-colored cabinets and dark hardwood floors showed wear, but the surfaces were spotless. Copper pots hung from a rack over a square island. On its smooth butcher-block countertop, Dex opened a laptop. Flames crackled in a brick fireplace, filling the room with dry heat.

Morgan unbuttoned her coat with a sigh of pleasure. Lance removed his jacket.

Dex cracked open the kitchen window. "Sorry about the smell. I picked up a leg full of shrapnel in Operation Desert Storm. Weed isn't ideal, but I don't want to take anything stronger long term. The risk of addiction to opioids is too high. Pot helps me get through the day."

"My husband was in Iraq," Morgan said.

"Is he still over there?" Dex asked.

"No." Her eyes went sad. "He didn't make it back home."

"I'm sorry for your loss." Dex nodded, his brow dropping with commiseration. "Can I offer you some coffee?"

"No, thank you." Morgan shook her head.

"Let me get you a copy of that video." Grimacing, Dex lowered himself onto a stool at the island. He woke the computer and typed on the keyboard. "Do you have a specific timespan?"

Morgan said, "Eight p.m. Friday to eight a.m. Saturday."

Dex shoved a thumb drive into the USB slot. Two minutes later, he handed it to Morgan, apparently having forgotten that Lance existed.

Whatever worked.

"Thank you very much." Morgan smiled.

Dex smiled back. He pushed to his feet with a wince, the effort clearly taxing him. "Anytime."

He escorted them back to the door. "Would you let me know if you determine someone is casing the neighborhood? I can't afford a break-in."

"Yes, we will." Morgan buttoned her coat.

"Thanks for the help." Lance shook Dex's hand.

Lance and Morgan stepped outside, and the door closed behind them.

Back in the Jeep, she marked the thumb drive as evidence and noted its origin.

"That was easy." Lance put the Jeep in gear.

"Yes, though I don't like lying."

"But that's one of the few benefits to not being a cop anymore." Lance drove away from the house.

"That's great as long as no one calls you on it."

Chapter Twenty-Six

"There he is." Sharp pointed to his computer screen. On the black-and-white grainy night image, a BMW sedan drove through Kieran Hart's gates.

Excitement rushed through him. Could they have found a viable suspect? He was afraid that he wanted Haley to be innocent so badly, he'd see signs of guilt in everyone else without the evidence to back up the theory. Thankfully, he had Morgan and Lance to keep him in line.

Standing behind Sharp and looking over his shoulder, Morgan said, "Kieran Hart drives a metallic-gray BMW 750i sedan."

"The license plate matches," Sharp verified. "It's definitely his car."

"What does the time stamp say?" Morgan asked.

"Four o'clock." Sharp took a screenshot and noted the time and date in the corner of the video.

He'd spent the entire afternoon reviewing the surveillance footage. He rubbed his aching eyes and followed Morgan back to her office. She went to the whiteboard, picked up the marker, and wrote under Kieran's photo. *Where was Kieran until four a.m. Saturday?*

"If we can get him to agree to another interview, we can ask him," Morgan said. "But this is the type of question that will prompt him to turn us away, phone his personal attorney, and file a harassment claim. The only reason he consented to the first interview is that he thinks he is smarter than everyone else." Morgan stood back and stared at the board.

"I don't want him to completely shut down on us yet. There might be more information we can get out of him. For now, just add the new information to our files."

"If we ask him, he's going to lie, so it's pointless to tick him off," Lance agreed.

Morgan got up and set her mug on her coffee machine. "Kieran has no alibi yet. He said he went for a drive. Who else has no alibi?"

Sharp stared at the whiteboard. "Piper was home alone."

Morgan added a pod to the machine and pressed "Brew." "Haley had hurt her feelings, Piper was jealous of Noah, and she was anxious when we interviewed her. Do we have any other suspects?"

"Adam?" Sharp suggested. "We know the boy has a temper. He planned that attack on Morgan."

"Would he kill his own brother?" Morgan asked.

"He might not be stable or rational." Rubbing his stubbled chin, Sharp studied the board.

"Haley has received more than a dozen additional email threats." Morgan lifted her cup from the machine and sniffed her coffee as if the aroma alone would perk her up. "Where do we stand on tracing those? The sheriff promised to look into them, but I have more faith in Lance's mother."

"Jenny hasn't had any luck tracing the email threats or identifying the source of that GIF of McFarland punching you."

"If they can be traced, Jenny will do it." Morgan rubbed her eyes. "On the bright side, we've found no motivation for Haley to kill Noah. She has no history of violence. She even said she liked him. Ordinary, law-abiding people don't murder people without good reason."

"I know, but I'm afraid I'm not objective. I want her to be innocent so badly that I'm afraid I'll see clues where there aren't any."

"You don't have to be objective in this case. The evidence doesn't add up to the prosecutor's equation."

"No, it doesn't. Unless Haley suffers from a previously undiagnosed mental illness." Sharp's phone rang. "It's Eliza."

He took the call.

"We have an incident going on here." Eliza sounded worried. "I thought you'd want to know."

"What happened?" Sharp asked.

"One of the protesters climbed the gate. So far, he's just shouting nasty things from the front lawn, but I've called the sheriff's department. They're sending a deputy."

"What are the rest of the protesters doing?"

"Milling around behind the gate," Eliza said. "They don't seem to have a plan."

"I'm on my way." Sharp went into his office. "Do you want to stay on the phone?"

"No. I'm sure everything will be all right." But her voice wavered. "The security guard is here."

"I'll be there in twenty minutes. Call me back if anything changes." Sharp ended the call and relayed the incident to Morgan and Lance. Then he went to the safe in his office and took out his sidearm.

"We're going with you," Lance said.

"Thanks." Sharp grabbed his jacket. "Though the deputy should get there first."

And hopefully remove the protesters before the situation escalated.

Worried, he drove out of town and took the exit to Route 47. Lance and Morgan followed right behind him in the Jeep. Sharp pushed his Prius hard and cut the drive down to seventeen minutes. When he reached Eliza's driveway, there wasn't a cop in sight.

Where was the sheriff's department?

The crowd of protesters waved signs and yelled, but they moved aside as Sharp drove up to the gate. He didn't stop, so they didn't have much of a choice. Eliza must have been watching, because the gate opened before he pressed the intercom button. Sharp drove through the opening. In his rearview mirror, he watched Lance's Jeep follow him. The gate closed behind them.

The figure on Eliza's front lawn was the lean shape of a young man. He stood a few yards shy of the porch, shouting through a bullhorn. "I know you're in there, Haley Powell. You're a murderess. A killer. You're going to burn in hell for your sins."

Two more men were running up the driveway toward the house. One held a baseball bat. The other waved a section of pipe. They must have followed their buddy over the fence. Sharp parked his car and got out as the two newcomers rushed up the front lawn toward the front porch. The man with the pipe outran his pal and leaped onto the porch.

Sharp jumped out of his car and ran toward the house. He heard Lance's vehicle door close. Sharp ran every day, but Lance was twenty years younger. It was no surprise when, a few heartbeats later, Lance blew past him and took the three steps to the front porch in one huge stride. Mr. Pipe raised his weapon over his shoulder, ready to swing at the front window.

Seeing Lance in the reflection of the glass, Mr. Pipe turned and swung at him. Lance had played hockey for many years, and he had a significant size advantage over the young man. Charging like a bull, he hit Mr. Pipe with a full body check. They went sailing over the porch railing into the bushes.

Sharp headed for Mr. Baseball Bat. Unarmed, Bullhorn Guy could wait.

Mr. Baseball Bat faced Sharp with the bat over his shoulder, ready for a swing. "Come on, old man."

Part of Sharp wanted to beat the snot out of the jerk, but he had more important things to do with his day than teach a punk a lesson.

"I am too old for that tackling bullshit." Sharp pulled his gun and pointed it at the asshat's face. "Put down that bat, or I will shoot you."

"You can't." Mr. Baseball Bat didn't sound very sure.

"Put the bat on the ground." Enunciating each word clearly, Sharp lowered his weapon until it pointed at the man's groin. "Now."

Mr. Baseball Bat dropped the bat like it was on fire. It bounced off his own foot. Then he turned sideways and lowered his hands over his crotch, as if that would stop a bullet. What an idiot. "Don't point that thing at my junk, you crazy old fucker."

"Facedown on the ground," Sharp instructed. "Hands stretched out at your sides."

"You can't do this. You're not a cop," he whined as he assumed the position. "I'm going to sue you."

"Good luck with that. You're trespassing." With one knee in his lower back, Sharp took a zip tie out of his pocket, pulled off Mr. Baseball Bat's gloves, and secured his hands behind his back.

"Hey! That hurts," Mr. Baseball Bat protested.

Sharp scanned the front yard for Bullhorn Guy.

Where is that little shit?

"Don't move." Sharp stood.

On the porch, Lance was hauling a zip-tied Mr. Pipe to his feet. He half dragged the assailant down the steps. "Get on the ground with your friend."

"Where did the guy with the bullhorn go?" Sharp scanned the front of the house.

"He ran."

Sharp and Lance spun around at the sound of Morgan's voice.

She was striding across the grass toward them. "And jumped back over the fence into the crowd."

"Hear that, boys? Your buddy deserted you." Sharp nudged one of the teens on the ground.

"Fuck you," one of them said.

"Watch your language in front of the lady." Sharp turned to Morgan. "Did you get a look at him?"

She nodded. "He was far away, but it looked like Noah Carter's younger brother, Adam."

Sharp raised his brows. "The guy who tried to douse you with the homemade pepper spray?"

"The same," Morgan said. "He was wearing jeans and a black jacket."

"His parents must have bailed him out." Lance propped his hands on his hips and stared down the driveway. "We need proof that it was him."

A sheriff's department vehicle came through the front gate and parked. The deputy climbed out. "Sorry for the delay." He sized up the two young men on the ground.

"There were three trespassers." Sharp summed up the incident. He pointed to Mr. Pipe. "He tried to break the window. His buddy had the baseball bat. I didn't see any weapons on number three, who Ms. Dane thinks was Adam Carter."

Another sheriff's vehicle drove through the gate.

"We'll take care of it." The deputy reached for the radio mic on his shoulder.

Leaving the young men with the deputies, Lance, Morgan, and Sharp headed for the house.

A burly man dressed in khaki pants and a polo shirt bearing a security firm logo opened the door for them. A Glock was holstered at his hip. "I'm Eric."

"Where are Eliza and Haley?" Sharp asked.

"In the basement." Eric gestured toward the door that led downstairs. "I wanted Mrs. Powell and Haley out of sight."

"Do we have a picture of the man with the bullhorn?" Morgan asked Eric.

"I'm sure the surveillance system captured the whole incident, but I took a video of him. The images on my phone should be clearer." Eric angled his phone so they could view the screen, and they gathered around it. "Do you know him?"

Lance leaned in. "Adam Carter."

The deputy knocked on the door. Eric let him in. They showed him the video.

"The two men outside are Brandon Webster and Kyle Dixon. They are both twenty-one years old and attend the local university with Adam."

"Are they friends?" Sharp asked.

The deputy hooked a thumb in his duty belt. "They won't say. They're already demanding lawyers."

Occasionally, Sharp longed for the good old days before everyone and his mother was an expert on crime.

The deputy handed Eric a business card. "On my way back to the station, I'll stop at the Carters' house and see if Adam is home. Please forward the video to me."

The deputy took statements from each of them. "I'd like to speak with Mrs. Powell."

"This way." Sharp led him through the basement door. "Eliza?" He didn't want to spook her.

She appeared at the bottom of the staircase. "Is something wrong?"

"No. Everything is being handled." Sharp descended, stepping off the last stair onto a concrete floor. The basement was large and unfinished. Boxes filled a row of utility shelves against one wall. In the middle of the space, an open box sat on a long worktable.

Eliza hugged her arms, as if her heavy sweater and fleece boots weren't enough to keep her warm. In the middle of the room, Haley stood in front of an easel. Dressed in black yoga pants and a thick hoodie, she swirled a paintbrush in frantic circles on a canvas.

"Two of the three trespassers are on their way to the sheriff's station." The deputy gave their names and showed the women their photos on his cell phone. "Do you know either of these men?"

Eliza and Haley shook their heads.

"The third man was Adam Carter, Noah's brother. Don't worry. We'll find him," the deputy assured them. Then he took statements from Eliza and Haley and left.

Sharp scanned Eliza's face, then Haley's. Eliza's face was strained. Fresh lines fanned out from the corners of her eyes. The overhead fluorescent lights didn't help, but Haley was gray. Her eyes were haunted and dark, and the purple circles under them weren't from this afternoon's incident. She clearly hadn't slept in some time.

"Are you both all right?" he asked them.

"Eric assured us we weren't in any danger." Eliza shivered. "But I admit, the incident was disconcerting." She glanced back at Haley, whose paintbrush trembled. "I'm glad he was here, and tonight at six a new bodyguard will take his place."

Sharp wanted to hug them both but felt too awkward. Guilt flooded him. He'd let Ted down. He'd promised to take care of his family, and he didn't even know them well enough to comfort them when they needed it.

"I didn't know you were an artist." He crossed the concrete floor and stood behind Haley. He nearly flinched when he saw her painting. The entire canvas was covered in shades of red.

"I haven't painted in a long time." Haley mixed thick red and black paint on a square of white glass.

"The psychiatrist suggested art therapy." Eliza slid off her stool and joined Sharp. "I dug out Haley's box of art supplies. It hadn't been opened since we moved into this house." Her eyes widened as she took in Haley's artwork. Sharp and Eliza shared a concerned look. Then she glanced away.

"Sounds like a great idea." Sharp stood back a few feet, trying to make sense of the chaotic painting. He could sense there was a bigger picture in all the shadows and subtle differences in color, but he couldn't see it. To him, the painting looked like smeared blood.

Like the crime scene.

Chapter Twenty-Seven

Morgan stood in the foyer of Eliza's house. Through a tall window next to the front door, she could see activity at the bottom of the driveway. Cameramen were packing up equipment as reporters climbed into vans. It seemed as if one or two news vans had already left.

"Is something going on?" she asked the deputy zipping his jacket at the front door.

"Yes, ma'am." He settled his hat on his head. "The sheriff just announced that the female body found this morning has been officially identified as the missing woman, Shannon Yates."

The media would want to jump on the new story. Maybe they'd leave Haley alone for a while.

"You'll let us know if you have news about Adam?" Morgan asked.

"Yes, ma'am." The deputy let himself out.

Morgan locked the door behind him.

Lance and the bodyguard were conferring down the hall. Morgan headed for the basement door. She wanted to check in with Haley and see how her appointment with the psychiatrist had gone. The basement was chilly, and the smell of sawdust made her sneeze. Haley was painting at an easel. Eliza and Sharp were standing behind her, looking over her shoulder with worried eyes.

Haley looked battered. Her eyes were sunken, her face ghostly.

"Art therapy?" Morgan walked closer, her heart clenching. The poor girl.

"Yes." Haley didn't look at her. Her painting held all her attention. "I'd forgotten how much I like to paint."

Morgan drew up as she took in the red on red of the canvas. At first glance, the swirls seemed chaotic, but the shape of two hands, palms up, soon took shape. Two immediate associations came to mind. First, the literal interpretation of Haley seeing her hands covered in blood. But a second, more metaphorical, meaning nagged at Morgan. Had Haley been caught red-handed?

She touched Eliza's forearm. "I'd like to speak to Haley alone for a few minutes."

"I need to speak with Eric before he leaves anyway." Eliza turned toward the stairs. Sharp went with her.

Morgan stepped up next to Haley.

Silver glittered on the girl's arm as she put her paintbrush to the canvas. An ID bracelet.

"You found your medical alert bracelet?" Morgan turned her head to read the inscription.

Haley shook her head. "Mom bought me a new one."

"Have you remembered anything else?" Disturbed, Morgan watched the brush push and blend the thick red paint on the canvas.

"No," Haley said too quickly. With shaking hands, she set the glass palette and brush on the worktable. She drew in a hitching breath, clearly battling for control.

"What's wrong?"

"I try not to cry in front of my mom, but I can't hold it inside." Haley covered her face with both hands and sobbed.

Morgan rubbed her shoulder. "What is it? You can tell me."

She inhaled sharply, lowered her hands, and hiccuped. "I had a dream last night." Haley's voice dropped. "It happened the other night too."

Morgan had to lean closer to hear the soft words.

Haley's eyes filled with tears and lost focus, as if she were looking inward—and seeing something horrific. "There was blood all over me. Noah was on the floor. Dying. He whispered that I killed him." Her brows lowered. "Or at least I think it was him. His lips weren't moving, but he seemed to say, 'You killed me.'"

Sharp had theorized that someone else was in Noah's house Friday night. That the unknown visitor had killed Noah and very carefully framed Haley for the crime. Given the amount of blood, it wouldn't have been easy. But then, he had all night to do it. And if the physical evidence against Haley was strong enough, the police were unlikely to look for other suspects.

But Haley's nightmare put a new perspective on the crime.

"The voice was male?" Morgan asked.

"I don't know. I think so." Haley changed her tone, as if to mimic the voice. "'What have you done to me?'" Haley shuddered and then turned dark, lost eyes on Morgan. "It was a whisper, so I can't identify the voice."

Pity welled up in Morgan's throat. Haley must be overwhelmed thinking she might have committed a violent crime. The ugly question reared in Morgan's head again. Should she pursue an insanity defense?

"This must all be so shocking for you," Morgan said.

A tear rolled down Haley's cheek.

"What did the psychiatrist say this afternoon?" Morgan wrapped an arm around the girl's shoulders. The psychiatrist would issue an official report for Haley's defense, but that would take time. Morgan wanted to know the gist of the diagnosis now.

Haley's slight frame quivered as she inhaled. "She said that my symptoms are consistent with post-traumatic stress disorder. But I could also have been drugged. The holes in my memory are similar to those of drug-facilitated rape victims. Many date-rape drugs cause amnesia.

My imagination can make even more frightening assumptions because I don't know what actually happened to me."

Frustration filled Morgan. If only Haley had gotten medical treatment last Saturday. They wouldn't be left guessing if she had or hadn't been given a drug.

"The doctor also said," Haley continued, "that emotionally traumatic events can trigger dissociative amnesia without the addition of any drug. Whatever happened to me could have been traumatic enough that my brain could be suppressing the event until I can handle the reality. Unfortunately, there is no way to predict whether or not that will ever happen. The memory loss could be temporary or permanent. With either scenario, the nightmares could be dreams or flashbacks or some combination of both."

"We shouldn't rely on the nightmares as truth." Not that Morgan would have done so.

"Right. Since I know what happened to Noah, my imagination could be filling in the details." Haley reached for her paintbrush. "She wants to see me twice a week. She says therapy can help."

"What about your insomnia?" Morgan asked. Lack of sleep could exacerbate symptoms. In turn, Haley's sleep would be even more disturbed. It was a dangerous loop that needed to be broken.

"She gave me medication to help me sleep. It's supposed to suppress nightmares." But Haley looked doubtful. "I'm still afraid to close my eyes. The nightmares seem so real. I don't *want* to sleep."

"I know." Morgan didn't discuss their theories on the case. She didn't want to do anything that might interfere with Haley's true memories or trigger her imagination to work overtime.

Haley leaned on Morgan's shoulder. "But I'm so tired."

"Haley, the doctor is right. You need sleep."

"But I can't control what I see when I'm asleep." Pulling away, Haley put the paintbrush down again and sat on a stool, hugging her knees to her chest. "It's like Friday night is happening all over again."

"I'm sorry this is happening to you," Morgan said. Was Haley remembering more details? Or was she slipping farther away from sanity? "But the doctor said the medication would suppress nightmares, so I think you should try it."

Haley sighed with her whole body. "I know."

"Have you eaten dinner?" Morgan asked.

Haley shook her head. "I'm not hungry."

"But you still need to eat." Morgan worried about the haunted look in the girl's eyes. "Why don't we go upstairs?"

"OK." Haley slid off the stool and followed Morgan up the steps.

In the kitchen, Eliza pasted a fake smile on her face. "Would you like some mac and cheese?"

Haley settled at the island. "Yes, please."

Lance introduced them to a burly armed man in black cargos and a plain black polo shirt. Eric's replacement. Haley paid him little attention. She didn't seem interested in anything, not even food.

But there wasn't any more that Morgan could do to help her tonight. She and Lance said goodbye and went outside. At nearly seven o'clock, darkness had fallen. The protesters had left with the media, and the quiet night seemed almost disconcerting.

"Is there anywhere you need to stop?" Lance asked, getting into the Jeep.

"No. I'd like to be home to put the girls to bed. I already missed dinner with them." One of the benefits of being her own boss was the ability to set her own hours. "I keep reminding myself that big cases are the anomaly. Most of the time I'm home for my girls when I want to be."

Morgan told Lance about her conversation with Haley as he turned the Jeep around and headed down the driveway. "She wasn't even certain that the voice was male. She assumed it was Noah's voice from the context. We don't even know if the voice was real or imagined."

The electronic gate opened, and they went through.

"I talked to the deputies while you were in the basement." Lance stopped by the side of the road and plugged his phone into his mobile charger. "Shannon Yates's body was IDed today. In addition to being raped, beaten, and strangled, they also found zolpidem and alcohol in her system."

"Yes. The deputy told me about Shannon Yates," Morgan said. "Refresh my memory. What is zolpidem?"

"A common medication for insomnia—one of the big brands is Ambien. There's no record of her ever being prescribed sleeping pills of any kind."

"Raped and drugged the week before that Haley was possibly raped and drugged," Morgan wondered aloud.

"We have no evidence linking the two cases." Lance made a left onto the road and pressed on the gas pedal. "But I don't like the coincidence."

"Me either."

The Jeep accelerated. Movement caught Morgan's attention. A shadow shifted in the woods. She squinted into the darkness. The shadow moved toward the road at a determined pace. Alarm burst through Morgan.

"Watch out!" she shouted.

But Lance was already braking.

She barely recognized the figure of a man stepping into the road before a loud crack sounded, and the windshield split into a thousand spider cracks. An object sliced through the glass and bounced off the center console.

Morgan ducked and grabbed for the armrest.

Cursing, Lance steered the Jeep to the shoulder of the road. Wind blew through a hole in the center of the windshield. In addition to the gaping hole, fissures covered most of the glass. The laminated glass had held. Instead of shattering, the broken piece hung down, still attached to the windshield at its base.

If it weren't for the safety glass, Morgan and Lance would have been sliced by flying shards. Lance's heartbeat stuttered as he processed the narrowly avoided danger.

"What was that?" She swiveled in her seat, searching the car.

Lance glanced into the rear seat. "A rock."

Morgan looked over her shoulder. The rock was the size of a brick. She turned her head farther and squinted out the back window. The figure had disappeared. Had he gone back into the woods or was he still back there? Considering reaction time and braking distance, she wasn't sure how far the Jeep had traveled before Lance had been able to bring it to a stop.

"Lock the doors." He jumped out of the vehicle, gun in hand.

"Wait. You can't go running after him alone." Heart thumping against her breastbone, Morgan drew her weapon, took the flashlight from the glove compartment, and followed him.

Morgan broke into a jog, but Lance was way ahead of her. He sprinted down the road like a running back. In the best of times, she was no athlete, and today was not the best of times.

She hadn't jogged a hundred feet before her head began to pound. She slowed to a walk and called the sheriff's department to report the incident. By the time she reached the place where the figure had been standing, Lance was examining the shoulder of the road. She shone the beam of her flashlight on the road.

"Is there any sign of him?" All she saw was dirt and darkness.

"No." Lance straightened. "He's long gone."

He took out his phone.

"I already called the sheriff's department," Morgan said. Her head hurt, and her stomach had gone queasy from the exertion. "I really need to get in shape."

Lance shook his head.

"Yes, I know I've said it before, but this time I mean it. As soon as the weather warms up." She put a hand on her forehead.

"In this case, I suspect it was your concussion rather than lack of fitness that slowed you down. I'd better call Sharp and warn him in case the rock thrower sets up another ambush."

Morgan stared down the road into the darkness. "He could have killed us."

Grim-faced, Lance followed her gaze. "Yes. We were very lucky."

Chapter Twenty-Eight

Lance watched the taillights of Stella's car disappear in the darkness. Morgan had called her sister, and there had been no reason for her to sit and wait for the tow truck, especially since she was clearly feeling ill.

He pressed a hand to his solar plexus, where tension gathered. A sheriff's department vehicle sat behind his Jeep, the red and blue strobe lights swirling in the night.

The same deputy who had responded to the protesters call earlier now took photos of the interior of Lance's Jeep. He opened the rear door and removed the rock with gloved hands. He hefted it in one hand. "This sucker must weigh four pounds. Good thing it didn't hit either of you."

Every time Lance pictured the incident in his head, he wanted to hyperventilate. If the rock had broken through the windshield eighteen inches to either side, it would have hit Morgan or him. There was nothing he could have done to prevent it. He'd had no warning and no time to react.

"Any luck finding Adam Carter?" Lance asked.

The deputy carried the rock back to the rear of his patrol car, put it into an evidence box, and labeled it. "No. He wasn't home. His parents thought he was in his room, but he'd gone out the window. They're as desperate to find him as we are."

"I'll bet." Lance couldn't imagine losing one son and having the other go missing. The Carters must be devastated. The depths of their grief would only be aggravated by their guilt over not keeping better tabs on Adam. He might be an adult, but they would still feel responsible for whatever happened to him.

"We're looking for him." The deputy closed his trunk.

The pepper spray incident had been worrisome enough, but no one had been at risk of dying.

"That rock could have killed both of us," Lance said. "If Adam threw it, his anger is escalating."

Lance's gaze returned to his windshield.

This was an act of rage.

Had it been planned? Had he been waiting for them or had he been running from Eliza's house, seen them coming, and grabbed the rock from the ground? Lance considered the darkness.

"Look, we don't *know* that Adam was responsible for this. You're speculating. It could have been a random act of violence committed by any one of the dozens of protesters that were at Ms. Powell's house today. How could he have known it was your Jeep coming in the dark? He would have seen headlights and maybe recognized the general shape of an SUV, but there's no way he could have identified the actual vehicle approaching."

Lance reviewed the incident in his head. "Unless someone was watching the house, saw us leave, and relayed our position to him."

"Now you think more than one person was involved?" the deputy asked, his voice skeptical.

"It's just one possibility," Lance admitted. "But we already know he brought two friends. Maybe there were more."

"We'll consider it." The deputy's voice implied that Lance shouldn't count on it.

The rough surface of the rock would be all but impossible to fingerprint. Yellow strobe lights blinked in the darkness as a flatbed approached. It pulled onto the shoulder of the road and beeped as it backed up to the Jeep.

"Let me get back to work. I'll let you know if we find Adam." The deputy got into his car and drove away.

While the driver hoisted the Jeep onto the flatbed, Lance called Morgan to give her the update.

"I could come over there and sleep on your couch tonight," Lance offered. "I'm worried. At this point, we need to operate on the assumption that he threw the rock and that he's clearly angry beyond reason. He either wants to hurt you for representing Haley or he wants to stop you."

"Stella is staying over," Morgan said. "And she brought good news. McFarland was denied bail. We don't have to worry about him for a while."

"That is good news."

"And Grandpa says we can use his car tomorrow. Do you want me to pick you up in the morning or meet you at the office?"

Lance lived six blocks from Sharp Investigations.

"I'll meet you at the office." He would walk over. He wanted to go in early, and she would be tied up getting the kids off to school.

The truck driver waved at Lance. "I have to go," he said to Morgan.

"See you in the morning then." Her voice turned husky with emotion. "I love you."

"I love you too." His brain told him that Morgan and her sister were more than capable of taking care of themselves, but his heart didn't listen to reason, and he would still worry. "Get some sleep."

"I will," she said, and the line went dead.

More than an hour later, the tow truck driver dropped Lance off in front of his house. The Jeep had been left at the body shop in town. Lance stared at his house. The lights were on. Someone was inside. Only two people had keys, and he'd just talked to Morgan.

"Thanks." Lance tipped the driver and walked to the front step. It was doubtful that a burglar would have turned on the lights, but better careful than dead. Standing to the side of the doorframe, he unlocked the door and pushed it open.

"It's just me," Sharp called out.

Lance went inside. Removing his jacket, he hung it in the hall closet, then walked back to the kitchen.

Sharp was pouring whiskey over ice. Other than the occasional organic beer, Sharp rarely drank alcohol. Normally, his whiskey consumption was limited to a single glass on Christmas Eve.

"I couldn't settle down and decided to go for a walk." He took down a second tumbler, poured a finger of whiskey into it neat, and handed it over.

Lance took it. "Been a hell of a day."

"It has." Sharp sipped his whiskey, wandering out of the kitchen. He walked past the grand piano that sat in the dining room in lieu of a table and into the adjoining living room. Stopping in front of the glass patio doors, he stared out into the blackness of the yard.

When he hadn't spoken for a few heartbeats, Lance went to his piano and sat. Sharp would talk when he was ready. Lance took a swallow, then set his whiskey on top of the piano. He stretched his fingers over the keys, not thinking. The first few chords of "Desperado" felt right. Always his outlet, the music flowed through him and cleared his head.

After the final notes faded away, Sharp rattled the ice in his glass. "Haley's first birthday was a hard day for Eliza. Ted should have been there. He'd been gone about nine months by then. Eliza didn't have any family in Scarlet Falls, but she threw a party anyway. Some of the SFPD came. I was there early, did the things Ted would have done. Went out for ice and beer. Put burgers on the grill. Eliza did her best to celebrate an important milestone. After everyone left, she put Haley to bed. I cleaned up for her. Then we sat out in the backyard with a couple of beers, not talking, just being sad and missing Ted."

Sharp drained his glass and stared at the ice. "I don't know how it happened, but before I could think, I was kissing her, my best—dead—friend's wife. And I was married then. I felt like a total shit. I didn't even apologize. I just left." Sharp shook his head, disappointed. "I felt so damned guilty. It wasn't even sexual. Not really. Eliza and I didn't have a romantic relationship. What we shared was pain. There wasn't anything healthy about starting something between us, and we both knew it."

Lance picked up his glass and swallowed some whiskey.

Tension radiated from Sharp as he drew in a deep breath. It hissed out between his teeth. "A week later, she called me to tell me she was moving. She needed a fresh start. But I also think she wanted to put some distance between us. It was almost like neither one of us could heal. Whenever we were together, our grief amplified. It's supposed to be the opposite, right? Friends help each other cope. But not us. We were trapped in some mutually destructive pattern, and she was the one who was brave enough to break it."

"That was a long time ago." Lance sipped his whiskey.

"My wife left not too long after that. My marriage was in trouble before Ted died. Afterward, I spent more time helping Eliza and Haley than making any attempt to save my own relationship. But the divorce followed right on top of Ted's death and Eliza leaving town. There were no shining moments in my life at that time."

Lance counted the years. Soon after all this had gone down, Lance's father had disappeared, and SFPD detective Sharp had been assigned the case.

"I assume you lived up to the cop cliché and threw yourself into your work?"

Sharp's grin was ironic. "You know it."

Was the fact that his personal life had been in shambles part of the reason Sharp had immersed himself so deeply in Lance's father's case and taken a paternal interest in Lance?

Lance didn't want to think of how his life would have turned out if he and his mentally ill mother had been on their own. Sharp had made all the difference. Once he'd figured out that anxiety crippled Jenny Kruger, Sharp was the one who made sure Lance had a ride to hockey practice. He gave a scared, lonely boy a safe place to stay when his mother had especially bad times. He'd gotten Jenny help too.

He and Sharp had been brought together by multiple tragedies. But as a young boy, Lance had been oblivious to anyone's pain but his own. Now it seemed that he'd given something back to Sharp.

Sharp sighed. "I promised Ted I would look after his family, but I let them walk away. I never called her. I didn't check up on them."

"Eliza was the one who left, Sharp. You couldn't make her stay."

"Maybe." Sharp let out another long breath. He walked into the kitchen and put his glass in the sink. "But I was the one who drove her away. All these years later. I barely know the family I'd promised to protect."

"Eliza came to you for help. She knew you'd support her."

The overhead kitchen light created shadows on Sharp's thin face. For the first time ever, he actually looked his age. "But how am I going to keep Haley out of prison?"

Lance tossed back the last swallow of his drink and got up from the piano. He walked past Sharp on the way into the kitchen.

Slapping him on the shoulder, Lance said, "You're not alone in this. Morgan and I will do everything we can."

"I appreciate everything you've already done. I hated asking Morgan. She shouldn't be working."

"She wouldn't have it any other way." Even if Lance didn't like her working with a concussion either.

"I'm going to head home." Sharp turned away.

"I'll be in early tomorrow."

Sharp nodded. "Me too."

Lance let him out and locked the door. With an early morning ahead, he took a hot shower and went to bed, tossing and turning for an hour, Sharp's words on his mind.

How *were* they going to keep Haley out of prison? And what would it do to Sharp if they couldn't? Even worse, what if the girl *was* a killer?

Chapter Twenty-Nine

The sound of glass breaking woke Lance from a dead sleep. He sat up, adrenaline streaking through his veins. Cold air blew into the room, and a sharp scent hit his nose. Gasoline! In two heartbeats, he took in the smashed window, the broken bottle on the floor, the cloth and small flame, the liquid spreading across the hardwood and area rug.

Shit.

Fire erupted with a whoosh. Heat rushed over him as the blaze surged toward the bed. The fire alarm blared, lights flashing from the overhead units.

He swung his legs over the side, grabbed his gun from the night stand, and rushed toward the door. Leaving the bedroom, he ran down the short hall toward the front door, passing the guest room and a bathroom.

Another bottle came through the window near the front door and smashed on the floor. Liquid splattered. Fire bloomed in the foyer, engulfing the welcome mat and blocking his exit to the door.

Lance turned back. Smoke filled the hall. He lived in a one-story house. He just had to find a window that wasn't on fire.

He covered his mouth and nose with his hand and headed for the guest room. Before he could get close to the window, another Molotov cocktail came crashing through the glass. It landed on the wood floor next to the guest bed and erupted into a ball of flames. The bedding caught fire. Flames rushed toward the ceiling.

Lance backed out of the room.

Whoever was trying to kill him was still outside, running around the house and tossing incendiaries through every window, trapping him inside.

What were his options?

He had damned few.

The hall bath was an interior room. With no windows, it was a death trap.

The bedrooms had too much fuel. Soaked in gasoline, bedding, mattresses, and area rugs would catch too quickly. Smoke was pouring from both doorways.

But if he continued to stand still, he was dead. The whole house would be engulfed in a few minutes. Modern houses, full of synthetic materials, burned hotter and faster and emitted more toxins than houses in the past.

Heat enveloped him. Sweat broke out on his skin. The smoke darkened and filled his lungs.

With no other choices, Lance raced back toward the front hall, toward the fire. With no fabric save the welcome mat, the fire would spread more slowly there. He could exit through the dining room windows or patio slider.

Provided the arsonist didn't beat him to the back of the house.

Flames danced across the floor in front of him. Without breaking stride, he dug deep, pushed off the floor, and leaped over the fire. Pain licked at his bare feet and roared through his bad leg as he landed, but adrenaline blocked the pain as quickly as it registered.

Eyes stinging, lungs burning, Lance coughed. He stumbled across the living room toward the sliding glass patio doors.

Through the glass, he saw a flaming bottle soaring toward him like a missile. Anticipating another explosion, he ducked and covered his face. But the bottle broke on the outside of the thicker glass of the patio door. Liquid splattered the glass and patio. Flames rushed across the concrete, then, lacking additional fuel, went out.

Lance opened the slider. Air flooded the house. Behind him, the fire rushed toward the fresh oxygen. Leading with his gun, he staggered through the opening into the darkness. His focus tunneled down to the potential threat. Smoke clogged his throat, and his racing heartbeats echoed in his ears.

A shadow ran toward him. A man. Sweat dripped down Lance's forehead, mixing with soot and smoke, and ran into his eyes. He blinked, but his vision was still too blurry to identify the man.

"Stop!" he shouted, aiming his gun at the dark figure.

"Whoa," the figure yelled. "Don't shoot me. It's Bill."

Lance wiped his eyes, which didn't help much. He squinted, and his vision clarified enough to see his skinny next-door neighbor standing on the back lawn, hands in the air. Shirtless, he wore only pajamas bottoms and sneakers, the laces untied.

Lance lowered the gun. A wave of heat hit his back, and he staggered a few yards farther away from the house. "Did you see anyone?"

Sirens blared. One big advantage to living in town was the proximity to the fire and police stations.

"No!" Bill yelled over the din of the fire and approaching emergency vehicles. "Is anyone else inside?"

Lance shook his head. Now that he was alive and likely to stay that way, his body busied itself with exchanging smoke for clean night air. He leaned on his thighs and hacked up what felt like an entire lung.

The winds kicked up. Something hot pricked Lance's shoulder. He swatted an ember from his skin. Glancing over his shoulder, he saw the fire swallow his roof. Flames reached into the dark sky, and smoke billowed across the moon.

"Dude, we gotta get away from here. Let me help you." Bill slung one of Lance's arms over his shoulders and half dragged him to his own backyard, around his own house, and out to the street. Bill's wife stood on the sidewalk in a long bathrobe. She clutched their toddler on her hip. More neighbors emerged from houses and gathered on front lawns.

A fire truck parked, and firemen went to work, dragging hoses off the rig toward the inferno. Two more fire trucks and multiple Scarlet Falls police cars roared onto the street. An ambulance parked at the rear of the vehicle pack, three lots down the road. Patrol officers herded the crowd farther from the fire.

Sharp jogged down the sidewalk toward Lance. He wore jeans and sneakers, but his salt-and-pepper hair stood straight up on one side.

"You alive?" Sharp asked, scanning him.

Still coughing, Lance nodded.

"I'll take him from here," Sharp said to Bill.

Bill ducked out from under Lance's arm, and Sharp took his place. Lance wanted to tell him he could walk on his own, but he wasn't entirely sure about that. Faceplanting on the sidewalk would be embarrassing.

"Thanks, Bill," Lance croaked.

With a wave, Bill turned and jogged toward his wife and child.

"I heard the sirens and just knew it was you." Sharp hauled Lance to the back of the ambulance. Lance perched on the rear bumper. A paramedic slapped an oxygen mask over his face and handed him a bottle of water. Lance moved the mask to rinse his eyes and mouth. He spat onto the street then sipped water. The cool liquid soothed his raw throat.

The paramedic unfolded a blanket. Lance waved it off. He was still sweating from the fire.

Sharp took the blanket and shoved it at Lance. "You realize you're only wearing boxers?"

Lance hadn't. His attention had been focused on not burning to death.

He lifted the oxygen mask off his face. "Good thing I have my gun, or I'd feel naked." His voice was hoarse and speaking set off another wave of coughing.

"Just breathe." Sharp snapped the mask back into place, then wrapped the blanket around him. "You're giving that old lady down the street an eyeful."

The oxygen helped, as did sips of water.

The paramedic took Lance's vitals, then gestured toward the open doors of the rig. "Can you climb in?"

"I don't need to go to the ER," Lance said. His coughing had subsided, though his lungs still felt irritated.

"Have you seen your foot?" the paramedic asked.

Lance looked down. Blood dripped from multiple cuts. He propped one ankle on the opposite knee and examined the bottom of his foot. "It's not that bad."

And just like that, Lance's foot began to throb.

"But you should probably have the glass picked out," Sharp said.

Admitting defeat, he handed Sharp his gun, butt first. "Would you lock this up for me?"

"I will." Sharp slid it into his jacket pocket. "I'll run back to my place, get my car, and meet you at the ER."

"What time is it?" Lance asked.

"Two a.m., but yes, you should call Morgan."

"I hate to wake her."

Sharp stared at him. "How did she take it the last time you had an emergency and didn't want to bother her?"

Not well. Not well at all.

"You're right. She'll want to know. But my phone is in there." Lance gestured to his house. The firemen were giving the blaze their best effort, but his house was not salvageable. The best they could hope for at this point was to keep the fire from spreading to his neighbors' homes.

"I'll call her." Sharp nodded. "Be right behind you."

"Thanks. There should be spare clothes in my office closet." Lance turned and climbed into the back of the ambulance. The paramedic strapped him in. Through the open door, he watched his roof collapse. Sparks showered into the sky. The firemen retreated, spraying the houses on either side of Lance's.

It suddenly occurred to him that he had nothing. He didn't even have any clothes on his back.

His second big realization was that he didn't care. He hadn't built a life here. He'd used his house to sleep and store his stuff. Other than some photographs and his piano—he was going to miss that—there was nothing he couldn't replace.

His life was with Morgan and her kids.

"Wait," he said as the paramedic started to close the door. "I need to see a cop. Just for a minute."

The paramedic jumped down and flagged down a cop.

The Scarlet Falls patrol officer climbed into the back of the ambulance.

Between coughing bouts, Lance gave him a three-sentence summary of the firebomb attack.

The officer took notes. "I'll call the arson investigator and start knocking on doors. Maybe one of your neighbors saw something."

But the fire wasn't just arson. It had been attempted murder. Lance had thought someone was after Morgan, but it seemed he was also a target.

Who had he angered recently? Adam Carter came to mind first. Noah's brother was beside himself with grief and rage. He was also missing.

But Adam wasn't the only person with a personal grudge against Lance. What if Kieran Hart had discovered his photos were missing?

Chapter Thirty

It was still dark when Morgan rushed down the ER hallway. Sharp had said Lance was OK, but until she saw him for herself, she would not be able to draw a full breath.

"Morgan, over here," Sharp called from a doorway.

She hurried over. At the sight of Lance, her eyes welled with hot tears. Her first deep breath felt like it cracked her wide open.

Lance was sitting up, bare chested, with a hospital blanket pulled up to his waist and an oxygen mask on his face. An IV dripped into the back of his hand. His face was splotched with soot, and his eyes were red. A doctor wearing magnifying glasses bent over his foot.

Lance pulled the mask off his face. "Hey, come here. Sharp was supposed to tell you I was OK."

But there was no stopping the tears once they started. She'd lost both her parents and her husband. She'd never thought she'd find another man to love. *That* had seemed nothing short of a miracle. But now . . . she couldn't bear to lose him.

"He did." She swallowed a sob.

Sharp moved into the hallway to give her space. As she passed, he gave her shoulder an awkward pat.

Lance reached a hand toward her. She took it, and he pulled her close. She pressed her face into his bare shoulder.

His hand stroked the back of her head. "This is all minor stuff."

"I know." She couldn't explain her unexpected emotional outburst. Relief? After Sharp had called, she had dressed and driven calmly to the hospital.

She straightened and swiped a tear from under her eye. "I'm sorry."

He squeezed her fingers.

"Two stitches." The doctor sat up and snipped off a thread. He set down his scissors and removed his gloves. "We'll get that foot bandaged. As soon as the X-ray and blood test results come back, you can be on your way."

"What happened?" Morgan asked. "And don't gloss over the details."

"Someone tossed Molotov cocktails through my windows."

Shocked, Morgan eased into a plastic chair next to his bed. "How's your house?"

Lance shook his head. "Gone, I expect."

"Oh, no. Your piano." Morgan loved to sit next to him while he played.

He grimaced. "The piano can be replaced. But I will miss that one. I've had it for a long time."

She leaned over and kissed him on the mouth. Then she replaced the oxygen mask on his face. "I'm sorry your house burned down."

He lifted the mask. "It's only a house."

Clearly, neither one of them had fully processed the fact that someone had tried to burn Lance alive.

Sharp returned with a Styrofoam cup in his hand. He offered it to Morgan. "I thought you could use some coffee."

"Thank you." She took the cup and sipped it. "I must look like a disaster if you are bringing me coffee."

"I'm not going to answer that, but addicts can't go cold turkey," Sharp said. "I assume you're taking him home?"

"Yes." Morgan wasn't letting Lance out of her sight.

"I'm going to head home." Sharp nodded toward an athletic bag on the counter. "I put an extra change of clothes in the bag."

Morgan stood and pressed a kiss to Sharp's cheek. "Thank you for calling me."

"Take care of him." He gave her a quick hug and left the room.

"I will." Easing back into the chair, she clasped Lance's hand in both of hers.

"I should go to a hotel," Lance suggested. "What if whoever set my house on fire follows me?"

"We've both been targeted, so the chances that he'll come after me are just as good." Morgan had been attacked in her home before. Being the only physically sound adult was frightening. She simply couldn't protect three children, her grandfather, and her sick nanny all by herself. She'd always feel safer with Lance in the house. "And I talked to Stella. A patrol car will sit outside our house tonight."

It was nearly four o'clock before he was released. Morgan drove him back to her house in her grandfather's Lincoln Town Car.

Morgan parked in front of her house. Once inside, Lance greeted the dogs and limped toward the sofa.

"No." Morgan took his hand and led him back to her bedroom. "I know I didn't want to share a bed with the kids in the house, but this is silly. We are not having a fling."

"No?" He turned to face her.

"That's not how I view our relationship." She wrapped her arms around his neck. "Am I wrong?"

"No. This is the real deal for me too."

"Then you are sleeping with me. I'm keeping an eye on you, and I'm too damned tired to get up and check on you all night." She rose onto her toes and kissed him. She wanted to be able to reach out during the night and touch him, to feel him warm and alive and breathing at any time. That was the only way she'd be able to close her eyes. "The girls will be up in a few hours. We'd better try and get some sleep."

"Would you mind if I take a quick shower?" he asked. "I smell like smoke. The only part of me that's clean is my foot."

"Go ahead." Morgan changed from her jeans back into her flannel pajamas. She climbed into bed. Lance pulled off his T-shirt and went into the attached bathroom. She heard the shower spraying on the tile. He emerged a few minutes later, his skin and hair still damp and smelling of her soap. Sitting on the edge of the bed, he put a clean bandage on his foot and climbed into bed in his sweatpants. She curled against him, the solid feel of his body against hers and the heat of his skin reassuring her that he really was alive.

She rested her head on his broad shoulder. "I love you. I don't know what I'd do if you—" The sob choked off her words.

"Shh." He pressed a kiss to the top of her head. "I love you back, and I'm not going anywhere."

Morgan usually didn't have any trouble sleeping. With three young children, she generally fell asleep instantly, like a combat soldier. But tonight, she lay still, listening to Lance's steady breathing and thinking about how much she couldn't bear to lose him.

Chapter Thirty-One

Lance cracked his eyelids, a being-watched feeling stealing over him. Seeing a small figure next to the bed, he startled.

Sophie stood less than a foot away, staring at him.

"How long have you been there?" he asked. The words scratched his raw throat.

"A long time," she said.

Wasn't that creepy?

She pointed to the hour digit on the bedside clock. At three, her ability to tell time was limited. But she was learning her numbers. "Mommy said I couldn't wake you until this number was a seven. Is that a seven?"

"Yes. Where's Mommy?"

Sophie nodded. "She's in the kitchen with Grandpa. Gianna is making pancakes. If you want some, you hafta hurry before Grandpa eats them all."

Lance sat up. He swung his legs over the edge of the bed. His legs were hot in his sweatpants. If he was going to stay with Morgan and her girls, he was going to have to buy pajamas, along with everything else.

Sophie handed him his T-shirt, and he tugged it over his head.

"You hurt your foot." She frowned. "You hurt yourself a lot."

Truer words . . .

"It's just a scratch." Lance didn't feel as badly as he'd expected. His throat was sore, his lungs felt a little wheezy, and his foot hurt, but all his injuries were minor, nothing that would keep him from working. He was a lucky man.

Sophie grabbed his hand and pulled him from the bedroom. "Come *on*."

"I'm coming." Lance let her drag him down the hallway.

Morgan was at the table, drinking coffee. Her eyes brightened as he walked in. She'd clearly already showered. Sophie steered him toward a chair and pushed him into it.

Art gave him a critical once-over then nodded. "Glad to see you up and around. Someone was worried."

Morgan got up and poured him a cup of coffee. As she set it in front of him, she leaned over and kissed him on the mouth. "Good morning."

"Morning." Warmth crept over him that had nothing to do with the coffee.

Gianna brought him a plate of pancakes, eggs, and bacon. "I thought you'd be hungry."

"Thanks. I am." Lance dug into the food.

Ava and Mia appeared in the doorway, still in their pajamas. "Lance!"

They rushed him for hugs. He dropped his fork and hugged them back.

He checked the clock on the microwave. "Why aren't you ready for school?"

"No school today!" Ava bounced. "Grandpa and Gianna are taking us to the library."

"School is closed for a teacher in-service day." Morgan set her own coffee on the table. "Girls, why don't you get dressed?"

The girls skipped out of the kitchen.

Morgan picked up her coffee again and drained the cup. "How do you feel?" she asked Lance.

"Pretty good, considering." He finished his breakfast. "Thank you, Gianna. That was great."

Smiling, Gianna collected his plate. "You're welcome. We were worried about you." The girl's eyes were misty.

Lance wasn't accustomed to having so many people take care of him, but it wasn't a bad feeling.

Morgan refilled her coffee and warmed up his. "Are you sure you feel up to working today?" asked the woman who'd been working for days with a concussion.

"Yes." He drank more coffee, waiting for the caffeine to kick in.

Sophie bounced over to stand in front of him. "If you're sick, you can stay home wif me. Today is Friday. I don't hafta go to preschool. If you stay home 'cause you're sick, you get to watch extra TV."

Lance scooped her into his arms. "Is that so?"

"Uh-huh." She leaned on his chest.

"But I'm not sick, and your mom needs my help today."

Sophie pouted. "OK. But it woulda been fun." She leaned close to his ear and whispered, "I like it when you sleep over."

Lance's heart squeezed. He whispered back, "Me too."

Sophie squirmed. The child had the energy of a squirrel on Red Bull.

Lance set her on the floor and stood, turning to Morgan. "I'm going to call my mom. She'll be up by now. I don't want her to read about the fire on the internet. Then can I use the shower?"

"The bathroom is all yours," Morgan confirmed.

Lance called his mother, told her about the fire, and promised to stop at her house that morning so she could see for herself that he was alive. He had a second cup of coffee. By the time he'd showered, he was feeling mostly human.

He and Morgan said their goodbyes, left the house, and climbed into Art's huge sedan. Lance drove to an electronics store on the interstate to buy a new phone before heading out to his mother's place.

Jenny Kruger still lived in the house he'd grown up in. After his father's disappearance, she'd refused to sell. She'd retreated from life in every way. They'd been isolated in the countryside until he'd turned sixteen and gotten his driver's license. If it hadn't been for Sharp, Lance would have been stranded. Those lonely years came back to him as he drove down the rural highway that led out to his old home. As the miles rolled by, fields and forests replaced houses.

He parked in the driveway, and he and Morgan climbed the steps to the front porch and waved at the surveillance camera. The motion detector would let his mother know they were there. She'd always been plagued by anxiety, but her paranoia had increased sharply since being attacked. Lance had upgraded her security system over the winter. Now the president would be safe in her little three-bedroom ranch.

Lance used his key to let them in. Morgan shed her coat in the foyer, and they walked through the living room and into the kitchen of the one-story home. "Mom?"

Though his foot throbbed, he did not let himself limp. His mother would be worried enough.

"Oh my goodness. Your poor face." His mother stood in the doorway to the kitchen, her gaze on Morgan. She hadn't seen Morgan since the incident at the courthouse on Monday.

"I have quite a bruise, don't I?" Morgan grimaced, then lied without missing a beat. "It's more ugly than painful."

Jenny didn't look convinced, but she nodded and turned to Lance. "Your eyes are red. Is that from the smoke?"

"Yes." Lance gave her a heavy sigh. "If only the house fared as well as I did."

"You're lucky to be alive." Her crow's feet deepened with worry. His mom's anxiety burned off as many calories as she managed to eat. Frailty and stress had aged her far beyond her sixty years. "Do the police think that same man who sprayed you with pepper spray set your house on fire?"

"They don't know, but it's a reasonable theory." Lance didn't mention the rock that had been thrown through this windshield. "He's young and grieving. He isn't thinking straight."

"You never did anything criminal when you were young and grieving," his mother said.

"I was perfect." Lance grinned. "But look at all the situations the kids on my team get into." He coached a hockey team of at-risk youths. Most of them had less than ideal home lives and were frequently in trouble. "Young people react to emotion. Controlling their impulses takes practice and maturity."

His mother sighed, and he wondered how much of his teen years she really remembered. Mentally, she'd been absent more than she'd been present. He needed to distract her. "Do you have any other information for us?"

"Actually, yes." Jenny turned and walked toward her office at the back of the house. Her two cats followed her like dogs. When she sat down, her eyes were more focused, and her expression less strained.

The office had once been the smallest bedroom in the house. Jenny sat behind her desk. Morgan took a chair facing her.

"Any luck on tracing the origin of that GIF of McFarland's attack on Morgan?" he asked, leaning over his mother's shoulder.

"Not yet. Once something goes viral, it becomes hard to trace its source." His mom nodded toward the screen. "And that video clip is everywhere. I still can't believe he punched you like that."

"It was a surprise," Morgan agreed.

"Aren't you afraid to go back to the courthouse?" Jenny only left the house for her weekly group therapy and for an occasional trip to the psychiatrist, and she needed medication for those brief outings.

"No," Morgan answered in a firm voice. "What McFarland did wasn't just unusual, it was stupid. He was already facing jail time. Now he's going to be incarcerated much longer. The prosecutor isn't going to offer him any sort of deal. He committed assault in the courthouse, in front of dozens of witnesses, in full view of the surveillance feeds, with a dozen deputies just steps away. Most criminals aren't *that* dumb."

He appreciated Morgan's effort to downplay the risks of her profession, but it didn't matter what she said. The unpredictable and random nature of the courthouse incident made it the exact sort of thing that fed his mother's anxiety. People who didn't suffer from anxiety could rationalize that the assault had been an aberration. But his mother's mental illness translated the event into: if one wasn't safe at the county courthouse, then one wasn't safe anywhere.

Lance brought the conversation back to the case. Working was the one thing that seemed to distract his mother from her crippling fears. "So what did you find out?"

"I traced the first email threat to Haley and the one to Morgan to an email address registered to Adam Carter." His mother flexed her arthritic fingers over the keyboard. Her getting-back-to-work gesture made Lance feel like a dunce for not realizing she needed to be needed.

"The police are already looking for Adam," Morgan said. "Please send me the evidence, and I'll forward it to the sheriff and prosecutor."

"OK. And if the police can get a search warrant for Adam's computer, their forensic tech will be able to tell if he also originated the GIF."

"Great." Morgan entered a detailed reminder into her phone. "I'll mention that in my email. This is a huge help, Jenny."

Jenny beamed. "I also uncovered something interesting about Justin O'Brien."

Morgan balanced her notebook on her lap. "What do you have?"

"Justin was arrested for date rape during his junior year of college," Jenny began. "He brought a girl home from a party and slept with her. In the morning, she accused him of taking advantage of her while she was too drunk to walk straight, let alone give consent. In an interesting defensive move, his attorney claimed that Justin was also drunk and didn't remember most of the night. He threatened to countersue the girl for sexual assault."

"Sounds like a nightmare of a case." Morgan lifted her pen.

Jenny looked up from her computer screen. "In the end, the charges against Justin were dropped for lack of evidence."

"I'd call it a classic *he said, she said,* but if neither of them remembered what happened, then I don't see how either of them could be held responsible." Lance paced the tiny office. "What else did you find?"

His mother continued. "Isaac has nothing but a misdemeanor drug possession on his record from when he was eighteen. He was found with a small amount of pot. I didn't find any criminal charges against Chase."

"What about the Powells? Did you learn anything about Haley or her mother or Eliza's company, Wild?" Morgan asked.

Jenny consulted her list. "Wild has a few lawsuits from people claiming the cosmetics damaged their skin."

"With the success and size of the company, I'd expect a certain number of lawsuits," Morgan said. "There are always people looking for easy money. Do any of the cases look valid?"

"Not really." Jenny tucked a gray hair behind her ear. "The company's research and testing seem adequate. No doubt some will settle for low dollar amounts simply because it would be cheaper than going to court. None of the claims are for serious injury. No one went blind or died from using Wild products."

Morgan looked up from her notepad. "Did you find anything unusual about the victim and/or his family?"

His mom ran a finger down her own paper notes. "Nothing on Noah Carter, but Adam has a record for assault. In his senior year of high school, he and another student turned in identical test papers. The teacher gave them both Fs. Adam claims the other boy cheated off his paper. He went to the boy's house and waited for him to come home, then attacked him."

"How badly did he hurt the other kid?" Lance asked.

"The other boy suffered a broken nose and fractured cheekbone. Witnesses stated that Adam 'lost his mind' and 'went berserk.'" Jenny added, "He didn't go to jail. His parents paid a fine, he got probation, and attended mandatory counseling. He was charged as an adult, so the record wasn't sealed."

Morgan looked up from her notes. "Adam has a history of violent reactions and no impulse control."

"I wonder where he was Friday night," Lance said.

And how Adam felt about fire . . .

Morgan twirled her pen. "He said he was angry with us for representing the person who killed Noah. Would he really kill his own brother?"

"We both know it's possible. People can rationalize anything. He wouldn't be the first man to kill his brother. We've both seen family members tear each other apart. Guilt would amplify his grief. What if he blamed Haley for an argument he'd had with Noah?"

"You're right," Morgan said. "But we don't know where he is, and he's already wanted by the police. Even if he's found, we won't have access to him for a long time."

"I'm still digging. I might have more for you tomorrow." His mom set her list down on her blotter and frowned at Morgan, then at Lance. "You should both get some rest. You look exhausted."

"I'm fine," Morgan assured her. "Thank you for all this information. We really appreciate the help."

Jenny sat back. "I'm glad you came to me. I thought maybe you lost confidence in me after what happened last fall."

"No." Lance jumped in, hating that she'd been thinking that all winter. "Not at all. That was not your fault. We didn't want to give you any additional stress while you were recovering. You're teaching, and you have your own business to run."

His mom smiled. "Honestly, I wish you would have asked me anyway. I would have welcomed the work. I don't like to be idle. Gives me too much time to think."

And overthink.

"OK, then," Lance said. "Consider yourself back to work."

She smiled. "Wonderful."

"How's Kevin?" Morgan asked.

Jenny only saw her boyfriend once a week at their group therapy session. But Jenny and Kevin talked via video call every evening.

"Very well. His son is getting married," Jenny said, glancing back and forth between Morgan and Lance.

Was that a hint? Whatever it was, Lance was glad his mother's relationship had survived the winter. She needed someone her own age in her life.

"That's wonderful." Morgan stood.

"We have to go. Bye, Mom." He kissed his mother on the cheek, then straightened and moved out of the way as Morgan rounded the desk to give his mom a quick hug.

They left the house. Lance locked the front door, and they climbed into the Town Car.

Morgan tucked her giant bag next to her feet. "We have two strong possibilities for the arson: Adam, and Kieran, if he discovered that you stole his photographs."

"Good thing I locked those in the office safe."

"We don't have a motive for Adam as a suspect for his brother's murder, but as you pointed out, families are complex, and we have little information about the brothers' relationship. We need to learn more."

"Sharp is tracking down Noah's ex-girlfriend Callie Fisher today." Lance opened his phone and typed a text to Sharp. "He's going to see her this morning. Maybe she can tell us more about his family. I'll send him a message to ask about the relationship between the brothers."

"Have we discounted Piper as a suspect?"

"We shouldn't write her off just yet, but she's moved down my list. Her motivation doesn't seem as strong."

"Unless there's something we haven't learned about her yet. Kieran's motivation for killing Noah is clear. He was jealous."

"What about Justin and his arrest for date rape?" Lance started the engine.

"I think we'd better talk to him today too."

"Maybe we should ask Isaac or Chase about it first. If Justin killed Noah, then Isaac and Chase are covering for him by providing him with an alibi. We could explain how that makes them accessories."

"We will make no appointments this time. I want to question them individually, and I don't want them to be prepared to see us."

"Right." Lance leaned across the console and planted a kiss on Morgan's mouth.

"Not that I didn't enjoy it, but what was that for?" She smiled.

"For understanding my mother and trying to minimize her fears." Lance settled back into his seat.

"I know it didn't work, and I feel bad that McFarland's attack will affect her too."

"Some things are beyond our control."

"I know, but I love your mom. She's part of the family." Morgan fastened her seat belt.

Family.

The more time Lance spent with Morgan and her family, the less he wanted to live alone. Before their relationship, he thought he was content enough. But now he knew what he'd been missing. He wanted to help her get the kids ready for school every morning. He wanted to go to sleep with her every night and wake up with her by his side.

He wanted to be a part of her life rather than an accessory to it.

He was ready to make their relationship a formal commitment. Despite the events of the day, warmth filled him. Six months ago, the mere thought of becoming a stepfather to three little girls would have sent him into a panic attack. But now the idea filled him with happiness and memories of Christmas morning. Morgan's kids racing into the family room at dark o'clock. Their high-pitched squeals of joy as they ripped through wrapping paper, the excitement of the day alone making them—and Lance—happy. Lance and Morgan sitting on the floor with the children, drinking coffee, very much feeling like a couple.

That's what he wanted every day.

But what did Morgan want? Was she content living in Scarlet Falls and working as a defense attorney, or did she miss being a prosecutor more than she would admit?

"I can't help but feel awful for Noah Carter's family." Morgan rested her head against the window.

"I appreciate that you can see both sides of the case, but there's no point torturing yourself." Lance started the engine. "There isn't anything you can do to help that family."

"No. Defending Haley is our job." Morgan looked over at him, her eyes bleak. "Who do you want to talk to first?"

"Let's try Isaac and Chase." Lance turned onto the highway and pressed the accelerator, not feeling half of the confidence he'd tried to project. They had theories and possibilities to investigate but nothing concrete. Juries loved fingerprints and DNA and everything else they'd seen on *CSI*. The prosecutor had a mountain of physical evidence that pointed directly at Haley as the killer.

Chapter Thirty-Two

At eleven o'clock Friday morning, Sharp handed Noah Carter's ex-girlfriend a business card through the open door of her apartment. "I'm investigating Noah Carter's death. I was hoping you would answer a few questions about him."

Callie Fisher lived in the residential district of downtown Scarlet Falls. The huge colonial had been converted into apartments.

"I can try," the young brunette said. Instead of inviting Sharp into her apartment, she stepped out onto the long porch and pulled her door closed behind her.

Sharp approved of her lack of trust. *Smart girl.*

On the long front porch, four white wicker chairs faced the street. Callie walked to one and sat down. Sharp followed her, angling his chair so he could see her face.

She pulled her knees to her chest and hugged them. "I couldn't believe it when I heard he'd been killed."

Sharp commiserated with a nod. "How long did you date him?"

"Not long, less than two months." She stared at the street, her focus inward.

"When was the last time you saw him?"

"I ran into him in the grocery store a few weeks ago." She plucked at a hole in the knee of her jeans. When she looked up, her expression was wry. "This is a small town. You can't avoid seeing an old boyfriend."

"No. I imagine you can't. Were there hard feelings between you and Noah?"

"Aren't there always?" Her lips flattened, as she carefully considered her answer. "If the relationship had been perfect, we'd still be dating."

"Good point." Sharp nodded. "Did you break up with Noah, or did he break up with you?"

Her jaw tightened. "I broke up with him."

Sharp heard nothing but honesty and sincerity in her voice. He waited to see if she offered a reason, but she didn't seem anxious to share. Her reluctance piqued his interest.

"Why did you break up with him?" he prompted.

She swallowed, her gaze returning to the street as a minivan cruised by. "Look. I don't really want to say bad things about him. He's dead. His parents are suffering enough. They don't need to read about their son's faults in the newspaper."

"I'm not a reporter," Sharp said.

Callie turned critical eyes on him. "Who are you working for?"

Sharp had hoped to keep his association with the defense to himself for now. Presumption of innocence was a legal term. Most of the time, the public assumed the defendant was guilty, and Callie seemed more loyal to Noah's parents than to his memory.

But asked directly, he couldn't lie. They might need her to testify.

"The attorney hired to defend Haley Powell," Sharp said.

Callie didn't look surprised. But then, Sharp had already established that she was intelligent.

"Noah had his good points," she began. "He was cute in a geeky way. Sometimes he was disarmingly adorable." The corner of her mouth quirked up, as if she were remembering something specific.

Sharp waited. He could sense a big, fat *but* was coming.

"But every time we'd hang out, I'd wake up with the worst hangover. I was no angel in college. I had my share of evenings to regret. But after the first year or so of college, the partying grew old. These days, I'm a one-or-two-drink girl. I teach grammar school at the Young Academy."

"The private school on Oak Street?" Sharp asked.

"More specifically, the Christian private school. The last thing I need is for a picture of my sloppy-drunk self to show up on social media. The parents of my students would go ballistic. One whiff of scandal, and I would lose my job."

"So what does this have to do with Noah?"

"He had—how can I say this tactfully? Noah's sexual appetites were a little more adventurous than mine." A blush stained her cheeks. "I like fruity, girly drinks. No matter what I ordered, he would bring me a double. If we were at his house, he added extra alcohol to mine. Face it, after a drink or two, particularly doubles, I wasn't thinking clearly. I'm embarrassed to admit this, but it took me a while to figure out what he was doing. When I did, I felt incredibly stupid."

"Did you confront him?"

"I did. He said I was a prude, and he was just trying to loosen me up." The red of her cheeks darkened with anger. "I broke up with him immediately. Who would date a guy she can't trust?"

"Smart of you."

"Look, I'm not saying Noah was a terrible person. He didn't deserve to die. But he wasn't perfect."

"No one is," Sharp agreed. "How well do you know Noah's friends?"

"We hung out with them a few times." She folded her hands, and her head tilted. She was deciding whether to tell him something.

Sharp waited. He'd questioned enough people to know when to push and when to be patient. Callie needed patience. If he pushed her, she'd toss him off her porch.

"Honestly, I didn't like hanging out with his friends, and Noah spent *a lot* of time with them."

"Every man needs some guy time." Sharp had his retired cop buddies.

"True." Callie nodded. "Maybe I'm being too harsh, but they all seemed to resent me. They didn't have girlfriends. I definitely felt like the fifth wheel."

"How did Noah get along with his family?"

"His parents are nice. Maybe too nice."

"Can someone be too nice?" Sharp asked.

"Noah and his brother were indulged." She laughed, but the sound was tight and strained. "Maybe I *am* just too uptight."

When she went quiet, Sharp pressed for more. "How did Noah get along with his brother?"

"Adam has issues." She watched the mail truck move from house to house across the street, her mouth turned down, as if she were deciding how much to reveal.

"I know you probably feel like you're betraying confidences, but Noah is dead. The right person should be convicted of killing him. If you know something, holding back might put an innocent woman in prison."

Callie turned to face Sharp again. Her eyes narrowed as she studied him. "You really think she's innocent?"

Since he was asking for her complete honesty, Sharp offered his to her. "I think so. But I want to be one hundred percent sure."

Her head dipped in a small nod. "I never witnessed any fight between the brothers, but Noah did tell me about a few incidents from his childhood. When Adam was five, he stabbed Noah in the neck with a pencil. Noah had a small scar from it. When he was seven, Adam tried to set the house on fire in the middle of the night. The family's retriever gave him away." Callie's eyes hardened. "A week later, the dog died. Noah suspected Adam had poisoned her."

Sharp leaned back and absorbed the information.

Adam was a psycho.

"That's all I know." Callie stood.

"Thank you for talking to me." Sharp rose and shook her hand. "Can I call you if I have more questions?"

"I suppose, but I'd rather you didn't." She wrapped her arms around her middle.

"Call me if there's anything else you want to tell me." Sharp jogged down the porch steps and hurried to his Prius.

Could Adam have killed his brother? And why?

Chapter Thirty-Three

"They're avoiding us." Eating the last bite of her chicken sandwich, Morgan stared through the windshield at Isaac's house. Though his car was parked out front, he hadn't responded to their knock on his door. He'd also ignored her phone call. Chase had done the same. She crumpled the sandwich wrapper and stuffed it into the fast-food bag. Lance had already finished his lunch.

"That's what I would do if I were them." Lance turned the car around.

Morgan's phone pinged with an incoming email. She read the display. "Let's stop at the office. A forensic report just came in."

Lance drove into town and cruised past what had been his home.

Caution tape and barricades blocked off his lot. Smoke curled from the burned-out shell that had been his house. One fire truck still sat out front, no doubt waiting for the ashes to stop smoldering.

"Oh, my God, Lance." Morgan pressed a palm to her chest. Emotions clogged her throat. The bed he'd been sleeping in was in that pile of charred debris. "When I think you were in there . . ."

She'd known at the hospital that he could have died, but seeing the evidence was a slap of reality. He was very lucky to be alive. Gratefulness filled her. *She* was lucky he was alive.

Lance reached for her hand. "It didn't look like that when I was in it."

"With multiple points of origin, it must have gone up very quickly."

"Let's go to work." Lance put the car in gear. "This is just a house. Haley's life is much more important."

But the investigation was dragging them into dangerous places. *Again*. But then, what did she expect? They were pursuing a killer, who presumably didn't want to be caught.

Lance cruised the six blocks to the office. Sharp's Prius was parked out front when they arrived. They went inside and found him in the kitchen brewing tea.

"Oh, good, you're here." Sharp rubbed his palms together. "Want to know what I learned from Callie Fisher?"

"I hope it's a break in the case. We really need one of those." Morgan deposited her coat and bag on a chair and eased into the next seat.

"It might be more than one." Sharp bounced on his toes with more energy than he'd shown in days.

Lance leaned on the wall. "What did she say?"

"One, Noah liked to give her extra booze, and two, his brother, Adam, sounds like a psychopath." Sharp poured three cups of green tea while he gave them the details on his interview.

Then Lance filled Sharp in on his mother's report.

Sharp studied Morgan's face. "You should take a cat nap."

Morgan realized she must still look terrible, because Sharp placed an organic oatmeal cookie on a plate and laid it next to her. She blew across the steaming cup of tea to cool it. "A forensic report just came in. The trace evidence has been processed."

"Lance and I can read through it." Sharp's jaw set. "This is a team effort."

Morgan wanted to argue, but the throbbing of her head stopped her. "You're right. I'll close my eyes for twenty minutes."

Sharp's brows dropped. "You're not arguing?"

She nibbled on the cookie. "If I rest for a little while, I'll be more useful in the long run."

Morgan walked into Sharp's office and stretched out on the couch. Her eyelids slammed shut as soon as she was horizontal. When she opened them, a glance at her phone told her that someone had turned off the alarm she'd set for twenty minutes. Nearly two hours had passed. She sat upright, annoyed. But the pain in her head had been replaced with grogginess.

She stopped in the kitchen to reheat her tea in the microwave and grab another cookie. She found her partners in her office. Lance sat behind her desk reading his laptop. Sharp had spread out printed pages on the opposite side of the desk.

When she walked in, he put the cap on his yellow highlighter. "You look better."

"I feel better," she admitted as she took a bite of the cookie.

"You need something to eat. Be right back." Sharp bustled out of the room.

Lance got up from behind the desk and gestured to it. "I need to pace anyway."

Morgan took her place in her chair.

Sharp carried a steaming bowl back into her office and set it in front of her. "Chicken soup."

"Thank you." Morgan inhaled. Her stomach rumbled. "Did you make this?"

"Yes." Sharp looked offended. "Do you think I'd feed you something processed?"

"No, of course not." She lifted the spoon to her lips. "I just didn't know when you had the time."

"It was in my freezer." Sharp dropped into the chair facing her desk.

She savored the soup. "Have you talked to Eliza today?"

"Yes," Sharp said. "Haley had a bad reaction to the medication the psychiatrist prescribed."

"What kind of a reaction?" Morgan asked.

"She was dizzy." Sharp ran a hand through his short hair. "Probably low blood pressure caused by her Addison's disease. The doctor prescribed a different medicine. Eliza said she did sleep last night, though."

"That's something," Morgan said.

Sharp rubbed his eyes. "Yes, but Eliza is worried about any potential reactions to the new meds. I'm going to stay there tonight so Eliza can get a decent night of sleep."

"That's good." Morgan dipped her spoon in the bowl again. "Haley needs more than just a bodyguard. She needs emotional support."

Cheered by less pain in her head and more food in her belly, Morgan ate the entire bowl in five minutes. "Did you find anything while I was sleeping?"

Lance's face brightened. "We most certainly did."

"What?" Excitement over a potential lead cleared Morgan's head even more.

"Dog hair." Lance grinned. "Black dog hair. Found on the collar of Noah's T-shirt. The lab is testing for the specific breed. But guess who has a black dog?"

Morgan hadn't seen the dog, but from the look on Lance's face, he could only be talking about one person. "Kieran Hart?"

"Yes." Lance clasped his hands behind his back and rocked back on his heels.

"That's a pretty damned good lead." Morgan scraped up a few drops of soup remaining in the bottom of the bowl.

Lance nodded. "Do we call the sheriff first or go ambush Kieran with the information?"

Morgan pushed the empty bowl away. "I know you like Sheriff Colgate, Sharp, but I already have multiple calls in to him. He is simply ignoring us."

"Yes, he is," Sharp agreed. "Colgate is a straight shooter, but he's in way over his head."

"So you vote for ambushing Hart?" Lance smiled.

"Yes." Morgan drank her tea. "The sheriff hasn't responded to my previous messages. He will not be able to claim we withheld information."

Lance nodded. "Finish your tea, then we'll go pester Kieran about his alibi."

They would not mention the dog hair. There was no reason to tip their hand to Kieran.

"I'm heading to the pub to see what the boys know about Noah's murder case." Sharp picked up Morgan's empty bowl and left the room.

Sharp was the youngest of his retired cop friends, but he referred to the group affectionately as *the boys*. They gossiped more than any women Morgan knew.

"I'll bring my tea with me." Morgan poured her tea into a stainless steel travel mug. "Do you know where Kieran is?"

Lance whipped out his phone. "Let's find out." Three calls later, he smiled. "He's in the family trust office this afternoon. Do we want to talk to him there or go to Justin's house now and wait to see Kieran at home later?"

"He's going to be angry." Morgan put on her coat and gathered her bag. "His office would be more public. He likely has surveillance cameras and other employees there."

Lance walked out of the room. He reappeared in a few seconds wearing a jacket. "You're right. His mansion is private. It would be too easy for him to kill us and have his majordomo dispose of our bodies."

"I was thinking about the dog. You already have holes in your pants and boot. I'd rather not have them in your person."

"Excellent point. The office it is."

They went outside and climbed into the sedan. Lance drove toward the interstate. A few miles down the highway, he took the exit for Route 32. In three-quarters of a mile, the GPS prompted that they'd reached their destination, a four-story office building made of green-tinted glass.

They went into the lobby. Morgan read the directory. "Fourth floor."

They rode the elevator and stepped out. Gold block letters on a glass door spelled HART FAMILY TRUST.

Lance held the door open, and Morgan led the way inside. The office was larger than she'd anticipated.

A slim, blonde woman sat at a black lacquer and glass reception desk. She wore a navy-blue sheath dress, heels, and pearls. Behind her, a half dozen employees manned phones and computers at open work-stations. Morgan and Lance crossed a few yards of thick gray carpeting and stopped in front of the blonde.

She greeted Morgan with a cool smile but gave Lance a not-so-cool once-over and lifted a haughty brow at him. "May I help you?"

"We'd like to see Kieran Hart." Morgan reached into her pocket for a business card. She could have been invisible, because the blonde completely ignored her.

"Allow me." Lance handed his card across the desk.

The blonde glanced at it. "Do you have an appointment, Mr. Kruger?"

"No. But Mr. Hart will want to see us." Lance smiled at her.

She smiled back. "Then I'll tell him you're here." She stood and pivoted. She treated Lance to plenty of hip sway as she sashayed toward her boss's office. In case he didn't know the performance was for his benefit, she glanced over her shoulder and sent him a heated look before she knocked on the door and went inside.

Lance leaned close to Morgan's ear. "You want to roll your eyes, don't you?"

"So much," Morgan said under her breath. But she couldn't blame the woman. Lance, with his chiseled face and jacked body, attracted plenty of female attention.

The blonde emerged a few minutes later. A harried frown replaced her sexy attitude. "You can go in now."

Kieran was no doubt a difficult boss, and he was likely not thrilled about their visit.

Morgan led the way into Kieran's office. He sat behind a huge black desk, his features fixed in a neutral expression. A low growl pulled Morgan's gaze to the giant black-and-brown dog that sat next to him. The irony of the dog's presence was not lost on her. The dog locked its attention on Lance. Its lips peeled away from its giant white canines.

Morgan felt confident handling Kieran, but a 120-pound Rottweiler with a head the size of a bear's made her hands sweat. She was a dog lover, but the giant black beast did not look friendly.

Kieran stroked the dog's back. Like the dog, his focus was locked on Lance. "It seems that Luther doesn't like you. I can't imagine why."

"Me either." Lance's tone was bland.

Morgan wiped a palm on her thigh. How fast could that dog get across the office? Too fast.

Next to her, Lance's hand flexed next to his weapon.

Kieran sneered. "You would shoot such a magnificent creature?"

"Who said I would shoot the *dog*?" Lance reached behind him and pulled the door closed. But they didn't move any closer to Kieran and Luther. "Now let's get down to business. We know you were out all night Friday."

Kieran scratched under his dog's chin, but Luther was fixated on Lance. "I wasn't watching the clock."

"You left Beats at ten thirty and arrived home at four o'clock the following morning," Lance pressed. "Where were you during all that time?"

"I told you I went for a long drive."

"For nearly six hours?" Lance asked.

"What are you suggesting?" Kieran's voice dropped an octave.

Lance took a step closer. "That you followed Haley and Noah to his house."

"That's ridiculous." Kieran stood.

Luther growled. The two men stared at each other for a few seconds. As two alpha males, neither would back down.

Sensing a stalemate, Morgan butted in. "Mr. Hart, we're not suggesting anything. But given your recent breakup with Haley, it would certainly ease our minds if you could verify your location at some point during the night."

Kieran's gaze shifted to her, his expression only slightly less aggressive. "I don't have to give you an alibi. You aren't the police. I don't even have to speak to you."

"This is true." Morgan lifted her hands, palms out, surrendering. "We'll be happy to pass our information along to the sheriff. Then you can speak directly with him." She turned toward the door, taking Lance's arm and spinning him around. Being charged with harassment would only hinder their investigation. Better to leave and try to get information from other sources.

"Wait," Kieran called.

Morgan pivoted.

Kieran's lip curled and his face pinched, as if cooperating with them was the equivalent of wading through raw sewage. He opened the center drawer of his desk and took out a slip of paper. He held it across the desk. "I found this in the console of my car after we spoke last time. It's a copy of a gas receipt. I was in Syracuse at one a.m."

Morgan reached for the receipt. The dog's growl grew louder. Sweat dripped between her shoulder blades, and her shirt stuck to her back as she read the slip of paper. The receipt was time-stamped 1:17 a.m.

"I had nothing to do with that man's death." Kieran sat back in his leather chair. "I trust you're satisfied?"

"Thank you for sharing the receipt," Morgan said.

Kieran's nod was curt. "We're done here. I've been more than cooperative. I am not answering any more of your questions."

Morgan took a step backward toward the door. The dog's gaze shifted to her. Kieran's eyes were cold, and there was a darkness in them that made her believe that deep down, he wanted to set the dog on them. She knew he wouldn't. He wasn't stupid. But he wanted to.

Lance moved sideways, angling his body between her and the dog.

"Oh, and Ms. Dane?" Kieran's lip curled. "Thank you for the warning. I'll put my attorney on notice in case the sheriff comes calling."

"Do you think you're going to need him?" His arrogance grated on Morgan. "Is that the same attorney who convinced the Connecticut authorities to drop the stalking charges?"

"It is." Kieran smirked, then his expression darkened further. "Now please get out of my office. If you wish to speak with me again, you can contact my lawyer."

"I'll speak with your attorney anytime," Morgan said. She wasn't afraid of Kieran or his lawyer. The dog was another issue all together. Anyone with a brain would be wary of a huge, angry canine.

Kieran said nothing as Morgan and Lance backed out of the room. Lance shut the door behind them. He detoured to the blonde receptionist's desk on the way out of the office. "Mr. Hart has one big dog. Does he bring it to the office often?"

"Yes." The blonde's forehead furrowed. "All the time." She glanced back at her boss's door, the set of her lips and curl of her shoulders implying she was not a fan of Luther.

Morgan led the way back to the elevator. Relief swept over her as the heavy steel doors closed. "I love dogs, but I'll pass on petting that one."

"Me too." Lance wrapped an arm around her shoulders. "What do you think of Kieran's alibi?"

"Syracuse is roughly two and a half hours from here." Morgan buttoned her coat. "The receipt was time-stamped just after one a.m. His neighbor's surveillance camera caught him arriving home at four a.m. That wouldn't leave him much time to kill Noah."

The elevator doors opened, and Lance followed Morgan through the lobby and outside. They crossed the parking lot and climbed into the car. "Assuming Kieran can't be the killer because he was driving all over New York State while Noah was being stabbed, where does that leave us?"

"Is there any way he could have faked that receipt?"

"I suppose the slip could have been altered. But he used a credit card for payment. If the DNA on the dog hair is verified to be a Rottweiler, then we'll have grounds to subpoena his credit card statement to support the transaction. There isn't anything else we can do with Kieran until we get that report, which we both know could take weeks or months."

"We'll back-burner Kieran as the lead suspect for now."

Morgan reached for her travel mug. She chugged the lukewarm liquid, then rubbed her temple. The dull ache in her head had returned. Extra-strength pain relievers had little effect. Sleep was the only remedy.

Lance frowned at her. "How's the headache?"

"The same." She dropped her hand. "It's no worse. I'm just frustrated with the case."

"Maybe we should call it a day? It's getting late."

She stared out the passenger window. Clouds had blown in during the afternoon. It would be dark soon. "That two-hour nap you let me take ate up too much of our afternoon. Let's at least try to talk to Justin before we wrap up the day." Morgan would spend the weekend reading and rereading every piece of evidence they had accumulated so far.

Her phone rang, and she answered the call. "Hi, Sharp. You're on speaker."

"I just left the pub. No one knew anything about Noah's murder case. Colgate was furious when the initial case details were leaked to the press. Now he's keeping information under tight wraps. But I did learn something very unexpected. Shannon Yates was at Beats the Saturday night before Noah was murdered."

Morgan stared at the phone. "But the news report said she'd last been seen at work the previous Friday. The sheriff's department claimed that's when she went missing."

"That's what the sheriff's department previously thought," Sharp said. "Apparently she went to the bar alone and paid cash. There was no record of her visit. The police just learned she'd been there. One of the bouncers came forward yesterday after seeing her picture on the news."

Static sounded over the connection.

Morgan leaned closer to the phone. "This *is* a surprising development."

"That's all I got." Sharp's words were broken with spaces of dead air. "The deputies I knew in the department have all quit. We need a leak from someone who is still there. I wonder . . ."

A few seconds of quiet passed.

"Sharp, are you still there?" Lance asked.

"Yes," Sharp said. "Sorry. I was thinking. We're losing our connection. I'll get back to you."

The line went dead.

Lance said, "I was curious about the Shannon Yates case, and I didn't like its coincidental timing and similarities with Haley's, but I didn't predict a link this strong between the two cases."

"No." Morgan tapped her lower lip with a forefinger. "I don't want to get ahead of the investigation, but this could change everything. We need to know where all of our suspects were the night Shannon Yates went missing."

"Definitely."

"Shannon Yates was just identified yesterday." Morgan used her smartphone to search for more information. "According to the local news, Shannon worked at the Lakeview Inn in Grey's Hollow. Her boss is the person who reported her missing."

"Shall we take a ride past the Lakeview Inn and talk to Shannon Yates's employers?"

"Yes." Morgan pulled up the inn's website on her smartphone. "The inn is owned by Carol and Bob Shaker."

"Here's hoping the Shakers will talk to us."

"It's frustrating that we can't compel anyone to answer our questions. As a prosecutor, I had some authority. Now witnesses treat me like I'm a criminal."

"Just in this case. In previous investigations, we've found people who think the cops are the criminals."

"Where are all those people now?" Morgan asked.

Lance sighed. "There aren't enough career criminals in this case. No one is afraid of the police."

"But not because they're law-abiding citizens. Kieran is a voyeur and a pervert and has a history of stalking. Noah liked to sneak extra alcohol into his dates' drinks, Justin was once accused of date rape, and the victim's brother has a history of violent behavior and assault." Morgan rested her head against the seat. "This time, it isn't innocence that is making witnesses shut down on us. It's guilt. Unfortunately, they all think they'll get away with whatever they've done."

Chapter Thirty-Four

Lance slowed the car and took in the impressive property.

The Lakeview Inn sat on a large chunk of prime waterfront real estate. The main building was an old Victorian mansion with an enclosed front porch that spanned the length of the building and a two-story round turret that ended in a spire. The inn was beautifully maintained. Freshly painted gingerbread trim gleamed white against dark-gray clapboards. Several smaller buildings were spread out on the lawn behind the main building. Behind them, the late afternoon sun shimmered on Grey Lake.

"I can't believe what I'm seeing." Morgan's voice was stunned.

"What is it?" Lance doubted it was the gorgeous view that Morgan was gawking at.

She pointed out the passenger window.

He followed her finger to the side yard of the inn. "I don't see . . ." And then he did.

Stuck in the grass next to the neatly trimmed shrubs was a bright-green McFarland Landscaping lawn sign.

"I can't say that I've been truly speechless very many times in my life, but I actually don't have words to describe how I feel." Morgan turned to Lance. "McFarland has been to the inn where Shannon Yates worked."

"That does seem to be a whopping coincidence." The parking lot was full, and Lance drove up and down the rows looking for a spot. "McFarland punched you and has a record of violent assault. I would have no difficulty believing that he killed Shannon Yates."

"He has no connection to Noah that we've seen."

Thankfully, McFarland had been denied bail. If he was tied up in the case, at least he was safely behind bars.

"We don't know that the cases are definitely connected." Lance parked the Town Car, and they entered the inn. The lobby was just as well maintained as the exterior. An open doorway opened into a restaurant. Inside, glass clinked as staff arranged place settings on white tablecloths. A sign announced that the dinner hour started at five o'clock. Lance glanced at his watch. Four o'clock.

"Good timing," he said. "This place looks like it'll be hopping in another hour or two."

"It's Friday. The restaurant will probably be busy tonight." Morgan walked up to the registration desk tucked into an alcove under the curving staircase.

The slim woman behind the desk was in her fifties, but a sleek bob and funky gray-tinted glasses made her look younger, as did her wide smile. "Can I help you?"

"Are Mr. or Mrs. Shaker in?" Morgan asked.

The woman lowered her glasses from her nose. "I'm Carol Shaker."

Morgan fished a business card from her bag. She glanced around. Two guests studied a display of activity brochures near the window. "Is there any way we could talk privately? We'll try not to take up too much of your time."

Carol replaced her glasses and read the card. Her smile faltered, as if by reading it she knew what they'd come to discuss. "Yes. Just give me a moment."

She summoned a young man in a suit. "Tony, please cover registrations for a few minutes."

"Yes, ma'am." Tony took her place behind the desk.

"Follow me." Carol led them down a hallway to a meticulously neat and organized office. Carol rounded the antique mahogany desk and sat behind it. She gestured to two equally old schoolhouse chairs that faced her. "Is this about Shannon?"

Morgan perched in the wooden chair. "Yes."

"You're a lawyer. Have they arrested someone in her death?" Carol asked.

"Not that I've heard." Morgan introduced Lance. "We're actually working another case, and we've come across something that might tie the two together."

Carol leaned back in her chair. "I'll do anything I can to help find the man who hurt Shannon."

The old chair creaked and shifted as Lance sat on it. "How long had Shannon been working here?"

"A few months. She started right before the Christmas holiday." Carol took a long breath. "I hired her as a favor. Her mother is a friend of a friend, and Shannon had been out of work for some time."

"Was she a good employee?" he asked.

"Very." Carol rocked forward and leaned her forearms on her desk. "Shannon was reliable. She worked her butt off. She appreciated the job, and it showed." Carol blinked back a tear. "I reported her missing to the police. When she didn't show up for work, I knew something was wrong."

"Did she act normally the last time you saw her?" Morgan used a gentle voice.

"She seemed perfectly normal," Carol said. "I still can't believe—" A sob cut off her words. Her eyes filled with tears. She plucked a tissue from a box on her desk. "I'm sorry."

"Take as much time as you need." Morgan waited until the woman took several deep breaths and collected herself. "When did you last see her?"

Carol wiped her nose with the tissue. "Friday, February 23. She had the weekend off and wasn't due back until Monday."

Lance leaned forward. "Is it unusual to give your staff weekends off? Aren't those your busiest days?"

Carol nodded. "Only one or two employees can have off each weekend. They rotate. It was Shannon's turn." Carol pressed the tissue to her face. "It was her first weekend off."

"But she didn't mention any specific plans?" he asked.

Had Shannon been excited for her weekend off? It would have been her first opportunity to spend a Saturday night at the club.

"No." Carol tossed her tissue in the trash can under her desk and took a fresh one.

Morgan slipped her phone from her bag and pulled up a picture of Roger McFarland. "Do you recognize this man?"

Carol put her glasses on and glanced at the phone. "No. Who is he?"

How could she not know her own landscaper? Lance wanted to call bullshit, but he saw no duplicity in her face.

"Would you look closer?" Morgan handed her the phone.

Carol took a second, longer look and frowned. "He still doesn't look familiar."

"His name is Roger McFarland, and his landscaping sign is in your side yard." Lance studied her face.

"Oh." Carol shrugged. "I've never met the owner of the company. A foreman and crew come out once a week to cut the grass in season. They also handle our spring and fall cleanups and take care of snow removal. Neither Bob nor I can handle the backbreaking work anymore."

"You don't know if Mr. McFarland has ever been to the inn?" Lance asked.

"My husband handles the outside maintenance." Carol handed Morgan's phone back. "Would you like me to ask Bob?"

Morgan slid her phone back into her bag. "That would be very helpful."

Carol sent a text. "He should be here in a minute."

True to her word, a middle-aged man in gray slacks and a blue button-down shirt came into the office. He gave Morgan and Lance curious looks.

His wife introduced them. "They're here about Shannon."

Bob's eyes softened, and he closed the office door. "We're all very upset about her death."

"We're sorry to dredge it all up again," Lance began. "But can you tell us if Roger McFarland has been to the inn since Shannon was hired?"

Bob took off his wire-rimmed glasses and cleaned them on his shirt, his head cocked, as if he were thinking. "I don't think so. I haven't seen Roger since September, when we met to discuss the fall cleanup and the replacement of a couple of shrubs. Usually, I deal with his foreman."

Disappointment slipped thorough Lance. "But the crew has been here to clear snow?"

"Yes." Bob hooked his glasses behind his ears. "We had quite a few snowfalls this year. We're very happy for the early spring."

The winter had been cold and snowy.

"Is there any way to know for sure if Shannon was working on any of the days that McFarland's crew came to do snow removal?" Lance asked.

"Why?" Bob's eyes narrowed. "Is Roger mixed up in this?"

"We have no evidence of that," Morgan said quickly. "The fact that he contracts with your inn is probably a simple coincidence."

"I don't have a record of the times he came to plow and shovel. I pay a monthly fee, and he removes any snow deeper than a couple of inches." Bob propped a hand on his hip. "His company contracts with many of the local businesses. In fact, I got his name from Peter Wence, who owns that retail strip down the road. I believe you'll see McFarland's yard signs all over this area."

253

Lance considered the information. As a previous offender with a history of violence and no respect for women, Roger McFarland was an excellent suspect. On the other hand, linking McFarland to Shannon's murder might sever the connection with Noah's case.

"Do you need anything else?" Bob asked, glancing at his watch. "The restaurant will be opening soon."

"Just one more thing." Morgan opened her tote and took out some photos in an envelope. She turned them to face Carol, dealing them out on the desk like a game of solitaire: Kieran, Isaac, Justin, Chase, Noah, and Adam. "Do you recognize any of these young men?"

Both Carol and Bob scanned the pictures and nodded without any hesitation.

Bob tapped Justin O'Brien's picture. "Justin made a new logo for the inn. The old one was terribly outdated. We had new menus, business cards, and brochures printed last month."

"Did Justin come to the inn?" Excitement gathered in Lance's gut.

"Just once. We found him through an online freelancer site. We discussed our needs in a phone call and emails. But he did come to the inn to show us a dozen potential designs. He didn't seem thrilled about the face-to-face meeting. I understand that most business today is conducted online, but I'm afraid I'm old-fashioned. I like to meet the people I'm going to do business with. And Justin was local, so there seemed to be no reason to make an exception."

"What did you think of Justin?" Lance kept his voice level, but inside he was encouraged for the first time since they'd taken this case.

"He was awkward and a little shy, but then I suppose he spends most of his day on the computer." Bob shook his head. "Young people today are losing their ability to talk to other people."

"Do either of you remember if Shannon was working when he came to the inn?" Morgan asked.

"We don't have to remember." Bob took out his phone. "I'll check my calendar."

Carol turned to the desktop computer on the other side of the L-shaped desk. She moved the mouse. When the screen brightened, she typed in a password.

Bob looked up from his phone. "Justin was here at five p.m. on January 9."

Carol tapped on the keyboard. "Shannon worked the registration desk that day from two to ten p.m."

Justin had been at the inn at the same time as Shannon.

Chapter Thirty-Five

Sharp paced his office, frustrated. Lance and Morgan had called to bring him up to speed on the case. If Shannon Yates had been at Beats the night she'd gone missing, then how was her case related to Haley's? Could Justin O'Brien be a serial rapist and killer? Even if he was and he killed Shannon, how did they tie the murder of Shannon Yates to Noah's death? Raping and strangling a woman was a very different crime from stabbing a man.

Justin O'Brien had done work for the inn where Shannon Yates had been employed. McFarland's landscaping sign had appeared at the same inn. Justin's link strengthened a connection between the cases, but McFarland's suggested the cases were unrelated.

What Sharp needed were more details on Shannon Yates's case, but how could he get more information when all his sources at the sheriff's department had quit or retired?

An idea wormed its way through his gut.

Who else had sources?

No.

He couldn't.

He'd feel like a traitor, like he'd be dealing with the enemy. Would Luke go to the Empire for help? No frigging way.

He crossed the floor of his office and spun around, his mind scrambling for other options.

Damn it!

Moving behind his desk, he opened the center drawer and fished for the business card. Then he pulled out his phone and dialed the number. Luke had been tempted by the dark side, and Sharp was more of a Han Solo than a Luke Skywalker anyway. And Solo was a smuggler. So what the hell.

The line rang twice, then she answered. "Olivia Cruz."

"Lincoln Sharp here." He swallowed his pride in one big gulp. "The last time you came to my office, you talked about working together."

"I did." Her voice was as smooth and cool as glass. "And you have my attention."

"I'm looking for information on the Shannon Yates case."

"Isn't everyone?"

"Look." Exhaustion weighted Sharp's shoulders. He dropped into his chair. Games irritated him. "I don't have time for banter. Bad things are happening to good people. Do you know anything or not?"

The line went silent. Sharp heard her take a breath. When she spoke again, her voice was serious.

"Actually, not much. I've had my head down in my writing project." She paused. "But I assume your question means there's a link between the Shannon Yates case and the murder of Noah Carter."

He knew she'd make the connection. Reporters were naturally nosey creatures. Ms. Cruz shouldn't be able to resist the lure of a mystery.

Sharp dangled the bait. "Shannon was at Beats the night she went missing."

"Oh." Her one-syllable response was loaded with surprise and interest. In the seconds of silence that followed, Sharp could practically hear her synapses firing over the cellular connection.

But Sharp's patience had worn razor thin. He was tired of waiting for a break. The case had put Lance and Morgan in danger. "I could probably get Shannon's case details on my own, but I'm short on time. Someone tried to kill my partner."

"I heard about the fire." Her voice was grave. "Your investigation has clearly made someone nervous."

"Only guilty people get nervous as an investigation proceeds."

"I could make a call."

"Would you?" Sharp asked.

"Give me an hour. Then you can meet me at this address." She rattled off a number and street in Scarlet Falls, barely a mile from his place.

"Thank you." Sharp ended the call feeling disconcerted. That had been too easy. Ms. Cruz had been far too agreeable for a reporter. He didn't trust her. Not at all. *Remember when Han trusted Lando?* Look where that had gotten him—frozen in carbonite and shuttled off to Jabba the Hutt.

Sharp drove to the address Ms. Cruz had given him and parked his Prius behind hers. He checked the number on the front of the white bungalow. Was this her house? He took in the picket fence, porch swing, and tidy garden. Except for the solar panels on the roof, the little cottage was small-town traditional. With her fashionable coat and skinny-heeled shoes, Sharp had expected her to live in something swanky, not homey.

He walked to the front door and knocked.

Ms. Cruz answered the door.

Sharp drew back, surprised. Instead of a polished outfit and pointy heels, she wore very worn jeans and a loose sweatshirt. Her feet were bare, and her toes sported candy-pink nail polish. Again, not what he'd expected.

"Are you coming in?" She stepped back. Without her shoes, the top of her head was barely level with his chin.

"Um. Yes." Sharp was uncomfortably short on words. He was uncomfortable period. Ms. Cruz wasn't falling into line with his preconceived notions.

She locked the door and led the way down a narrow hall into a bright, recently remodeled kitchen. A fan of all things renewable and sustainable, Sharp approved of the dark bamboo floors and gray recycled-glass kitchen counters. The scent of something spicy filled the air. In the center of the island, a bottle of red wine stood open to breathe next to a laptop computer.

"I like your house." He removed his jacket and hung it over the back of an island stool.

"So do I." She moved behind the laptop. "My aunt left me this house when she died. It isn't what I'd ever imagined I'd want, but I have good memories here, and I've made it my own. Now I can't imagine living anywhere else. Would you like some wine?"

"No, thank you." Though he did note that it was a very nice organic pinot noir. He did not want to let down his guard. Not around her. "I'm not much of a drinker."

She poured herself a small glass. "Before we start, I have to ask. Why did you call me today?"

Sharp leaned a hip on the island. After a minute, he decided on honesty. He was, after all, asking for a favor. "I spent all day trying to get details on the Shannon Yates case. But the sheriff is keeping the investigation sealed tighter than a mason jar. I started thinking about leaks and other possible sources. That train of thought led to you."

She sipped her wine. "I've already provided two good pieces of information for free."

Sharp corrected her. "Only the first one was gratis." *Just like a crack dealer.* "You bargained with Morgan for the second."

She nodded. "But I haven't received payment."

"You will." Sharp pulled his shoulders back. "Morgan is the most ethical, honest person I've ever worked with. You do not have to doubt her integrity."

"I don't." She swirled her wine, studying him. "Nor do I doubt yours."

The statement surprised him. He did not feel the same way about her.

259

She set down her wineglass. "I do my homework. Your firm and Morgan's have stellar reputations for pursuing the truth."

"She'll make good on her promise."

Ms. Cruz's fingers spread over her keyboard. "Do you have anything to offer in *this* exchange?"

So much for reporters seeking the truth for its own merits.

Frustrated, Sharp rocked on his heels. He had nothing. "No."

Would she refuse to help?

The smile that spread over her face was Cheshire-pleased. "Then I suppose you'll owe me a favor."

Damn. It.

"I'm sorry." Her lips curved more. She was enjoying this. "I didn't hear your response."

Had he said it out loud?

"Yes. I will owe you a favor." Sharp gritted his teeth. "With the caveat that the favor owed must be commensurate with the usefulness of the information you provide on the Shannon Yates case."

Laughing, she flexed her fingers. "You've been hanging out with a lawyer too long."

"Do we have a deal?" Sharp extended a hand over the island.

With a grin far too mischievous for Sharp's own good, Ms. Cruz wagged a finger at him. "I have a condition of my own to impose on this transaction."

"What is it?" Sharp snapped. Reporters were a giant pain in his—

"You must call me Olivia."

Sharp froze. "That's it?" Was she yanking his chain or was she serious?

"That's it." She nodded.

"OK, Olivia." Sharp drew out her name. What the hell? When you're neck-deep in league with the enemy, you may as well get to know her better.

"I will call you Lincoln."

"No one calls me Lincoln."

"I know." With a too-satisfied curve of her mouth, she scrolled and clicked on her computer. "What do you know about Shannon's case?"

He recited the basic facts the police hadn't been able to keep quiet: where she worked, the places her vehicle and body had been found, and the cause of death.

Olivia nodded. "This is what my source says. Shannon worked weekends at the inn and hadn't made any friends in Grey's Hollow yet. She was young and frustrated with the smallness of Grey's Hollow and its microscopic social scene. She was last seen at the nightclub Beats on Saturday, February 24. Surveillance videos of the club entrance and exit show that she arrived alone. The club has only been open for a short time, and they've had a few technical glitches."

Like missing video feeds.

"The night Shannon was there, the fire alarm and sprinklers in the kitchen went off at 11:32 p.m. Patrons were evacuated to the parking lot. Given the late hour, the club closed for the night."

"Everyone left at once."

"Yes," Olivia agreed. "The police have not been able to trace her movements after she left the club. She lives in a studio apartment over a private detached garage. Her landlord was on vacation. No one was there to see if she came home that night."

"Or if someone followed her home from the club." Sharp always assumed foul play and hoped to be pleasantly surprised if none had happened.

"Her apartment was clean and exceptionally neat," Olivia continued. "Her bed was made. There was no sign of a romantic rendezvous or break-in or struggle."

"If she met someone at the club, she could have gone home with him." Sharp paced the tiny kitchen.

"She did not show up for work on Monday. Though she'd only been at her job for a few months, her boss said she had proven herself to be very dependable. Shannon's boss is an older woman and has a reputation as the motherly type. She sent a coworker to Shannon's apartment to check on her. There was no answer, but her car wasn't there. The boss thought maybe she'd simply made a mistake. But when she didn't show up for work a second day, her boss called the police."

"The cops must have her credit card records."

"Shannon had declared bankruptcy two years ago. She'd been out of work multiple times before getting the job at the inn. She did not use credit cards."

"What about her cell phone?"

"It hadn't been used since the Thursday evening before she disappeared, when she called her mother in Maine. She prepaid for her minutes and used them sparingly. The phone was with her body. The battery had been removed."

"No one could track its location."

"Exactly." Olivia looked up from her computer.

"What about the body?" Sharp pivoted.

"We know Shannon Yates was raped, beaten, and strangled, and that she died with alcohol and zolpidem in her system," Olivia said. "I don't have a copy of the autopsy."

"No source at the medical examiner's office?" Sharp tried not to look disappointed. But none of this information was deal-with-the-Empire worthy. She hadn't provided many more details than weren't publicly available on the latest news channel. So far, the case was baffling, but he wasn't seeing any parallels to Noah's murder, except for the fact that they died a week apart after visiting Beats, and they both knew Justin O'Brien.

Sharp rubbed the back of his neck, a detail nagging at him. "Those lab results came back on Shannon Yates's autopsy awfully quickly. Usually, forensic toxicology reports take weeks or months. The only way they would have been expedited is if the ME was specifically looking for something."

Olivia's gaze snapped to his. "Do you think the ME has run across a similar case and was checking for similar details?"

"That would make a lot of sense."

She attacked her keyboard with renewed zeal.

National crime databases like the National Crime Information Center and the Violent Criminal Apprehension Program could be accessed only by law enforcement. If someone in the sheriff's department was performing a NCIC or ViCAP search for Olivia, he could be fired—not that Sharp was going to turn anyone in. Curious, he tried to casually peek over the top of her computer.

She tilted the screen down. "I will share the information. I cannot share the source."

Sharp resumed his pacing. "Now what?"

"We wait."

"I was afraid you were going to say that." Sharp huffed. "I don't like waiting."

She sipped her wine and licked her lips. "How about some vegetarian chili? I promise it's not poisoned."

Sharp hesitated.

She sighed and ladled chili into a bowl. "You might as well eat. Those return emails might take a while."

"All right."

Olivia handed him the bowl, and he sat on a stool and spooned chili into his mouth without tasting it, his mind on the case. She ate standing, one foot propped on the opposite knee like a stork. A ping sounded from her computer, and she tapped a few keys.

Excitement lit her eyes. "Last summer, the body of twenty-six-year-old Adele Smith was found in the woods in Redhaven. Adele had been beaten and raped. She had bruises around her neck consistent with choking, but the cause of death was a lethal combination of zolpidem and alcohol."

Sharp's blood chilled. "Since Redhaven is within Randolph County, the same medical examiner's office would have handled both Shannon's and Adele's autopsies."

"And Shannon's case was similar enough to Adele's to be flagged by the ME." Olivia scrolled on her computer. "Adele went missing after a big music festival. It was a huge outdoor event, so no surveillance cameras, lots of drugs and alcohol, and a few thousand out-of-towners. The Redhaven police got nowhere with their investigation. They found DNA from multiple sources on her body, but CODIS didn't turn up any matches."

The Combined DNA Index System (CODIS) was the national database of DNA collected from known offenders and recovered from suspects, victims, and crime scenes.

"Whoever attacked her wasn't in the system. Adele could have been his first victim."

"Possibly." Olivia nodded. "The sheriff's department and Redhaven police now suspect that Shannon's and Adele's murders could be related."

"Both women were raped, beaten, choked, and had zolpidem in their systems." Sharp slid off the stool, deposited his bowl in the sink, and resumed his pacing.

"But how are their murders connected to Noah Carter's?"

Shannon was connected to Noah through Justin O'Brien. But telling Olivia that felt like an overshare, so Sharp kept his mouth shut.

Her computer pinged again. Olivia narrowed her eyes like a cat that has just spotted a mouse. "I just received the surveillance footage from Beats for the night Shannon disappeared."

Sharp rubbed his palms together. "Now you're talking. We can see who interacted with her."

He moved to go around the island so he could see her computer screen. Maybe she'd be distracted and he could sneak a peek at the name of her source.

She closed her laptop. "I can show the videos on the television. It'll be easier to see. The screen is larger."

"Good idea," Sharp conceded.

She carried her laptop and wine into the next room, a cozy den. She set down the computer and glass, then turned on several lamps.

Sharp sat on the sofa. He leaned his forearms on his knees and waited. And sulked. Being on the favor-asking end of their relationship sucked.

Settling in a chair, she opened her laptop and angled it so that he couldn't see the screen.

"I thought we were working together," he said, frustrated.

"You're holding back information from me." Olivia arced a stubborn brow. "Don't try to deny it. I can see your mind spinning, and yet you say nothing."

"I have client confidentiality concerns." Moral superiority lifted Sharp's chin.

"And I have confidentiality concerns of my own. I do not have excellent sources because I'm careless with their identities. If you want to work with me, you'll have to give me the same amount of professional respect you demand for yourself."

"You're right." Sharp leaned back. She wasn't going to put up with any of his bullshit. He was going to have to let go of his need to control everything, or he was going to end up with nothing. "I apologize."

With a stiff bob of her head, Olivia started the first video. "This is the feed from the camera that covers the tables next to the dance floor."

Nothing but static showed on the TV screen.

Sharp tossed her a good-faith tidbit. "The same camera wasn't functioning the night Noah was killed."

"The club is new. Glitches are to be expected, but it's disappointing." Olivia tapped on her keyboard. "Let's try the video of the club entrance."

Though slightly grainy on the big TV screen, the image of the front doors of the club began to roll.

Sharp settled back, his irritation with Olivia gone as he focused on the faces of the people arriving at Beats.

His instinct, honed by many years of investigation experience, began to tingle. Thirty minutes into the video, Sharp's spine snapped straight.

"Isn't that Noah Carter?" Olivia asked.

"Yes." Sharp noted the location on the video. "Looks like the whole gang was at Beats that night, just like they said in their initial interview. There's Noah, Chase, Isaac, Adam, and bingo—Justin."

Sharp pulled out his phone and dialed Lance, but the call wouldn't go through. Sharp sent him a text instead.

Justin had crossed paths with Shannon at Beats the night she went missing.

Chapter Thirty-Six

Lance steered the Town Car around a deep pothole in the road leading to Justin's house. He was unable to avoid the next crater, and the car bounced over it. The car's undercarriage scraped on a rise in the dirt, and he wished his Jeep's windshield were fixed. Tall trees lined both sides of the road, casting deep shadows in the fading daylight.

Lance switched on the headlights. "I never like the coincidence of two murder cases so close together, but I never really expected to discover a link this strong between them."

In the passenger seat, Morgan stretched her neck. "Me either, but for the first time, I'm encouraged about Haley's case."

Lance turned onto a skinny gravel driveway and drove a hundred yards. The headlights swept across a barnlike building. Time had faded the exterior to a color between brown and gray. Light seeped through blinds covering the windows, and a Toyota sat in front of the sliding double doors.

Lance parked next to Justin's vehicle. "Looks like he's home."

They stepped out of the car. Lance doubted that the sun penetrated the thick forest even in the daytime. In early evening, damp cold hung in the air. Moss grew between the trees, and a large patch of mold crept up the side of the building.

Melinda Leigh

Morgan rounded the front of the vehicle and stood next to him. She hunched her shoulders against the chill. "I supposed artists like solitude."

"Serial killers like privacy too."

Morgan started up the walk, a loose row of broken slate that led from the parking area to the door. "The mere fact that Justin and Shannon were both at the inn at the same time does not make him a serial killer."

"You're right," Lance said. His phone buzzed with a text. "It's from Sharp. He says Justin was definitely at Beats the night Shannon was killed. Now *that* puts him at the top of our suspect list."

They walked to the door and knocked. He didn't see a peephole or a surveillance camera, but the big picture window provided a view of the front door. Justin would know who was standing on his stoop. The door rolled open. Justin slumped in the opening. Surprise lifted his chin. He obviously hadn't looked through his window. Had he been expecting someone else?

Lance expected him to shut the door in their faces. That's what he would have done if he'd been in Justin's shoes.

"What do you want?" Justin asked. His eyes were red, and ruddy patches covered his face. He'd been crying.

"We have a few follow-up questions," Morgan said. "It'll only take a few minutes of your time."

"I don't know." His eyes darting to the woods behind Lance and Morgan, Justin raised a hand to his mouth and bit off a chunk of fingernail. His twitchiness reminded Lance of a drug addict who needed his fix.

Had Lance read him wrong?

He scanned the dim room behind Justin. The inside of the house was as messy as the outside. Clothes, trash, and junk mail had been tossed at random. It appeared as if it had been ransacked, but Lance got the feeling that's the way it looked all the time. Was Justin normally a slob, or was the neglectful state of his living conditions a sign of depression, drug addiction, or something else?

Justin's face screwed up with resentment, and he folded his arms over his thin chest. He glared at Lance. "I don't have to talk to you."

And yet he'd opened the door when neither of his friends had.

"We know," Morgan coaxed. "And we appreciate your cooperation."

Lance waved a hand. "If you don't want to meet with us, we can leave and take our concerns to the sheriff. Would you be more comfortable talking to Sheriff Colgate?"

Justin gave him an insolent stink eye. "Just ask your questions and go."

Morgan lifted her tote strap higher onto her shoulder. "We learned that you were once accused of date rape."

He froze, his mouth gaping. "The . . . the charges were dropped," he stammered.

"But you were arrested." Lance unzipped his jacket for quicker access to his weapon.

Justin's gaze shifted to Lance. "How can you even know that? There was no trial or anything."

"Arrest records for nonconvictions are supposed to be sealed in New York State, but that doesn't always happen," Lance explained. "Your lawyer should have followed up."

Justin obviously hadn't known. His eyes filled with moisture. "That's not right."

"Right or wrong, that's the way it's done." Lance lifted a palm. "If they dropped the charges, then it couldn't have been too bad, right?"

Justin's face reddened. "She lied. She fucking lied. We were both drinking and having a good time. She came back to my apartment with me. We drank some more. We ended up in bed." He gripped his head with both hands. "I didn't wake up until noon the next day. She was gone. I was too hungover to think about it much. I assumed she did her walk of shame early. I went back to bed. When the police knocked on my door . . ."

Lance nodded. "You must have been shocked."

"Shocked doesn't even begin to cover it." Justin tugged at his hair. "I'd had a lot to drink too, so the details of the night are hazy. But she never said stop. She was totally on board with the sex."

"But a drunk girl can't really consent, can she?" Morgan's voice was uncharacteristically judgmental. She was baiting him, hoping his anger would override his common sense. He was under no obligation to answer any of their questions. If Justin was thinking clearly, he'd shut the hell up.

But he wasn't thinking at all. He was reacting.

Justin's eyes snapped back to her. The animosity in them drew Lance a step closer.

"I was drunk too," Justin said, resentment shining over the moisture in his eyes. "Maybe she took advantage of me? If both parties have been drinking, why is it always the guy who takes the rap?"

"That's a good question." Lance countered Morgan's hard-ass lawyer routine. "Why is all the responsibility on the man's shoulders?"

"The cops questioned me for hours." Justin's voice rose with his emotion. "I didn't have the money for a fancy lawyer. If it wasn't for Isaac's dad and his attorney, that bitch might have put me in prison. For nothing. Just because she woke up in the morning and regretted sleeping with me."

"Isaac's dad fixed it for you?" Lance asked.

Justin nodded, but he continued to stare at Morgan, his chest heaving, his nostrils flaring.

"This is why bros have to stick together." Lance took a step closer to Morgan. Justin was fixated on her like Kieran's dog had been focused on Lance.

Morgan's eyes narrowed, just a millimeter. It was her interrogation, slam-dunk face. If Lance hadn't been looking for it, he would have missed it.

She stepped forward. "Where were you on Saturday, February 24? Were you at Beats?"

Justin's head snapped back as if she'd slapped him. His mouth opened, then closed.

"Do you know Shannon Yates?" Morgan pressed.

"No." His eyes shifted away.

Liar. Liar.

"Are you sure?" Morgan raised her voice. "Because we know you designed the new logo for the inn where she worked."

His gaze flicked back and forth between them. Lance could see the panic building. At his sides, his fingers curled and uncurled into fists. Sweat broke out on his forehead and upper lip. So much guilt, so little time.

"Haley is starting to remember what happened," Morgan lied smoothly. Lance was impressed.

Then Justin broke. His breath hitched, and his face screwed up. Then his eyes turned pink and filled with tears. "I can't do this anymore."

"Do what?" Morgan asked.

"Lie. I've been lying." Justin squeezed his head between his palms, as if he could hold himself together with the pressure of his hands. "So many lies. I can't keep them all straight."

Had he killed Noah?

"Why not just tell the truth?" Lance scanned Justin's pockets. His skinny jeans were too tight to conceal weapons.

"It wasn't my fault. I didn't mean to do it." Justin dropped his hands to his sides.

"What did you do?" Morgan asked.

Justin shook his head. "Bad. It was bad. I just want the nightmares to end. I want it all to go away." He stopped moving. He'd made a decision. Resignation shut down the emotions in his eyes. "There are some decisions you can't take back. Things you do that can't be undone."

"Why don't you just come clean?" Morgan's voice was smooth now, coaxing. "You'll feel better if you get this off your chest."

Tears streamed down his face. Gesturing for them to follow him inside, he took a half step backward.

The crack of a rifle shot split the quiet air. Justin dropped like a sack of meat.

"Get down." Lance pulled Morgan to the ground and covered her with his body. His heart took off like a racehorse. Justin groaned, but Lance couldn't spare him a glance.

Where is the shooter?

A second shot rang out.

"Get inside." Lance rose to his hands and knees, trying to keep his body between Morgan and the woods.

Drawing his weapon, he spun around just in time to see a muzzle flash in the trees. A bullet hit the door, bits of wood exploding from the impact. He returned fire, then glanced over his shoulder. Morgan scrambled over the threshold. She grabbed Justin's hand and tried to drag him inside but couldn't move him.

"He's too heavy for me." She drew her own handgun. Standing behind the doorframe, she peered around the edge and aimed her gun at the woods. "I'll cover. You get Justin inside."

Lance didn't like her plan, but he couldn't argue with its practicality. "The shooter is behind that stand of fir trees at six o'clock."

Morgan popped off two shots in the general direction of the shooter. Lance ducked into the house, taking Justin by the arm and dragging him through the doorway. Blood poured down the man's face. Morgan backed away from the opening. Lance shut the door and flipped the dead bolt.

He hauled Justin through the living room and into the attached kitchen. The cabinet footprint formed a U. Lance pulled Justin behind the metal oven, which provided better protection than drywall and wood. Bullets could penetrate the exterior walls of frame buildings.

Morgan grabbed her bag from where she'd dropped it by the door and followed Lance into the kitchen.

She took her phone from her purse and called 911. Then she turned her attention to Justin. "The bullet hit him in the temple."

"Are *you* hurt?" Lance asked Morgan.

"No," she said. "You?"

"I'm fine." Adrenaline was mainlining through his body. His heart thudded in his chest, and his pulse echoed in his ears as he swept through the first floor, making sure all the rooms were clear. He checked the rear door lock. Then he went to the front window and peered around the window frame, using one finger to separate the blind slats. "I don't see him."

"I suspect he ran as soon as you returned fire."

Lance hoped so, but he didn't like not knowing where their attacker had gone. He wanted to chase the shooter, but he wouldn't leave Morgan and Justin unprotected.

Morgan took a pair of vinyl gloves out of her bag and put them on. She grabbed a dish towel from the counter, folded it, and pressed it to Justin's wound. "The best I can do is try to stop the bleeding."

"I'll secure the upstairs." He headed up the steps. Three doors opened off the hallway. Two rooms faced the rear of the property. Lance cleared the first two rooms. Through the second-story window, he scanned the rear yard but saw no one. He crossed the hall to the master bedroom. After checking under the bed and in the closet, he looked through the window that overlooked the front yard. There was no sign of the shooter.

Morgan was probably right. Whoever had shot Justin was not likely to stick around now that he'd been fired on. He also had to know that the police had been called.

Justin was just as sloppy in his bedroom as in the rest of the house. Dust and dirty dishes covered the nightstand and dresser. Clothes littered the carpet, and the room smelled like sweaty feet. Lance stared at the bed. Photos covered the blue comforter. The photos on the left side of the bed showed four friends at college graduation, smiling for the camera in their blue caps and gowns, their arms looped around each other's shoulders. More snapshots depicted them skiing and partying. A few appeared to be a spring break beach vacation. The right side of the bed was all Noah. Justin had been staring at these images, grieving.

Lance's gaze swept over the nightstand. Three prescription vials stood next to a full glass of water and a box of tissues. Used, crumpled tissues littered the floor.

Lance move closer to read the prescription labels. Justin's name was printed on each of the bottles. They were all the same medication— zolpidem, the same drug that had been found in Shannon's body. The first prescription was dated the previous summer. Roughly two-thirds of the original thirty tablets were missing. Had Justin stockpiled the pills to use on young women? Is that why he'd refilled the sleeping pills even though he wasn't using them?

Pulling out his phone, Lance snapped photos. He pictured Justin crying over the photos of his friend Noah and thinking about taking all the sleeping pills. The scene appeared to be an impending suicide. But was Justin motivated by guilt or grief or both?

He found nothing else out of the ordinary in the bedroom and moved on to the bathroom. He opened the medicine cabinet and found another prescription bottle. He recognized the medication as an antidepressant.

He jogged downstairs and checked his watch. Ten minutes had passed. The police would be here in another five or so.

"Is he still alive?" Lance asked Morgan.

"Yes." She knelt on the floor next to Justin. Blood was seeping through the towel she held to his head.

Justin's eyes opened halfway. "Let me die."

Lance wouldn't have minded. Justin had probably raped and killed Shannon Yates. He'd also likely killed Noah, drugged Haley, and framed her for the crime. But Morgan had a higher moral standard than Lance did. Besides, they wanted explanations, and dead guys couldn't sign confessions.

But who had shot Justin?

"You're not going to die." Morgan stacked a second towel on top of the first. She sounded more confident than Lance suspected she felt. The wound was still bleeding heavily. "At least not today."

"I'm cold." Justin's words trembled.

Lance grabbed a blanket from the couch and spread it over him.

Blood continued to pour from the wound, soaking through the dish towels. Morgan applied more pressure to the towels by overlapping her hands and leaning on them. Her quick glance at Lance betrayed her concern.

Justin's eyes fluttered and closed. His lips moved. Morgan bent close to his mouth. When she straightened, worry darkened her eyes.

"What did he say?" Lance asked.

"I killed Noah."

"It's not a signed confession, but I'll take it."

Morgan shook her head. "He also said Haley was the next target."

"Does that mean Justin intended to kill Haley next? Or is there someone else who was targeting her?"

"I don't know, but I'm texting Sharp just in case. He can check on Haley. We're going to be tied up here for a while."

Chapter Thirty-Seven

"Hal-eeeey," the whisper calls.

Leave me alone, *she cries.*

She draws her knees to her chest and pulls the blanket up over her shoulders, hiding from the voice. Why won't it leave her alone?

"Why did you kill me, Haley?"

She whimpers.

There is no escaping it. The voice echoes inside her own mind.

She shakes her head. No. I didn't. I wouldn't. I couldn't.

"The knife was in your hand," the voice whispers. "You killed me. The blood. Remember the blood."

She sees it now, spreading across the floor, coming toward her, a wave of red.

A sea of guilt. Pointing at her. Reaching for her.

"You'd better run, Haley. Run away. I'm coming back for you."

But this time, she doesn't wait for it to catch her. She can't. She can't stand it anymore. She can't let it touch her. If it gets on her skin one more time, she'll never be able to wash it away. It will stain her forever.

Sliding away from her hiding place, she slips from the room. She'll find another hiding spot, one where the voice can't find her.

Her bare feet are silent on the carpet as she runs.

Chapter Thirty-Eight

The taillights of the ambulance disappeared into the darkness. Morgan turned to the woods in front of Justin's house, where a handful of deputies searched for evidence with high-powered flashlights.

"I'm worried about Haley." Morgan leaned back against the Town Car.

"Me too." Lance paced in front of her. "Justin is out of commission. He can't hurt her."

"But we don't know that *he* was the one who was targeting her, and he can't tell us. He might never regain consciousness. And whoever shot Justin is still out there."

Lance checked his watch. "Sharp should be with her by now. She also has a private bodyguard."

The sheriff walked out the front door. Even in the darkness, his exhaustion was evident in the hollows of his cheeks and under his eyes.

Next to Morgan, Lance folded his arms in a rigid line over his chest.

The sheriff conferred with the lead deputy before approaching Lance and Morgan. "Did he really confess to killing Noah?"

Morgan nodded. She'd already given a statement to the deputy, but she recited Justin's exact words again for the sheriff. "We don't know what he meant by 'Haley was the next target.'"

"Considering he confessed to murdering his friend, I'd think it means that he was going to kill Haley next." Sheriff Colgate pressed a fist to his sternum. He didn't seem resentful that they'd solved the case for him, just relieved. The porch light cast his face in shadows. The skin appeared slack, as if he'd lost weight. "What made you suspect him?"

"We found out that he'd once been arrested for date rape," Morgan said. "The charges were dropped, but it made us take a harder look at him. Then we found out that he'd also crossed paths with Shannon Yates at the inn where she worked."

"When I was clearing the house, I saw the bottles of zolpidem in the bedroom," Lance added.

"That's the same drug that was used on Shannon." The sheriff swept his hat from his head and scratched his scalp. The sheriff glanced at Justin's front door. "It sure looked like he was planning to commit suicide. But Justin has an alibi for Noah's murder. He was with his friends all night."

"I see two immediate possibilities. One, Isaac and Chase are lying for him." Morgan extended one finger then a second. "Two, Isaac said that Chase and Justin slept on his couch. They'd all been drinking. What if Justin slipped out and killed Noah while the other two were sleeping?"

"I suppose that's one theory." The sheriff removed his hat and swept his hand through his wispy hair.

"But why would he have killed Shannon *and* his best friend?" Morgan asked. "The two crimes are very different. There's no pattern."

"Maybe Noah knew what Justin had done to Shannon," Lance offered. "Then Justin killed Noah to shut him up."

"But who tried to kill Justin tonight?" Morgan rubbed the ache in her temple. Thinking made her head hurt.

"Adam is still on the loose." Lance scanned the dark woods, as if the shooter might be out there somewhere. "He has a temper and a history of violent behavior. Our computer expert tracked some of the threatening emails Haley has received to Adam Carter's house."

"But how would Adam know that Justin killed Noah?" Morgan couldn't connect the dots.

"We won't know until we find Adam." The sheriff sighed. "Do you know why Justin would have killed Shannon Yates?"

"No." Morgan shook her head. "But he has access to zolpidem, he knew Shannon from his business with the inn, and the surveillance videos at the club show that he was there the night she went missing."

"Shannon's rapist used a condom." The sheriff scrubbed both hands down his face. "But several other DNA samples were found on her body. We'll see if Justin's DNA matches any of them." He gestured behind him. "We still have a whole scene to process. And *if* Justin survives, hopefully he'll be willing to talk." The sheriff set his hat back on his head. "Standing around here yakking won't help. I'll get back to the scene."

"Now that Justin has confessed to killing Noah," Morgan said, "I'd like the charges against my client dropped."

"I will look at the charges after all the evidence has been examined." Colgate nodded.

Frustrated, Morgan tensed. "Zolpidem would explain Haley's amnesia. If Justin killed Noah, then we think he gave the drug to Haley so he could frame her for the murder."

"I will review all the evidence and talk to the DA." The sheriff used a nonnegotiable tone.

Morgan wanted to thump the sheriff upside the head. "Justin admitted to killing Noah. You can hardly keep Haley under arrest for a crime another person has confessed to committing."

"You are the only one who heard that confession. What if you didn't hear him correctly?" Colgate pulled a roll of antacids from his pocket and put two in his mouth. "I promise you that the case will receive a thorough review. If the evidence bears out, then the charges will be dropped against Haley."

Morgan protested, "Sheriff—"

Colgate held up a hand. "Ms. Dane, have patience. If Justin killed Noah Carter and Shannon Yates, then he is no longer a danger to anyone. I will not rush into anything. You'll have to let the process work itself out."

"The same process that was going to put my client away for a crime she didn't commit?" Morgan shot back.

"It isn't perfect," the sheriff admitted. "But it's all we have to work with. I wish you'd have come to me with this information instead of handling it yourself." The sheriff chewed and swallowed two more antacid tablets. "Then maybe Justin wouldn't have been shot, and I'd have a signed confession."

"Sheriff." Morgan raised her voice. "I have left you numerous messages over the past few days. You haven't returned any of my calls."

The sheriff exhaled, his chest deflating. "I have a hundred and eighty voice mails." He pulled at his collar. "And I don't even know how many random messages."

Sharp had been right. Colgate was clearly in so far over his head, he couldn't see the surface.

"Are we free to go?" Morgan swallowed her irritation.

"Yes. We have your statement. I'll call you if I have additional questions." The sheriff walked back toward the house.

She turned to Lance. "I don't like this."

"Me either. Haley deserves to have her name cleared ASAP. But that's a technicality. What I like even less is the fact that whoever shot Justin is still out there." Lance pulled out his phone, pressed a button, and held it to his ear. He lowered his phone. "Sharp isn't answering."

"There are places out toward Eliza's house with poor reception." But worry filled Morgan. "Let's drive out to Eliza's house. Haley deserves to know what happened as soon as possible. She didn't kill Noah, and there's a solid explanation for her amnesia."

"And we'll both feel better if we keep an eye on Haley until the shooter is brought in." Lance turned and opened the car door. "The sheriff might be right. The answer to our questions could come from the evidence they collect tonight or from an interview with Justin."

Morgan hurried to the passenger side. "But this case is so strange, I'm not comfortable making assumptions. The more people protecting Haley the better."

Chapter Thirty-Nine

Sharp sped out to Eliza's place in record time. He'd called to let her know he was coming, and she opened the gate as he drove up. There were no protesters in sight. Maybe the bastards had tired of tormenting Eliza and Haley.

Eric the bodyguard let him in and led him back to the kitchen. Eliza sat at the island drinking from a mug. The sheets shrouding the great room still felt claustrophobic.

"Where's Haley?" Sharp couldn't wait to tell her some good news for a change.

"She took a sleeping pill." Eliza greeted him with a quick hug. Her body felt thinner, frailer than it had just a few days ago. "She's out cold."

"I suppose it's good that she's getting some rest." But disappointment filled Sharp.

"It's a relief." Eliza's body sagged. "She's been completely exhausted. I didn't know what to do for her. Do you want some tea?"

"Not now. Sit down. I have news." Sharp stood back and waited until she eased back onto her stool. "Justin O'Brien confessed to killing Noah." He told her what happened at Justin's house that evening. "It'll take the police a little while to sort through the evidence, but Morgan will push to have the charges against Haley dropped ASAP."

Eliza's mouth gaped for a few seconds. "But Justin and Noah were close friends."

"Yes. Our best theory is that Justin killed Shannon Yates and Noah found out about it. Justin wouldn't have much of a choice but kill his friend to save himself."

Sharp also suspected Justin might have been involved in Adele Smith's death, but they would likely have to wait for the DNA samples to be analyzed.

"But then who shot Justin?" Eliza asked.

"We don't know yet. Adam's still on the loose. He has a history of violent behavior. We know he sent Haley threatening emails. He was one of the trespassers on your lawn. If he somehow learned that Justin killed Noah . . ."

They also didn't know who'd thrown a rock through Lance's windshield or who'd set Lance's house on fire. Was Adam angry enough to do all those things?

Eliza shuddered. "I hope he's satisfied that it was Justin and not Haley who killed his brother."

"The police are still looking for him. They'll find him eventually." If Adam *had* shot Justin, Sharp thought Adam would either run or he'd try to finish what he started by attacking Justin at the hospital. Either way, Sharp couldn't see Noah's brother bothering with Haley if he knew Justin had murdered Noah.

"I just want all of this to be over." Eliza set her teacup down. Exhaustion lined her face.

Sharp covered her hand with his. "You look like you haven't slept much in days."

"I haven't." She yawned. "I know we still have plenty of questions, and this isn't over yet. But I'm so relieved we know who killed Noah. I feel like I could sleep for a week."

"Eric is on duty, and I'll sit up and listen for Haley." Sharp squeezed her hand. "Go get some sleep. I'll wake you if anything happens. We'll talk about the case in the morning. Morgan and Lance will have more information by then anyway."

"OK." Eliza nodded. "Thank you, Lincoln."

Sharp watched her walk down the hall. Ten minutes passed. The house was quiet. Eric came through the kitchen on his rounds, checking windows and doors. Sharp got up and went to the stairwell that led to Haley's private suite. He felt a little awkward as he reached for the doorknob, but he needed to see Haley sleeping soundly with his own eyes.

He eased the door open and peered inside. The light fell across her bed. The sheets were tossed back, and Haley was gone.

Don't panic.

But fear bubbled in his chest anyway. Where could she be?

She was probably in the bathroom. Sharp hurried across the carpet and pushed the door open. The bathroom was empty. He checked under the bed and in the closet, then searched the sitting area. But there was no sign of Haley.

Sharp turned toward the door. He took a deep breath. Haley had to be somewhere in the house, or the burglar alarm—and her ankle bracelet—would have gone off.

"Hal-eey." A low whisper floated through the room.

Sharp froze. What the fuck? He spun, his hand on the butt of his gun, his gaze searching the room. Was someone here? Sharp had just searched Haley's suite. No one was here. Where was the voice coming from? The TV was off. He checked Haley's computer, but it was turned off as well.

"Hal-eey." There it was again. Sharp drew his weapon and moved toward the voice.

"What have you done?" the whisper asked.

Sharp scanned the entertainment center in the sitting area across from the bed. On it sat a cable box and game console. The game console's light was on. Sharp stared at it. Could that be the source of Haley's "voices"?

"Hal-eey," the voice whispered again. "You'd better run. I'm coming for you."

It was definitely the game console. How the voice had gotten into the machine didn't matter right now. Any device connected to the internet could be hacked, and there were multiple ways it could have been done.

Anger rolled through him. Haley wasn't crazy, but someone wanted her to think that she was. But who? Who would want to torment her like that?

Sharp left the room. He had to find Haley and keep her safe, then he'd worry about solving the case.

At the top of the steps, he looked for the bodyguard, but Eric wasn't in sight. Sharp's gaze locked on the open basement door. Either Eric was checking the basement as part of his hourly rounds, or that's where Haley had gone.

Sharp jogged down the stairs and crossed the wood floor to the basement door. A light was on. Bending forward, he peered down the steps. He could just see the legs of Haley's easel and her bare feet standing in front of it. A deep breath eased the tension inside him. She was safe.

"What's wrong?" Eric walked into the room from the front of the house.

"Haley is in the basement."

Eric frowned. "I didn't see her go down there."

Sharp explained about the voice coming out of the game console. "It must have frightened her."

Frowning, Eric said, "The easiest way to get into the device would have been to hack the router."

Had a terrified Haley run from the voice?

"I'll get her." Sharp turned to the basement and called softly, "Haley?"

She didn't respond. He went down two steps and bent to watch her. She was dabbing gobs of red paint onto the canvas, but her eyes were unfocused, and she didn't respond to his call. The basement was cold and damp, and Haley was barefoot. Her feet had to be freezing. Sharp stared as red paint dripped from her brush and onto the floor and her feet. She had no idea what was happening around her. "I think she's sleepwalking."

"Probably from the meds." Eric nodded from the top of the steps.

"I'll try to get her back to bed." Sharp turned toward the basement. "Can you determine if they hacked the game console or the router? We need to shut that down ASAP."

He and Eric shared a look. Was someone listening in on them now? How many devices could be compromised?

"I'll take care of it." Eric turned away.

But before he could walk ten feet, an explosion rocked the kitchen. The force picked up Eric and flung him into the wall. The blast hit Sharp like an 18-wheeler. The impact hurled his body backward. The stairwell disintegrated beneath him. Arms pinwheeling, he plunged downward, landing on the concrete with a blinding rush of pain.

Debris rained down on top of his stunned body.

Blackness encroached at the edges of his vision. His ears rang, and sound was muffled. His last thought before the pain and darkness consumed him was that he couldn't save Haley after all.

I'm sorry, Ted.

Chapter Forty

"No." Lance braked at the base of Eliza's driveway. His heart stuttered. The house above was engulfed in flames, and at least four people were inside—including Sharp. But there would be no one to open the gate. "Hold on tight."

Next to him, Morgan grabbed the armrest.

He put the car in reverse and backed up as far as he could. Then he shifted into drive and punched the gas pedal to the floor. The Town Car crashed through the metal gates and bounced up the driveway. He stopped next to Sharp's Prius.

Lance shoved the gearshift into park and jumped out of the car. Morgan was on her phone calling for help.

The alarm system would have summoned the fire department, but the rigs wouldn't get all the way out to Eliza's house that quickly. Unlike Lance's house, which had been just blocks from the station, Eliza's house was remote. It could burn to the ground long before help arrived.

"Just making sure." She lowered her phone.

Lance ran toward the front of the house. He pulled on the door handle, but the door was locked. "We'll need to break a window."

He backed up and scanned the ground for a rock. Flames raced up the kitchen side of the house, the fire rapidly eating its way across the roofline. A car roared up the driveway.

Esposito climbed out, dressed in jeans and a sweatshirt. He jerked a thumb over his shoulder. "I saw the fire from my house down the road."

Lance went back to the Town Car and pulled a heavy metal flashlight from the glove compartment. He raced to the front of the house and swung it at the window. The glass cracked. He hit the window again, smashing through the panes, then used the flashlight to clear the larger shards around the window frame.

"How many people are inside?" Esposito yelled above the roar of the fire.

"At least four," Lance shouted back as he climbed through the broken window.

Esposito was right behind him. Smoke and heat filled the house. Lance couldn't see more than a foot in front of his face. He pulled his jacket collar over his mouth and nose. He felt Esposito's hand grip his shoulder. They shuffled down the hallway toward the back of the house.

Lance's boot tripped over something. He stopped and reached down. His eyes watered, further blinding him. He groped at the body. Too small to be Sharp.

Eliza.

He shook Esposito, gestured to Eliza, and shouted, "Take her outside."

Esposito stooped and picked her up. Lance continued down the hall, crouching to get below the worst of the smoke. In the entrance to the kitchen, he found the bodyguard.

Lance wanted to keep looking. Haley and Sharp were still inside, but he had to get Eric outside first. He dragged the big man by the armpits down the hallway and out the front door. Behind him, the fire crackled, the smoke thickened, and the heat intensified as he stumbled through the opening and into the cool night air.

Esposito rushed to Lance and grabbed Eric's feet. Together, they carried the bodyguard across the grass to a safe spot away from the house.

Eliza was on her hands and knees, coughing and choking, definitely alive. Morgan rolled the bodyguard to his back.

Lance's lungs revolted, spewing soot and smoke, as he climbed to his feet and turned back toward the inferno.

Was Sharp dead? Haley?

Lance couldn't stop. Sharp and Haley were still inside. He turned back, his legs wobbling as he forced them to move toward the fire.

A hand snatched at his arm.

Esposito. His face was covered with black grime, his eyes bloodshot. "You can't go in there!"

Lance shook off the hand and ran through the front door.

"Sharp! Haley!" he shouted, but the fire drowned out his voice.

The inside of the house was filled with black smoke. The heat sucked the air from Lance's lungs as he stumbled farther inside.

Where were they?

Chapter Forty-One

Pain jolted through Sharp like a bolt of lightning. It flooded every inch of his body until he could feel nothing but agony. He opened his eyes but couldn't see through the smoke and haze and liquid dripping into his eyes. He let them drift closed again, anything to let go of this bulldozer of pain rushing over him.

"No," a woman cried. "You can't die."

He forced his eyes open. Haley. Her tears fell onto his face. On her knees at his side, she clutched his jacket lapels and shook him. The motion of her hands ignited blasts of pain that stole his breath.

She lifted her hands. They came away covered in blood.

Sharp tried to form words with his lips. The effort was ridiculously difficult. "Where are we?"

"The basement," she said. "The house is on fire."

The explosion came back to Sharp with a rush of images and sensation. Eric going flying. Sharp falling.

Pain.

They were trapped. The house above them was burning. Over Haley's head, Sharp could see smoke and flames. The only reason they were still alive was that heat rose and the basement held a pocket of air. But it wouldn't last. As the fire burned through the house, the floor would give way. It would collapse right on top of them.

Sharp grabbed for her hand. His lungs screamed as he forced the words out. "Go. Get help."

He added the second part to convince her to leave him. Although he suspected the house would fall down on top of him before she could get back, at least she'd be out.

Shaking her head, she sat back on her heels. "No. I won't leave you."

Sharp tightened his grip on her fingers. "You have to."

"No. You have to come with me. I can't let you die." She wiped her bloody hands on her sweatshirt, the gesture defiant and determined. "I can't. I'm not going without you."

She stood, grabbed his ankles, and tried to pull him toward the rear of the basement, where two windows looked over the rear yard. But she simply wasn't strong enough to budge him.

There was no getting around it. Sharp was going to have to move his own ass.

He levered onto an elbow to look at his injury. White-hot agony erupted, splitting him in half. A large chunk of wood protruded from his side. The sight of it sticking out just below his ribs just about made him pass out.

He gritted his teeth. "Tie something around the wood to hold it still. Don't pull it out. I'll just bleed more."

He couldn't afford to spring any more leaks. He couldn't let Haley down. He had to get her outside the burning house. Once she was safe, then he could die all he wanted.

Rushing to her paint easel, she gathered some clean rags and brought them back to him. She opened his jacket, the widening of her eyes showing Sharp how badly he was injured.

"Use my belt." He felt her hands working it from his belt loops and heard his holster and gun hit the concrete with a clunk.

She tightened the belt around his middle, stabilizing the shaft of wood. Pain burst through Sharp, sucking the air from his lungs as much as the smoke and heat were. He blinked to clear his vision. Embers fell from the first floor burning over their heads. A glowing bit of fire landed on Haley's shoulder. She swatted it away. No time for a pity party. They had to go.

"Help me up." He held out his hand.

She rose to her feet and grabbed hold. Sharp braced himself for the agony of movement. Haley pulled, and Sharp rolled to his knees.

Light-headed, he sucked hot air into his lungs and gestured toward the window at the back of the room. "Let's go."

Haley dragged the workbench under the window. Climbing on it, she flipped the lock and shoved the window open. Cool air poured in. Above them, the fire answered, flames rushing at the fresh oxygen.

"Come on." She jumped off the bench and hurried back to him.

Sharp crawled to the base of the bench and pulled himself upright. His knees shook as he put one knee onto the wooden table.

Don't think. Don't stop. Don't feel.

Keep moving.

He focused one inch ahead. No farther. If he looked all the way out the window, he couldn't possibly see himself making it. But he could crawl one more inch. And then another.

Haley was behind him, pushing, as he dragged himself onto the workbench. Without stopping, he put his arms and shoulders through the open window. With Haley lifting his legs, he went out like a foal being birthed. He hit the ground with a jolt of pain that blanked his vision for a few seconds. Warm liquid gushed down his side.

A thud next to him announced that Haley was out the window too. Then she was at his side dragging him by the arm, her voice breaking with sobs as she cried, "Move. Please."

The clean air in his lungs—and the hope that at least Haley would live—gave Sharp a small charge of energy. Unable to get to his feet, he crawled through the dry grass to the back of the yard, an inch at a time, trying to reach a place where the worst of the burning embers and flying bits of fire couldn't reach.

Probably only a couple of minutes had passed, but it felt like hours to Sharp. Each movement sent another gush of blood from his wound.

Finally, Haley knelt and tugged off her sweatshirt. She pressed it to his wound and leaned on it. Tears streamed down her cheeks, cutting through the sooty grime. "The wood came out."

Sharp couldn't believe they were alive. Haley hadn't given up on him. As the night air rushed into his lungs, feeling returned to his body.

And pain. Loads of it.

He put a hand to his middle. The belt had come loose during his slide out the window. The wood in his side had been knocked free, and blood was flowing. The rags she'd used to stabilize the wood impaling him were gone.

Sharp lifted his hands. They were coated with blood. Haley's horrified eyes took it in.

Sirens approached.

She clutched his hand. "They're almost here. Please don't die."

"I'll try," he croaked and stared up at the sky. A thick cloud of smoke blew across the stars. The sight was deadly but beautiful. Would it be the last thing Sharp saw?

"I'll get help." Haley stood and turned toward the house. She'd have to give it a wide berth to get to the front of the property, where the fire trucks would arrive.

Even if he didn't make it, Haley was going to survive. He hadn't failed her. He hadn't failed Ted.

She turned away from him. Sharp let his eyes close. He'd rest until she came back. The darkness pulled at him.

"You're not going anywhere, bitch," a voice said.

Sharp forced his eyelids open. A figure approached, silhouetted against the fire. He pulled a gun and pointed it at Haley.

"No!" she sobbed, her body wavering, her legs shaking.

"Stop," the man shouted. The firelight played over a thin face that Sharp recognized from the photos on the whiteboard.

Isaac McGee.

Shocked, Sharp reached for his weapon, but his hand slapped nothing but his bloody hip. His gun had fallen from his belt in the basement.

"You're coming with me," Isaac said to Haley.

"No!" Sharp reached forward, digging his fingers into the dirt and trying to drag his body between the man and Haley. But it was no use. They were defenseless.

If Isaac took Haley away, she would die. Just like Ted. Sharp knew it with every fiber of his being. She'd be better off being shot here, with emergency responders on the way. Most bullet wounds were survivable with prompt medical attention. Ted had been unlucky.

Sharp drew in some air and forced out three words. "Don't go, Haley."

With his gaze locked on Haley, Isaac gestured toward Sharp with his gun. "Come with me, or I'll shoot him."

"Don't listen to him," Sharp croaked. "I'm dying anyway."

"She doesn't have a choice," Isaac said.

Haley stared at Sharp. Tears glistened on her face. Were they both going to die?

No. They weren't completely out of options.

Haley knew the trails around her house. Hopefully, Isaac did not. In her black yoga pants and gray T-shirt, Haley would be a tough target in the dark.

He met her gaze in the flickering firelight. She knew what he wanted her to do, and it was clear she didn't want to leave him. But Sharp couldn't run, and he couldn't fight.

Sharp mouthed, "Run."

Chapter Forty-Two

Morgan lifted her fingers from the bodyguard's neck. His eyes stared blankly at the sky. The man was dead.

She stood on shaky legs and scanned the lawn. Esposito staggered away from the burning house.

Terror gripped Morgan's heart when she didn't see Lance. She grabbed Esposito's shoulder. "Where's Lance?"

The ADA spun around and jerked a thumb at the blazing house. Anger narrowed his bloodshot eyes. "Your boyfriend is an idiot," he yelled, then choked, bending forward and spitting on the ground.

They turned toward the house. A roof beam collapsed at the front door, sending a shower of embers high into the air. A figure stumbled out of the smoke-filled doorway.

Lance.

Esposito raced forward. Draping one of Lance's arms over his shoulders, Esposito half dragged him away from the burning house.

Lance shook off the assistance a few feet away from the house. "I'm going to try to get in through the back." He pointed at the ADA. "Someone has to direct the fire crews."

"I think they'll find the fire on their own." The ADA followed Lance around the house.

Morgan ran after the men. Someone had to keep a lookout for whoever had set this fire. She knew without a doubt that this fire was not an accident. Someone wanted Haley dead. But why?

Nothing made sense.

Morgan jogged through the grass behind Lance and Esposito. They made a wide detour around the house and ran into the small backyard. Embers and debris rained down on them. A pinprick of heat seared Morgan's cheek as she scanned the back of the house. She brushed the ember off her skin.

"Look!" She pointed to smoke pouring from an open basement window. "Someone must have gotten out."

Wood creaked and groaned. Then a moan sounded, soft and low. The fire or a person? Lance and Esposito both froze. Morgan strained to listen. The moan came again.

Lance dropped to a knee and touched the ground. "Blood."

Crouching, he followed it through the tall grass. "Sharp!"

Morgan rushed to Lance's side, her head pounding from the exertion and smoke. Sharp lay on his back in the grass, unmoving, eyes closed. Was he breathing?

Morgan scanned the yard. Where was Haley? She glanced back at the house, now almost completely consumed by fire. Anyone who was still inside that building wasn't coming out alive.

Dropping to her knees, she pressed her fingers to Sharp's throat. *Please.* His pulse throbbed weakly against her fingertips. "He's still alive."

But barely.

His hand clutched a balled-up sweatshirt pressed against his belly. Morgan lifted it and took in the volume of blood seeping out of the wound in his abdomen. She quickly pressed it down again. He needed help. Now.

"I have a first aid kit in my car." Esposito doubled back and ran toward the front of the house.

Lance knelt on Sharp's other side.

Morgan took Sharp's hand in her own. His fingers were cold and bloodless. "Sharp, where's Haley?"

Sharp's eyes cracked a millimeter, just enough to show his complete defeat. She couldn't hear him over the roar and crackle of the fire. Morgan leaned closer.

"I don't know." His voice was weak. "She ran." He gasped. "Isaac." Sharp drew in another labored breath. "Chased her."

Isaac?

Morgan had no time to process Sharp's revelation.

He lifted a hand and pointed to the fence and steep drop-off beyond it. The gate to the lookout path stood wide open. The bike lock was on the ground.

"You stay with Sharp." Lance wiped soot from his face with his forearm and headed toward the gate.

Sharp tugged on Morgan's hand and mouthed, "Go with him."

Morgan put Sharp's hand on the balled-up sweatshirt. "Press as hard as you can."

Sharp's eyes closed.

"Sharp!" Morgan touched his arm.

His eyelids opened halfway.

"Don't you dare die." Morgan wiped tears from her face with her sleeve. "Lance needs you."

"Nah." Sharp gave her a small headshake. "He has you. Now go. He needs backup."

Esposito would be back in a minute. He'd have to look after Sharp. Morgan wasn't letting Lance face a dangerous man alone. But leaving Sharp felt wrong.

Esposito's shadow appeared around the side of the house. He was carrying a first aid kit and a blanket. Morgan stood and stared at the gate and trail beyond it. Her head throbbed, and nausea churned in her belly.

She'd never be able to catch Lance, not with her concussion. Even if she wasn't injured, he was just too fast. Whatever was going to happen would be over long before Morgan caught up with them.

But she couldn't just stand here. She had to do something.

Ignoring the pain in her head, Morgan broke into a run.

Chapter Forty-Three

Haley ran through the gate. Adrenaline had swept the dregs of her sleeping pill from her brain. The fire roared and crackled behind her. Her own heartbeats and footfalls drowned out the sound of Isaac giving chase.

But he was there. She could sense him behind her in the darkness.

Her brain didn't bother to try and sort out the reason for his attack. She could only focus on surviving it.

She made a sharp left and kept to the narrow path cut into the side of the ravine. Using moonlight, the glow from the fire, and her muscle memory, she moved along the trail at a steady pace.

She might not be big or strong, but she knew the trail. She and her mom hiked down to the overlook practically every weekend.

The trail dropped, and the left-hand side became a wall of rock. Ten feet to the right, the slope fell off.

The roar of the fire faded as she moved farther away. She paused for a breath. The night's chill blew against her sweaty T-shirt. Her ankle bracelet had begun to vibrate, and she hoped the alarm summoned more police. Rocks shifted on the trail. Isaac was behind her. Somewhere.

She moved faster, determined to put some distance between them. The rocky ground bit into her bare feet, and her lungs burned as she ran. But adrenaline charged through her bloodstream, wiping out all traces of pain.

Pushing off a boulder, she rounded a turn in the trail. On the right, the wooded slope dropped off at a steep grade. If she went over the edge, she'd tumble at least a hundred feet through tree trunks and brush. The slope was too steep to navigate without a rope. Broken bones would be a sure thing.

She went around a stand of trees. Shadows from their branches fell over the path. She picked her way along the trail with care. A twisted ankle would be the end of her. Lungs heaving, Haley slowed her steps to catch her breath and listen again. Her pulse echoed in her ears. She held her breath for a few seconds. Straining, she could hear him scrambling on the trail behind her. Was he farther away now? Had she increased the gap between them?

Hope charged her and lent her speed. She could do this. She could get away.

She might not be an athlete, but neither was Isaac.

She raced around a huge dead oak tree. Its trunk had been split nearly to the ground by a lightning strike. The overlook was just ahead. And beyond it, the trail that led to the road.

And maybe her escape.

Emergency vehicles would be coming up the mountain. There would be people on the road. Surely, once she reached it, she'd be safe. Thoughts of safety and survival led back to Sharp, bleeding in the grass.

Was he still alive?

His blood on her hands had cooled. Her breath caught on a sob, and her toe snagged a tree root. She stumbled but didn't go down.

Focus.

Nothing she could have done would have helped Sharp. If she had stayed, Isaac would have shot them both. She'd seen the intent to kill in his eyes. Her only option had been to draw Isaac and his gun away from Sharp and hope that someone else saved him.

Surely the fire trucks would be there soon.

Pebbles broke loose on the trail behind her.

Isaac.

With all her attention on the trail, she burst onto the ledge of the overlook. Once she crossed it, she'd start up the other side. The uphill, harder part of the climb would hopefully put more ground between her and Isaac.

But a shadow stepped out from behind a tree, blocking the trail on the other side. Someone was here. She opened her mouth to shout for help, but the word died on her lips. The moonlight glinted on the metal of a gun in his hand. It was Noah's friend, Chase.

Haley skidded to a stop. The metal barrier of the overlook was on her right, a solid wall of rock on her left. Isaac's footsteps on the trail behind her drew closer. She spun around, turning her back to the rock wall, as Isaac emerged from the trail and staggered to a halt.

Panting, he raised his gun, pointing it at her head. "You're done."

Panic ripped through her bloodstream.

She was trapped.

Chapter Forty-Four

Lance's chest burned as he moved down the path. The terrain—and his smoke-filled lungs—kept his pace to an agonizingly slow jog. He blocked the image of Sharp and his heavily bleeding wound from his mind. Saving Haley from Isaac had to be his sole focus.

Sharp wouldn't have it any other way, and Lance would not let his friend down.

But in the back of Lance's mind was the thought that Sharp was, at that very moment, dying in Morgan's arms. Would she be able to stop the bleeding?

The trail sloped downward. Lance's boots ate up the ground. Parts of the trail were narrow. One wrong step and he'd go over the side. Then he wouldn't be able to save anyone.

A split tree shone in the moonlight ahead. The overlook wasn't much farther. Lance eased off the speed as he approached.

A voice floated to him on the breeze. "Stop right there, bitch. I said stop."

Lance slowed and quieted his steps. He didn't want Isaac to have any warning that he was coming.

The trail opened onto the overlook clearing. Isaac stood in the mouth of the trail, his back to Lance, the gun in his hand pointed at Haley.

Placing each step carefully and silently on the trail, Lance eased up behind him and pressed the butt of his own gun into the back of Isaac's head. "Drop it."

Isaac froze for a second, as if he needed time to process his failure. Then his gun hit the ground, and his hands shot into the air.

Relief flowed through Lance. Haley was going to be all right.

But across the clearing, a voice said, "I don't think so."

Lance glanced ahead. Haley stood in the center of the clearing, about ten feet away from Lance and Isaac. Fifteen feet in front of her, at the entrance to the path that led up to the road, Chase Baker stood with a rifle in his hands, pointed at the sky. He lowered the barrel until it was aimed at Haley. Chase had cut off her escape route.

"Put the gun down or I'll shoot her." Chase handled the weapon with the comfort born of a lifetime of use.

Lance's brain whirled. Now what? If he dropped his gun, then he and Haley were dead. Chase would shoot them, or even worse, take them to a secondary location and kill them there. Then Chase and Isaac would roll them off the overlook or bury them in the woods somewhere. Giving Chase control over the situation would not increase Haley's and Lance's odds of survival. Isaac and Chase had come here to kill Haley. They weren't going to walk away after all the effort they'd gone through to get to her.

If Lance didn't lower his gun, Chase might shoot Haley. But Lance would definitely be able to take Isaac down. Then he'd only have to worry about Chase. Haley might survive a bullet wound if help came quickly.

"I like my odds with the gun," Lance called out. If he shifted his aim over Isaac's shoulder, could he hit Chase before Chase shot Haley?

Chase was twenty-five feet away from Lance, too far away for an accurate handgun shot in the dark. Haley was in the way, and Lance's vision was blurry from the fire.

"I mean it." Chase wagged his rifle. "I can't miss her at this distance." His long gun was a much more accurate weapon.

"Why do you want her?" Lance asked.

"Fuck you!" Chase yelled. "And drop the gun, or I'll blow a hole right through her."

"You're going to shoot her anyway." Lance kept his voice calm. "And I'm going to blow the back of Isaac's head clean off. Then I'm going to shoot you. However you look at it, I'm the one who's going to survive."

He tried to sound as if he didn't care that much if Haley was shot, but the fury building inside him—and the soot he'd swallowed—wouldn't let him. His voice was Clint Eastwood harsh.

"I'm going to count to three, and then she's dead." Chase raised the rifle to his shoulder. "One. Two." Something snapped.

Lance's heart skipped a beat.

A gunshot blasted. Haley dropped to the ground and rolled toward the overlook. To Lance's horror, she slid beneath the metal barrier and went over the edge.

Chase had shot her.

Holding Isaac by his ponytail, Lance leveled his gun over Isaac's shoulder at Chase. But Chase's rifle barrel tipped toward the ground. His hands opened and released his grip on the stock. The weapon clattered to the earth. A heartbeat later, Chase dropped to his knees and fell on his face in the dirt. Behind him, on the dark trail that led up to the road, Morgan aimed her Glock at the place where Chase had been standing. Her face was frozen with shock, as if she were surprised at what she'd just done.

Chase hadn't shot Haley.

Morgan had shot Chase.

For one full breath, Lance just stared. Then Morgan seemed to wake up. She walked closer to Chase, bent down, and placed her fingers on his neck. "He's dead."

Her tone was too matter-of-fact as she shifted her aim to Isaac. "I'll cover him. See if Haley . . ." Her voice broke.

Lance burst into action. He scooped Isaac's gun out of the dirt, shoved it into his waistband, then lunged toward the overlook barrier. Leaning over it, he called, "Haley!"

Where could she be? He hadn't heard her body strike the ground or crash through the branches of the trees below. Could she be hung up on the slope somewhere?

He pulled his flashlight out of his pocket and played the beam of light into the ravine. It was too deep for him to see the bottom. He searched the side of the gorge.

"Do you see her?" Morgan called.

"No." Lance called out, "Haley!"

"I'm here." Haley's voice startled him. She was closer than he'd expected.

Lance turned the light toward his feet. Haley was splayed upright against the side of the ravine, her face and body pressed into the earth, both hands holding on to the bottom rung of the metal barrier. Her bare feet dug for purchase in the side of the cliff. Finding none, she dangled.

She was alive. She hadn't fallen over the side. She'd intentionally dropped over the edge.

Lance let out the breath he'd been holding. He extended a hand toward her. "Give me your hand."

She shook her head. "I'm afraid to let go, but I don't think I can hold on much longer."

Lance aimed the flashlight on the slope below her feet. "There's a boulder nine inches from your right foot. If your foot is at six o'clock, the rock is at two o'clock. Prop your foot on it, then reach for my hand."

Haley raised her leg. Her bare toes felt for and found the rock. She braced against it, then looked up at him. Her eyes were white-rimmed with fear.

Lance reached for her hand. "You can do it."

Their gazes met. Haley swallowed, and determination tightened her jaw.

She pushed off the boulder, released one hand from the barrier, and stretched toward him. Lance caught her by the wrist and pulled her up and over the rail. Her feet hit the earth, her knees buckled, and she began to sob.

Lance turned his attention to Isaac, forced him to his knees, and secured his hands behind his back with a zip tie.

Morgan rushed to the girl's side, wrapped her arms around her, and told her, "It's all right. It's all over."

Morgan supported Haley with an arm around her waist. "Let's get you out of here. You're freezing."

"Where did you come from?" Lance asked Morgan.

The breeze blew her hair across her face, and she shoved it back. "I knew I wouldn't be able to catch you, so I drove to the other end of the trail and circled down from the road."

She was so smart, he thought with a giddy burst of pride.

Haley was wearing only thin yoga pants and a T-shirt. She'd used her sweatshirt to stem Sharp's bleeding. Lance took off his jacket and wrapped it around her. Looking at Haley's bare feet made him think of his own, and his stitches began to throb. He suspected his dash down the trail had torn them.

A small price to pay for surviving. Not that he'd had much to do with that in the end. Morgan had saved them.

Esposito and two state troopers ran into the clearing. Lance handed Isaac over. Then he moved to Haley's other side to support her. She was moving gingerly, both of her feet hurting. The cold, rocky trail must have been brutal in bare feet.

He caught Morgan's eye over the girl's shoulders, then scooped Haley into his arms. She weighed nothing. But she'd survived.

Toughness had nothing to do with bulk and brawn and everything to do with determination and the ability to think under duress.

He glanced at Morgan. She defined grace under pressure. As she fell into step beside him, he knew that was exactly the way he wanted to spend the rest of his life: with her at his side.

Morgan grabbed Esposito's arm. "How is Sharp?"

"I don't know." The ADA looked at the ground and shook his head. "He didn't look good. I'm sorry."

Lance's heart squeezed as he carried Haley up the trail to the road. He couldn't imagine life without Sharp. Dread fisted in his gut.

"Obviously, I shot Chase, so I can't leave the scene," Morgan said to him. "You take Haley to the hospital. You both should be checked out. I'll come as soon as I can."

"I love you." Lance kissed her. Even through the grief that threatened to take hold of him, he was more grateful than ever that she'd come into his life. He couldn't imagine facing this without her.

"Love you back." She opened the passenger door. "Don't discount Sharp just yet. He's tough."

Lance set Haley in the car, rounded the vehicle, and slid behind the wheel. Morgan crossed her arms and stepped back. The wind blew her hair across her face, but he could see the worry in her eyes. They both knew how much blood Sharp had lost.

Chapter Forty-Five

In the corner of the ICU, Morgan filled two Styrofoam cups with coffee. Across the way, she could see through the glass partition into Sharp's room, where Lance sat at the bedside. She rooted through a drawer and found a stash of shortbread cookies.

Her stomach rumbled. Daylight filtered through the blinds, and she blinked. She hadn't even noticed that the sun had risen.

The door opened, and Esposito walked into the unit. He spotted her and altered his course. He set a cup on the pod-style machine and pressed "Brew." "How's Sharp?"

"He had a lacerated liver and lost a lot of blood. But the surgery went well. He made it through the night, and the doctors are hopeful." Morgan filled her pocket with little packs of cookies. "Who else survived the night?"

Her bullet had caught Chase in the center of the back and had penetrated his heart. He'd been dead when he'd hit the ground. She wasn't sure how she felt about killing him, and she imagined her conscience would trouble her when she fully processed it. But she'd made the right decision. Chase would have shot Haley, and Morgan couldn't have let that happen. Lance's opinion had been good riddance.

Morgan picked up the two coffee cups and walked back toward Sharp's room. Lance spotted them through the window and walked out into the hallway to join them. He turned, keeping one eye on Sharp through the open door, as he'd done all night long.

Morgan did a quick scan of Sharp's machines. Nothing had changed. He was breathing. His heart was beating. She said a prayer that he continued to do those things. She handed Lance his coffee and offered him a pack of cookies from her pocket.

"No, thanks." He shook his head.

Morgan opened the plastic with her teeth and ate a shortbread.

Lance sniffed his coffee and lowered the cup. "I don't suppose Isaac has started talking," he said to the ADA.

"No. The only words Isaac spoke were to request his lawyer." Esposito drank his coffee and made a disgusted face. The ADA must have stopped home to shower and change his clothes, because he was wearing a suit instead of jeans. The only signs of the night before were a burn on his jaw and the shadows under his eyes. He tossed his half-full cup in a nearby trash can. "But Justin woke up during the night, and his mouth has been on a confession marathon. He got lucky. The bullet grazed him. Lots of blood, no real damage."

Morgan's sister had brought her a change of clothes, and Lance wore a pair of hospital scrubs donated by an orderly.

Lance perked up. "He seemed ready to break."

"He's so guilt ridden, it's pathetic," Esposito said. "He signed a ten-page confession. Justin and Isaac are both going to prison forever."

"Justin, Chase, and Isaac were in it together?" Morgan had been pondering possibilities all night.

"Yes." Esposito took a deep breath. "Justin says it all began last summer at a music festival. Noah wasn't with them. He ditched them to spend the day with a girl. Isaac, Chase, and Justin were all pretty steamed that he'd blown them off again. They ran across a very drunk woman named Adele Smith in the parking lot and decided to have sex with her. They took her to a secluded spot and gave her more alcohol. Isaac slipped a few of Justin's Ambiens into her vodka, but he wasn't patient enough to wait for the pills to work. They all raped her. She struggled and yelled a little at first. Isaac smacked her around and even half choked her to make her shut up. Eventually, they all passed out. When they woke up, she was dead. They'd given her too much Ambien on top of all the booze. They'd used condoms, and none of them had any felony convictions. Their DNA was not in the system. They thought they were in the clear. They left her body by the side of the road and went home."

"Shit." Lance drank his coffee and crushed the empty cup. "They're animals."

"There's more." Esposito folded his arms. "They took pictures."

Appalled, Morgan felt her mouth drop open. She wasn't sure if she was more surprised by their callousness or stupidity.

"And Noah saw some of the pictures," Esposito continued. "They lied to Noah, telling him it was an accident. They were all drunk and didn't even remember most of it."

"Obviously that was bullshit." Lance's arms tensed.

"How could it have been an accident?" Morgan needed more coffee for her brain to make all the connections. "They gave her Ambien."

Esposito gave her a patient look. "They lied and told Noah that they didn't know what drugs Adele might have taken."

"Right." Morgan sighed. "And that detail wasn't made public, so Noah wouldn't have known."

"Yes. As for our recent cases, they were at Beats the week before Noah's murder. They ran into Shannon. Justin remembered her from the inn. They'd talked for a few minutes, apparently. She'd asked him for the names of the local hot spots, and he'd directed her to Beats."

"Then it wasn't a coincidence that she was there," Morgan said.

"No." Esposito shook his head. "Adam was at the club that night too. He'd had too much to drink, so Noah left early to drive him home. Isaac, Justin, and Chase were in the parking lot after the fire alarm went off. They found Shannon wandering around. She couldn't find her car.

They thought they'd gotten away with it once before, so why not do it again? They repeated the ploy, taking her out into the woods, giving her alcohol. This time they only slipped one pill into her drink. But she woke up while Isaac was raping her and screamed. He strangled her. Again, they thought they couldn't be tied to her murder. Except when Noah heard about her disappearance, he started looking at them funny. Then he started asking questions about what they'd done that night after he'd left the club."

"So they killed him."

Esposito nodded. "Justin said Noah let them in that night. He was irritated that Haley had passed out on him right after they'd had sex. The three men had previously agreed to each stab him once so that they were all equally culpable. Justin had slipped Haley two sleeping pills at the club. They'd planned on framing her all along, but after they'd stabbed Noah, she was standing there. At first, they thought she was watching, until Isaac figured out she was sleepwalking. They put the knife in her hand and pushed her into the puddle of blood. She slid and fell. She scrambled and ended up covered in blood. Justin said it couldn't have been easier."

"They killed their friend to cover up their own crimes," Morgan said.

"When Haley was arrested for Noah's murder, they thought they were home free." Esposito gestured from Morgan to Lance. "Until you two started asking questions. They were particularly concerned when you"—the ADA pointed at Lance—"told them she remembered parts of the night. They didn't like the questions or the direction of the investigation, which is why they set Lance's house on fire. They thought if Morgan and the PI firm were out of the picture, they'd be safe."

"How did they start *this* fire, tonight?" Morgan asked.

"The arson investigator thinks Isaac shot a hole in the propane tank," Esposito said. "The initial explosion is probably what killed the bodyguard."

"Why did they decide to kill Haley?" Lance asked. "She was taking the fall for their crimes."

"Yes. At first, Isaac thought they could make her seem crazy," Esposito explained. "He hacked into the router and whispered nasty things to her through her game console. But Isaac and Chase must have decided they needed a clean slate. Justin was losing his shit. He'd become a risk. Haley might have been remembering that night. If Haley and Justin were both dead, there would be no witnesses."

"But Justin wasn't dead," Morgan said.

"They didn't know that," Esposito said. "As for incriminating evidence, Justin said their clothes only had a little bit of Noah's blood on them. Isaac's final stab wound was the only one that had bled heavily. They'd managed to keep their shoes out of it. They'd disposed of their clothes and gloves by burning them in a barrel behind Isaac's house. The black dog hair you pointed out on the forensics report belongs to a coonhound. Chase's father happens to own several, including a black-and-tan dog that he uses for hunting. And we found Haley's medical alert bracelet in Isaac's house. He'd kept an earring that belonged to Adele and a scarf that belonged to Shannon. Trophies of his crimes, I guess." The ADA shrugged. "We're hoping he starts talking once he learns that Justin has turned on him."

"Who shot Justin?" Morgan asked.

"Chase," Esposito said. "He and Isaac knew Justin was near the breaking point. Justin had talked on the phone to Chase a half hour before you showed up at his door. He admits he was freaking out and telling them he couldn't keep lying. The guilt was too much for him."

"But not for Isaac and Chase." Lance tossed his empty cup into the trash can.

"No." Esposito's phone beeped. He pulled it out of his pocket and checked the display. "They had no remorse. Isaac still doesn't."

"Psychopaths." Lance glanced at Sharp, then turned back to Esposito. "Have the police found Adam?"

"Actually, yes." Esposito's phone beeped again. "He was hiding out in the woods about two miles from Eliza's house. A friend had fixed him up with a tent and camping gear. But he didn't have a computer, so that's why he hadn't sent any more threatening emails. He has some emotional issues. He admitted to making that GIF of Morgan being hit by McFarland and throwing the rock through your windshield. He will be spending some time in jail."

"Good to know." Lance nodded.

"Have the charges against Haley been dropped?" Morgan asked. Eliza and Haley were sharing a room on the third floor of the hospital. Eliza was being treated for smoke inhalation. Haley had several deep cuts on the bottoms of her feet. But they would both recover—physically, anyway. Haley would no doubt have lingering emotional issues.

"Yes." Esposito nodded. "She is free to go."

The knot in Morgan's belly finally unraveled. Haley was not going to prison. Morgan and Lance were all right. Hopefully, Sharp would recover from his wounds.

Morgan would have questions about the case for Esposito in a day or two. But she'd heard enough for now. She couldn't take in any more information.

"You're not going to admit that Morgan proved your case wrong?" Lance asked.

Esposito shrugged. "Since we didn't go to court, no one won or lost. I'll still get credit for Isaac's and Justin's convictions. I'll let you know if I need any paperwork signed." Esposito turned and left.

Lance watched him leave. "I guess it's too much to ask that he acknowledge that you kept another innocent person out of prison when he was happy to railroad her into it."

"I don't expect acknowledgment or accolades." Morgan ate another cookie. "And at least we now know that he's not evil."

"No. Not evil. But he's still an asshole."

"He went into a burning building with you," she said in a *really?* tone.

"I still don't like him. All he cares about is his reputation, not seeing justice done." Lance wrapped a hand around the back of his neck. "Speaking of people I don't like and justice not being served, remind me to have a bonfire with Kieran Hart's photos tomorrow. I wish there was something we could do to him."

"He hasn't broken any laws, just the trust of the women he dated. Think of it this way. Even with all his money, women see through him, and he is still alone." She offered him a cookie. This time he took one and crunched it down in three bites. "Does that make you feel better?"

"A little." He reached for another cookie and froze. "Sharp's waking up."

Morgan turned to see Sharp's body shifting ever so slightly on the bed. His eyelids fluttered.

Calling for the nurse, Lance bolted into the room.

Chapter Forty-Six

Sharp cracked an eyelid. Bright light stabbed his eyeballs, and he squeezed his lids shut again. Was he dead? If he was, then the bright light and tunnel weren't all bullshit.

But if he was dead, why did his stomach feel like someone had parked a train on it?

Maybe he hadn't gone to heaven.

He squirmed, sending bolts of pain through him that made him think about letting the darkness suck him under again.

A familiar voice broke through the haze of agony. "Sharp."

He opened his eyes. Everything was blurry. *Lance?*

He'd intended to say the word, but his throat felt like it was filled with ash, and all that came out was a rasping choke. He blinked until his vision cleared. Lance hovered over him, his blue eyes filled with worry.

"Can he have some water?" Lance asked someone.

A minute later, a straw found his lips, and Sharp sucked a tiny amount of water into his mouth. He held it there and savored it before swallowing. With his mouth moist, he had one question to ask. "Haley?"

"She's OK." Lance set the cup and straw on the rolling tray next to the bed. "Eliza too. But Eric didn't make it."

Sharp nodded as images of the explosion rushed back at him. He whispered, "Close to the explosion."

"Isaac shot a hole in the propane tank."

"Isaac?" Sharp had wondered who had been in league with Justin.

"Isaac, Chase, and Justin were all in on it together."

Sharp couldn't wrap his brain around Lance's revelation. His thoughts were mush. Drugs, probably. He tried to reach for his cup of water, but all he managed to do was make his fingers twitch. Still the movement was enough for pain to slice him in half.

Lance gave him another sip of water. "I'll give you the details another day. Right now, you look like you need your pain assessed."

"OK," Sharp agreed. Breathing shallowly, he waited while the nurse and doctor reviewed his vitals, shined lights into his eyes, and then injected some blessed morphine into his IV line.

He curled his fingers at Lance, who leaned closer. "Haley didn't imagine those voices. They hacked her game console. Little bastards. Tell her."

"She knows. Justin confessed." Lance straightened. Sharp didn't catch the rest of what he said. He floated away on a comfortably numb sea.

Sharp napped. When he woke in the afternoon, Eliza was in the chair next to his bed, and the pain was only a knife blade through his gut instead of a chain saw. Eliza looked worn-out, but her eyes looked brighter than he'd seen them since she'd first come to his office to ask for his help.

"Haley's OK?" His voice was not quite as raspy.

Eliza hesitated. "She's going to be. I won't lie. She's going to need some serious therapy after what was done to her, but at least now she knows what happened. She knows she's not crazy. She didn't harm anyone. Thank you. For everything."

Sharp reached for his water. He really wanted to do it himself, but he gave up when he could barely lift his hand an inch off the bed. Any movement sent waves of pain rolling over him like tsunamis.

"Let me." Eliza held it to his lips.

God, he wanted to brush his teeth. He had a beautiful woman tending to him, and his mouth tasted like ass.

He drank more water. As his head cleared, he blurted out an apology that had been building for decades. "I'm sorry."

Eliza stopped, her expression bewildered. "Sorry? For what? You and your friends saved Haley. Without them, she would be going to prison, and the men who killed Noah Carter would have walked away from their crime free and clear. I have no doubt of that."

"For kissing you." Even through the drugs, he knew he was bungling this. "Way back when."

"You don't owe me any apology." Eliza cupped the side of his face, her touch soothing. "It was too soon. I didn't know what I wanted. Any relationship I would have started back then would have been a mistake. You were one of my best friends. I couldn't bear for something to happen between us and then end badly."

"You had enough grief. You didn't need the pressure I put on you." Sharp hadn't planned on kissing Ted's widow. It had just happened. "You left right after that."

"It's not your fault that I left," she said. "You didn't drive me away. Ted's memories did. I couldn't get over him there, in his place, with all his things." She leaned back, her hand falling from his face. "We were both hurting. We shared that pain. No one else really understood what we were going through. Did I ever thank you for all you did that first year? I wouldn't have gotten through it alone."

Sharp felt the warmth rise into his cheeks. "Still shouldn't have kissed you."

Eliza touched his hand. "You know I love you, but not that way."

"I know." Sharp nodded. The wound in his side throbbed with its own heartbeat of pain.

"It was hard to leave you. You were my rock that first year. But it was equally important that I was forced to make it on my own. In the city, there was no one else to handle Haley while I crawled back into bed. I had to get up every morning and get on with the day. With my life."

What they'd shared hadn't been romantic love, at least not on her part. It had been shared trauma. Sharp wasn't sure if he'd loved her or not back then. But then, he supposed it didn't really matter, did it? They hadn't been good for each other.

Eliza straightened. "Haley and I are going to Seattle. There's nothing left for us here. The house is gone. The memories in this place are, once again, horrible enough to bury us both."

"Start fresh," he said. Then he realized his kiss really *hadn't* driven her out of town. Eliza walked away from painful situations. It was what she did.

She nodded. "Haley needs to heal. She can't do that here."

Sharp thought maybe Haley needed to face what had happened to her instead of running away from it, but who was he to say?

"She's outside. She'd like to say goodbye." Eliza released his hand.

She wasn't wasting any time.

He nodded. "Sure."

She leaned over and kissed his face. "I can never thank you enough for what you did. You saved her."

"No," Sharp corrected. "Haley saved me."

She hadn't given up on him. If she had, he'd be buried under a burned house.

Eliza walked to the doorway and waved. Haley hesitated at the threshold, then came inside, her eyes filled with tears.

"I'll give you two a few minutes." Eliza left the room.

Haley crossed the floor and took Sharp's hand. "Thank you so much. I don't know what would have happened if you and Morgan and Lance hadn't stepped in." Her gaze dropped to their joined hands. "I don't remember my dad, but I think he'd be grateful."

"If your dad were still alive, he'd have handled this himself." All Sharp could muster was a tiny squeeze of her fingers. "And don't forget. You saved me too."

"I guess we saved each other." Haley nodded, leaned over, and kissed him on the cheek.

She was definitely Ted's daughter.

Emotions clogged Sharp's throat. He cleared it. "Your dad would be proud of you."

"I wish I remembered him." Haley smiled, her eyes shining with tears.

With his throat tight with emotion, Sharp could only squeeze her hand again.

"I have to go and talk to the police again. I already gave them a statement, but they want more."

Sharp frowned. "Take Morgan with you."

"I am." Haley released his hand and left the room without a backward glance. She was Eliza's daughter too. That was for sure.

Eliza came back in and sat in a bedside chair.

"You're not leaving?" Sharp shifted his legs, trying to get comfortable. But the pain was building at a steady pace. Each breath was harder to draw than the last. He should call the nurse, but he didn't want the interruption.

"I promised Lance I'd stay until he returned," Eliza said.

"I don't need a babysitter," Sharp grumbled.

"I promised." Eliza settled back in the chair.

The nurse walked in, checked his vitals, and injected a shot into his IV. Sharp wanted to talk with Eliza until she left. Who knew when or if he'd see her again. But in a few heartbeats, his eyelids felt like they weighed eight hundred pounds.

Eliza was gone when he opened his eyes again. A small shape stood in front of the window. His ICU room was Grand-friggin'-Central. His eyes focused on a khaki trench coat tossed over the bedside chair.

No. Who the hell let her in?

This time, it *really* bothered him that his mouth tasted like ass. He was not letting Olivia Cruz hold his fucking water cup. He was going to brush his fucking teeth and act like a man.

If only he could move his arm far enough to push the call button. His fingers scratched on the bedding.

Shit.

Not going to happen.

His humiliation was complete.

"I'm glad you're not dead, Lincoln." Olivia walked to the bedside. He could hear the rap of impractical skinny heels on the tile. Her mouth curved in a wicked smile. "You still owe me a favor."

Chapter Forty-Seven

Morgan was going to die, and she hadn't even had her coffee yet.

"How far have we run?" She panted. The April morning was chilly. Her leg muscles burned, but the rest of her body was freezing. She pulled the sleeves of her jacket farther down over her hands. Under her gloves, her fingers were numb. At seven o'clock in the morning, the sun wasn't strong enough to provide any real heat yet.

Nearly a month had passed since she'd suffered her concussion, and she was finally well enough to exercise.

"Do you want to walk for a while?" Next to her, Lance was barely jogging. Black running pants and a gray hoodie covered his big, buff body. He moved with the grace of a natural athlete.

Morgan did not.

She felt like a giraffe in running shoes. A lame giraffe.

She sucked in another lungful of damp spring air. "You didn't answer my question."

He winced. "About a half mile."

"That's it?" Morgan slowed to a walk. Her side cramped. She bent forward and pressed a hand against it, her gait limping and pathetic. She hated running with every cell in her body.

"You want to stretch out the cramp"—Lance demonstrated by raising his hands over his head—"not compress it."

She mimicked him. The cramp eased a little.

Lance pivoted and jogged backward in front of her. "You don't have to do this. It was your idea."

"I know."

"Improve your fitness if that's what you want to do, but don't feel like you need to do it for me. You're perfect. I wouldn't change one thing about you."

"But I can't keep up," she gasped. "I can never keep up."

"Physically, maybe not. But your brain runs circles around mine. And in Haley's case, if you had run after me, we'd all probably be dead. You used your head. One of us has to remember to do that."

The cramp seized up again. She stopped to catch her breath. She wanted to be fit. If only getting in shape didn't involve so much effort.

"Maybe next time we should try this later in the day, after you've had your coffee." He stopped next to her.

"I need to be done before the kids get up," she wheezed.

"Just stop for a minute." He took her hand. "Catch your breath."

"What?" She swiped a piece of hair out of her face.

They'd followed the path that ran along the river behind her grandfather's house. With Lance's place burned to the ground, he was still living with her. She never wanted him to leave.

Lance looked down at her. "I love you."

She smirked. "I know."

He rolled his eyes. "You love me back."

"I do." More than he'd ever know.

"This might not be the most romantic place in the world, but this is probably the only time we will be alone all day."

"With three kids underfoot, that doesn't happen too often." She laughed.

"I've noticed," he said dryly.

The river flowed next to them. Water tumbled over rocks. The trees around them budded with new foliage. Despite the morning's crispness, the air smelled of spring.

"And *I* think this place is *very* romantic." She waited for a kiss, but Lance just looked down at her, his face turning contemplative.

"I know we haven't been together that long, but I've known since the beginning that you were it for me. I want you by my side for the rest of my life. I love you and your kids and the rest of your family. I will never try to replace the girls' father with you or them, but I promise to be the best husband and parent I can."

Husband? Was he going to propose? Her breath caught in her throat.

His face went serious. "When that prosecutor in New Jersey called, at first, I didn't want to be the reason you turned him down, but now I don't care. I love you, and I want to be with you more than I need any stupid gesture of pride."

"I never thought I'd find love again." Morgan's heart fluttered. "Now that I have, with you, I will not give it up. There is no job in the world more important than you. *You* make me happy. You are a priority in my life, whether or not you want to be. You'll just have to live with that."

"I think I can manage."

She settled her hands on his shoulders. "There are many reasons I didn't want to interview for that job. But you *are* one of them. I love you. But I also like being my own boss. When I'm not on a big case, I'm home every night to be with my kids. ADAs work night and day. I'd barely see my girls. I don't want to leave my grandfather either. He took care of me most of my life. Now he needs me. It's my turn to look after him. Plus, this is my girls' home. They've already had one big shake-up to their lives. I won't drag them away from their family without a damned good reason. And I want to be with you too. I like working together."

"We make a damned good team."

"We do." She took his face in her hands. Happy tears dampened her cheeks. "But if you were the only thing keeping me in Scarlet Falls,

I still wouldn't leave. I would not walk away from you. *You* are enough."
And she couldn't believe her good fortune in finding him.

"In that case . . ." Lance dropped to one knee and took a small box
from his pocket. Inside, a diamond ring nestled on black velvet. ". . .
marry me. I want to wake up with you every morning for the rest of
my life."

They'd talked about commitment and the serious nature of their
relationship, so his proposal wasn't a complete surprise. But she hadn't
expected it this morning. Joy bloomed through her. It didn't matter
that her hair was a mess, she wasn't wearing makeup, and she was all
sweaty.

She'd found a good man, one she loved, one who accepted the extra
responsibilities of three small children without any hesitation. How did
she get so lucky?

"Yes. I will marry you." She didn't know what she'd done to deserve
a second chance at love, but she wasn't going to waste any time mull-
ing it over. Life was short and filled with uncertainty. She was going to
seize her opportunity and hold on to it with every ounce of strength
she possessed.

He slid the ring onto her finger, and she pulled him to his feet.
Lance wrapped his arms around her waist, pulled her close, and kissed
her hard.

She kissed him back. "You're sure about this, right? My life is crazy."

"But it's the good kind of crazy." He looped an arm around her
shoulders, and they turned back. "Not the psychopathic kind. I was also
thinking, after my house is rebuilt, that I'll sell it. We can use the money
to renovate the kitchen and maybe add a master suite to the house."

"Technically, it's Grandpa's house, but I think he'll be all for it. We
could use a little more room."

"With three girls in the house, another bathroom would be useful
too. They're going to be teenagers someday."

"It'll happen before we can blink." Morgan leaned on his shoulder. "But I don't know if this running thing is really for me. Maybe I should try yoga."

He laughed. "That sounds like a plan."

They climbed the deck steps and went into the house. Morgan drew back. Gianna, Grandpa, and all three girls were waiting, their gazes eagerly searching Lance's. Even Sharp was there, holding a white bakery bag and a bottle of champagne.

They knew?

"Well?" Sharp asked. "Did she say yes?"

"She did." Lance squeezed her tightly.

"Yay!" Sophie bolted across the room and leaped at Lance.

He released Morgan and caught the little girl in midair.

"You're going to be our new daddy." She squealed and wrapped her arms and legs round him.

Mia and Ava hugged his legs, and Lance squatted to scoop them up too.

Gianna was wiping her eyes. "I'll make breakfast. We're having mimosas."

"Make bacon too," Grandpa said as he opened the bag Sharp had brought. "*You* brought donuts?"

Sharp grinned. He wasn't ready for a marathon anytime soon, but he was healing and looking stronger every day. "Sometimes you gotta live a little."

Morgan helped herself to a donut. "Indeed."

Lance set the children down. Gianna brought a tray of champagne glasses. She handed the girls three plastic flutes filled with orange juice. She was far too prepared.

"So how long have you all known?" Morgan took a glass from the tray.

Gianna blushed. "Since yesterday."

"I wanted to ask the girls first." Lance lifted a glass. "I wanted to make sure they were OK with having me as a stepdad."

"We are." Sophie bounced on her toes.

"You were awfully sure of yourself. What if I had said no?" Morgan turned her hand to admire her ring.

Rolling his eyes, Sharp took a glass. "You were never going to say no."

"You're right." Morgan wrapped her arm around Lance's waist. Two years ago, she'd been devastated. She hadn't thought happiness would ever be possible for her. But now, anything seemed possible.

Lance tapped his glass against Morgan's. "To us. To all of us."

"Yay! We're gonna be a family." Sophie rapped her plastic flute too hard against Ava's. Orange juice splashed to the tile. The dogs rushed in to lick it off the floor. Morgan tripped over Snoozer, and Lance caught her before she hit the floor.

Gianna snatched a dish towel and mopped up the mess.

Pulling Morgan away from the chaos, Lance kissed her.

"You're sure about this?" She laughed.

"I've never been surer of anything in my life," he said.

Neither had Morgan. "Life around here is a whirlwind."

He kissed her again. "But it will never be dull."

Acknowledgments

As always, credit goes to my agent, Jill Marsal, and to the entire team at Montlake Romance, especially my managing editor, Anh Schlucp, and my developmental editor, Charlotte Herscher.

Special thanks to writer friends Leanne Sparks, Rayna Vause, and Kendra Elliot for much-needed motivation and help in finishing this book.

About the Author

Wall Street Journal bestselling author Melinda Leigh is a fully recovered banker. A lifelong lover of books, she started writing as a way to preserve her sanity when her youngest child entered first grade. During the next few years, she joined Romance Writers of America, learned a few things about writing a novel, and decided the process was way more fun than analyzing financial statements. Melinda's debut, *She Can Run*, was nominated for Best First Novel by the International Thriller Writers. She has also garnered Golden Leaf and Silver Falchion awards, along with nominations for two RITAs and three Daphne du Maurier awards. Her other novels include *She Can Tell, She Can Scream, She Can Hide, She Can Kill, Midnight Exposure, Midnight Sacrifice, Midnight Betrayal, Midnight Obsession, Hour of Need, Minutes to Kill, Seconds to Live, Say You're Sorry*, and *Her Last Goodbye*. She holds a second-degree black belt in Kenpo karate; teaches women's self-defense; and lives in a messy house with her husband, two teenagers, a couple of dogs, and two rescue cats.